HEROES FOR SALE

AFSIC Kampfental was a very special military establishment tucked away in a corner of the Bavarian Alps. In
1944, with every German front collapsing, the Armed
Forces Special Instruction Centre was allegedly still
training men for 'the last decisive battle of the war.'
AFSIC Kampfental was of course top secret and sealed off
from the outside world, but within it an elaborate
hierarchy existed, and layer upon layer of bureaucracy,
designed – like the orgies in the camp 'recreation centre' (a
former chapel) – to ensure that its supermen were screened
from the hell awaiting them in the Third Reich's final
collapse.

Into this strange, surreal world, in which women as well
as men were manipulated, came a certain Corporal Singer
and his friend Lieutenant Kersten who had not quite lost
touch with reality, especially when it was represented by a
Field-Marshal's lovely daughter. In different ways they
attempted to bring AFSIC Kampfental to grips with the
situation existing beyond its perimeter, with the hilarious
result that bureaucracy was soon bureaucratically dismantling bureaucracy. But their attempt was dearly
bought. In a world where all standards had vanished, only
one remained: survival. Never mind at whose cost.

Hans Hellmut Kirst, already well known for some
eighteen novels chronicling the worst absurdities and
excesses of Nazi Germany, here chronicles brilliantly and
bitingly the ultimate in absurdity and excess.

HEROES FOR SALE

—— ⟪o⟫ ——

HANS HELLMUT KIRST

Translated by
J. MAXWELL BROWNJOHN

COLLINS
St James's Place, London
1982

William Collins Sons & Co Ltd
London · Glasgow · Sydney · Auckland
Toronto · Johannesburg

First published in Germany under the title *Ausverkauf der Helden*
First published in the UK 1982
Copyright © C. Bertelsmann Verlag, GmbH, München 1980
© in the English translation
by Wm Collins Sons & Co Ltd 1982

British Library Cataloguing in Publication Data

Kirst, Hans Hellmut
Heroes for sale.
I. Title   II. Ausverkauf der Helden.   *English*
833'.914[F]   PT2621.I76

ISBN 0 00 222396 1

Photoset in Imprint
Made and Printed in Great Britain by
William Collins Sons & Co Ltd, Glasgow

The supreme law is supreme injustice.
Roman Proverb

Enjoy the war—peace is going to be terrible.
Popular saying in Nazi Germany

I

'Well, get a load of that!' There was a commanding note in the bright and breezy voice – a whiff of the parade ground. 'Just what we've all been waiting for.'

The object of this salutation trailed his field pack across the dusty forecourt of Hölzbach station. Blinking in the glare of the midday sun, he saw a uniformed figure lounging against a tarpaulin-covered truck – a sergeant with a ruddy complexion and eyes like gimlets.

'Think you're here for a rest cure, do you?'

The new arrival, a corporal, instinctively grasped that this was a reference to the civilian suitcase he was carrying in addition to his pack and kitbag. He put it down and produced a rather lopsided salute.

'What was that meant to be?' The amusement in the voice was tinged with menace. 'Are you trying to make a monkey out of me?'

'Certainly not, Sergeant.' The corporal sounded genuinely eager to please. Four years of war service had made him something of an expert at cultivating the impression that he was a useful subordinate to have around, but the sergeant remained to be convinced.

'All right, do it all over again, and this time do it properly. Get back inside there at the double!'

The corporal retreated in double-quick time. Once inside the shabby booking hall he divested himself of his baggage by simply letting it drop. Then, with an impassive choirboyish face, he smoothed down his crumpled uniform and re-emerged into the sunlight – drillbook fashion.

Five paces short of the sergeant he halted and tried to click his heels. Straining to preserve a regulation stance, he went through the motions expected of him. Though not a prize performance, his salute conveyed the best of intentions. The sergeant, who was still leaning nonchalantly against the truck, seemed to recognize this, but no experienced drill instructor could have left the matter there.

'Hit the deck!' he barked.

The corporal barely hesitated. Then he obeyed like a well-trained dog.

'You see?' the sergeant said happily. 'You can do it if you try. On your feet!'

The corporal stood up, not leisurely but not like a jack-in-the-box either. He knew the prescribed barrack-square sequence: flex right leg, brace left leg, support weight on hands, resume position of attention.

The sergeant followed this procedure with a connoisseur's eye. He also noted that the corporal refrained from patting the dust off his uniform right away, and the sight of him meekly awaiting further orders was an invitation to benevolence.

'Right. Name and destination?'

'Corporal Singer, Sergeant, posted to Kampfental Camp.'

'A trainee, eh? You've rolled up too soon, soldier. Our next survival course doesn't start for another ten days.'

'I'm on assignment to permanent staff, Sergeant.'

'You don't say. Who assigned you and why?'

'No idea, Sergeant. My movement order just says "Kampfental Camp, Hölzbach District".'

'Where are you from?'

'Munich, Sergeant. No. 9 Field Hospital.'

Corporal Sebastian Singer had just spent six weeks recovering from a chest wound sustained on the Eastern Front. A Polish sniper's bullet had punctured his lung.

'Bought yourself a ticket home, eh?' the sergeant said knowledgeably. 'Very nice too. I suppose you've been lying around eating yourself sick for months – *and* screwing some cuddly little nurse. Well, you've had your fun. This is a tough outfit, so you better get used to the idea.'

Beyond the sergeant stretched an expanse of glorious South Bavarian countryside, with rolling green foothills, dense tracts of darker green forest, isolated farmhouses and dusty white roads. In the background, seemingly within touching distance, were the Bavarian Alps, a rugged and indestructible panorama bathed in picture-postcard splendour.

Corporal Singer wrenched his eyes away from the scenery and focused them on what mattered – the man in front of him. His uniform fitted snugly, his belt was highly polished, his pants had knife-edge creases, and his almost dust-free shoes shone like glass. All in all, he looked like a military tailor's dummy.

Detecting the sergeant's slightly less acid expression, Singer provisionally tagged him as one of those superiors who could be semi-human as long as you tickled their self-esteem by obeying them to the letter – but only then.

'Gerner's my name,' said the sergeant. 'By rights, I should make you double the three miles to camp in full marching order, the way we do with all new arrivals. Being kind-hearted by nature, I'll give you a lift to the gate.'

Singer registered intense gratitude. 'Thank you, Sergeant.'

'But not till you've helped me load up. Kind-hearted I may be, but I'm not from the Salvation Army.'

Chuckling at his own brand of humour, Gerner climbed into the cab, started up, and backed the truck towards the small freight depot beside the station. A prolonged blare on the horn produced results. The deserted platform was enlivened by the appearance of a grizzled old porter.

'Here we go again,' Gerner called. 'I brought some reinforcements this time.' He indicated Singer.

The porter gestured languidly at a stack of cartons. 'That's them.'

Gerner had already lowered the tailgate and was standing beside it with his thumbs hooked in his belt. 'All right, let's go.'

Singer began to hump the cartons on to the tailgate one by one. They were not particularly heavy, but there were fifty of them.

'Hurry it up!' Gerner exhorted him.

Still suffering from the effects of his wound, Singer was soon out of breath and unsteady on his feet. His face streamed with sweat and his hands shook.

Gerner had meanwhile joined the porter on a bench. They appeared to be enjoying themselves hugely. 'These youngsters,' said the porter, wagging his head. Gerner clicked his tongue. 'And that's what we're expected to win the war with.'

Singer completed his fiftieth round trip and slumped against the tailgate, breathing hard. Gerner sauntered over and slit the top of a carton with a pocket-knife. Six champagne-style bottles of German fizz – 'Henkel Extra Dry' – came to light. The sergeant extracted three of these and handed two to the porter, who accepted them as his due. The third was thrust into Singer's hands with a well-meant admonition.

'Here, sonny-boy – just to show you what a good sort I am, so don't you forget it. Keep your nose clean and you won't go far wrong – and keep your mouth shut, or you'll need a new set of teeth.'

Singer was privileged to stow himself and his belongings among the cartons in the back of the truck, which roared off at once. Dust swirled high above the potholed road, reducing visibility to zero.

*

Minutes later the truck braked so sharply that Singer went sprawling. He tossed his pack, kitbag and suitcase into the road and bailed out just as Sergeant Gerner slammed the truck into gear and roared off again with his load of fizz. He didn't waste a backward look on his temporary passenger.

Singer stood there feeling rather forlorn. Above him loomed an eight-foot fence of closely woven barbed wire stapled to massive timber posts. The heavy gate swung open, and two soldiers advanced on him. Their armbands identified them as camp policemen of some kind.

'Papers,' said one.

Singer surrendered his movement order, which was accepted without so much as a glance.

'In there,' said the other man. He jerked his thumb at a hut on the right of the gate.

Singer toted his gear inside. It was a crude, boxlike building with a concrete floor and two small windows – a former storehouse, from the look of it. A desk and chair were the only furniture. Resignedly, Singer perched on his suitcase and waited.

After fifteen or twenty minutes – hospital had made him indifferent to the passage of time – another two MPs appeared. In masterful silence, they took his items of baggage and emptied their contents on the floor.

'May I ask – '

'Shurrup.'

His dirty underwear was contemptuously tossed aside, followed in quick succession by two books – superfluous equipment for a corporal of infantry. All a dogface was expected to cart around was a rifle, some ammunition, and a spare pair of socks and underpants – clean ones – but this specimen actually went to war with crap like Goethe's *Faust* and Heine's *Buch der Lieder* in his gear.

'What are you, a bloody choirboy?'

Sebastian Singer grinned and said nothing – ignorance on the part of those in authority always gladdened his heart. Although Goethe obviously rang a bell with these two uniformed oxen, they'd mistaken Heine's 'Book of Songs' for a hymnal. By now, however, their attention had zoomed in on something of far greater interest : a bottle of Henkel Extra Dry.

'What's this?'

'Field rations.'

'Like hell. No drinking allowed in camp except on authorized premises at authorized times. This bottle's confiscated, get it?'

Singer got it all right. He could have cited the donor of the gift, but he decided not to. He could also have asked for a receipt, but he resisted the temptation.

'In that case,' he said good-naturedly, 'cheers!'

The MPs gave him an approving grin before retiring with their acquisition. He had shown due respect for authority, and that was just as it should be – that was the way things worked at Kampfental.

Singer knelt down and gathered his things together. Books first, then underpants, then the remainder of his gear. He was still crawling around on his hands and knees when a shadow moved across the floor and came to rest. Screwing up his eyes against the glare from the window beyond, he identified its source as a thickset lieutenant of infantry with several medal ribbons on his chest.

'Wagner – Lieutenant Wagner,' said the officer, sounding quite affable. 'Assistant Adjutant to the camp commandant, Colonel von Feuerfresser. My official designation is Staff Officer, Grade Three, Intelligence. That makes me responsible for security, discipline and counterespionage.'

Singer's jaw dropped. Officers who formally introduced themselves to enlisted men were few and far between. 'How does that affect me, Lieutenant? Will I have something to do with security, discipline and counter-espionage?'

'We all do in this outfit, Corporal. Take your cue from me and you'll be all right.'

'To the best of my knowledge, Lieutenant, grade three intelligence officers also act as National Socialist Guidance Officers. Or am I wrong?'

'Far from it.' Lieutenant Wagner could barely conceal his surprise at this display of expert knowledge on the part of a mere corporal. 'You seem to know your stuff.'

'I heard it somewhere, that's all.'

Wagner felt impelled to explain. 'My responsibility for the political guidance of camp personnel is a purely automatic assignment, Singer – a secondary function, but one I perform to the best of my ability. Kindly take note of that.'

'Yes, Lieutenant.'

Wagner's manner remained benign. 'So now you've been posted to Kampfental. I hope it won't take you long to grasp what that means – and what a very special obligation it imposes on you. For a start, I'd like you to sign this statutory declaration.'

He opened a slim folder and removed a sheet of paper which he held aloft like a banner before handing it over. 'Read it through carefully, Singer. Ask me any questions you like, as long as they're relevant. Then sign.'

Singer mouthed the words as he read them to himself. 'I, name, rank, number, date and place of birth, hereby confirm that I have been informed that the Armed Forces Special Instruction Centre at Kampfental, near Hölzbach (authorized acronym: AFSIC), to which I have been officially attached, is a military installation whose purpose and function are classified Top Secret.'

Singer's jaw dropped again. Having spent years familiarizing himself with the rules of the army game, he knew at a glance that he had landed in a military pressure cooker. 'Top Secret' was the third and highest rung on the security ladder, the first two being 'Confidential' and

'Restricted'. It was seldom employed except by army and army group commanders, who used it daily as a matter of course.

'The signing of that document,' Lieutenant Wagner continued in a mechanical tone, 'pledges you to utter secrecy in respect of all you see and hear, or think you see and hear, within the precincts of this camp. At no time and under no circumstances is any outsider to be informed, even in outline, of what goes on here, because all that goes on here is done by order of the Führer and for the good of the state. Unquestioning compliance with the said regulation is your natural and bounden duty – is that clear, Singer?'

'Absolutely, Lieutenant.' Singer qualified his prompt response with a discreet enquiry. 'But may I ask a purely theoretical question? What would happen if someone felt unwilling or unable to comply?'

Wagner, who had installed himself behind the desk, sat back and regarded him with the narrowed eyes of a sniper sizing up an awkward target. 'Does that apply to you?'

'Of course not, Lieutenant – naturally I'll sign. It's just that – well, everyone does a better job if he knows where he stands.'

'In that case, Singer, I'll tell you.' Reassured by the newcomer's docility, Wagner had regained his sovereign calm. 'If, having signed that declaration, you were tempted to do something foolish, the consequences would be extremely serious. You might even be charged with high treason, and I'm sure you wouldn't want that. So much for point number one.'

'And number two?'

'If you refused to sign at all, we'd simply write you off and transfer you out. Not to put too fine a point on it, you'd find yourself crouching in a foxhole inside twenty-four hours – somewhere where the shit was really flying.'

Singer, who found this prospect equally unattractive,

signed the document without more ado. Lieutenant Wagner took possession of it, relieved that all had gone smoothly after a minor hiccup in routine.

'This declaration will be inserted in your personal file,' he said blandly. 'Your movement order has still be be checked, so stay here till further notice. You won't be assigned any specific duties until our double-dyed doctor has given you a clean bill of health. We don't have room for wheelchair cases at AFSIC Kampfental.'

The lieutenant marched out just as the medical officer sauntered in, almost colliding with him in the process. A small man of almost frail appearance, the MO was carrying an index card and wearing thick-lensed glasses whose sole purpose might have been to conceal the eyes behind them.

'Let's make ourselves comfortable,' he suggested, seating himself at the desk. 'Pull up that suitcase and park your butt. I've an aversion to people looking down on me.'

His voice sounded hopelessly unmilitary and his manner was equally so, though this could have been a witch doctor's device to gain his patients' confidence. He removed his glasses, unveiling a pair of shrewd blue eyes, and looked at Singer closely.

'Königsberger's the name,' he said at length, ' – Captain Königsberger, but don't let that worry you. I'm only a doctor in uniform.' To Singer's surprise, he went on, 'If you've any questions, I'll be glad to answer them as fully as I can.'

Singer bit back the host of questions on the tip of his tongue and limited himself to one. 'The lieutenant called you "our double-dyed doctor" just now. Mind telling me what he meant?'

'Only that I took two degrees in succession.'

A southerner from Bamberg, Königsberger had gone on studying for as long as he possibly could. After becoming a doctor of medicine, he had whiled away some more of the war by switching to psychology and adding a PhD to his name. Then he had been drafted, rapidly promoted, and posted to the select establishment known as AFSIC Kampfental.

'How about you, Singer – what brings you here?'

Innocent curiosity or a trick question? Singer, who was already feeling like a man in a minefield, decided to play it safe. 'No idea, Captain. All I know is, they discharged me from No. 9 Field Hospital and posted me straight here.'

The MO accepted this explanation with a sympathetic smile. 'I've sent for your medical record but it hasn't arrived yet. According to the rundown they gave me on the phone, you were wounded in the right lung. Two clean punctures, almost healed. Anything else the matter with you?'

Never be surprised at anything, however long the war lasts – Sebastian Singer had made this resolution some time ago, but he couldn't suppress a pang of misgiving at this unusual interest in his person. His face must have given the game away, because Königsberger's smile broadened.

'Don't worry, Corporal, this is just our standard routine. You've been posted to the Army's equivalent of the Vatican, and nobody gets in till he's gone through an inquisition. A sound mind in a healthy body, that's the local motto. It may be nonsense, but it's compulsory.'

Singer's nod told the MO that he could put his stock questions without risk of further misunderstanding.

'Right, Singer. Any homosexual tendencies?'

'Not that I'm aware of, sir – that's to say, no.'

Königsberger didn't relish this aspect of his job – in fact he found it repugnant. Eager to get it over, he hurried on. 'You mean you're actively heterosexual?'

'Not as active as I'd like.'

The MO smiled. 'You're unmarried, I assume. Are you

16

engaged? If not, are you involved in any form of binding relationship with a member of the opposite sex?'

'No.'

'Any specific diseases in your family? Infectious diseases? Hereditary diseases?'

'Anyone in a bughouse – that sort of thing? No, not so far.' Emboldened by the double-dyed doctor's easy-going manner, Singer felt he could afford to be candid. 'Those papers you've asked the hospital for – it so happens I've seen them.'

'How did you manage that? It's strictly against the rules.'

'Maybe, but any medical orderly'll sell you a peek at your record sheet for ten cigarettes or a bar of chocolate – or a bottle of wine. There's nothing on mine but details of my wound and the way they've treated it.'

'If you're hiding something, Singer, don't bother. This is only a preliminary interview. I'll be putting you through the hoop properly in the next few days, so you may as well come clean right away.'

'Are you speaking as a doctor, or what?'

The MO gave a wry laugh. 'You fancy yourself as an original, don't you? You may be only a corporal but you aren't one of the common herd, eh?' He shook his head. 'Well, I'm not amused – for your sake. Eccentricity doesn't pay in this place. Better drop it.'

'I'll do my best, Captain.'

'And I'll forget what I've heard so far. That's all for now.' Königsberger stood up. 'Report to Sergeant-Major Schulz in the administration block. He won't know what's hit him.'

The Armed Forces Special Instruction Centre – AFSIC for short – occupied a site between Lake Kampfental and the forest that fringed the sides of the valley from which it took its name.

17

The heart of the establishment was a former country mansion with the thick walls, small windows and cavernous rooms of a castle in miniature. It boasted a banqueting hall of grandiose design and two terraces, one facing the lake and the other looking out over the camp itself.

The whole complex, including stables and servants' quarters, had been requisitioned by an army planning department back in World War I, so huts had been constructed, even at that stage, for the storage of files and equipment.

Between 1919 and 1923 the site was misappropriated with the connivance of various local authorities, all of which disclaimed responsibility for it. An illegal right-wing volunteer corps styling itself 'The German Eagle' was raised and trained on the premises. Although its terrorist squads carried out summary executions during the chaotic postwar period, it never went into action as a single unit and was soon disbanded.

From 1925 on, Kampfental was taken over by the Boy Scout movement, which converted it into a large-scale youth hostel complete with sports facilities and playing fields.

In 1933, the picture changed radically. For some months, Kampfental became a serious rival to Dachau concentration camp. The mansion was lavishly re-decorated for the benefit of the commandant and his staff, the stables were enlarged to house SS guards, and additional huts were built to accommodate the reluctant inmates, who were now cut off from the outside world by a massive barbed wire fence.

Later on, when the camp was inspected by Hitler's deputy, Rudolf Hess, its backcloth of lofty German mountains and primeval German forests stirred him to the core. 'Men, comrades,' he exclaimed with habitual missionary fervour, 'this just won't do. Kampfental is a health resort, not a suitable environment for self-confessed enemies of the state.'

That settled it. By 1936, the Kampfental site had been expensively re-renovated and converted into a training centre for male and female Labour Corps functionaries. One new feature was a spacious communal canteen where film shows and ideological lectures could be staged, not to mention weekend dances and ceremonies marking red letter days in the Greater German calendar.

In 1939, when World War II broke out, the Army moved in. Kampfental now did valuable service as a recreation centre and convalescent home for wounded warriors whose every need was satisfied by female nursing staff of impeccable German stock.

Midsummer 1942 saw the arrival on the scene of a Lieutenant-Colonel (soon to be Colonel) von Feuerfresser, holder of the coveted '*Pour le Mérite*'. Invested, despite his rank, with all the powers of an army corps commander – powers granted him by the Armed Forces High Command, reportedly at Hitler's personal behest – Feuerfresser took one look at Kampfental and said snap. More precisely, he said, 'I requisition this establishment in the Führer's name!' He had the site evacuated in short order and developed, enlarged and revamped to accord with its latest role. Construction workers descended on the peaceful valley like an army of termites.

By the time the camp reopened on 1 May 1943, it had become a complex unequalled anywhere else in Greater Germany. After completing his preliminary tour of inspection, General (soon to be Field-Marshal) Wedell was able to inform Hitler that the Wehrmacht had acquired 'a unique installation – and perfectly geared to our requirements'.

Once a rather gloomy-looking edifice, the mansion was now resplendent in snow-white stucco with warm brown door and window embrasures. Its spacious terraces had earned it the nickname 'Feuerfresser's Sans Souci' – an allusion to Frederick the Great's palace at Potsdam.

Captain (Med.) Königsberger raced up the steps of the main terrace, two at a time, and hurried into the adjutant's office.

'About time too!' Lieutenant Wagner, who was already there, gave a snort of disapproval, delighted at this renewed opportunity to chide the MO for his unsoldierly conduct. It stuck in his craw that Königsberger technically outranked him. He glanced at the adjutant, Captain Tauschmüller, in quest of support.

Tauschmüller, a short, sturdy man with a grave and watchful expression, never wasted words. 'The Colonel's expecting us,' he said.

'And you're late as usual,' Wagner chimed in.

Königsberger grinned at him belligerently. 'I always do a thorough job, unlike some I could mention. That takes time.'

'Gentlemen, gentlemen!' said Tauschmüller, raising both hands in entreaty. 'Never air your differences in the Colonel's presence, or one of you will have to go – and you know what that means. Our field commanders are crying out for replacements.'

The gamecocks relapsed into silence. Having captured their attention, Tauschmüller made the most of it.

'I presume you know what's on the agenda?'

They didn't, but they took care not to say so. In any case, conferences with Feuerfresser followed an invariable and well-established pattern. The Colonel began by stating his own views and then asked his subordinates for theirs, a procedure which assured him of their wholehearted agreement. Nothing more was expected of them.

Colonel von Feuerfresser's office, which was situated on the mansion's first floor, consisted of three rooms knocked into one by the demolition of two partition walls. Genuine

Persian rugs lay strewn across the gleaming parquet, and hunting scenes were much in evidence.

Majestically ensconced behind a colossal baroque desk, like royalty personified, sat the Commandant. His strongly chiselled features and unwinking gaze were reminiscent of a mountain eagle.

Colonel von Feuerfresser's uniform was immaculate and carefully pressed. Not a single order, decoration or medal marred its virgin surface, though everyone knew he had plenty, including two Iron Crosses First Class of which the first had been earned in World War I. That was when he had also won his '*Pour le Mérite*', the Kaiser's highest award for gallantry in the field, but he disdained to wear such fripperies except on very special occasions.

Feuerfresser not only modelled himself on Moltke, the great Prussian general whose motto was 'Be more than you appear!', but expected his trusty subordinates to do the same. He nodded to them as they filed in but left them standing just inside the door, patiently awaiting whatever orders he chose to give them. With perceptible deliberation, he leafed through some papers on his desk. Then, at long last, he raised his head.

'We've just been sent a man named Singer,' he said thoughtfully, ' – a corporal. Rather an abnormal proceeding, wouldn't you say?'

The Commandant of Kampfental enjoyed extraordinary powers, one of them being the right to select his own personnel from any source he cared to tap – combat units, home-based formations, or trainees undergoing instruction in the camp itself. Singer's unheralded transfer was an exception to this rule.

'Where did he come from?'

The adjutant cleared his throat. 'A Munich field hospital, sir. He was posted to us direct from there.'

'At whose instigation?'

'Army Group Headquarters, Colonel – or so I've since discovered.'

'Nothing so exceptional about that, Captain Tauschmüller. Not on the face of it.'

The Colonel made a practice of addressing subordinates whose performance met with his satisfaction by their rank and name. If he dropped their rank and called them 'Herr' instead, they were in trouble. Today, all seemed right with the world.

'If I ventured to draw the Colonel's attention to this matter,' Tauschmüller said discreetly, 'it wasn't because the initiative came from Army Group proper. We've had one or two similar postings in the past six months. As I see it, the unusual feature of the case is that the man was transferred on direct orders from Field-Marshal Wedell's staff – more precisely, from Colonel Schlumberger.'

Lieutenant Wagner shrugged. 'Nothing so exceptional about that either.'

He had no need to explain his meaning, nor did he even hint at it in the presence of a commanding officer as ultra-correct as Feuerfresser. The fact was that not all transfers were prompted by strictly military considerations. There could be quite different reasons for them – reasons of a personal and private nature. Wagner, who clearly thought this a case in point, felt obliged to say more.

'I've taken a look at the man,' he reported. 'A pretty insignificant type, but no fool. I suspect that's why he seems quite glad to have landed up here instead of being sent straight back to the front. Still, I propose to keep a close watch on him for security reasons.'

Colonel von Feuerfresser nodded approvingly and turned to Königsberger. 'What do you think, Doctor?'

'I don't entirely share Lieutenant Wagner's opinion of Corporal Singer – not that I feel qualified to form a definite assessment at this stage. This much I can say, however. To judge by some of his remarks, he seems to have a mind of his own.'

'We'll soon cure that, Doctor,' Wagner interposed with a ferocious grin. 'Our methods have never failed yet.'

'For all that,' Tauschmüller said cautiously, 'a few discreet enquiries might be . . .'

Feuerfresser took the hint at once. 'Get me Army Group Headquarters,' he decreed.

Captain Tauschmüller got through in two minutes flat, invoking the magic words 'top priority'.

'Colonel Schlumberger, please. Colonel von Feuerfresser calling.'

Passing the phone to Feuerfresser, Tauschmüller picked up the extension earpiece and reached for a pencil. The ensuing conversation, whose gist he carefully noted down, went as follows:

SCHLUMBERGER: Glad you called, my dear chap. I was just about to phone you myself and warn you to expect a call from the Field-Marshal. Something terrible's happened – a flap of the first order.

FEUERFRESSER: All in good time, Schlumberger. I'm always at the Field-Marshal's service – 'nough said. You've just sent us a new boy named Singer. Why?

SCHLUMBERGER: Singer? Ah yes, I remember. A trivial matter – one of those things that land on your desk by accident, if you know what I mean.

FEUERFRESSER: I think I understand. You transferred him at the Field-Marshal's suggestion?

SCHLUMBERGER: No, no, don't run away with that idea. The decision was mine.

Colonel von Feuerfresser made his adieux and hung up with a faintly mocking smile. The position seemed clear enough. Nepotism was a deplorable but commonplace phenomenon in Nazi Germany. Singer, he assumed, enjoyed protection. He was either the son of a Party member with important connections, or the nephew of someone on somebody's staff . . .

'We could always ship him off to the front, Colonel,' suggested Wagner. 'It might save us all a lot of trouble.'

'There are other ways of handling these things,' Captain Tauschmüller put in quickly, 'certainly here at Kampfental. No need to upset higher authority by unloading him right away.'

'May I hazard a suggestion?' said Königsberger. 'Having been deprived of my personal orderly a few days ago – for reasons which remain a mystery – I suppose I'm entitled to a replacement. Singer might be just the man.'

Wagner pricked up his ears. 'You'd take him in hand yourself?'

'Why not?' said Captain Tauschmüller. 'If we have to keep tabs on him, where better than in the officers' mess?'

Wagner was quick to exploit the underlying inference. 'Well, yes – as long as the MO is prepared to assume full responsibility for the man.'

'Well,' said Tauschmüller, 'are you?'

With the eyes of all present upon him, and especially those of the Colonel, Königsberger had no choice.

'Of course,' he said, 'why not?'

Colonel von Feuerfresser wound up the meeting fast. 'Very well, Doctor, he's all yours.'

After being instructed to report to Sergeant-Major Schulz in the administration block, Corporal Sebastian Singer set off along the road from the main gate. Nobody helped him with his gear, but that he took for granted.

The road led straight to the heart of the Kampfental complex. Twenty feet wide, its asphalt surface had a foundation strong enough to support the heaviest armoured vehicles. Everything that met Singer's eye as he trudged along it in the glare of the summer sun looked new, neat, and carefully maintained. Stretching away on the left, with Lake Kampfental glinting beyond them, were training areas, rifle ranges and playing fields, including a football pitch. On the right of the road stood rows of huts whose fresh paintwork and spotless windows looked positively inviting. They were temporarily unoccupied because they belonged to the Training Wing, and the next course was still ten days off.

The few soldiers who passed Singer hardly deigned to acknowledge his existence. He also sighted a gaggle of the uniformed females known as women staff auxiliaries. They eyed him with curiosity before swiftly averting their gaze as though forbidden even to look at a member of the opposite sex.

The central part of camp made a far less deserted impression. Lazing in the sun outside a sort of chapel on the left of the main thoroughfare were several exotic-looking girls, some of them rather scantily attired. On the right stood more trim huts whose surroundings had been embellished with birch hedges, flower-beds and ornamental shrubs. In the background, overlooking the lake, was a snow-white building of baronial dimensions.

Everything in this sector of the camp seemed strictly regimented. There were scores of notice boards bearing injunctions and prohibitions such as 'No Admittance', 'Keep off the Grass', 'Maximum Security Zone' and 'Officers Only'. The signposts were so numerous that only an illiterate could have gone astray.

Obediently, Singer followed the signs that were relevant to him: 'Permanent Staff', 'Main Administration Block' and 'Orderly Room'.

Innocuous as it sounded, Singer knew from long experience that the latter term masked the real nerve centre of any military installation because, in the German Army, the orderly room was the home of the sergeant-major.

Sergeant-majors were the backbone of any unit. Most of them were hard-core professionals versed in every aspect of their trade and capable of sorting out every conceivable and inconceivable problem that might crop up in the sphere of military administration. No commanding officer could dispense with their wealth of experience, so they had, albeit reluctantly, to be treated with respect.

The sergeant-major who presided over AFSIC Kampfental answered to the undistinguished name of Schulz. At thirty-one, he should – in his opinion – have been commissioned long ago. Far from resenting his lack of promotion, however, he preferred to lead a life of his own.

Schulz's manner was gracious and patronizing – even sympathetic. It was years since anyone or anything had impressed him. Although he could roar like a pride of lions when he chose to, he had discovered better ways of getting what he wanted.

When Singer appeared, he was lounging in a chair with his boots off and his feet propped on the desk. There was an open beer bottle in his left hand and a half-empty glass in his right. His welcoming grin was distinctly affable.

Affable or not, Singer's sixth sense told him that the man was dangerous. He deposited his belongings on the floor, stiffened to attention like a recruit on parade, and barked out the regulation form of words.

'Corporal Singer reporting for duty!'

Sergeant-Major Schulz shifted his position just enough to signify approval.

'Smart lad, eh? Stay that way and you'll be all right. Keeping in step, that's what counts, and I call the tune round here. If there's anything you don't understand, ask me. Get it?'

'Yes, Sergeant-Major.'

'Lieutenant Wagner's still got your papers, but after that they'll come to me. Then I'll decide what to do with you.' Abruptly, Schulz added, 'Ever play cards?'

'Yes, Sergeant-Major.'

'For real money?'

26

'Any stakes you care to name,' Singer assured him, instinctively sensing that he could afford to omit the ritual 'Sergeant-Major'.

'Fine, I'll hold you to that – maybe tomorrow. What about women? They say there's lots of hot stuff in Munich. Speaking man to man, can you slip me a couple of good phone numbers?'

'Yes, Sergeant-Major, if that's what you want.'

'You're starting to grow on me, Singer.'

'Glad to hear it, Sergeant-Major.' Singer was unabashed. 'Mind if I ask you a question?'

'Shoot.'

'Why so interested in phone numbers? You've got all you need right here on the doorstep – gorgeous girls in uniform, luscious-looking hired help from abroad. What more do you want?'

Schultz gave him a pitying smile. 'You may be smart, Singer, but you've still got a lot to learn about Kampfental. With us, the Colonel's word is law. He likes everything organized down to the last detail, and I mean everything.'

'Sex included?'

'This installation is vital to the war effort – indispensable, more like. We think of everything, that's why there's a first-class brothel on the premises. The only trouble is, a man with a position to keep up – ' he obviously meant himself – 'can't afford to be seen there too often. You'd do well to steer clear of the place yourself.'

'What about the ladies stationed here?'

'Those, my friend, are what the Colonel refers to as "splendid specimens of German womanhood". Anyone who messes with them and gets caught can kiss the girls goodbye for good, so I wouldn't advise you to risk it. Mind you, all the regulations in the world can't stop a man wanting to do what comes naturally.'

'So what about the brothel? Doesn't that fill the gap?'

'Anyone who shows his face there goes down in the book

– Lieutenant Wagner inspects it once a week. Name, rank, number, date, time, expenditure, details of condom consumption, type and quantity, sanitary precautions, et cetera.'

'Sounds enough to put you off your stroke.'

'That's why it's mainly designed for trainees. My own men are strictly forbidden to use the place. They can keep in practice on their weekends in Munich, but for that they need some nice reliable phone numbers. I tell you, anyone in camp with a decent address book can really make friends and influence people.'

It wasn't hard to discern the sergeant-major's list of priorities: skat, skirt and schnapps, though not necessarily in that order. Singer and Schulz grinned at each other, one with dawning optimism and the other with dawning approval.

Just then, the telephone rang. Captain Tauschmüller, who doubled as adjutant and HQ Company commander, was on the other end of the line.

'You've got a Corporal Singer with you, Schulz. I suggest you assign him to Sergeant Gerner's detail in the officers' mess. Any objection?'

That kind of suggestion was an order – Schulz offered no objection. Although he betrayed no resentment at Tauschmüller's cavalier failure to sound him out first, if only for form's sake, he felt piqued. Maybe the new man wasn't such a welcome acquisition after all.

'Good idea, Captain. Just what I was going to suggest myself.' Schulz replaced the receiver and turned to Singer. His manner was as casual as ever. 'By agreement with the company commander, I'm assigning you to the officers' mess. That's a plum job, so you'd better not let me down.'

On his way to the officers' mess, which proved to be part of the big white building he'd noticed in the background, Singer had to negotiate another barbed wire fence. The checkpoint was manned by a beetle-browed military policeman.

'Hands above your head and brace them against the gatepost,' the MP said briskly. 'Spread your legs and shut up.'

Singer was expertly and thoroughly searched – even his crotch came in for a vigorous squeeze. Satisfied, the MP straightened up.

'Carry on, you're clean. Who do you want?' Singer mentioned Gerner's name. 'Straight on, main building. See the terrace? Through the small door on the right.'

Behind the small door Singer came face to face with his one-man reception committee at Hölzbach station. Mess Sergeant Gerner beamed with pleasure.

'So it's you again.'

'Yes, Sergeant,' Singer said humbly.

'Hit the deck!'

Singer obeyed in a flash.

'Up! Down! Up!'

Sweat erupted from Singer's brow.

'We can keep this up for hours if you like, but you're too smart – you know which side your bread's buttered. Feel like saluting till your arm drops off, or bailing shit out of a cesspool, or scrubbing the floor with a tooth-brush? No? Well, you don't have to, not if you toe the line.'

Singer preserved a docile and attentive silence. His next test took the form of an innocuous-sounding question.

'What about that bottle of fizz I gave you? Drunk it yet?'

'Afraid not, Sergeant. It was confiscated by the camp police.'

'You only had to tell them it came from me.'

'But I didn't, Sergeant. I thought it might be out of place – not what you'd want, I mean.'

Gerner rewarded this correct answer with an approving nod.

'Good lad, that's the ticket. I'll replace it, naturally – in fact I'll make it two this time.'

'I'm very grateful, Sergeant.'

'And so you should be. From now on, you're mine. Either I roast you alive or we end up buddies – it all depends on you.'

'So what do I do?'

'Every damn thing I say. First we'll get you properly kitted out, then I'll teach you how to feed and water the livestock. I want you on duty in the mess this evening.'

Singer was dispatched to a small room next door, which was lined from floor to ceiling with shelves holding tablecloths, napkins, towels and bedlinen. Lolling on a heap of blankets in the middle of this cubbyhole was a well-fed young man with a boyish, friendly face. He was cradling a bottle of schnapps in his arms.

Sergeant Eugen Priewitt's present rank had little significance. A few days earlier he had been a staff sergeant; tomorrow he might be a corporal, next week a master-sergeant. His status was determined by the Colonel alone, and his continual demotions and promotions provided Feuerfresser with a perfect means of demonstrating the full extent of his authority. As Feuerfresser's personal orderly of several years' standing, Eugen Priewitt was responsible for his comfort and well-being at every hour of the day and night. He also acted as mess supervisor, which meant in practice that he presided over all mess stores including a wine cellar of Lucullan profusion and variety.

Priewitt's well-groomed exterior – his immaculate uniform and aura of expensive *eau de toilette* – was not lost on Singer. Instantly recognizing the plump young man as a person of importance, he clicked his heels with appropriate vigour.

'Corporal Singer reporting as instructed, Sergeant.'

Eugen Priewitt flapped an indulgent hand at him. 'Take it easy, friend, we're all in the same luxury liner.' His expression implied that it was bound to sink sooner or later, but all he said was, 'No need to bust a gut. Some people think there is, but I'm not one of them. You can call me Eugen when there's no one else around.'

'Fine – Eugen it is. My name's Sebastian. What happens now?'

'For a start, Sebastian, I'm going to fix you up like a mess waiter.' He eyed Singer appraisingly. 'Medium build,' he said. 'No problem.'

Priewitt heaved himself up off the heap of blankets, still clutching his bottle, and pulled back a curtain on the far wall. It concealed more shelves, all crammed with articles of clothing. A dazzling white linen jacket fluttered in Singer's direction, followed by a pair of dark serge trousers with knife-edged creases, a pair of black patent shoes, and some snow-white pure silk gloves.

'Terrific,' said Singer, marvelling. 'In that gear I'll feel like something out of a grand hotel dining-room.'

'There's a bit more to it than that, Sebastian.' Priewitt came over and sniffed him like a rabbit. 'I'm not saying you reek, but you don't smell fit for an officers' mess.'

'What do you have to smell of for that, Eugen?'

'Nothing, preferably. If you smell of anything at all, it better be soap. Come on, you're going to have a proper shower – I'll be glad to help. Then you can get dolled up for the mess.'

Priewitt draped his arm round Singer's shoulders and gave him an affectionate squeeze. 'I like you, sonny – you can share my quarters. Let's go.'

CURRICULUM VITAE OF SEBASTIAN SINGER
or, The Reluctant Rebel

I was born in Uhlandstrasse, Charlottenburg, Berlin, on 1 April 1922, the fifth of six children. My father was a fitter in the loco-building division of Siemens. My mother just kept house, though she sometimes worked for an office-cleaning firm.

The stench of proletarian poverty – that was probably his earliest impression. One WC for each floor and a cold tap on the landing alongside. Eight people sharing three cramped rooms. The kitchen served as a dining-room and living-room for the entire family. The children slept in one room containing two beds, a pair of boys in one and the girls in the other. During babyhood, the youngest child slept beside its parents in a laundry basket in the third room, which was a sort of attic with a narrow sky-light.

Screams, scuffles and noisy altercations were the order of the day – as, for instance, when arguments raged over who should wear what or be first to pee in the communal bucket. Frau Singer usually put a forcible end to these squabbles by swooping on the children and cuffing them apart, though only with the flat of her hand. Sebastian nearly always managed to escape such treatment because he soon learned how not to provoke it.

His father, a small, wiry man with the wrinkled brow of a worried dachshund, was seldom to be found in the bosom of his family. Sunday lunch was the only function he did attend with a fair degree of regularity – they sometimes had meat: mince loaf, hashed calves' lights, or pigs' trotters with sauerkraut – because he was a very busy man. His brood had to be clothed and fed, but politics came into it too. Papa Singer was an active trade unionist and a member of the German Social Democratic Party. He tried to explain his apparent neglect at lunch one Sunday.

'It's all for the sake of the future – yours and everyone's. I don't expect you to understand right away. Sebastian's the only one that might.'

'I don't get much of what's going on,' said Sebastian. 'All I know is, the world's a pretty lousy place.'

I went to elementary school in 1928 and left in 1936, when I was fourteen. My father died in the spring of 1933. Killed in a road accident, or so it said on his death certificate.

Sebastian's teachers, who prided themselves on being educators too, began to take an interest in him very early on. He soaked up all they taught him like a sponge. 'Bright as a button,' said some. 'A born troublemaker,' said others, whose suspicions had been aroused by his questions during their patriotically slanted lessons in modern history.

'I'm puzzled by what happened after the Great War,' he once remarked, meaning the war that was later re-christened World War I. 'Millions of men were killed, the Kaiser went into exile in Holland, and his generals and field-marshals all got pensioned off – all except Field-Marshal von Hindenburg. We made him our President. Why was that?'

This interjection, which could not fail to excite the deepest disfavour, was construed as a slur on Germany's fallen heroes and an insult to the head of state. Summoning the misguided boy's father, the headmaster declared that his attitude was insupportable.

Tolerant man that he was, Papa Singer not only agreed but promised to talk some sense into his son. He was a patriot as well as a Social Democrat, and authority had to be upheld.

Then, in the springtime of Hitler's new era, Papa Singer died under the wheels of a truck. His death was no mischance, for the said vehicle had been pressed into use as a war chariot by Brownshirt bullies on the look-out for socialists and other treacherous elements. Although the so-called accident was witnessed by several people, they declined to testify, being anxious to live a little longer than its victim. The police, who arrived on the scene soon afterwards, could only record it as a hit-and-run case.

33

Because it was claimed that Father's negligence had contributed to his death, the family were very short of money. My eldest sister, Anna, who was then fourteen and later married a local Party boss, took over the housekeeping. Mother got herself an office-cleaning job in Father's old factory. In 1936 I joined the firm myself, as a management trainee. In 1938 I was drafted into the State Labour Corps.

Shortly before Sebastian left school, he was involved in an embarrassing incident which came to the notice of the school authorities: the janitor caught him making improper advances to a girl pupil in the basement. The headmaster sent for his mother, who was now head of the family.

'Your son Sebastian,' he told her, 'is not only mentally warped but in grave moral danger. I shall be obliged to make a note to that effect in his school record.'

Horrified, Frau Singer took her son to task. 'How could you do this to me?' she wailed.

'But I didn't do anything to you, Mother,' he retorted. 'Nor to the girl. She led me on and I was curious, that's all.'

'But aren't you ashamed of yourself?'

'No,' Sebastian said simply, 'why should I be? It was quite good fun.'

The youngster seemed to attract trouble like a magnet. No sooner had he started his job in the offices of the Siemens locomotive plant than he showed signs of managerial precocity. He criticized what he regarded as superfluous paperwork, had the gall to propose several administrative short cuts, and even drafted a new personnel structure. The head of his department was outraged.

'What the hell are you trying to do?' he snarled. 'After my job, is that it? Well, get this: you're only a trainee, so act like one.'

Sebastian's departmental chief was doubtless relieved when the Labour Corps called him up. The new recruit was sent to northern Pomerania, to a unit engaged in land reclamation, otherwise known as draining a swamp.

The miasma of his childhood – sweat, excrement, putrefaction – enveloped him once more. The patriotic young labour conscripts were not only obliged to wade knee-deep in gurgling swamp water with mud-bespattered faces; they had to sing as they did so.

Songs with guitar and squeezebox accompaniment were likewise a regular feature of their evenings around the blazing camp fire. Here the youngsters were sometimes joined by inmates of the neighbouring Labour Corps camp for girls. On the first such occasion, their buxom leader's haughty gaze fell on Sebastian and roamed no further. He had obviously taken her fancy.

Sebastian Singer possessed a magnetism that attracted women as well as trouble – quite why, it was hard to fathom. He was nothing much to look at, but one of his admirers thought he had a 'gentle' expression and another enthused about his 'graceful' hands.

The Labour Corps chieftainess came straight to the point. 'I fancy you,' she told him. 'Do you fancy me?' Sebastian replied in the affirmative, and that was that. He survived the remainder of his spell in camp very nicely.

In 1939, as soon as I'd finished my stint in the Labour Corps, I was drafted into the Army. In 1941 I made corporal, which was as high as I ever got. My unit didn't see action in the French campaign, and I stayed in rear echelon jobs for the next three years. I was sent to the Eastern Front in 1944 but wounded almost at once.

Nothing ever seemed to discourage Sebastian Singer. He patiently submitted to the rigours of primary training, the traditional hazing and bullying of raw recruits. Once it was over, he avoided further unpleasantness by quickly transforming himself into a useful and obliging subordinate.

After the French campaign, that glorious page in the annals of the Third Reich, Sebastian landed up in Dreux, a small town fifty miles from Paris. It was there that his talents developed to an extent that surprised even him.

He was attached to the local garrison headquarters, where he soon established a sort of travel bureau whose unofficial motto was 'Make the most of France while you can.' Sebastian specialized in sightseeing trips to Paris, complete with guided shopping tours, gastronomic orgies and room reservations in selected brothels. His commanding officer, a major, received a citation from Army Corps HQ for outstanding devotion to the morale and welfare of his men, and Sebastian basked in his reflected glory.

He also chalked up some personal successes. Lilo, the delectable *commère* of a vaudeville theatre in Paris, fell flat for him when he presented her with a bouquet from his infatuated CO, who had really meant it for Édith Piaf, one of the current show's attractions.

Their affair continued to flourish until Sebastian's CO, who had since been promoted lieutenant-colonel, transferred his attentions to Lilo. Lilo gave him the brush-off, which infuriated him. 'Singer,' he said to his usually ultra-dependable factotum, 'how dare you cross me for the sake of a little French floozy! I'd never have thought you capable of such ingratitude.'

The fruits of the new lieutenant-colonel's wrath did not take long to mature. Sebastian was packed off to the Eastern Front and assigned to an infantry battalion in training for house-to-house fighting in Warsaw. He was badly wounded on his very first operation, while jumping out of a truck.

That was how he found himself in a hospital near Munich, where he met Lieutenant Kersten, who had also been wounded, and became his regular opponent at chess.

That, in turn, was how he came to meet Barbara Wedell. And that, as he sensed with characteristic speed, was a watershed in his life.

Corporal Singer took up his duties in the officers' mess at AFSIC Kampfental on the evening of 20 July 1944, but not before he had liberally soaked and soaped himself under a piping hot shower. As soon as Eugen Priewitt had decked him in his mess waiter's uniform, which fitted like a glove, he was given his first assignment by Sergeant Gerner.

'You're to open and close the doors,' he explained. 'Smartly, but don't overdo it. This isn't a parade ground.'

The double doors in question – slabs of plate glass in ebony frames – led from the anteroom into the banqueting hall. Those who passed through them were confronted by a long refectory table swathed in white damask and laden with antique china, solid silver cutlery, and fine cut glass. Overhead sparkled an ornate chandelier.

The officers assembled in quick succession. First to arrive was Captain Tauschmüller, camp adjutant and commander of HQ Company. Once through the doors, which were assiduously opened and shut by the new mess waiter, he was greeted by Sergeant Gerner and escorted to the table. Tauschmüller inspected Gerner's preparations with an expert eye – needlessly, because nothing fell short of Colonel von Feuerfresser's exalted standards.

Tauschmüller's inspection was rudely interrupted when the radio, which had been burbling in the background, began to broadcast the unlikely-sounding news that someone had tried to assassinate Adolf Hitler. He listened with a dubious expression.

His air of scepticism persisted when Lieutenant Wagner appeared, closely followed – indeed, almost pursued – by Captain (Med.) Königsberger, who was, incidentally, the only person to acknowledge Singer's presence. He found time to give him a friendly wink before hurrying after Wagner. The two men went over to the radio set and listened, one with head-wagging indignation and the other with unemotional interest.

'Thanks to the workings of Providence . . . the Führer himself . . . only minor cuts and bruises . . . sad to state, some loss of life among members of the Führer's entourage . . .'

'Hell's bells!' exclaimed Wagner. 'Might as well switch off – we'll get the details officially in a few hours' time. We can dispense with that crap.'

'Are you implying that it's enemy propaganda, Lieutenant?' The MO cocked a provocative eyebrow. 'I'd remind you that we're listening to the Greater German Broadcasting Service.'

Wagner lapsed into furious silence and Captain Tauschmüller looked studiously vacant. The MO edged nearer the radio. He had his back to the room, so he missed the nightly entrance of two key figures. It was no great loss, though their arrival never failed to tickle him. Shoulder to shoulder and marching in step came AFSIC's production managers, Majors Kastor and Pollandt, who planned and ran the courses that were Kampfental's *raison d'être*. One was plump and of philosophical bent, the other thin as a rail and abrim with fighting spirit, but both had an unmistakable awareness of their own importance.

Immediately behind them, like their sword- and shield-bearer, strode Lieutenant Lahrmann, an erect, heroic-looking, gladiatorial man of few words and granite physique. It was Lahrmann, that most faithful of subordinates, who translated the instructional theories evolved by Kastor and Pollandt into rugged, combat-oriented practice.

The threesome converged on the radio, which Königsberger had turned up even louder.

The next arrival was female – flaxen-haired, robust and

athletic, but dignified and decorous of bearing. As soon as Sergeant Gerner had drawn his attention to the lady's presence, Captain Tauschmüller made for her like a homing pigeon.

Frau Klarfeld was in charge of AFSIC's three dozen women staff auxiliaries. The Colonel treated her with the utmost respect and chivalry – she was, after all, Erika, Countess von Klarfeld, even if she did insist on being addressed by her surname alone.

Tauschmüller hurried across and kissed her hand, then feasted his eyes on her. The high-necked, ankle-length gown in dark grey silk did nothing to conceal her outstanding feminine attributes.

'May I?' Tauschmüller gallantly offered his arm and escorted her over to the radio, which had just announced that the Führer and Reich Chancellor, Adolf Hitler, would now address the German people.

'My God,' breathed Frau Klarfeld, deeply moved, 'the trials our Führer has to endure! What a magnificent example he is to us all!'

Nobody contradicted her.

Singer, who had been watching the scene with interest, felt a dig in the ribs. It was Eugen Priewitt.

'Get those doors open fast, Sebastian – wide open. The Colonel's coming.'

And come he did. Colonel Viktor von Feuerfresser strode into the banqueting hall with measured step and majestic mien. As though alerted by a fanfare of trumpets, all present turned in his direction. Beyond them, sounding positively obtrusive in the respectful hush, the Greater German Broadcasting Service droned on.

'Switch it off!' hissed Lieutenant Wagner.

'Louder!' commanded Feuerfresser. He might have been emulating his hero, Frederick II, King of Prussia, known as 'the Great' – the monarch who, when confronted by an unflattering caricature of himself while out riding in the streets of Berlin, had loftily ordained that it be hung in a more conspicuous position.

The radio, obediently turned up full by Königsberger, filled the room with Hitler's hoarse, rasping voice: 'A small and isolated clique of shady individuals ... unworthy to be described as German officers . . . mentally deranged, infected by Marxist propaganda . . . if not actually bought and paid for by Moscow . . . but in vain!'

'Well,' said Feuerfresser, clearly unmoved, 'that's that. Frau Klarfeld, gentlemen, to business. Shall we dine?' He paused as though struck by a sudden thought. 'But not, I think, to music.' Another pause. 'Not tonight.'

The meaning of this ban eluded Singer. The day had been one long series of surprises.

'Permit me, dear lady,' said Feuerfresser, with a courtly bow. Frau Klarfeld laid her hand on his slightly flexed arm and moved off. The others trailed along behind.

The long table was flanked by hard, leather-seated chairs. The Colonel took his accustomed place at the head. Frau Klarfeld was privileged to sit on his right; Captain Tauschmüller, his trusty henchman, on his left. The rest of his staff disposed themselves in accordance with a carefully devised seating plan. Nothing, it seemed, was left to chance in Colonel von Feuerfresser's sphere of command.

'The soup,' he decreed.

At once, two mess waiters sprang to life. One was carrying a Meissen tureen on a silver salver, the other a gleaming silver ladle. They doled out soup with the practised dexterity of trained hotel staff under Sergeant Gerner's eagle-eyed supervision.

Singer had meanwhile stationed himself beside the door to the kitchen, which afforded a better view of the assembled company. It struck him that the Colonel was served last, not first. He was inclined to regard this as an act of courtesy until he realized that its underlying motive was strictly practical. No one could start eating before him, so the others' food cooled off while his arrived hot on the plate.

They all spooned up their soup in silence. It was cream of vegetable with beaten egg – savoury and sustaining – but they were given little time to enjoy it. Having briefly sampled the contents of his plate, Feuerfresser pushed it away. This was an unmistakable signal, and everyone hastily followed suit. Galvanized by a whispered order from Sergeant Gerner, the mess waiters sprang to life again.

The Colonel had evidently resolved to put the interval between soup and main course to good use. He turned to Lieutenant Wagner.

'This latest business,' he said. 'I'd be interested to hear your views on it.'

As local intepreter of the National Socialist scriptures, Wagner plunged into his element. '*Tempus edax rerum,*' he proclaimed. 'Time devours all things, as the Romans so aptly put it.' His ensuing spate of words had clearly been culled from innumerable Party pamphlets and textbooks. 'Everyone has enemies, even the noblest of mortals – even the Führer. The more exalted a man's station, the more persistent the attempts to lay him low. Such was the fate of Siegfried, that uniquely Germanic figure from the realm of legend. He too was compassed about by treacherous dwarfs intent on his destruction. Just as murder quenched his Germanic radiance, so traitors have tried to assassinate our beloved Führer – without success, of course. It isn't the first time.'

Feuerfresser nodded thoughtfully, whether or not in agreement it was impossible to tell. Captain Tauschmüller gave his commanding officer an inquiring stare. Majors Kastor and Pollandt just ruminated in silence, but Frau Klarfeld emitted a rosy glow of enthusiasm which visibly delighted the heroic Lieutenant Lahrmann, whose adoration of her was plain to see.

41

Captain (Med.) Königsberger had been sitting there like a spider in a web. 'Except,' he said mildly, 'that this time the treacherous dwarfs were senior German officers who disagreed with their supreme commander on matters of policy.'

This version was hotly disputed by Wagner, who felt assured of his Colonel's approval. 'You obviously fail to see this outrage in its true historical context, Doctor. I advise you to try harder.'

'I'd appreciate your help, Lieutenant.'

Wagner fortified himself with a sip of Franconian wine, which was second only to sparkling hock as the favourite mess beverage. He then proceeded to summarize his analysis of modern German history under three main headings:

1. Even before the Führer came to power, a few notorious dissidents tried to bar his upward path. One of them was Gregor Strasser, the Party's chief political organizer. He was duly disposed of.

2. In 1934, a certain Ernst Röhm, chief of staff of the Party's brown-shirted private army, staged a revolt. Having always been regarded as one of the Führer's most devoted comrades in arms, he turned out to be a perverted and overweeningly ambitious homosexual. In consequence, he too was condemned and eliminated – by a bullet.

3. It later transpired that moral decay was rife at the very top of the armed services. General von Fritsch, said Wagner, had himself been unmasked as a fairy. As for Field-Marshal von Blomberg, the earliest and most senior of the régime's military supporters, he not only got mixed up with a prostitute but went to the lengths of marrying her.

Frau Klarfeld, who felt satisfied that she had seen to the

heart of Wagner's dissertation, announced her findings with solemn fervour. 'No matter what burdens are imposed on our revered and beloved Führer,' she declared, 'his superhuman spirit will prevail.'

'Spoken like a true daughter of Germany!' cried Wagner. He almost toasted her with upraised glass but stopped himself just in time, remembering that this was the Colonel's prerogative.

Feuerfresser laid a soothing, commendatory hand on his table companion's upper arm but was distracted from the sight of her devoutly heaving bosom by an interjection on Königsberger's part.

'There have always been assassins and idealists with homicidal tendencies, I grant you, but the people behind this attack weren't any of those. They appear to have been army officers from the Führer's personal entourage.'

'How would you know, Doctor?' Wagner's tone was fraught with menace. 'You weren't on the spot, and I trust you weren't involved, directly or indirectly. Very few details of this dastardly crime have yet been released, so kindly don't jump to conclusions.'

Everyone but the Colonel glared at Königsberger, who remained unruffled.

'It so happens,' he said, 'that I'm familiar with the Führer's East Prussian headquarters, *and* with the level of security maintained there. Access to the inner sanctum is restricted to a small, select band of the Supreme Commander's personal associates and military advisers, and even they have to submit to repeated checks.'

Once again, only the Colonel seemed indifferent to Königsberger's remarks and the surprise they aroused. From his post beside the door, Singer noted the buzz of agitation with interest.

Wagner's voice rose. 'Are you telling us, Doctor, that you've actually been inside the Führer's headquarters? If so, when and why?'

'I don't feel called on to explain, Lieutenant, not to you.'

'That's enough!' Colonel von Feuerfresser had stepped in at last. Whether or not he was tired of the MO's cat-and-mouse game, he evidently thought it incumbent on him to offer the rest of his staff a partial explanation.

'In the first place, Captain Königsberger spent a week at the Führer's headquarters in May of this year. He did so with my consent and at the request of Dr Morell, the Führer's personal physician, in his capacity as a medical practitioner and qualified psychologist. During that time he drafted a written opinion whose contents are naturally subject to the strictest secrecy.

'Secondly, where today's events are concerned, I have since telephoned an old friend and brother officer of very senior rank.' He had no need to elaborate: Field-Marshal Wedell was not only their army group commander but the founder and sponsor of the whole establishment. 'He assured me that the Führer is alive. This latest attempt on his life has failed like all the rest. The inference is plain.'

'Yes indeed.' Frau Klarfeld sighed ecstatically. 'Providence was at work!'

Almost everyone nodded. To the faithful, even a near catastrophe had somehow to be imbued with purpose.

Wagner put it into words: 'The Führer is our all. If he still exists, so do we!'

Ever practical, Majors Kastor and Pollandt held a brief whispered conference. 'In other words, Colonel,' said the lanky Pollandt, 'we carry on just as before?'

'Certainly,' Feuerfresser rejoined. 'AFSIC Kampfental remains in operation. And now, *bon appétit!*' He waited until the sucking-pig had been served before continuing, in an oracular tone, 'The impossible is never beyond the bounds of possibility. If it were, our lives would be meaningless.'

Having eliminated the Afrikakorps, the Allies were free to land in Sicily, then Italy. The so-called Rome-Berlin Axis began to crumble, menaced by the imminent collapse of the Fascist régime. Mussolini was 'taken into protective custody', or arrested, by Italian troops claiming to be patriotic royalists. He was soon released by a special German task force of airborne troops under SS command. Only a few months later, he was shot by his fellow countrymen and hung up by the feet.

Stalin appointed himself 'Marshal of the Soviet Union' – deservedly, from his point of view. His armies began to wipe out the German invaders and drive them westward on a broad front. They entered Polish territory. The surviving inhabitants of the Warsaw ghetto launched an insurrection with the crudest of weapons – home-made pistols, hand grenades and rifles – but were bloodily subdued. Not long afterwards, the Polish 'Home Army' followed their example. Though better armed, the Polish insurgents were defeated after weeks of ferocious fighting. Tens of thousands died, and Warsaw was reduced to rubble. The Red Army, already poised to take the city, stood aloof.

Troops of the Western Allies – British and Americans – managed to establish a bridgehead in Normandy under the command of General Eisenhower. This 'longest day' of the war – a phrase coined by Rommel – was followed by one of the most costly weeks in the conflagration which Hitler had so wantonly ignited. It soon became clear that the invasion had succeeded. The Western Allies, too, began their march on Germany itself.

2

Corporal Singer took up his duties as the MO's orderly the very next morning. He did so in accordance with a schedule laid down by Mess Sergeant Gerner.

'Right. Unless otherwise instructed, stick to the following timetable: in this camp, reveille for all noncommissioned personnel is at zero six hundred. The sergeant-major expects every butt to be clear of the bedclothes in sixty seconds flat, understand?'

'What about officers' butts, Sergeant?'

Gerner chuckled at this man-to-man jest, but only briefly. 'Officers and gentlemen have to be dressed and in their right minds by zero eight hundred. Their orderlies are responsible for that. In the MO's case, that means you.'

'What if he won't budge?'

'He will. Everyone in the Colonel's orbit does. If he finds it hard you have to give him a little help – tactfully, mind you, but firmly. If you don't, you'll be transferred out, get me?'

Singer was beginning to. To be on the safe side, he sought further information from his new-found friend Eugen Priewitt. The disastrous result of these first-hand tips from the Colonel's major domo was that Captain (Med.) Königsberger received almost the same privileged treatment as his commanding officer.

The members of the mess had been installed in a wing of their own on the ground floor. Each set of quarters comprised a small vestibule, a bathroom, and a bed-sitter furnished with a wardrobe, desk and bed.

Singer knocked at the door marked 'Königsberger' – twice. Then, faithful to Priewitt's tuition, he opened it a crack and called, 'Morning, Captain! Zero seven hundred and a nice sunny day!'

His ears detected several plaintive grunts and groans, followed by a hoarse injunction to go jump in the lake. Forewarned against just such a response, he walked over to the window, drew the curtains, and flung it open. Dazzling sunshine streamed into the room. The MO, who was sporting black silk pyjamas, heaved himself erect. His face looked pale and sweaty.

'Ugh!' he groaned, kneading his forehead. 'I must have overdone the brandy last night.'

'Wish I could say the same, Captain,' Singer said brightly. 'Unfortunately, Sergeant Gerner keeps the key to the cellar.'

'Know what I could use right now? Some icewater.'

'I'll turn the cold tap on full, that should do the trick. I'm told our water comes straight from the mountains. You cool off while I go and organize the sort of breakfast you need in your condition.'

Singer bustled off to the mess kitchen, a big tiled room with an array of well-stocked shelves. Its focal point was a huge wood-fired range bristling with ovens and hot plates. Presiding over it at this early hour was the third of Kampfental's chefs.

Number One was a top-class chef who had been drafted straight from the Black Horse in Wiesbaden. Number Two, likewise a chef of the highest calibre, came from Munich's famed Four Seasons. These two were responsible for lunch, dinner and intermediate repasts. Breakfast was handled by Number Three, who had originally trained as a breakfast chef at the Dorchester in London.

This trio of culinary virtuosi owed their presence at Kampfental to Captain Tauschmüller's unerring grasp of essentials and numerous excellent connections. They always worked with a will despite their lowly rank, presumably because they reflected that wielding a ladle was preferable to toting a rifle through the snows of Russia, and never made trouble because that was the quickest way of getting into trouble themselves. The breakfast chef was mindful of this when the new boy, Corporal Singer, breezed into his domain.

'Breakfast for the MO, please. Something really solid on a big silver tray, right?'

'Officers' breakfasts are served in the small dining-room,' he was politely informed, 'any time between seven and eight hundred hours. Your boss has his in there with the rest.'

'Up to now, maybe. This time he wants it in his room.'

'But it isn't usual. Only the Colonel gets room service.'

'Unusual doesn't mean forbidden, does it?'

'No, not necessarily.' The breakfast chef's experience was not confined to hotels of international standing. It also extended to the ways of AFSIC Kampfental, which was why his marzipan visage puckered into a worried frown. 'All the same, it isn't the done thing.'

'Look, friend, stop yakking or the coffee'll get cold. Just sling some breakfast on a tray, the way you do for the Colonel.'

The breakfast chef reluctantly complied, not forgetting to cover himself with a time-honoured formula. 'Fine,' he grumbled, 'if you say so. It's your funeral, not mine.'

Singer returned to the MO's quarters with his booty: three oven-warm rolls, a big pat of butter, three fried eggs on smoked ham, and half a pint of fresh milk. Also on the tray was a whole pot of strong black coffee abstracted with Priewitt's connivance from the Colonel's personal supply.

These princely offerings met with the MO's unqualified approval. Having freshened up and shaved in the interim, he quickly restored his spirits by slurping hot coffee and munching ham and eggs.

'Take a pew somewhere,' he told Singer, 'perch on my bed, if you like.' He himself was sitting at his desk. 'There are times when the world doesn't seem so bad, even now – even in this place. A decent breakfast does wonders for your morale. I'm feeling quite perky.'

'Even after what happened yesterday, Captain – or what didn't happen?'

'It's best not to dwell on these things. We're living on another planet, my friend, and we don't do too badly. That bomb won't change a thing, not in here. Besides, it'll soon be forgotten. There are too many people around with a vested interest in oblivion.'

'And you're one of them?'

Königsberger wagged a finger at him. 'I'll give you some good advice, Singer: stop poking the fire. With me you don't have to, and with the rest it could be risky. If you ever feel tempted, take a leaf out of Lieutenant Wagner's book – and I mean that literally. He's got a big fat collection of Roman proverbs, most of which he knows by heart. Here's one for you: *Carpe diem*. Roughly translated, it means grab what you can while the going's good.'

'Right, Captain. If that's the house rule, I'll try to act accordingly.'

'That's better, Singer – you catch on fast. If you want any more tips, just ask me.'

'Thanks, Captain. I do have a question, as it happens. Sergeant Gerner puts his mess staff through the mill twice a week, so I'm told, and the next work-out is scheduled for ten this morning. Do I have to turn up?'

'The Colonel approves of Gerner's keep-fit classes,' said Königsberger. 'Being a soldier to his fingertips, he doesn't want you cooks and bottlewashers running to fat before your time. Gerner's well aware of that.'

'But I'm not too keen on the idea. One good turn deserves another, if you know what I mean.'

The MO realized that his superlative breakfast had

carried an invisible price tag. He frowned. 'Look, Singer, you're obviously trying to get me to meddle in HQ Company business. Field training for mess personnel is standard procedure. Sergeant Gerner requested permission to hold these sessions, Captain Tauschmüller approved them in writing, and Sergeant-Major Schulz has them down in his duty roster. What do you mean, you're not keen? You want me to certify you unfit, is that it?'

'Not exactly, Captain. I'm just out of hospital. You only have to say you're still running tests on me. At least that would give me a breathing space. How about it?'

'Oh, all right.' Königsberger shook his head, partly in surprise at his own acquiescence. 'You're a sly dog, Singer. I'm fond of dogs, especially smart ones, but this is a war on wheels. Mind you don't get run over.'

Military fun-and-games for mess personnel took place every Tuesday and Thursday, starting at 10 a.m. Duration: ninety minutes to two hours. Sergeant Gerner always took advantage of the occasion to impress on his minions that they were common or garden soldiers, and that he was their lord and master.

Some two dozen mess waiters and other ancillary staff turned out on parade. They included cooks, orderlies, laundrymen, gardeners, and the recreation centre supervisor, alias brothel superintendent.

Training sessions, which took place on the greensward in front of the palatial mess, directly in the Colonel's line of vision, presented a spectacle that never failed to attract curious onlookers. Lieutenant Wagner regularly cast an expert eye over the proceedings. Captain Tauschmüller seldom attended, but Sergeant-Major Schulz was invariably present. As AFSIC's senior noncommissioned officer, he despised the mess personnel who came outside his immediate sphere of command and relished seeing them sweat.

Faithful to his usual custom, Sergeant Gerner opened today's session with a long and appreciative look at his victims – semi-military creatures in dappled camouflage suits, field packs ballasted with four bricks apiece, belts adorned with sidearm and ammunition pouches, shoulders supporting 98K carbines, vintage 1898.

'Take cover!' yelled Gerner.

They all hit the ground and cowered there awaiting further orders – all, that is, save one. Corporal Singer was still on his feet.

Gerner stared at him in disbelief. 'What are you playing at?' he demanded. Singer stood fast while the sergeant advanced on him like an ogre in seven-league boots. 'Lost your marbles, or something?'

Singer's response was crisply military. 'Begging the Sergeant's pardon, but I'm excused field duty till further notice.'

'What gives you that half-baked idea, you idle shower of shit?'

'MO's orders, Sergeant. Light duties only, pending further medical examination.'

Gerner advanced another step. They were eyeball to eyeball now. 'Are you trying to give me trouble, you little turd? *You* give *me* trouble?'

'Certainly not, Sergeant.'

'Well, that's what it looks like, you miserable streak of piss. This is your second black mark since reveille. You broke mess regulations. I wasn't there, worse luck, or I'd have booted your backside from here to kingdom come, but this takes the cake. Better think again, you conniving bastard!'

'It's the MO's decision, Sergeant. I'm only obeying orders.'

Their exchange had naturally been overhead and savoured with glee by the others, who were still lying prone. One of them sniggered and another let off a thunderous fart. But Singer still wasn't through.

'So I can fall out, can I? Unless, of course, the Sergeant cares to take full responsibility for . . .' He left the rest unsaid. Although it was only a ritual precaution, the present context made it sound like downright defiance.

Gerner tried to save face and partly succeeded. 'Don't think I'm through with you yet, dogface!' He spoke with conviction. Nobody had ever eluded his clutches, not in the long run. 'Fall out? Like hell you will! As of now, you're reassigned to our beginners' squad – it's all you're fit for.'

Singer showed no outward sign of shame at his demotion because it promised a temporary respite from the worst that Gerner could do. The beginners' squad consisted of only three men – the three chefs. They, too, had to parade in the interests of fairness. Never having received any basic military training, however, they were unfit subjects for Gerner's refresher courses. What was more, a hint from the Colonel had sufficed to ensure that they were handled with kid gloves.

Sergeant Priewitt, whose responsibility they were, made a habit of marching his charges into the far distance. What he described as 'basic training' was a leisurely affair. This time he had comfortably installed his squad on a bench in the sun, there to practise dismantling and reassembling a 98K carbine.

Singer joined the little group as ordered. Priewitt nodded a welcome. 'As far as I'm concerned, you can mosey off into the bushes and practise personal camouflage. If you take a nap while you're at it, never mind me.'

His suggestion was not declined.

Meanwhile, Sergeant Gerner was putting the rest of his men through their toughest-ever work-out. His jaw muscles bulged with determination and his guts churned with fury at his recent skirmish with Singer as he showered them with spittle and words of command.

Gerner's victims crawled along on their elbows, carbines held crosswise, leapt to their feet and sprinted, flung themselves headlong while running full tilt, and crawled along once more. Gerner chivvied them relentlessly, pushing them to the limit. They toiled across the turf with surprising stamina until three of them finally collapsed. One of the trio, a hospital case, was borne off on a stretcher by a pair of medical orderlies who had been prudently stationed on the edge of the training area.

At this point, Sergeant-Major Schulz strolled up. 'Pretty good going, Gerner, but you don't look too happy. Anything wrong?'

'It's that bastard Singer,' snarled Gerner, while his squad continued to crawl lakeward like clockwork toys. 'He's a troublemaker. The day's hardly started, and this is the second time he's tried to put one over on me.'

'He wouldn't be that dumb.' Schulz spoke as an expert on the mentality of underlings. 'All his type wants is an easy life. He doesn't know the rules yet, that's all.'

'If you ask me, somebody's laid an egg in our nest. I've got a nasty feeling about Singer.'

'You're imagining things. Anyway, if he won't co-operate we'll unload him fast.'

'There's more to it than that, Schulz. He's trying to dig in behind the MO, the crafty son-of-a-bitch. They could be in cahoots.'

Gerner gave the sergeant-major a detailed account of Singer's breakfast-time gaffe. Schulz listened with growing interest while the mess waiters crawled on. By the time Gerner was through, they had reached the lakeshore and were gasping in the shallows like stranded fish, unheeded by either of the NCOs.

'If that's the way it is,' said Schulz, 'we'll have to fire a shot across their bows. Leave it to me.' He lowered his voice. 'It's no use telling Captain Tauschmüller – he'd only try and paper over the cracks. Lieutenant Wagner's our man. Wagner's got it in for Königsberger, and Königsberger's responsible for Singer. A hint to Wagner – just a hint, not a formal report – that ought to do the trick.' He winked malignly. 'I don't like doing these things, but it can't be helped.'

Schulz's machinations bore fruit at lunch that day. As soon as the main course had been disposed of, Colonel von Feuerfresser sat back and eyed his table companions in turn. Frau Klarfeld was spared this ordeal, but Captain (Med.) Königsberger found himself transfixed by a lingering, intense, almost sorrowful gaze. Feuerfresser seemed only moderately satisfied when the object of his scrutiny began to fidget.

Ever alert to the Colonel's unspoken wishes, Captain Tauschmüller dismissed the mess waiters. Sergeant Gerner, who had been expecting this order, shooed them into the kitchen, where they swooped like vultures on the left-overs.

It was only then that Feuerfresser launched into one of his celebrated performances. His voice was bland, with an unmistakable dash of vinegar.

'Is it true, Captain Königsberger, that you cherish certain ambitions outside the purely medical sphere – ambitions of a nature hitherto concealed from me?'

In his obvious bewilderment, the MO blundered badly. 'The Colonel must be joking!'

'Joking?' Feuerfresser's eyebrows rose. 'You consider me a frustrated comedian, Doctor?'

'Certainly not, Colonel – I mean, I'd never be so presumptuous.'

Captain Tauschmüller came in on cue. 'In that case, perhaps you're one yourself. How else are we to interpret your attempt to claim privileges exclusive to the Colonel?'

The light of understanding dawned in Königsberger's eyes. 'I never claimed anything,' he protested. 'It simply happened. The tray was brought me by Corporal Singer, my new orderly.'

'On his own initiative? If so, he'll have to be dealt with. You agree?'

'The whole thing was a mistake, I'm sure. Singer doesn't know his way around yet. He may have misunderstood me.'

'Purposely misunderstood, or was he put up to it?' Lieutenant Wagner had inserted his oar, presumably hoping to court the Colonel's favour. 'Somebody's to blame. If it isn't you, it must be him.'

'Not necessarily.' Captain Tauschmüller was demonstrating his usual talent for compromise. Königsberger, he knew, possessed some influence and was not without his uses. Singer, who had been posted to Kampfental on direct orders from Army Group HQ, could not be jettisoned at once. 'The possibility of an error can't be entirely ruled out. The man was probably misinformed at the wrong moment.'

'By whom?' Feuerfresser shot his adjutant an appreciative glance. To the experienced observer, it seemed quite likely that their double act had been rehearsed beforehand.

'By Sergeant Priewitt, Colonel. He may well have given Singer the wrong impression – inadvertently, I'm sure.'

Eugen Priewitt was summoned at once. He snapped to attention in front of the Colonel, a dutiful and submissive figure. His face was expressionless, but the faintest twinkle in his eye conveyed a secret fondness for the role he was called on to play from time to time. Königsberger started to speak, but Tauschmüller silenced him with a peremptory gesture. He knew his own role by heart.

'This breakfast business, Priewitt – you gave Corporal Singer the wrong idea, didn't you?'

'Could be, sir.'

Majors Kastor and Pollandt shook their heads in silent reproof. Their gladiatorial sidekick, Lieutenant

Lahrmann, did likewise but far more vigorously. Frau Klarfeld seemed unaware of what was going on, but Lieutenant Wagner, the camp's custodian of National Socialist ideology, emitted a scornful, triumphant laugh: the culprit had been found!

'Sergeant Priewitt,' said the Colonel, looking grave in the extreme, 'this should never have happened. Your irresponsible remarks were a threat to routine, and routine is the cornerstone of military efficiency. Undermine that, and you jeopardize the entire war effort. I cannot let this incident pass, do you understand?'

'Yes, sir,' Priewitt said simply.

'Since you have been found guilty, and since you admit your misdemeanour, I am left with no option. On disciplinary grounds, I hereby reduce you to the rank of corporal.'

The brand-new corporal accepted his lot without a flicker of emotion. He saluted, performed a smart about-face, and marched out.

Lieutenant Wagner seized the opportunity to produce another of his Latin tags. '*Principiis obsta*,' he exclaimed. 'Roughly translated, that means "nip an evil in the bud".'

'And now,' ordained Feuerfresser, 'the pudding.'

It turned out to be oven-fresh apfelstrudel with vanilla sauce. Only Captain Königsberger took no pleasure in this culinary delight.

Sebastian Singer, who had secretly witnessed the performance through a crack in the kitchen door, followed Priewitt down to the room they shared in the basement. Priewitt unbuttoned his fly and peed nonchalantly into the wash-basin. Singer looked apologetic.

'Sorry, Eugen, that was the last thing I wanted.'

Priewitt shrugged. 'Don't let it worry you. You've still got a lot to learn about this place.'

'No reason why I should do it at your expense.'

'Bullshit,' Priewitt said consolingly. Instead of buttoning his trousers, he removed them for comfort's sake. 'You haven't got the hang of the system, that's all.'

'I like a bit of fun, Eugen, but this is going too far – I mean, what the Colonel and his cronies did to you just now.'

'Let me put you straight.' Priewitt opened the door of his locker. 'Here, get a load of those.'

Hanging inside were three uniforms, each with different badges of rank: a staff sergeant's, a sergeant's, and a corporal's. 'See?' said Priewitt. 'Sometimes I'm one thing and sometimes I'm another. It all depends on the mood of the moment.'

'Don't you mind going up and down like a yo-yo?'

'It's one of my special functions, buddy.' Priewitt, who had unbuttoned his shirt, scratched himself pleasurably, then stripped off his underpants. 'Feuerfresser uses me as a scapegoat. I help him show off his authority – or his kindness and generosity, whichever.'

'You mean he can walk all over you?'

'It's not just me. The way he treats me is an object lesson to the rest of his underlings. It shows them what he can do if he has to.'

'And you take it lying down?'

'It isn't a question of that, Sebastian. Feuerfresser's a big shot. I know what makes him tick – I should do, after all these years. He can do more than promote and demote people. He can reassign or transfer them, which pretty well gives him power of life and death. Mind you, appearances can be deceptive.'

'Really?' Singer said quickly. 'You mean there's another side to him?'

'That's my business. Anyway, everything's fine as far as I'm concerned. I'm still the CO's personal orderly, and that gives me a fair amount of clout.'

'Regardless of rank?'

'Screw that,' Priewitt said cheerfully. 'It doesn't matter what rank I happen to hold at any given time, I always draw a staff sergeant's pay. What's more,' he added with dignity, pink as a piglet in his birthday suit, 'I expect to be treated like one. Look, I've swiped us a nice big magnum of burgundy – vintage 'thirty-three, CO's personal reserve. Let's go for a shower and take it along with us. We've earned a little relaxation.'

That afternoon a heavily laden, tarpaulin-shrouded Henschel twenty-tonner trundled into Kampfental Camp and headed straight for the officers' mess. It was not waved down at any of the checkpoints.

Lieutenant Lahrmann, who had been alerted by a phone call from the guard commander, was waiting on the main terrace. The truck pulled up with a squeal of brakes, and out of it jumped a burly master-sergeant in a camouflage suit white with dust. He pounded up the steps and saluted.

'Mission completed, Lieutenant,' he barked.

Lahrmann returned his salute before giving him a comradely handshake. 'Any problems, Heinz?'

The master-sergeant stared at Lahrmann, with his spotless uniform and gleaming Knight's Cross. His faint air of surprise seemed to ridicule the question, but his response was crisply formal.

'No problems, Lieutenant.'

Lahrmann nodded and made his way down to the truck. Heedless of his best uniform, which was *de rigueur* for lunch in the mess, he clambered up the tailgate, pulled the covers aside, and conducted a preliminary examination of the crates, cartons and sacks in the interior. His hands were soon black with grease and his uniform badly in need of a visit to the cleaner's.

'Very creditable, Heinz,' he said at length.

'Nearly twice my quota, Lieutenant.' Master-Sergeant Heinz spoke with a touch of pride, as befitted AFSIC's weapon-training ace. 'You want them on display?'

'As usual.'

This was not the first such exhibition on the main terrace. Within minutes, a fatigue party was hard at work unloading the truck and unpacking Heinz's haul of captured equipment. It included a quick-firing anti-tank gun, anti-personnel mines, tommy-guns, hand grenades, and snipers' rifles. All, apart from a few British items, were of US manufacture. Once they had been sorted and arranged, Majors Kastor and Pollandt made a simultaneous appearance. They surveyed the collection in gratified silence, nodding judicially. Then Kastor turned to Heinz.

'Where did you get all this stuff?'

'From three of our army corps on the Western Front, Major.'

'Did anyone dispute your authority?'

'Only once, sir, but I followed instructions. A phone call to Colonel Schlumberger at Army Group HQ cleared the bottleneck.'

The two majors embarked on a leisurely and detailed inspection of Heinz's arsenal. Rifles and sub-machineguns were checked for weight, balance, ease of operation and standard of manufacture. Pollandt was the first to pass judgement on them.

'High-grade articles, but not robust enough for prolonged use under combat conditions. The Russians have a better instinct for these things.'

Sergeant-Major Schulz and Sergeant Gerner were also in attendance, though more in the role of interested spectators. Schulz nodded at the huge array of weapons.

'Reckon we'll have to enlarge our museum,' he said. By 'museum' he meant the camp armoury, which already occupied a lot of real estate. No. 1 Section was devoted to German military equipment, No. 2 to Russian.

'I don't get it,' said Gerner. 'Some of these popguns look

as if they've hardly been used, but they're covered in rust.'

'Ignorant sod!' sneered Master-Sergeant Heinz. 'That's not rust, that's blood.'

Before Gerner could think of a suitable retort, the Colonel appeared with Captain Tauschmüller at his elbow and Corporal, formerly Sergeant, Priewitt bringing up the rear. Feuerfresser curtly acknowledged the rigid salutes of all present and set off on a tour of inspection. He took his time, scrutinizing each exhibit in turn but touching none. Then he turned to Heinz.

'Good work, Sergeant, I couldn't be more pleased.' His next words were addressed to Lieutenant Lahrmann. 'Kindly ensure that all these weapons are fully serviceable by the time the next course starts.'

Major Kastor clicked his heels. 'You wish us to modify our methods of instruction, Colonel?'

Feuerfresser quelled him with a martial glare. 'I shall advise you of any such changes in good time, Major, but I can promise you one thing: this next intake will be the most important we've ever handled.'

The following day found Corporal Singer stretched out, stark naked, on an examination table in the camp medical centre, coughing and taking deep breaths under Captain Königsberger's direction. The MO had been sounding his chest.

'Well, my friend,' he said with a smile, 'you'll never be an Olympic athlete, but I can certainly classify you as average cannon-fodder.'

'You mean I'm fit again, Captain? I don't feel it, believe me.'

'Really? You don't strike me as a very sick man.'

'What about my lung?'

'It's healed up very nicely.'

Königsberger ran a professional eye over Singer's operation scar. 'First-class butcher's work – they really did you proud in Munich.' He went to a side door and opened it. 'Fräulein Mauerland,' he called, 'get me Singer's medical record, would you?'

Singer heard the tiptap of approaching footsteps. Through the door came a lissom brunette with a virginal, madonna-like face. She was wearing a white gown fractionally too big for her and carrying a buff envelope. Having deposited this on the patient's genitals, as though for propriety's sake, she made a graceful exit.

Singer propped himself on his elbows and stared after her. 'Wonders never cease in this place. Who was that?'

The MO chuckled. 'Down, boy, or I'll certify you fit for combat duty.'

Singer subsided again. 'Be fair, Captain. A girl like that would put anyone's pulse rate up, even when he's as sick as I am. I could use some physiotherapy. How about it?'

'I wouldn't advise you to try,' said Königsberger.

'Why not? Does somebody have first call on her services – you, for instance?'

'Keep your insinuations to yourself, Corporal. Fräulein Mauerland only helps me out part-time. She's one of Frau Klarfeld's staff auxiliaries, and the Colonel keeps them under his personal supervision.'

'What, *all* of them?'

'Every last one. Nobody's allowed within arm's reach of them, and vice versa.'

'What if – '

'Oh, it's been tried a few times, naturally, but the upshot's always the same: summary punishment and transfer. The score to date is one officer, two sergeants and three corporals. They were all caught *in flagrante* and sent to the front overnight. They've never been heard of since.'

'Human emotions don't seem to count around here.'

'Of course they do, Singer, as long as they're patriotic. The authorities have also catered for your baser instincts, so called. They've installed a really first-class brothel here.

61

I should know – I'm responsible for the health of its staff and clientele.'

'The whole idea makes me want to throw up. Anyway, Doctor, I still don't feel fit. I get these sudden attacks of deafness. There are times when I can't hear a word people say.'

Königsberger's good humour had returned. 'That,' he said, 'sounds like a brand-new complaint – one that could prove an asset if the symptoms declared themselves at the right moment. I'll make a note of it. Anything else?'

Singer stretched luxuriously. 'Not for now, but I may think of something later.'

'Very well,' said Königsberger, who had been glancing through his medical record. 'Your lung was last X-rayed three weeks ago. I suggest we take another picture of it in a week or two. Till then you can concentrate on looking after me whenever you aren't on duty in the mess, all right?'

It was. Singer jumped briskly off the examination table and got dressed. 'Fine, I'll try and get acclimatized to the place, meaning come to terms with the inevitable. Does that include what happened on July twentieth?'

The MO's response was surprisingly brusque. 'Drop it! That – er – incident is over and done with. In a place like this, run by a bunch of officers like ours, it doesn't even rate a mention.'

'I see,' Singer said drily. 'Funny, you didn't sound as if you thought so in the mess the other night, when you were arguing with Lieutenant Wagner.'

'Come off it, man!' Königsberger was striving to control himself, but his voice shook with some anonymous emotion. 'Lieutenant Wagner can't stand me and I can't stand him. He thinks I'm redundant – a square peg in a round hole. I think he's an arrogant jackass, but that's as far as it goes.'

Singer was undeterred. 'So you aren't interested in the events that led up to the attempt on Hitler's life?'

'Do me a favour!' The tremor in Königsberger's voice had communicated itself to his hands. He clasped them together like a man at prayer. 'Humanity's sick and getting sicker. Accept the fact.'

'Just like that?'

'For God's sake, Singer, surely you aren't proposing to do something about it? If so, I didn't hear you. You see? Your deafness must be catching.'

'There isn't much a corporal *can* do, but every little bit helps.'

'Well, don't expect any help from me. The most I can do is offer you an occasional constructive suggestion.'

'Like what?'

'Like keep your nose clean. Get the measure of the place before you go off half-cocked. Apart from that, you can pay a call on Frau Klarfeld and take her a copy of my scheme for reorganizing the medical centre. I'd be interested in your views on it, Singer – and on her. Would you mind?'

'Why should I?' said Singer.

Shortly after three o'clock that afternoon, Corporal Singer made his way to the women auxiliaries' block. It was situated on the right of the main thoroughfare, not far from the officers' mess, in a compound enclosed by its own barbed wire fence. A sentry stood guard over the only entrance.

Standing orders stated that these precincts were off-limits to anyone not in possession of a special permit signed by one of the six officers on Colonel von Feuerfresser's staff, though this applied to daylight hours alone. Nobody, but nobody, was allowed in or out after 9 p.m. and before 7 a.m. Only the Colonel could approve exceptions to this rule, one of them being Frau Klarfeld, who enjoyed complete freedom of movement at any hour of the day or night.

Armed with a visitor's pass signed by the MO, Singer gained access without difficulty. The sentry jerked his thumb at the block where Frau Klarfeld had her office and living quarters, which proved to be a spotlessly clean and elegantly furnished suite of rooms.

Erika Klarfeld, who favoured sober colours, was seated behind her desk in a simple grey costume. She eyed her visitor with a trace of curiosity and waved him into an armchair. Then she indicated a capacious silver teapot in front of her.

'I prefer tea, myself – Indian, with a dash of rum. Would you care to join me?'

While admitting that he was no connoisseur, Singer politely accepted. One sip from the wafer-thin china cup in his hand left him hugely impressed. Contrary to her description, Frau Klarfeld's favourite brew consisted of rum with a dash of tea.

'And now, Herr Singer, I presume you've come to apologize.'

Singer choked on his second sip. 'I don't know why I should, ma'am, but I will if you think I ought to.' The 'ma'am' was a form of address adopted on Königsberger's advice. 'May I ask what I'm supposed to have done?'

Frau Klarfeld gazed at him sternly. 'You exhibited yourself to one of my auxiliaries in a state of total undress. It simply won't do.'

'I didn't mean to – it was an unfortunate coincidence. Captain Königsberger had just been examining me when Fräulein Mauerland entered the room at his request.'

'A lame excuse, Herr Singer.' Frau Klarfeld refilled her cup. 'You could have covered your nakedness when my little Melanie walked in – with your hand, say, or a handkerchief – but you did nothing of the kind.'

Singer racked his brains for some motive behind these reproaches, but without success. Although he had been quick to note the possessive pronoun in '*my* little Melanie', its precise implication escaped him. He gained time by asking for another cup of alcoholic tea.

'If you'll pardon my saying so, ma'am, Fräulein Mauerland seems to be quite a favourite of yours.'

Frau Klarfeld drained her cup, nipped a hiccup in the bud, and gave him another reproving stare. 'You do not, I trust, suspect me of being emotionally entangled with a member of my staff?'

'Of course not, ma'am,' Singer said quickly. 'On the contrary, I get the impression – if you'll permit me to say so – that you're very much a woman and highly attractive to the opposite sex.'

'Do you indeed?' Frau Klarfeld sounded pleasantly surprised. 'You're a very forward young man.'

'Not as forward as I'd like to be,' Singer said boldly, 'but I know my place. All the same, ma'am, you can't blame me for stating the obvious when it's staring me in the face.'

'I'm flattered, Herr Singer.' Her expression seemed to confirm this. 'You're right, of course. I am a woman, but a woman with very special responsibilities.'

'One of them being Fräulein Mauerland?'

'That girl,' she replied with almost religious fervour, 'is only one of my three dozen charges, but to me she's a symbol. Melanie is a beautiful, clean-living, worthwhile member of our national community – German to the core and destined to become the mate of someone whose qualities match her own. In other words, Corporal, hands off!'

Never having meant to get involved with one of her girls in the first place, Singer was able to return an unhesitating 'Certainly, ma'am.' Then he rose to his feet, swaying slightly. Though undetectable in its effect on Frau Klarfeld, the rum was starting to percolate his system.

She leafed through the MO's reorganization plans, smiling to herself. 'I shall have to take a closer look at these,' she said, then redirected the smile at him. 'You may call on me again tomorrow or the day after, by appointment. We can discuss Captain Königsberger's ideas then. For the present, you may go.'

Situation Report No. 2

The attempt to kill Hitler on 20 July 1944, had been intended to hasten the end of a war that was degenerating into wholesale slaughter. Though not the first of its kind, it was certainly the boldest and most spectacular.

Colonel Count von Stauffenberg, a staff officer badly disabled by several war wounds, had been summoned to attend a conference at the Führer's headquarters. He left his lethal briefcase under Hitler's map table, where it duly exploded. Several people were killed or injured, but Hitler himself was almost unscathed.

Hitler's huge and carefully constructed manhunt-machine swung into action, directed by Himmler, co-ordinated by the Central State Security Bureau, and fully backed up – pursuant to the Nazi penal code – by the People's Court under Judge Roland Freisler. Many death sentences were passed and plenty of other scores settled on the spot, murder in the public interest being then the order of the day. Hitler had decreed that the whole 'subversive rabble' should be exterminated.

Some five thousand people died in consequence. They included socialists rounded up by the police as well as civil servants and armed forces personnel suspected of hostility to the régime. At a conservative estimate, seven hundred officers were executed. Many were tortured and humiliated before being suspended from meat-hooks with piano strings round their necks, so that they would expire as painfully and protractedly as possible. Their death-throes were filmed for Hitler's delectation.

The abortive revolt of 20 July 1944, was followed by an almost unimaginable increase in the carnage it had been designed to prevent. Both humanly and materially, the last nine months of the war doubled the ravages inflicted during its first five years. 'Total war' had become a consummate reality.

A few nights later, after successfully helping to serve a dinner of smoked trout, wild duck with red cabbage, and cheesecake with whipped cream, Sebastian Singer paid a visit to the brothel.

Officially sanctioned by the Colonel, this establishment occupied a site below and to the left of the administration block. It was under the overall supervision of Captain Tauschmüller, in his capacity as HQ Company commander, further supervised from the aspect of troops' welfare by Lieutenant Wagner, and still further supervised in matters sanitary and hygienic by Captain Königsberger.

Its nickname – 'the Chapel' – was not fortuitous, because it had originally been built *circa* 1895 as a place of worship dedicated to St Hubert, patron saint of huntsmen and the chase. Soon commandeered for other purposes, it became a stable and storehouse. Then, towards the end of World War I, the copper sheathing on the roof and the modest bell in the little tower were sent off to a gun foundry.

Still later, the erstwhile chapel had served as a venue for lectures and dances. It continued to do so until the arrival of Colonel von Feuerfresser, who announced that the combat troops to be trained under his command were entitled to the fullest possible 'recreational facilities'. The building was duly converted into the semblance of a hotel, with a foyer and bar downstairs and a dozen 'recreation rooms' flanking the passage on the extra floor that had halved the height of the original nave.

Patrons entered the premises from the rear, through what had once been the sacristy. This was presided over by the 'recreation supervisor' or 'lighthouse keeper' – an allusion to the discreet red lamp above the door. A sad but amiable little man with a perpetual smile on his wizened

67

face, Corporal Hausleitner looked as old as time but was only forty-five.

'You don't have a reservation,' he told Singer, checking the book on his desk. 'Never mind, maybe I can fit you in if you need it that badly.'

'I don't,' said his unexpected visitor. 'I'm here on duty. The MO told me to drop in – I'm his new orderly.'

Hausleitner looked uneasy. He was suspicious on principle, especially of those who turned up with no intention of sampling his wares. 'You mean he's sent you to keep tabs on me?'

'Take it easy,' Singer said soothingly. 'All he wants is an up-to-date list of the medical supplies you keep here, including contraceptives.'

'Why? Doesn't he trust me? Is he trying to pin something on me?'

'Is there something to pin, Hausleitner?'

The corporal was about to retort when Sergeant-Major Schulz and Mess Sergeant Gerner lurched into the whitewashed sacristy, arm in arm and slightly the worse for wear. One was brandishing some money and the other a bottle of fizz. They deposited them on Hausleitner's desk, then noticed Singer.

'Well, well,' said Schulz, 'look who's here!'

Gerner leered. 'You reckon he's after a piece of tail?'

'Why not?' the sergeant-major said magnanimously. 'The youngster's only human.'

Corporal Hausleitner, who had scrambled to his feet, produced two keys and two matchbox-sized packets, presumably of contraceptives. 'Here you are, gentlemen. Numbers three and seven, as arranged. They're ready and waiting.'

Gerner picked up the keys and contraceptives and split them between himself and Schulz. Then he loomed over Singer.

'You never saw us, is that clear?'

'Didn't I?'

'No, you didn't,' snapped Schulz, though his thoughts were clearly elsewhere. 'Not unless you're looking for trouble.'

'He isn't,' Gerner said confidently. He turned to Hausleitner and jerked an indulgent thumb in Singer's direction. 'Give him number five, that'll take his mind off things. He can have one on us if he likes.' He grinned at Singer. 'Pay us back next time around.'

'Over a hand of cards,' said Schulz. Muted laughter greeted this suggestion. Hausleitner, too, saw the joke; Singer didn't.

The sergeant-major and the mess sergeant took their condoms and keys for numbers three and seven – a Polish and a Hungarian girl respectively – and tottered purposefully upstairs. Hausleitner and the MO's representative regarded each other in silence for a while.

'What was all that about?' Singer asked eventually. His tone was faintly menacing. 'I thought this place was strictly supervised. Doesn't everyone go down in the book?'

Brothel regulations were known all over camp. First came the reservation procedure, preferably two or three days in advance because demand was heavy – though not, admittedly, during the two-week breaks between courses. Applicants were then registered and allocated to female 'operatives'. Finally, 'on completion', their names were recorded in a card index: red cards for permanent staff, green for the trainees who provided the establishment with its passing trade.

Hausleitner looked more worried than ever. 'Don't make trouble for me, that's all.'

'Why should I? You seem to be doing that very nicely without any help from me.'

'Don't say that! I follow my instructions to the letter.'

Under pressure, the little corporal went on to disclose some administrative details. Normal duration for enlisted men: one hour. Standard charge: thirty reichsmarks, of which careful account was kept. 'The operative gets ten reichsmarks – '

'Really? In hard cash, you mean?'

'Of course not. Ten marks per trick – or per hour, whichever – go to the paymaster, and he keeps an account for each of our girls.'

'Who dreamed that up?'

'It's all in my list of management procedures.'

'Fine, terrific. So the girls get ten marks an hour. What happens to the other twenty?'

'I keep ten to cover current expenditure on aids to comfort and personal hygiene: a change of sheets once a day, underclothes, towels, room cleaning, douching and showering facilities, et cetera. I can account for every last pfennig, too.'

'And the balance?'

'That goes into the camp welfare fund, which is also run by the paymaster.'

Singer did some rapid mental arithmetic. He quickly realized that the brothel was a lucrative concern. For eight hours' work a night, each girl pulled in two hundred and forty marks. Since there were a dozen of them on the premises, their annual turnover must exceed a million. He whistled through his teeth.

'Then it's not surprising that people like Schulz and Gerner can amuse themselves for free without going down in the book.'

'Forget it,' Hausleitner said urgently. 'You know what'll happen if you don't. Those two prize bulls will squash you like a bug – and me into the bargain.'

'Even if we joined forces? Even if we both said – '

'Said what, my friend? That they were here? Only conducting a spot check, Schulz would say, and Gerner would back him up. They'd swear they always suspected me of putting my hand in the till, and they'd find some way to prove it. They're fireproof, those two. We wouldn't stand a dog's chance against them.'

Hard as he found it, Singer was forced to acknowledge the truth of this. He still hadn't mastered the rules of the game, unlike Hausleitner, who seemed to have a thorough grasp of them.

'So what should I do?'

'Play along, the way they expect you to. They offered you girl number five. You can't afford to say no.'

'Who is she?'

'The pick of the bunch, so I'm told, but I've also heard she's a bit of a handful.'

'You mean you haven't tried her out yourself?'

'Me?' Hausleitner gave a broad, gnomelike grin. 'I'm as good as impotent, sonny – couldn't fail to be, in my job. Try sitting in a whorehouse yourself, night after night, and you won't feel a thing below the waist or anything else.'

'I'll take your word for it,' said Singer. 'But go on about number five. What sort of girl is she?'

'Russian, probably Jewish. If she takes a fancy to someone – and you could well be her type – she's supposed to be heaven on earth. If she doesn't – which happens pretty often, worse luck – they say it's like screwing Lot's wife. Some people rave about her and others accuse her of sabotaging the war effort – nothing in between. That's why I try and keep her free for very special customers – tactful, sensitive youngsters like you. Want me to introduce you?'

'Why not? I'd like to have a chat with her.'

'A chat?' The little man grinned again. 'That's one way of passing the time, except that you won't find it easy – she only speaks Russian. Know any?'

'Not a word. How do you get through to her?'

'By sign language, if I have to. Anna catches on quickly – she's a smart girl – but if I ever have to give her a real telling off I send for Natasha. That's our camp interpreter.'

'Could you send for her now?'

Hausleitner sighed. 'Why not let sleeping dogs lie, my friend? Me, I aim to get through this war without getting bitten.'

Fresh from his excursion to the Western Front, Master-Sergeant Heinz was gazing with reverence at his assortment of captured US hardware in the Russian section of the camp armoury. Weapons held a magical fascination for him.

Master-Sergeant Kainz of Lieutenant Wagner's Security Platoon was keeping him company and helping him finish a bottle of bourbon, likewise captured on the Western Front.

Heinz pointed at his loot with rapturous enthusiasm. 'How about that! Isn't it a sight for sore eyes?'

Kainz, nicknamed 'Bulldog' because of his squat but powerful physique, wore the Iron Cross First Class, like Heinz. 'Terrific,' he conceded. 'They'll look great on display.'

'Except that they're hot off the production line. They're too damn good to gather dust in here. They deserve to be used by experts, not pawed and gaped at by a bunch of lousy trainees.'

'You're the expert around here, Heinz. Everyone appreciates that, including your boss.'

'Lahrmann?' Heinz sneered faintly. 'You think so?'

He could afford this dig in his fellow sergeant's presence because they were cut from the same cloth. As effective head of camp security, Kainz shared Heinz's stark and simple philosophy of life. The only good enemy was a dead one. When in doubt, you blazed away with everything you'd got.

Kainz scratched his chin. 'Well,' he drawled, 'my boss –' he meant Lieutenant Wagner – 'hasn't been too happy

72

about him lately.' He lowered his voice. 'The way he sees it, Lahrmann's going soft.'

'Could be,' said the weapon fetishist. 'Lahrmann used to be a shit-hot instructor – keen as mustard – but now . . . He's turning out Boy Scouts, Kainz, not combat troops with hair on their teeth. Guns and cold steel are there to be used, I keep telling him, and what do I get in return? A load of theoretical bullshit!'

He reached for a hand grenade and held it on high. 'The latest US development – still in the experimental stage.'

Apart from a kind of red safety-ring, Kainz could discern nothing unusual about the grenade, which was conventionally pineapple-shaped. 'What's so special about it?' he asked.

Without a word, Heinz pulled the retaining pin and let the safety lever fly off. This would have caused any normal grenade to explode within seconds. Heinz held his exhibit under Kainz's nose. Kainz cowered away and glanced ostentatiously at the open window, but his friend made no move to toss the bomb outside.

Seven seconds passed, then ten, then twenty. Beads of cold sweat stood out on Kainz's forehead. Still no explosion.

Heinz gave an ecstatic guffaw. 'Unlike a traditional grenade,' he explained knowledgeably, 'this one isn't automatically detonated via a delayed-action fuse when the safety lever's released. It's got an acid detonator that functions on impact, not before. Isn't that terrific?'

'You can say that again.' Kainz, his whole face greasy with perspiration, was breathing hard.

'A great close-combat weapon for men with plenty of guts and judgement,' Heinz enthused. 'What's more, you can easily disarm it if you change your mind.' He retrieved the safety lever, folded it down and replaced the pin.

Kainz looked suitably impressed and steadied his nerves with a long pull at the bourbon bottle. Uncertain how to comment on this demonstration, he waited for Heinz to elaborate. He did not have to wait long.

'You see, Kainz? The war's getting more and more interesting. All kinds of possibilities are opening up, especially on the technical side, and we've got to make the most of them. The trouble is, nobody in this namby-pamby outfit's up to it. What we need is new blood – someone to point us in the right direction and pull the trigger.'

In response to a phone call from Corporal Hausleitner, Natasha presented herself at the reception desk within fifteen minutes. Kampfental's Russian interpreter was an austere young woman in a grey-green linen smock gathered at the waist by a broad leather belt. Her high cheekbones, thin lips and catlike eyes lent interest to a flattish face that would otherwise have been unremarkable.

'Well, Herr Hausleitner?' Her tone was cool and business like. 'What can I do for you?'

'For me, nothing, but my friend here needs your services badly. He wants a word with Anna.'

'It's not my job,' she said firmly.

'That's what I told him,' said Hausleitner. Pontius Pilate could not have been quicker to disclaim responsibility. 'There's just one thing, Natasha. Corporal Singer is Captain Königsberger's new orderly. He's here on the MO's say-so.'

This seemed to capture her attention. She took a closer look at Singer. 'I've heard of you,' she said. 'What do you want me to do?'

'Translate a few questions and answers, that's all.'

Surprisingly, she gave an acquiescent shrug. 'Very well, follow me.'

They went upstairs and along the central passage. Each of the doors flanking it bore a shiny brass number. Natasha opened door number five and walked in.

The room was dominated by a capacious bed. On it, wearing a white cotton shift, lay a pale, raven-haired girl of exceptional beauty. She sat up at once, her dark eyes filled with apprehension.

Singer remained standing near the door while Natasha sat on the edge of the bed and started talking, very softly, in Russian. Eventually she turned her head.

'Well, what do you want to ask her?'

'I'd be interested to know how she got here.'

'That's nobody's business,' Natasha said resolutely. 'I'm not translating that.'

'Isn't it your job to translate anything that's said?'

'Normally, yes.'

'So what's abnormal about my question, Fräulein Natasha?'

'Please don't call me Fräulein,' snapped Natasha. 'Nobody here calls me that. I don't like it – it's out of place. You probably don't mean to be sarcastic, but that's the way it sounds to someone in my position.'

'As you like.' Singer was beginning to enjoy himself, perhaps because of the unmistakable interest with which Anna was regarding him over Natasha's shoulder. 'But what was so abnormal about my question? I'm still waiting to hear.'

'Simply the fact that you asked it. Why ask Anna questions when the MO could answer them just as well? It isn't fair to her or me.'

'You're being obstructive, Natasha. In the wrong company, that could be dangerous.'

'I know, Herr Singer, and I also know that my time here won't last for ever.' It sounded like 'my days are numbered'. Natasha shrugged. 'They'll send me to a concentration camp sooner or later, but I can't see *you* putting me there.'

Singer took this as a compliment, which it was. 'Good interpreters are at a premium,' he said. 'Besides, there's a difference between being obstructive and bending a phrase here and there. You must be up to all kinds of tricks in your trade, and who's going to catch you out? Not me, for one.'

Natasha smiled for the first time. She turned back to Anna and addressed her in her mother tongue, presumably summarizing the course of their exchange. Anna started to smile too – at Singer.

He now learned that Natasha had been working at Kampfental ever since Colonel von Feuerfresser took it over. Her primary function was to teach his trainees basic Russian for use in anti-partisan operations.

'In your place,' Singer said brightly, 'I'd lead our budding heroes up the garden path – tell 'em *nyet* means yes, and so on.'

'It did cross my mind,' Natasha admitted. 'Fortunately, I found out just in time that one of your officers speaks Russian – not brilliantly, but well enough. It's Major Kastor, who runs the training courses, though he never lets on – always talks German to me and pretends he doesn't understand a word.'

'The plot thickens,' said Singer. He decided to change the subject. 'As far as I can judge, Natasha, the three of us are roughly the same age. You and Anna must have been born in the early 'twenties, like me. Any reason why we shouldn't reminisce about our childhood – where we spent it and how? Would you mind translating that sort of thing?'

Natasha shook her head and made room for him on the bed. He sat down beside her, feeling genuinely welcome at Kampfental for the very first time.

CURRICULUM VITAE OF VIKTOR VON FEUERFRESSER
or, Noblesse Oblige

Born 21 March 1895, on my parents' country estate at Pösenitz in Pomerania. Father: Friedrich von Feuerfresser, who attended the imperial coronation at

Versailles in 1871, after Germany's defeat of France. Mother: Hermine von Feuerfresser, née Baroness von Bernitz of East Prussia, a friend of the Hindenburg family. I was the second of three sons born at intervals of one year. In keeping with tradition, my elder brother was expected to take over the family estate. I joined the Army, and my younger brother entered the Church.

The three boys' spheres of responsibility were strictly defined and supervised from infancy onward. Their upbringing and education were entrusted to an English governess and a French tutor. German ideals and sentiments were instilled by their father himself, in company with his spouse. 'Our sons,' he often said, 'must be groomed for a great and brilliant future. We owe them nothing less.'

Every aspect of their lives was sedulously tailored to that future, one being the maintenance of a strict daily routine. They rose during the winter months at seven, in summer at six. Thereafter came cold baths, teeth-cleaning, ear inspection, and physical jerks. 'Discipline,' their father used to say, 'is everything. Discipline alone enables one to meet life's challenges and surmount them.'

There were, none the less, a few members of the fair sex prepared to console the hard-pressed youngsters, especially Viktor, who was a handsome lad, tall and wiry, proud and silent. His mother often took him in her arms and pressed her cheek against his. 'You're the best boy in the whole wide world,' she would tell him in a whisper, and the cook used to slip him extra helpings of the things he liked best. 'You appreciate them,' she used to say. 'That's because you've got good taste.' His English governess carried the process of consolation somewhat further by taking him into her bed and cuddling him close.

These matters did not escape the notice of his austere

male parent, though he was probably unacquainted with every last detail. 'Beware the wiles of women,' he adjured Viktor. 'Keep them at arm's length, or they'll destroy you before you know where you are. Always be a man, whatever happens.'

Viktor's revered father took him deer-hunting and taught him to ride. The promising youngster's inbred horsemanship manifested itself at an early age, and it was not long before he was given a mare of his own: Erika, a magnificent beast with a lustrous chestnut coat.

> *In 1905, when ten years old, I was privileged to enter the Cadet Academy at Potsdam. This came under the direct command of His Imperial Majesty, Kaiser Wilhelm II, who had long and successfully sponsored the formation of an élite officer corps. Many graduates of the institution went on to win our country's highest awards for valour and command its armies in battle. It was there that I met the fellow cadet who became my lifelong friend.*

No boy of Viktor von Feuerfresser's background was likely to be ruffled, still less cowed, by the iron discipline prevailing in this semi-monastic male community. His father's schooling paid off. By virtue of stamina and perseverance, Viktor passed every test of mental and physical efficiency with flying colours.

Deliberate deprivation of sleep and food, nightlong vigils in the depths of winter, immersion in horse-troughs of icy water – Viktor accepted these and other equally subtle educational methods as inescapable necessities. 'What must be, must be,' ran his motto. 'Only women complain.' He welcomed such demands on his willpower because they would later entitle him to make the same demands on others.

He was one of the best, if not the best, in his year. Only one other member of this élitist community could match his prowess. He and Viktor engaged in manly trials of strength and skill – hard fought but impeccably fair, as comradeship prescribed.

Viktor's comrade and friend-to-be was Herbert Wedell, who was one day older than himself. Although Herbert possessed no patent of nobility, unlike the vast majority of his fellow cadets, this proved to be no disadvantage. His father, a Hanoverian high court judge, was in line for the Ministry of Justice, and these things soon got around. Even more important, however, was the fact that his grandfather, Colonel Heinrich Wedell, had been the right-hand man of Helmuth von Moltke, the legendary Prussian field-marshal, and was reputed to have had a hand in his classic military victories.

So Viktor and Herbert were evenly matched in every respect. They might have been made for one another. Tucked up in adjacent dormitory beds, they whispered together for hours and dreamed of their common future. They were also side by side when the Kaiser himself turned up to inspect their year, rewarded them both with a gracious nod, and enjoined them to 'keep up the good work'.

In 1914 we were compelled to launch our great German war of national self-defence. The Russians invaded East Prussia but were put to flight by Hindenburg, a victory in which my friend Wedell and I played a modest but not wholly unimportant part. Then came the battles in France – Verdun, Douaumont, and the rest. We fought there too, and our spirits remained undaunted even when America's intervention in the war endowed our enemies with overwhelming material and numerical superiority. Despite this, we were never defeated in the field.

Viktor and Herbert continued to prove their mettle, initially as junior company commanders in the same regiment. They first saw action at Tannenberg, where they helped to ensure that the invading Russians were driven from the Fatherland like frightened rabbits. This brought a summons from their army commander, Field-Marshal Paul von Hindenburg, who personally invested them with an Iron Cross apiece – First Class, of course – and reiterated Kaiser Wilhelm's injunction to 'keep up the good work'. It was one of their happiest days ever, and one they never forgot.

The two aspiring lieutenants, whose simultaneous promotion to captain was only a matter of time, were then transferred to the Western Front. In the fighting around Douaumont, which claimed tens of thousands of lives on both sides, Viktor von Feuerfresser and his men succeeded in storming the bitterly contested ruins of an outlying fort.

For this stroke of military genius, he received Germany's highest decoration, the '*Pour le Mérite*', Military Division, from the Kaiser's own hands.

Herbert gave him a manly hug. 'If anyone deserves it,' he declared, 'you do.' Viktor's response, delivered with equal sincerity and conviction: 'Your day will come too.'

It did indeed, though not for some time. Their beloved Germany was now confronted by forces whose superiority in mere numbers and equipment would not, they both agreed, have been sufficient to lay the Fatherland low by itself.

In 1918, after the war had been pronounced lost by certain traitors styling themselves 'representatives of the people', I returned to my home at Pösenitz in Pomerania. Father had meanwhile died of heart failure, and our estate was being run by my elder brother. Mother, who retained a life interest in the place, welcomed me back with all the iron composure characteristic of true German womanhood.

Viktor's mother, Hermine von Feuerfresser, had not changed one whit. Prim, proud and Prussian as ever, she fondly embraced her favourite warrior son and escorted him to his room. Nothing had changed there either, except that her photograph on his chest of drawers had been joined by several silver-framed photographs of himself in uniform, complete with orders and decorations. The usual vase of fresh flowers was also in evidence.

Pleasant though this reception was, other aspects of Viktor's homecoming were less so. His elder brother, Waldemar, looked moody and morose. The estate was faring badly. The war bonds which 'the Old Man' – their father – had been patriotic and imprudent enough to purchase in such numbers had gone down the drain. What was more, their agricultural labourers had become politically contaminated and were mouthing communist slogans. Finally, to crown everything, Waldemar had married a plump, sensual-looking brunette with bedroom eyes.

'Your brother has married far beneath our station,' Viktor's mother told him sadly. She had perched on her favourite son's bed to say good night before retiring to her quarters, as she had done ever since his earliest childhood. 'The woman's background is suspect in the extreme. Her parents are employed by a third-rate provincial opera company, he as a conductor and she as a singer. Artistes, they call themselves, and their daughter behaves accordingly. Not a happy choice, I fear.' She gazed into Viktor's eyes. 'I feel sure, my son, that *you* will never make such a disastrous mistake. Your standards are far too high.'

'I shall either marry a woman like you,' Viktor earnestly assured her, 'or remain a bachelor.'

Hermine imprinted a maternal kiss of gratitude on his brow.

Some nights later, when the family – Waldemar and his wife, Viktor and his mother – were gathered round the fire after dinner, Waldemar broke the rather unconvivial silence with a question that had obviously been preying on his mind.

'What do you plan to do, Viktor? It only needs one of us to run this place, and that's me.'

Waldemar's wife gave him a smile filled with dark and smouldering sex appeal but saved a little of it for her handsome brother-in-law. To his mother's evident satisfaction, Viktor ignored the creature.

'Well,' he said, 'I know a bit about horses. I could go into the bloodstock business.'

'Out of the question,' Waldemar said quickly. 'The estate can't run to any chancy experiments – I'm only just keeping our heads above water as it is. Anyway, you're a soldier.'

'Not in this day and age, Waldemar – not under a Red republic which spits on military tradition and besmirches the memory of our glorious dead.'

'Since the ultimate decision rests with me,' Hermine announced, 'it shall be as Viktor wishes.'

And it was. Viktor von Feuerfresser was allotted a tumbledown stable block on the edge of the estate, together with half-a-dozen acres of grazing land. He started his career as a breeder with three mares and one stallion. Less than four years later he owned nine thoroughbreds of which three turned out to be first-class sprinters. The Feuerfresser stable flourished and became a byword in racing circles. Viktor was a somebody once more.

Viktor's friend and comrade Herbert Wedell spent the same period as a freelance man of letters. He wrote a number of strategic studies, one of which was pregnantly entitled *War: the Key to Peace*. Soon after its publication he was approached by the Reichswehr, that strangely multifarious defence force which Germany had been permitted to retain under the Versailles Treaty. Officially restricted to a total strength of one hundred thousand men, it possessed – again officially – no aircraft, tanks, or heavy artillery. General von Seeckt, who then commanded it, recognized Wedell's special gifts and offered him a place on his staff.

Seeckt was a far-seeing man, but even he underestimated the phenomenon called Adolf Hitler. Like most people, he dismissed him as a tub-thumping demagogue of minor political importance.

The two old friends made a point of meeting now and then. Viktor would invite Herbert to the family estate for hunting parties, mounted excursions on thoroughbred horses, and informal, country-house supper parties. Herbert, by now a major-general, reciprocated by taking Viktor and his mother to the opera in Berlin or giving them dinner at Horcher's – occasions on which they would be accompanied by his wife, a woman of quiet refinement.

'Herbert's wife and I have many qualities in common,' Viktor's mother told him approvingly. 'In Herbert, you have a friend who is truly worthy of you.'

In 1939, when war was forced on us yet again, I had to give up my racing stable because all our international contacts were severed overnight. My friend Wedell appealed to me, personally and on behalf of the German Army, to do my patriotic duty. I responded to his call without a moment's hesitation.

Viktor von Feuerfresser rejoined the Army as a colonel and was given command of an infantry regiment on orders from the Führer's headquarters, where General Wedell was serving as an adviser. He soon distinguished himself by capturing an important Warsaw suburb. Later transferred to France, he scored further successes while attempting to drive the British invaders into the sea near Calais. These earned him another Iron Cross First Class and put him in line for a Knight's Cross – but then, he already held the '*Pour le Mérite*'. The Führer sent him a personal letter of gratitude and commendation.

Wedell had since made full general and was now an army commander. Hitler regarded him as a man of iron and one of his staunchest supporters. 'Wedell,' he declared when the tide of war had turned against him, 'I wish I had ten more like you. We must mobilize all that remains to be mobilized. If anyone can do that, you can. You have my full authority to act on your own discretion.' He then promoted Wedell field-marshal and appointed him commander of an army group.

One of Wedell's first steps was to contact his oldest friend. He instructed Colonel von Feuerfresser to set up a special centre devoted to the training of crack troops for deployment against partisan hordes operating behind the German lines.

Having combed his regiment for subordinates of the utmost competence and reliability, Feuerfresser made them swear an oath of allegiance to his person. More first-class personnel were procured and dispatched to him by Colonel Schlumberger, Field-Marshal Wedell's chief of staff. Together with his own selections, they formed the nucleus of the unique team which moved into Kampfental under his command. Erika, Countess von Klarfeld, was another of its number. Somehow, she reminded Feuerfresser of his beloved mother. Although they were strongly attracted to each other, their relations remained platonic. 'I respect you deeply,' the Colonel told her one day. 'I admire you tremendously too, but you've already been married. That means you could never make me the sort of wife my mother was to my father. We shall simply have to accept the fact. Public duty must always come before personal inclination.'

Closer in spirit than ever after their joint visit to the brothel, Sergeant-Major Schulz and Mess Sergeant Gerner strolled back through the star-spangled midsummer night, arm in arm, to sink a final beer in the canteen.

'Tell me something,' said Schulz. 'Why are there dozens of different wines and spirits in the officers' mess when we have to make do with the same old beer and schnapps? Booze or women, I'm all for a bit of variety.'

'Leave it to me,' said Gerner. 'I can get any amount of beer from the main depot at Army Group HQ. Pilsener, Dortmunder, Löwenbräu – what do you fancy?'

'The lot,' jested Schulz, whose consumption was genuinely impressive. 'There's nothing to beat a decent beer, any time of the day or night. Eat, drink and be merry, that's my motto.' He took a long pull at his latest bottle, then frowned. 'Good times don't last for ever.'

'Why shouldn't they, the way things are? Tonight was a success, wasn't it? I'll bet that number three of yours did her stuff.'

Schulz confirmed this with a nod and simultaneously opened another bottle of beer. He put it to his lips and drained it in one, a feat betraying years of practice.

'I can take plenty,' he said complacently, 'but I'm still as sharp as a razor. Trouble I can smell a mile off, and that man Singer stinks to high heaven.'

'He worries me too,' Gerner admitted. 'Incredible how quick he catches on. You can't help being suspicious of the little jerk.' He took a man-sized swig of beer and belched luxuriously. 'Still, what is he? A lousy corporal! We'll dump him just like that, if we have to. We've never been beaten yet, either of us.'

'Did you hear what old Hausleitner whispered to me when we were on the way out?'

Gerner shrugged. 'Hausleitner's all wind and piss, even if he does have his uses. All right, so what did he tell you?'

'Singer was in with number five, he said, but not on his own. Natasha was in there too – you know, that crafty bitch Major Kastor warned me about. That means Singer wasn't screwing Anna, he was asking her questions – her, of all people. Anna's the complicated type, and complicated types are dangerous. Why should he be doing that?'

Gerner shrugged again. 'Maybe he prefers talking to screwing. Some people do, so they say.'

But Schulz's thought processes became more lucid the drunker he got. 'We'll have to take out some insurance against Singer – we don't have any option. The MO may be using him to get at us. If so, we'll pull the rug out from under him.'

'Sounds as if you've had another of your brainwaves,' Gerner said admiringly.

'Right first time.' Though slurred, the sergeant-major's voice was as supremely self-confident as ever. 'Everyone who visits the whorehouse has to be registered, correct? Well, we'll get ourselves put down on tonight's list for safety's sake. I don't like doing it, but there's no alternative. See what I'm driving at, old pal?'

'Great!' said Gerner. 'You're a genius! Singer'll be the one who didn't book in, and that's against standing orders. We've got him cold, Schulz – we can drop him in the dirt any time we like.'

'But not right away,' said Schulz, automatically reaching for another bottle of beer. 'We'll dig up something else against him first, then we'll see. It shouldn't take long.'

Gerner grinned. 'Not if I know you, it won't.'

'Trouble is, the youngster's obviously got friends in high places – and I don't just mean the MO. There must be somebody rooting for him at Army Group HQ, the crafty little skunk. He won't be that easy to get rid of. Short of dumping him, we'll have to defuse him somehow.'

'The best thing might be a transfer to the Training Wing,' Gerner suggested. 'Once Sergeant Heinz got his hands on him, he'd really be up shit creek without a paddle. Could you swing it?'

'Could I!' Schulz said thickly. 'I can swing anything if I put my mind to it.'

3

The next batch of trainees started arriving at Kampfental three days before 1 August 1944, when their course was due to begin. Poised to receive them were a team of expert instructors and a training system whose mechanics had been steadily perfected over the preceding months.

Although some hundred and forty candidates had been selected from various combat units, past experience foretold that only a hundred and twenty would show up, the others having been killed or wounded in action, laid low by disease, or prevented from attending by administrative blunders and inadequate transportation. On average, however, the six-week courses were survived by a hundred specialists in close combat, superbly trained and tough as tempered steel.

The southern sector of the camp became a hive of activity during the three-day warm-up, but its outwardly chaotic comings and goings were carefully supervised by Majors Kastor and Pollandt, those skilled organizers and zealous agents of the Colonel's will. These first three days, they often declared, were crucial to the weeks of intensive training that followed them.

In accordance with their movement orders, candidates travelled to AFSIC Kampfental via Munich, in a combined passenger and freight train which pulled into Hölzbach station at twelve noon. That was when Lieutenant Lahrmann's instructors went to work.

The procedure never varied. At Hölzbach the new arrivals were greeted by a reception committee consisting of a stentorian-voiced staff sergeant, two sergeants whose air of grim authority was founded on prewar parade-ground experience, and a pack of yapping, snarling corporals.

'Pick up your kit! Into the station yard, march! Shut up and get moving!'

Outside in the station yard, flanked by another two sergeants as rigid and unmoving as pillars of salt, stood Lieutenant Lahrmann. His legs were braced and spread, his arms folded on his beribboned chest.

'Fall in in three ranks facing me!' he ordered. The heroic herd obediently complied. 'Welcome, trainees. I shall not address you as men at this stage – that is what you're here to become. My name is Lieutenant Lahrmann. I am the officer in charge of your training. Let's start right away.'

His Knight's Cross glinted, enjoining respect, as he pointed to a blackboard set up beside him. It bore a sketch map of the surrounding area, drawn to scale. 'Point A is our present location. Point B is the main gate of the camp. From Point A to Point B, at the double, march!'

They doubled off. Lahrmann himself brought up the rear in his Mercedes scout car, spurring them on with appropriate words of exhortation.

Panting and perspiring after their three-mile trot in full marching order, the trainees reached the main gate to find themselves confronted by a staff sergeant who might have been the twin of the one at the station.

'Into line! I want each man's rank, name, number and unit. You'll be given a slip noting your exact time of arrival. Then take your kit and double to the gym – and have all your papers ready. Right, sound off!'

Next port of call: the gymnasium, where four trestle tables had been set up in line abreast. Seated behind each was an officer flanked by a grim-faced sergeant and two corporals of similar aspect.

The first table to be negotiated by the trainees, who

looked 'dazed by their brusque introduction to life at Kampfental, was occupied by Lieutenant Wagner. He subjected each man to a supercilious stare and intoned his unvarying formula in a tireless, businesslike monotone.

'Spread out your gear for inspection and strip off, but hang on to your movement order. You can collect your things when I've had them searched. Next!'

Table number two was presided over by Captain Königsberger, whose task it was to conduct a preliminary medical inspection. With consummate boredom, he eyed the succession of naked trainees and asked them a single stock question: 'Are you suffering from any disease or disability that might prevent you from withstanding extreme physical stress?' The answer, as expected, was negative in every case.

Poring over an array of lists at tables three and four, which were butted up together, sat Majors Kastor and Pollandt. Still as naked as the day he was born, each new arrival was instructed to present his movement order and state his name, rank, number and unit. As he did so, both majors took simultaneous note of his deportment, enunciation, and general appearance. Then, after a final searching glance at man and movement order, they unerringly reached a unanimous decision on which of two groups the trainee should be assigned to, A or B.

Once the procession was over, the trainees were permitted to retrieve their clothes and equipment from table number one. They then formed up in their separate groups and were marched to their quarters by Sergeant-Major Schulz.

The first of the three induction days was a peaceful prelude compared to the second, when the bulk of the intake had to be processed. It was late evening when Mess Sergeant Gerner told Singer to take some refreshments to the four exhausted officers in the gym. He brought them a large vacuum flask of the Colonel's own coffee, brewed very strong, together with four cups and saucers.

'Take a break!' ordered one of the majors, and fifteen minutes' blissful repose ensued. Some of the trainees, who received permission to park their naked rumps on the floor, were enterprising enough to use their movement orders as cushions.

As soon as he had filled the officers' cups with steaming coffee, Singer sidled up to the MO. 'Care to tell me what's going on here?'

'Puzzling, isn't it?' The MO's smile was sympathetic. 'I couldn't fathom it myself, at first. It took me months to grasp the startling simplicity of it all. To borrow another of Lieutenant Wagner's pet phrases: *divide et impera.*'

'Divide and rule?' Singer shrugged. 'I still don't get it.'

'Kastor and Pollandt have evolved a system of their own. They preface each course by dividing the trainees into two groups labelled A and B.'

'And play them off against each other?'

'More or less,' said the MO, 'except that there's a special twist. Personal friends and members of the same unit get split up on principle. The most promising recruits are assigned to Group B, which implies that they're second-rate. That boosts the morale of the second-raters in Group A and hurts the pride of the first-raters in Group B. Both groups can be relied on to bust a gut in training, the A types so as to stay in Group A and the B types in the hope of being upgraded.'

'Very subtle,' said Singer.

The MO nodded. 'Psychologically speaking, quite a shrewd exploitation of human behaviour patterns. I'm sure you'll be keen to observe the results, Singer, but watch your step.'

The coffee break continued – in fact the majors prolonged it a little, so strong was the brew and so delicious its flavour. Even Lieutenant Wagner made a relaxed, almost human impression, but Kastor and Pollandt steadfastly combined business with pleasure by leafing through their lists with one hand while wielding their cups with the other.

Just then, Natasha appeared at Königsberger's side. Ignoring Singer and the rows of naked men, some of whom hastily converted their movement orders into fig leaves, she bent down and whispered in the MO's ear.

Königsberger pushed his cup away, looking dismayed. 'My God,' he said softly, 'not another!'

'Can you come?' she asked.

'I'm not allowed to leave,' he said apologetically. 'Of course, if my professional services are needed – I mean, if there's still a chance the girl's alive – '

'She isn't,' said Natasha. 'She's very dead.'

'In that case,' he said, 'I'll come as soon as I'm through here. Till then, make sure nobody touches the body.'

'I've already seen to that.' She paused. 'Very well, I'll be waiting for you.'

'Meantime, why not let Corporal Singer escort you back?'

Natasha accepted the offer with a curt nod. Singer followed her out. She did not look round, and he had some difficulty keeping up with her.

The camp's main thoroughfare was bathed in evening sunlight. They were half way to the brothel before Natasha turned her head.

'Don't you want to know who it is?'

'I'm new to this place. The only four women I know by name are you, Melanie Mauerland, the Klarfeld woman, and Anna.'

'That's good enough. It's Anna.'

Singer preserved a shocked silence until they reached the brothel. There he saw her lying on her bed, scantily clad, sprawled and motionless, with a dead face whose beauty had not been altogether banished by its look of frozen despair.

'How did it happen?'

'An overdose,' said Natasha. 'Don't ask me how she got hold of the stuff. There's another question that matters more.'

'I know,' Singer said. 'What made her do it?' There were tears of impotent rage in his eyes. 'Who was to blame?'

Situation Report No. 3

After 20 July 1944, this most total of all total wars plumbed the uttermost depths of insanity. Those on the brink of death strove to drag as many fellow creatures as possible into the abyss. 'No quarter!' they trumpeted. 'No surrender! Scorched earth tactics – hold out at any price!'

Cities and towns were razed to the ground – German ones only, now – after the manner of Coventry, where the fashion for such methods had been set. Human beings died in droves, not just in battle but because they happened to live near factories, rail junctions and arterial roads, or merely because their homes were in densely populated areas. They perished in the rubble of collapsing houses, were torn to shreds by shrapnel, or stuck fast in asphalt melted by phosphorous bombs and blazed like torches in the street.

The one-time predators had become bewildered prey, unable to grasp what was happening to them, and still their ears were assailed by an unending stream of last-ditch slogans and appeals to the fighting spirit of Greater Germany. 'That which fails to kill us only strengthens us!' – 'The coward has no right to exist!' – 'He who surrenders is lost!'

Practical steps were taken to ram this message home. Judges did their 'bounden duty' several thousand times – ordinary judge advocates as well as members of summary tribunals. Their tally of death sentences constituted yet another all-time record in the annals of war.

Whether on the battlefield or at home in some bomb-blasted city, in jail or concentration camp, death now seemed quite commonplace – which it was. The living were preoccupied with survival; the victims of wholesale violence died unmourned by an obituary notice – many without headstones and unbeknown to their next of kin.

Rommel, once Hitler's favourite general, was relentlessly browbeaten into committing suicide at Hitler's behest. Field-Marshal von Kluge also took his own life, as did General von Tresckow and several other senior officers. They all knew that the war, which was as futile as war invariably is, could never be won by Germany. Others knew this too but refrained from saying so for numerous reasons. Meanwhile, the unwitting masses fought on with misguided loyalty or boundless stupidity, dazed and drugged by patriotic Nazi slogans.

Germany had become a gigantic mirror in which the human race could gaze upon itself and shudder at its hideous potentialities. There were many who preferred to close their eyes.

At the end of the third and last induction day, when all was in readiness for the start of the course next morning, 1 August 1944, another festive soirée took place in the officers' mess.

White was the predominant colour: white table linen, white china, white candles and, on Gerner's orders, a full turn-out of mess waiters in white jackets and gloves. The occasion – a very special one – was Lieutenant Lahrmann's thirtieth birthday. Poker-backed but not unmoved and visibly appreciative, he sat on the right of the Commandant he revered so greatly. Frau Klarfeld, whom he idolized, flanked him on the other side, and his brother officers filled the remaining places in a mood of good cheer.

At the birthday boy's request, the main course consisted of ultra-Bavarian roast pork with potato dumplings. This was preceded by eel soup with dill and followed by apple pie and whipped cream. All present chomped their way valiantly through this manual labourer's repast while background music oozed through the double doors, which had been flung wide. In an élite establishment like AFSIC Kampfental, commanded by a man of Colonel von Feuerfresser's calibre, great importance was attached to culture. It was known that the Colonel actually read books – Voltaire, for example, like the Prussian monarch whose qualities he strove to emulate. He also shared his hero's love of music.

Ever alert to Feuerfresser's wishes, Captain Tauschmüller had managed to secure the services of the celebrated Kunkel string quartet, together with those of a concert pianist named Weinheber who had recently made a name for himself. 'The choice is yours, gentlemen,' he had told the reluctant musicians when recruiting them. 'It's entirely up to you.' The implication was obvious: either they joined the staff at AFSIC Kampfental, or they exchanged their instruments for a rifle and bayonet.

Having reached the only possible decision, they were permitted to practise for two or three hours a day. The rest of the time they spent doing auxiliary work, usually in the medical centre, supply depot, or kitchen garden. At night, however, they were expected to play with a will. When not required in the mess, they were often loaned out to neighbouring units and hospitals.

Reinforced by further acquisitions as time went by, this squad of musicians had developed into a chamber orchestra whose direction was hotly contested by two of its members. Karl Kunkel, leader of the original string quartet, and Adolf Weinheber, a keyboard virtuoso of strongly National Socialist beliefs, were forever accusing each other of professional incompetence. Their skirmishes might have disrupted the whole ensemble but for Lieutenant Wagner, who felt additionally responsible for German art in his capacity as National Socialist Guidance Officer. He made the position crystal clear. 'Harmonize, men! If you don't, you'll be given a chance to play solo on the Eastern Front.'

So they harmonized willy-nilly, though they often felt musically frustrated. All their attempts to slip in a Handel concerto or a Haydn symphony were thwarted by the unflagging demand for Mozart's *Eine Kleine Nachtmusik*. Tonight, even their offer of Brahms's *Hungarian Dances* had been turned down. To mark the thirtieth birthday of Lieutenant Lahrmann, an outstanding soldier but a musical zero, they had been instructed to play melodies by Strauss, Johann – preferably waltzes.

Strauss seemed to be having an uncommonly mellowing and digestive effect. The Colonel was gazing meditatively into space. Frau Klarfeld was smiling at Lahrmann with what he fondly hoped was rosy-cheeked interest. Kastor and Pollandt, those twin exponents of the noble art of war, had their heads together as usual. Wagner was covertly eyeing Königsberger, Königsberger covertly eyeing Wagner, and Tauschmüller keeping the entire company under observation.

Feuerfresser turned to the majors. 'All teed up for tomorrow, gentlemen?'

'All set to go, Colonel.' Kastor and Pollandt spoke in unison. 'We look forward to another successful course.'

'No problems on the horizon?'

'None at all, sir.'

'Anything else?'

The majors exchanged a glance. Then Pollandt took the floor alone. 'As regards foreign-language tuition, Colonel, the trainees – '

'Good thinking, gentlemen!' Feuerfresser broke in, relishing the astonishment of all present. He liked to demonstrate his powers of clairvoyance. 'Delighted to see you've grasped the gist of my plans for the future, at least in outline. It's very reassuring.'

'One thing, Colonel,' said Königsberger. 'I'm sorry to say there's been another unfortunate incident in a certain – er, recreational facility.'

Captain Tauschmüller glared at him. 'That's beside the point, Doctor. The Colonel's question didn't relate to recreational facilities. Have a written report on my desk by tomorrow morning. We'll see where we go from there.'

'All the same,' Königsberger persisted, 'it *is* the second suicide in two weeks.'

'That's your sphere of responsibility, Doctor,' snapped Lieutenant Wagner. 'I'm told the girl was highly strung and of racially inferior stock. I'm also told she took an overdose, which makes me wonder how the creature gained access to dangerous drugs in the first place. Perhaps you'd care to explain?'

'Gentlemen, gentlemen!' Frau Klarfeld entreated. 'I thought this was a birthday party.'

'And so it is, dear lady.' Colonel von Feuerfresser spoke with characteristic dignity. He took her hand and gallantly went through the motions of kissing it, then swept the table with a sternly reproving glance which came to rest on the MO. 'There's a time and a place for everything, Captain Königsberger.'

'Precisely, sir,' Lieutenant Wagner chimed in. '*Festina lente,* as the Romans used to say – more haste, less speed.'

The Colonel conveyed that this interjection, though irrelevant, was well meant. He even gave an almost imperceptible nod of agreement. 'Nevertheless,' he continued in his calm and deliberate way, 'if some form of unpleasantness has occurred, far be it from me to sweep it under the carpet. Captain Königsberger, I direct you to conduct a thorough and detailed investigation of this matter.'

The MO left it at that. 'Certainly, Colonel.'

'And by thorough,' added Feuerfresser, 'I mean that you will ascertain the source of the medicinal substance which the deceased misused for such a nefarious purpose.'

Everyone in the room realized that Königsberger had fallen into a trap of his own making.

'And now,' commanded Feuerfresser, 'some champagne!'

Bohemian crystal goblets and ice buckets filled with bottles swathed in white damask napkins were ceremoniously borne in. The champagne was Pommery 1933, a vintage normally reserved for army commanders, government ministers and Reich Marshal Göring. Clearly, the key members of this élite training unit came into the same bracket.

As mess president, Captain Tauschmüller was responsible for any ritual procedures left unconducted by the Colonel himself. 'On your feet,' he hissed at the birthday boy. 'It's time for your speech!'

Lahrmann, who was not noted for his gift of the gab, rose. With a brimming glass in his right hand and his heroic face congealed into semblance of rigor mortis, he delivered the following address:

'Colonel, Countess, comrades – my thanks.'

The others exchanged understanding smiles. They rose too, glasses at the ready, as Lieutenant Wagner led them in the traditional birthday incantation:

> *'Hoch soll er leben,*
> *hoch soll er leben,*
> *drei – mal – hoch!'*

They sang the words in harmony, briefly united like some ill-assorted band of brothers. Priewitt winked at Singer, and Sergeant Gerner, who had already treated himself to an off-stage bottle of champagne between the roast pork and apple pie, took the liberty of joining in.

'And now,' said the Colonel, 'our guest of honour's favourite tune, the *Emperor Waltz*.'

'Ah,' said Wagner, in his most ideologically sapient tone, 'if only Johann Strauss had been privileged to live in our own glorious era, he would surely have called it the *Führer Waltz*.'

'If he'd lived in our own glorious era,' retorted Königsberger, improvising hard, 'he mightn't have written it at all. I believe he had a Jewish grandmother.'

No one but Singer paid any attention to this minor skirmish. The rest were listening intently to the strains of the orchestra, though some of them could not help noticing Lahrmann's steadfast adoration of Frau Klarfeld and Frau Klarfeld's answering smile.

The so-called 'welcoming' parade for the latest batch of trainees – a ceremony to which Colonel von Feuerfresser attached the utmost importance – began on the stroke of ten next morning.

It was held on the expanse of gravel in front of the officers' mess and conducted by Lieutenant Lahrmann, who showed absolutely no sign of his liquid birthday celebrations, with the active assistance of Master-Sergeant Heinz and other NCO instructors. Drawn up in three ranks, Groups A and B waited patiently for whatever the future might hold in store.

First to emerge from the former country mansion, rather like two heralds of old, were Captain Tauschmüller and Lieutenant Wagner. Having briefly scrutinized the motionless ranks, they stationed themselves a little to one side and came to attention. This could only mean that the Colonel was on his way.

He appeared a moment later, dignified and erect, with springy stride and searching gaze. Members of his permanent staff were quick to note a rare phenomenon: he was wearing the highest of his many orders and decorations, the 'Pour le Mérite', which lent him a supremely heroic aura.

Feuerfresser was escorted by the two majors, who flanked him one pace to the rear. Strolling casually along behind them came the indispensable Priewitt. Singer was watching the scene from a mess window, as were Sergeant-

Major Schulz, Mess Sergeant Gerner, and Master-Sergeant Kainz of the Security Platoon.

Lahrmann's latest batch of heroes-in-the-making had paraded in steel helmets and combat suits, but without arms. He stalked up to the Colonel and reported them present and correct. As soon as Feuerfresser had acknowledged this information with a nod, Lahrmann faced about and gave tongue:

'Front rank, three paces forward, rear rank, three paces backward – march!'

The movement, which had been practised several times, was performed with absolute precision. The Colonel then toured the ranks, pausing in front of each man. He uttered not a word, but his eyes conveyed an unspoken question with all the authority proper to one who modelled himself on a Prussian monarch.

Carefully rehearsed by Lahrmann, the trainees reeled off the salient details of their military career with due brevity: name, rank, number, unit, decorations, combat experience. They came from Norway and Denmark, from beleaguered Warsaw, from the German-held remnants of Italy and the Balkans, and from the Western Front, which still ran through French territory – but only just. All were seasoned veterans, all had been decorated, and many bore the scars of at least one wound.

Colonel von Feuerfresser regarded them, one by one, with profound satisfaction. They were tough, doughty fighting men who had passed through the fiery furnace of war as he himself had done at Douaumont so many years before. Then he faced the two groups and addressed them for the first time in a clear, resonant, commanding voice.

'I bid you welcome, comrades. You, who have fought with distinction on every front in the European theatre, are now about to undergo another test of courage and endurance. I know you will come through it like the true soldiers you are.'

They gazed back at him devotedly, as sons might have gazed at a father whose severity was tempered with justice and loving concern.

The majors exchanged a glance. Up in the mess, Sergeant-Major Schulz rubbed his hands with gleeful anticipation. Gerner grinned, and Master-Sergeant Kainz muttered, 'Here we go again.' The Colonel wound up his little speech as follows:

'The training you receive here, comrades, will hone you into razor-sharp weapons of war – combat specialists of the highest calibre. Your present rank is immaterial; any member of my permanent staff is entitled to give you an order and see it carried out. You may, however, be interested to know that I am authorized to promote you on completion of the course – if you deserve it. And so, comrades, into the fray!'

There was little more to be said.

'All right, why did she kill herself?'

Singer asked the question point-blank. He had arranged to meet Natasha at the brothel, and Corporal Hausleitner had obligingly left them alone in the former sacristy.

'Ask the MO,' she said. 'He knows.'

'I'd sooner not. He'd probably feel compelled to lie, and I'd sooner spare us both the embarrassment. You can understand that, can't you?'

'I wouldn't bank on it.' Natasha's manner was studiously remote and impassive. 'You ask me why a person like Anna should kill herself. Well, why shouldn't she? Sooner or later, and it won't be long now, one or two people in this place may be faced with the same decision – or don't you agree?'

'Frankly, no. I've yet to discover anything worth dying for.'

Natasha stared at him for a moment. 'Anna thought differently. She'd lost hope. She couldn't see any point in leading the life she did – she was at the end of her tether. Perhaps I'm partly to blame for her death. I could have devoted more time to her. Who knows, Herr Singer – you may have helped to push her over the edge yourself, with all your talk of happy childhood days . . .'

'Honestly, Natasha! We all bear a share of the blame for what goes on here, but there's no way of proving it. Naturally, it doesn't stop the powers that be from trying to do just that.'

'Let them,' she said curtly. 'It's none of my business.'

'You mean you really don't care if they pin the whole thing on Königsberger?'

'How can they?'

'Because she took some pills which only the MO's supposed to have access to. He could be held responsible for their improper use.'

Natasha indicated a massive oak press that had once been a repository for church vestments. 'Pills like that are kept in there, along with contraceptives and first aid equipment.'

'Are you suggesting that Hausleitner slipped the girl a lethal dose of sleeping pills from misconceived notions of charity?'

'Don't get me wrong, Herr Singer. I was merely giving you a possible lead, not pointing the finger at anyone.'

'All right,' said Singer. 'So you're fond of poor old Hausleitner, but you've also got a soft spot for your boy-friend the MO.'

'Captain Königsberger isn't my boy-friend,' she snapped. 'There's more than one explanation, that's all I'm trying to prove.'

Singer knew what she was driving at – he felt sure of it now. 'Very well,' he said, 'let's see if we can clear this business up.'

Hausleitner, who had obviously been lurking round the corner, appeared like magic as soon as Singer called him.

He shuffled in, doing his best to look like a tired old man, but there was a wary glint in his eye.

'What happened to Anna was lousy,' Singer said, 'but it wasn't your fault.'

The brothel-keeper gave a momentary start before vigorously shaking his head. 'You bet it wasn't. It's a lousy world, but that's not my fault either. I'm the innocent type – always have been. I was born that way.'

Singer set to work on the oak press. He tried to open the double doors, at first without success, then tugged at them with all his might. They gave with a sound of splintering wood, and the tongue of the lock snapped off. He inspected his handiwork, breathing hard.

'There,' he said. 'Hausleitner, you've been burgled. Somebody filched some of your medical supplies, but you didn't spot it right away – you couldn't have, being as busy as you are. Well, now you know.'

'Do I?' Hausleitner glanced helplessly at Natasha.

'Sure you do. You're a conscientious man, but how can you help it if somebody forces a lock? You'd complied with all the safety regulations, and you'll have witnesses to back you up. I'm sure the MO will, for one. Believe me, my friend, you're in the clear.'

'You mean it?' Hausleitner looked trustingly at Natasha, who gave him a reassuring nod. 'All right, that's the way it was.'

Captain (Med.) Königsberger was off the hook, at least for the moment. Details of the fake burglary were officially communicated to him by Hausleitner. With Singer's help, he cobbled together a watertight report and submitted it to the Colonel via the adjutant's office, as instructed.

Feuerfresser's verdict was brief: 'Not wholly convincing, but I suppose I'll have to accept it.'

Although the voice of authority had spoken, Lieutenant Wagner permitted himself a whispered comment: 'Our wily witch doctor has wriggled out from under, but only just. He won't get away with it for ever . . .'

'What's *really* going on here?' Singer asked Natasha a little later. 'Why does Hausleitner take his cue from you all the time? Do you know too much about him, or has he got something on you? For all I know, he may be acting as a mercy-killer with your approval – or even with your help. And how does Königsberger fit into the picture? Is somebody gunning for him, or is he out for somebody's blood?'

'Whether or not your suppositions are correct, Herr Singer, how would it be if you viewed things in the light of your Führer's favourite maxim: "Nothing is beyond a German!"?'

'Including the ability to make himself look ridiculous?'

'Perhaps, but ridicule can also be lethal.'

That afternoon, Lieutenant Lahrmann displayed the unswerving devotion to duty that was probably his greatest asset, true to the German belief that business should never be confused with pleasure.

Being a man of few words, he barked out his orders in a form so telegraphic as to be unintelligible to all save his NCO instructors, who knew exactly what they meant.

'Grading procedure, commence!' he bellowed.

The effect of this command was to plunge his hundred and twenty trainees into what felt like a qualifying contest for the Olympic decathlon. They spent almost every minute of the next three days on the sports ground or in the gymnasium, while Lahrmann himself stood erect on a chair or upturned crate like an all-seeing god of war.

Records were kept of each man's performance in the long jump, high jump and hundred metres, as well as at weight-lifting and chinning the overhead bar. During intervals between events, the group awaiting its next ordeal had to circle the track at a steady trot. Only two men collapsed on the first day, a fact which Lahrmann accepted as convincing evidence of his trainees' prime physical condition.

Their division into two groups, A and B, proved its worth yet again. A climate of merciless competition developed, especially in team sports such as tug-of-war, handball, football, boxing and wrestling. Although it gradually emerged that Group A's teams were weaker than Group B's, their alphabetical precedence spurred them to superhuman efforts. The men in Group B, who felt that they had been wrongly classified, were likewise driven to surpass themselves.

The Kastor-Pollandt system – total domination by means of careful segregation – seemed to be working as well as ever. The majors were confident that a deliberate split in the ranks would prompt their men to strain every nerve and sinew – and that, they knew, could only serve the cause of final victory.

That evening, Corporal Singer's presence was requested by Sergeant-Major Schulz. Politely disguised as an invitation, the summons was delivered by Mess Sergeant Gerner.

Gerner and Singer betook themselves to HQ Company orderly room, which looked exceptionally tidy. The desk was bare except for a brand-new deck of playing cards, and behind it sat Schulz. The sergeant-major welcomed his visitors with an amiable flourish. On a stool to his right stood a full crate of beer. He tossed a bottle apiece to Gerner and Singer, both of whom deftly caught his largesse, and opened a third for himself. Only then were his guests permitted to sit down.

Schulz began by taking a routine precaution. 'Just in case you're asked, Singer, I didn't send for you. You came of your own free will, for recreational purposes. Right?'

'Right, Sergeant-Major. Sergeant Gerner happened to mention you were short of a third man for skat, and I was only too happy to oblige.'

'This is a friendly game,' said Schulz. 'We generally play for ten pfennigs a point, if it's all right with you.'

Ten pfennigs a point was madness, as Singer realized only too well. Undeterred by the possibility of losing several hundred marks in no time if his luck was out, he nodded. 'Deal me in.'

Play began in a sternly businesslike way, with none of the usual verbal conventions. No running score was kept because the losers paid out in cash after every hand. To Gerner's unwelcome surprise and Schulz's grudging admiration, Singer won nearly a hundred marks in less than an hour.

'I could use a pee,' announced the mess sergeant. 'I'll bet you could too, Singer,' he added meaningfully.

Schulz sanctioned their departure with a casual wave of the hand. Then he reached irritably for another bottle of beer – his sixth.

'God Almighty,' said Gerner, when he and Singer were relieving themselves in unison against the outside wall of the hut, 'you must be crazy, trying to cheat him like that!'

'What do you mean, cheat?' Singer sounded genuinely outraged. 'I'm a pretty good player, that's all. It isn't against regulations, is it?'

Gerner gave an exasperated grunt. 'You're just a goddam corporal,' he explained. 'Schulz outranks you. That means he's bound to be better at everything, cards included.'

'Mm,' said Singer, gazing up at the starry sky, 'you've got a point there. I'm convinced.'

With Singer at his heels, Gerner strode back into the orderly room, where Schulz was impatiently awaiting their return.

The sergeant-major's fortunes fluctuated in the next

couple of hours. He took two hundred marks off Singer but promptly lost a hundred of them back. After a night's play, his profit and loss account stood at zero. Eventually, he flung down his cards with an exclamation of disgust.

'Let's call it a day. How about a return match some time, Singer?'

'Any time, Sergeant-Major.'

Singer delivered a reasonably smart salute and withdrew, leaving the noncoms to themselves. They exchanged an ominous look.

'I'm a first-class judge of character under any circumstances,' said Schulz, and his nod of grim self-approbation was partly justified. 'But over a card table – well, there isn't anyone I can't see straight through. X-ray eyes, I've got.'

'If you say so,' said Gerner, 'you must be right.'

'You bet your sweet life I am.' Schulz glowered. 'Didn't you see what Singer was up to just now? He was trying to cheat me – beat me at my own game, I mean, and him a lousy corporal. If anyone suckers anyone around here, it's me!'

Gerner suppressed a smirk. 'You could squash him like a bug if you wanted to.'

'There are better ways,' said Schulz, whose speech had grown a trifle blurred. 'Being thorough, I took the precaution of looking through his personal record.'

'To find out who dumped him on us, you mean?'

'God knows who did that, I don't – he was probably misrouted by some dozy office clerk – but I did turn up something in his papers that ought to interest Kastor and Pollandt.'

'Enough to get him out of our hair?' Gerner asked eagerly.

Schulz's face betrayed a glimmer of hope. 'Could be.'

The Training Wing's division of labour, a well-devised

system, was in perfect running order. While Lieutenant Lahrmann continued to grade his trainees with the aid of tape measure, stopwatch and performance charts, the majors were at work in their so-called planning centre.

This establishment – 'Admission by Special Permit Only' – was housed in a three-wing block which also contained the records office run by Frau Klarfeld and her women auxiliaries. Its nucleus was the planning centre proper, a large room plastered with maps and diagrams. The shelves were still empty, but the desks were laden with typewriters and duplicating machines. Girls in uniform flitted to and fro.

In the inner sanctum, which was reserved for the majors' sole use, Kastor and Pollandt were seated side by side at a pair of outsize desks littered with files, pamphlets, lists, charts and memorandum pads, deep in conversation.

'Remember what the Colonel said in the mess the other night, on Lahrmann's birthday?' Kastor was saying. 'It all seemed pretty straightforward.'

Pollandt nódded. 'He obviously plans to extend the scope of our syllabus by applying the lessons of the Eastern Front to operational requirements in the West. The latest batch of American weapons is a pointer in the same direction. If there's going to be a shift in the focus of our activities, we'd better start preparing for it right away.'

'There may be one or two snags, for instance from the personnel angle, but they're the Colonel's problem, not ours. So what's next on the agenda?'

The next item on the agenda was Corporal Singer, who had been waiting outside for the past half-hour.

'Sit down, Corporal,' said Pollandt, indicating a hard chair geometrically equidistant from both desks. He glanced at Kastor, who led off.

'According to our records, your previous unit was engaged in house-to-house fighting in Warsaw.'

'That's correct, Major.'

'If you saw action there,' Kastor went on, 'you must have gained some pretty specialized experience. Is that why you were posted here – as an expert?'

'An expert on what, Major?'

'The technique and tactics of street-fighting, of course.'

'If I were one, what would I be expected to do here?'

This was too much for Pollandt. 'Kindly confine yourself to answering a normal question in a normal manner.'

Singer's dull-witted expression was a tribute to his presence of mind. 'What happened in Warsaw that time – I didn't see a thing.'

'But you went into action there, Corporal. That's why we're interested in knowing the extent of your combat experience.'

'I don't have any,' said Singer. 'I was serving with an infantry unit in eastern Poland. One day they loaded us into covered trucks and drove us to Warsaw. Somebody shot me just as I was climbing out. I collapsed on the spot. The medics carted me off before I even had a chance to look round. That's all I remember.'

'But surely you'd been specially trained for your mission?'

'Not at all, Major. I was sent into action and wounded two days after joining the unit. When I came to, I was in a dressing station. As soon as they'd done a temporary job on me, they sent me to Munich for further treatment. Then I was posted here. There's nothing more to tell.'

The majors exchanged a glance. 'I see,' said Kastor. 'That seems to confirm a few of our own impressions.'

'We must put your statement on file,' said Pollandt. 'It may serve some future purpose.'

The majors instructed Singer to write down what he had just told them and submit it within twenty-four hours in the form of a detailed report, complete with names, times and places. He was then dismissed.

CURRICULUM VITAE OF HERMANN TAUSCHMÜLLER
or, An Eye to the Main Chance

I was born on 15 January 1915, at Aalen in Swabia. My father, Heinrich Tauschmüller, was plant manager of a machine tool factory. My mother Henriette, née Klein, came from Stuttgart. I was the eldest of their three children. My early years were spent in the snug security of a happy home.

Hermann enjoyed a sheltered and almost troublefree boyhood. He was a dutiful son and a hard-working, obedient pupil noted for his courtesy of manner. The Tauschmüller family owned a modest suburban house with a small flower garden in front and an orchard and kitchen garden behind. Father Heinrich, who earned a relatively good salary, was extremely well thought of by the owner of the factory he ran.

Being bright, young Hermann soon discovered why. His father was a born inventor and time-and-motion expert. Thanks to his numerous patents and the production methods and rationalization schemes he introduced, the firm had saved hundreds of thousands, if not millions, of marks. This, needless to say, had an immensely beneficial effect on the profits accruing to Herr Bredenbeck, the owner.

One fine evening, Hermann startled his father by asking, 'Shouldn't you be earning a whole lot more than you do?' His father's response – 'Don't worry, we're doing very nicely' – he privately dismissed as 'pretty naïve', though he would never have said so out loud.

His father was none the less privileged to attend Sunday service with his family in the pew immediately behind that occupied by Herr Bredenbeck, his wife and daughter. The latter was a rather plump and inarticulate girl, but in Hermann's eyes these drawbacks were heavily outweighed by her relationship to the prosperous industrialist, whose only child she was.

Every year on Christmas Eve, Herr Bredenbeck visited the Tauschmüller home escorted by a chauffeur bearing a laundry basket full of parcels and packages. Having graciously distributed these gifts, he would linger to partake of a cigar and a glass of wine with 'the most loyal and dependable' of his employees.

'Say thank you, my boy.' Hermann, who was prepared for this paternal injunction, obediently recited a poem of his own devising. It celebrated the generosity of them that give, the joy of them that receive, and the virtues of a truly Christian community.

Herr Bredenbeck was enchanted. 'What a promising youngster!' he exclaimed. 'You should be very proud of him, my dear Tauschmüller. We can't waste that sort of talent. He must go to high school – at the firm's expense.'

In 1929 I was sent to a high school in Stuttgart, where I lodged with my maternal grandmother, a war widow. I was able to visit my parents every weekend and spend the vacations with them. In 1933 I passed my finals with distinction.

Hermann proved just as much of a model child at high school, where his marks were consistently good. His teachers praised his diligence and adaptability. He was never boisterous, far less insolent, and foolish practical jokes were as alien to his nature as expressions of political opinion.

As head of his class, Hermann had the honour of delivering the valedictory address. He opened it with the words: 'Whatever our teachers have seen fit to impart, we have learned. They have equipped us for the future that lies ahead – a German future.'

Herr Bredenbeck, who had never lost sight of Hermann,

conferred with his father. 'Splendid boy, your son – we must hang on to him now we've invested so much in him. He'd be wasted, doing national service. We'll give him a job with us – after all, our output's vital to the rearmament programme. If we say he's indispensable, they won't be able to draft him.'

This was how Hermann entered the executive offices of the Bredenbeck Machine Tool Corporation. His official status was that of a management trainee attached to the president's personal staff. Bredenbeck seemed to be grooming him as a sort of salaried successor.

Hermann proved to be an outstandingly gifted organizer. He rationalized administrative procedures, making them more efficient and easier to supervise, introduced new methods of accountancy and sponsored the purchase of calculating machines – and this when he was barely twenty years old.

Herr Bredenbeck pronounced him an extremely talented young man, but his pleasure was somewhat marred when Hermann applied his talents to a different field of endeavour. He began to take an interest in Herr Bredenbeck's daughter, who had lost her puppy fat and found her tongue. She welcomed his attentions, with the result that they were soon sighted romping in the woods in a state of partial undress. An engagement seemed inevitable.

Herr Bredenbeck was furious. 'This simply won't do,' he told Hermann's father over a bottle of wine. 'It wasn't part of the bargain. He may get her pregnant, and then what?' There could, he said, be no talk of marriage until Hermann had 'been through the mill'.

In 1937 I decided to do my patriotic duty and volunteered for the Army. Being a high school graduate, I was automatically classified as officer material. After attending military academy, where I was one of the best in my batch, I obtained a commission. That was in 1940.

Hermann Tauschmüller passed every test with flying colours. He was a first-class soldier, a congenial subordinate, and an inspiring superior. His personal file contained the promising verdict: 'Extremely versatile.'

Now a second lieutenant, he visited Aalen for a reunion with his parents and the Bredenbecks. Though not unimpressed by Hermann's good military record, Herr Bredenbeck prevaricated when his daughter displayed some eagerness to become Frau Tauschmüller. 'First show me what you're made of,' he told Hermann. 'Then we'll see.'

Hermann did his best, which was plenty. On the strength of his administrative ability, he was assigned to District HQ, Cologne, and then to a supply depot in the Nuremberg area. Finally, as an ex-employee of a firm whose output possessed strategic importance, he was promoted lieutenant and transferred to the Munitions Procurement Office in Berlin.

The Bredenbeck Machine Tool Corporation soon received additional arms contracts which not only guaranteed it a full order book for several years to come but enabled it to expand considerably with the aid of generous government subsidies.

On his next visit to Aalen, Hermann was welcomed with open arms. He was also permitted to marry Herr Bredenbeck's daughter and beget a child on her with the blessing of the Church. To mark the occasion, Herr Bredenbeck threw a big party attended by numerous local dignitaries and a senior officer from District HQ, Stuttgart. Hermann's father was appointed vice-president of the corporation, though his new status brought only a nominal increase in salary.

Before long, certain of Bredenbeck's competitors began to feel hard done by. Accusations of malfeasance, preferential treatment and similar abuses were embodied in a letter addressed to the Commander-in-Chief of the Army, whose office promptly forwarded it to the relevant army corps commander, General Wedell, who just as promptly sent for his most dependable staff officer, Colonel Schlumberger. 'I want this business cleared up,' he declared. 'Either put that man Tauschmüller behind bars, or shoot his father-in-law's competitors down in flames. They're all profiteers in any case.'

Schlumberger's investigation was predictably thorough and painstaking. He scrutinized every document that might have shed light on the case – every file, memo, contract, tender, and requisition – but was finally forced to admit defeat.

'Tauschmüller,' he said, 'you're a really smart operator. I'm ninety per cent certain you've pulled a fast one, but I can't prove it. You can consider yourself cleared, but I'll be watching you like a hawk from now on.'

'May I ask what that implies, Colonel?'

Schlumberger studied Tauschmüller thoughtfully. He marvelled at the young man's failure to register any emotion, even relief. 'I admire the way you cover your tracks, Tauschmüller. Smart operators come in handy from time to time. I'm sure you'll be hearing from me.'

In 1942, having been promoted captain, I was assigned to Colonel von Feuerfresser's special training unit in the dual role of adjutant and HQ Company commander. This brought me into daily personal contact with a World War I hero who was also one of the leading strategists of our time. Our relations were uniquely harmonious.

Before fully accepting him, Colonel von Feuerfresser submitted his new adjutant to the most rigorous tests. Tauschmüller successfully based a complete set of standing orders on a few terse remarks from the Colonel, translated his cryptic suggestions into detailed plans of a far-reaching nature, and conjured a whole series of security regulations out of one brief hint from on high.

'You're my kind of man,' Feuerfresser told him, when he had performed these Herculean tasks with little sign of effort. 'All right, get down to work, and remember: mutual trust is everything.'

They got along splendidly and in almost unbroken silence. One nod, one look, and Tauschmüller knew at once what Feuerfresser expected of him – in fact he often knew in advance. Their teamwork might have stemmed from years of practice.

No problems arose until Erika Klarfeld, who commanded the women staff auxiliaries, began to take an interest in Tauschmüller, at first with ladylike discretion but later with unmistakable intent. This slightly perturbed him because he knew, from various sources of gossip, that a strange and rather inscrutable relationship existed – or had existed – between his commanding officer and the lady in question. The dangers of the situation were brought home when Feuerfresser summoned him for a confidential chat.

'Nothing ever escapes my notice,' the Colonel told him, 'so I'm well aware that certain approaches have been made to a certain member of my staff. I would only say this: as far as I am concerned, your private life is your own. Get caught, however, and there could be trouble.'

For once, Tauschmüller failed to interpret his master's Delphic style of utterance. He stared at him helplessly.

'Look at it this way, Tauschmüller,' Feuerfresser went on. 'Although I do not suffer from the baser urges that seem to afflict so many of my sex, I sympathize with those who do not share my immunity. Your case, my dear Tauschmüller, is complicated by my heavy dependence on your services. I'm sure I can rely on you to the hilt, come what may.'

Hermann Tauschmüller took this to mean that Frau Klarfeld was fair game, but he was mistaken.

Singer knocked at the MO's door and went in. 'Any dirty washing, Captain? Socks, underpants, shirts, handkerchiefs, pyjamas?'

'No, no,' said Königsberger, 'I don't propose to trouble you with that sort of thing.'

'It's no trouble, Captain.' Singer's eyes twinkled. 'My friend Corporal Priewitt's off to the main clothing depot in Munich tomorrow or the day after, to replace the Colonel's wardrobe. I thought I'd tag along and do the same for yours.'

'You're damned efficient, Singer.' The MO stroked his jaw. 'Maybe too damned efficient for a simple quack like me.'

'You picked me to look after you,' said Singer. 'That puts me in your debt.'

'And me. I owe you for sorting out that drugs business.'

'Save your thanks for Natasha. She deserves most of the credit.'

'Natasha's a very special kind of person,' Königsberger said, almost reverently. 'Don't you think so?'

'I certainly do. Very attractive too – *and* she's got a soft spot for you.'

'Stop playing Cupid, Singer. You know I couldn't afford to get involved with her, not in this outfit.'

'That depends, Captain. You could always start taking Russian lessons. Who knows, they might come in handy.'

'They might also lead to complications.'

'Nice complications. I'm sure she'd welcome your interest in her mother tongue. Natasha's in a kind of no-man's-land between the girls in the brothel and the girls in uniform, which must be pretty lonely for her. Besides, I don't want to make you blush, but there's no mistaking her interest in you.'

'You mean it?'

'I know it, Captain.'

Königsberger blushed despite himself. 'All right, I'll give it some thought.'

'Meantime,' said Singer, 'you might care to tell me what really goes on here.'

'AFSIC Kampfental,' said the MO, as though reading from a prospectus, 'is a centre devoted to developing, testing and teaching novel combat techniques for use in partisan-infested territory behind our lines, notably in Russia and Poland. More particularly, in difficult terrain such as swamps and marshes.'

'You're pulling my leg, Captain. We don't have any partisan-infested territory left. The Russians are breathing down our necks, or hasn't the Colonel heard?'

'Don't underestimate Feuerfresser or anyone else in here. AFSIC's original function was to train men for anti-partisan operations, and very successful it was. Since then, the Colonel and his majors have started converting it into a specialized training centre for close-combat and street-fighting techniques.'

'Just so their overweight organization can stay in business when it's outlived its usefulness?'

'We all live off the organization, Singer, even you – and we do pretty well.'

'Maybe, but at whose expense?'

'Everyone lives at the expense of others. One man's asset is another's liability, one man's luck is another's misfortune. Life's unfair, Singer, but we can always write that off as part of the human condition. All wars are fundamentally insane.'

Singer went on sorting underpants. 'Something's insane about this place, but I haven't put my finger on it yet.'

4

Since all at AFSIC Kampfental appeared to be going according to plan – *his* plan – Colonel von Feuerfresser could once more engage in his favourite pastime. He sallied forth each morning before breakfast with three Trakehnen thoroughbreds from East Prussia. One he rode himself, another was ridden by his groom, Sergeant Wonnegut, whose face and intellect resembled those of the beasts he tended, and the third trailed behind on a long leading rein.

As the Colonel's personal orderly, Priewitt was also required to escort him on these early morning rides through field and forest. In view of his proven incompetence on horseback, however, he was permitted to use a bicycle. Though further permitted to stick to the beaten track when Feuerfresser struck off across country, he had to remain within view and hailing distance at all times.

'The Old Man's one in a million,' Priewitt told Singer. 'I reckon the Führer must be much the same.'

'Really?' said Singer, who enjoyed this line of conversation. 'In what way?'

'Well, always worrying about the country – always on his toes and ready for anything. The Old Man even sleeps at attention, Sebastian, flat on his back with his arms glued to his sides. You could swear he was thinking.'

'What do you reckon he thinks about?'

'A big shot like him? The Fatherland, his job, his responsibilities – what else? He even reads books – Clausewitz, Hölderlin, Kant, et cetera. He reels off whole chunks of their stuff as if he'd written it himself. How about that!'

'Terrific,' said Singer. 'Does he also reel off chunks of Hitler's *Mein Kampf*?'

Priewitt cogitated hard. 'No,' he said at length, obviously surprised at having to concede this, 'I can't say he does. Now I come to think of it, he's funny about Hitler. He hardly ever mentions him, and even then he never calls him the Führer, always the Supreme Commander. But that's the Old Man all over – a soldier to his fingertips.'

'Hm, very interesting. You mean he refuses to say the name out loud?'

'I said no such thing!' Priewitt paled slightly. 'Don't put words into my mouth – especially words like that. It's just that he's different from the rest. He doesn't spend the whole time sounding off about the Führer – or God, for that matter.'

Ever conscientious, Singer continued to perform his duties in the mess and minister to the MO at the same time. He also continued to play cards with the sergeant-major, taking care to let him win on a modest scale. Captain Tauschmüller paid no attention to him, which was a boon. Nor did Lieutenant Wagner, AFSIC's ideological supervisor, which was even more of one.

Being blessed with plenty of spare time and more than his fair share of curiosity, Singer began to take protracted strolls round camp. These often brought him within sight of the training area where members of the latest intake were being relentlessly knocked into shape.

Several times a day, Lieutenant Lahrmann put on a special show with the aid of the Mercedes scout car and driver that were permanently at his disposal. Standing erect behind the windshield, which he topped by several feet, he sped through camp like a charioteer in ancient times. The more dust his driver managed to kick up during these brief but headlong excursions, the more Lahrmann enjoyed them.

One of his favourite ports of call was the rifle range on the southern perimeter, where squads from Groups A and B would be awaiting him in the care of their NCO instructors.

'Load!' commanded Lahrmann, mounting a table for better visibility's sake. 'And now, comrades, imagine that the targets in front of you are enemy partisans – subhuman scum in need of extermination. Fire at will, and make sure every shot finds its mark!'

At the same time, the first of the special close-combat classes was in progress in the gym under Master-Sergeant Heinz. He and his team, which comprised two sergeants and three corporals, worked on their would-be heroes in batches of ten.

'Alertness, determination, speed!' exhorted Heinz, a six-footer in full uniform and heavy marching boots, bulging with muscle but lithe as a panther. 'That's what you need in this business.'

Ranged along the wall of the gym were some dummies the size and weight of an average man. All wore Russian uniforms and had articulated limbs. Squatting on a mat with his back to them was the master-sergeant, flanked by his henchmen, and facing them stood the ten members of the first batch, who were in for three hours' solid instruction. Another batch would follow that afternoon, and so on for six days out of seven. This meant that the entire intake passed through Heinz's hands – or fell into his clutches – at least once a week.

The preliminaries seemed all very innocuous, not to say relaxed and leisurely. Heinz enlisted one of his stock phrases. 'A soldier's job,' he said, 'is to dispose of the enemy.' The word 'kill' was not used at this stage. 'The question is, how?'

His pupils thought they knew what he was driving at. No

bangs, no senseless expenditure of ammunition – just the subtlest and most refined of all the martial arts: hand-to-hand combat.

'Firearms are all right in the proper place,' said Heinz, 'but they're noisy. They attract attention. Maximum results with the minimum of noise, that's what counts at close quarters. Locate your enemy, sneak up on him, and dispose of him – but be quiet about it.'

Still talking, he withdrew a knife from his left sleeve, then whirled and flung it at one of the uniformed dummies. The blade transfixed its chest, dead centre, and stayed there. Ten jaws dropped at this demonstration of lightning speed and accuracy.

'Practice makes perfect,' was Heinz's terse comment. 'You'll be able to do the same by the time I'm through with you. Forget about your bayonets – they're only good for opening cans. That knife's a precision instrument.'

He went on to explain that it came from captured stocks of equipment intended for issue to crack US ranger units. 'They wear those knives in a sheath round their necks. Why? Because it's the most practical place, for instance when you're told to raise your hands and surrender. That puts you in a perfect throwing position. It's all over in a flash.'

The trainees were then taken in hand. They threw knives, practised the trusty crotch-kick and how to counter it by jerking an assailant's leg into the air, strangled dummies with wire nooses, applied neck-locks and slit throats from behind.

When Lieutenant Lahrmann turned up to check on progress at the end of the first three-hour class, he found Master-Sergeant Heinz flushed with triumph, his instructors looking satisfied, and his pupils close to collapse. One man was bleeding profusely from a gash in the neck, another writhing on the floor with a dislocated shoulder, and a third clutching his balls in agony.

Lahrmann took Heinz aside, looking concerned. 'What's going on?' he demanded. 'You're meant to be training them, Sergeant, not fighting a war.'

'I don't see the difference, Lieutenant.' Heinz struggled to suppress his rage at Lahrmann's unwarlike lack of comprehension. 'It's no use being soft with them.'

Lahrmann glared at him. 'Are you trying to teach me my job, Sergeant?'

Heinz felt tempted to do precisely that, but he swallowed the retort that rose to his lips. Kampfental needed new men at the helm, he told himself. You couldn't win wars with the ladylike methods favoured by officers and gentlemen.

Dinner in the mess was over. The spring chicken *flambé* had come and gone, and the resident chamber orchestra had wound up its programme with a minuet. Since the Colonel had requested no musical dessert and evinced no desire to play a game of chess or deliver one of his didactic monologues, the evening could be deemed to have run its course.

Feuerfresser rose, nodded graciously at his minions, and retired to his upstairs suite. Priewitt bustled on ahead, opening all the doors in his path.

The musicians hurriedly packed up their instruments and scuttled off. Frau Klarfeld and the officers exchanged good nights and dispersed to their quarters.

Before clearing up, Mess Sergeant Gerner and his six waiters joined the two chefs at the kitchen table. Apart from devouring the officers' left-overs, they were always regaled with something extra and even more substantial. Tonight's offering consisted of Wienerschnitzels and Nuremberg sausages washed down with beer.

'Work well,' Gerner proclaimed for the umpteenth time, 'and you eat well.' He looked at Singer as he spoke. 'Otherwise . . .'

By midnight, all was shipshape in the mess. Gerner, who

seemed content with his men's efforts, rewarded them with a bottle of beer and a looted Dutch cigar apiece. Singer took his spoils and went outside to relax in the balmy August night. He felt peculiarly wide awake and disinclined to go to bed.

Lolling on a bench midway between the mess and the women auxiliaries' block, he stared ruminatively at the moon as he drank his beer and puffed at his cigar. Summer 1944, the last of the Greater German era, had been exceptionally hot, and the day's warmth lingered far into the night.

The camp itself seemed drugged with sleep. Singer transferred his attention from the moon to the officers' mess. As he looked, an indistinct figure descended the terrace steps and headed towards him. He waited until the white-robed apparition came flitting past his bench on silent, slippered feet, then hailed it.

'Good evening – or should I say good night?'

The figure halted abruptly, as if brought up short by a brick wall.

'Who's that? Not Corporal Singer?'

'At your service, ma'am.' Singer spoke with the deference due to someone of Frau Klarfeld's rank and station.

She remained rooted to the spot. 'Have you been spying on me?'

'Certainly not,' he protested. 'I was just taking the air – I couldn't sleep. I wasn't waiting for anyone, least of all you.'

'Well, now you've seen me.' Frau Klarfeld, who was clad in a billowing bathrobe, resolutely approached the bench and loomed over him. He scrambled to his feet. 'Am I right in assuming that you also saw where I came from?'

'Yes, but what of it?' Singer drew on his Sumatran cigar, which glowed brightly. 'You could be out for a midnight stroll – just that. On the other hand, you may have been paying a social call on a good friend. I'd quite understand.'

'So you don't know for sure?' She sounded relieved.

'Even if I did, ma'am, what business would it be of mine?'

'Meaning what, precisely? Are you trying to ingratiate yourself, *Herr* Singer?' She drawled the last two words.

'Why not?' he retorted, quite unabashed. 'If you're looking for human understanding, ma'am, I'm brimming with it. I'd appreciate the same from you, but not for myself. There are a couple of other people who may need some badly before long.'

Frau Klarfeld seemed alive to the special nature of the situation. 'You're a rather unusual person, Herr Singer, or so Captain Königsberger claims. I should like to believe that. May I?'

'Try me,' said Singer.

'I've no choice, I suppose. However,' she added warningly, 'don't go playing any tricks, not on me – not on someone with my connections.'

'I wouldn't be that dumb, ma'am, if you'll pardon the expression.'

'In that case, good night.'

Frau Klarfeld nodded as though sealing a pact and strode off quickly along the moonlit path that led to the women auxiliaries' compound.

Singer struck a match and rekindled his dead cigar. He stared after Frau Klarfeld's receding figure with a sympathetic grin.

She was greeted at the brightly illuminated entrance to her quarters by Melanie Mauerland, her chief subordinate and confidante, who was wearing a pink nightgown. Singer could hear her voice from where he sat. It was vibrant with reproach.

'There you are at last! I've been waiting for you – waiting and worrying myself sick!'

'Don't be so emotional, my dear. And try to keep your voice down – I'm always having to tell you. You simply *must* understand my position. In times like these, there are some obligations that can't be evaded.'

Melanie gave Frau Klarfeld a contrite hug and escorted her inside. The door closed behind them. A minute or two later, all the lights went out.

For a moment, Singer felt completely in the dark.

Still deserted by the urge for sleep, Singer paid a visit to the brothel. Corporal Hausleitner, who was manning his post in the former sacristy, greeted him with a worried frown. Natasha, who was also there, looked faintly surprised. Singer sat down uninvited.

'You puzzle me, Natasha. I can hardly believe you feel at home in this place, so why spend so much of your time here?'

'Because she's needed,' Hausleitner put in quickly. 'Because of her languages, among other things.'

'What other things?'

Natasha, who still hadn't spoken, left Hausleitner to answer the question. 'Look,' he said, 'you don't have a clue what really goes on here.'

'I thought this was a whorehouse.'

'So it is. A damn good one too, the way I run it, except that my girls go to pieces sometimes – usually after working overtime. That's when they come squawking to me in Russian. Yakety-yak! I'd be lost without Natasha.'

'Herr Hausleitner's problem is this,' Natasha said deliberately, looking straight at Singer for the first time. 'All the drugs were removed from here after the last suicide, and the girls need tranquillizers and sleeping pills badly. A total ban is pretty drastic.'

Singer shrugged. 'So's a lethal overdose.'

'You can't blame them,' Hausleitner said in a low, earnest voice. 'For some people, it's the best way out. Who'd want to go on living in a lousy world like this? Only a fool or a coward.'

Singer stared at the strange little brothel-keeper, temporarily dumbfounded by his unexpected outburst. At last he said, 'You must have been at the bottle, Hausleitner. That sounds suspiciously like defeatism to me. If Lieutenant Wagner heard you, he'd have you court-martialled.'

'I'm not drunk.' The elderly corporal had risen to his feet. 'It's just that I see these girls dying, one after another, because they can't bear to go on living. Death is everywhere you look. Everybody turns a blind eye, but I don't. I can see it round every corner.'

He shuffled off. The other two watched him go. 'Does he often shoot his mouth off like that?' Singer asked. 'Doesn't he realize how dangerous it is?'

'Perhaps you should speak to Captain Königsberger. He's a psychologist, after all, and he listens to you.'

Singer pounced. 'Why not speak to him yourself?'

'No opportunity. We never exchange more than two words.'

'But he's only waiting for the chance.'

She gazed at him with mingled disbelief and pleasure. 'Then why doesn't he show it?'

'He's afraid you'd cold-shoulder him, I suppose.'

Natasha got up, looking uncharacteristically flustered. 'I have to go now.' She glanced at her watch. 'I'm due to give the trainees their first Russian lesson tomorrow – today, I mean. You ought to come – you and your Captain Königsberger. You might find it instructive.'

The trainees' first Russian lesson was preceded by a top-level conference in the Colonel's office. Apart from Feuerfresser himself, only Majors Kastor and Pollandt were present. Neither Priewitt nor Captain Tauschmüller had been summoned to attend.

Feuerfresser opened the proceedings on a dramatic note. 'Gentlemen,' he said, 'what I propose to tell you is highly confidential. Make a mental note of every detail, but discuss the matter with no one, not even indirectly.'

The majors barked their response in unison.

'On the assumption that your statistical and other records have already enabled you to form certain conclusions, I'd be glad to hear them.'

It was borne in on the majors, not for the first time, that Feuerfresser never made life easy for his subordinates. After a quick glance at Kastor, Pollandt took the floor.

'In accordance with our usual procedure, Colonel, we began by listing and evaluating all relevant particulars about the members of this latest intake. Comparison with previous courses indicates that an exceptionally high percentage of trainees have a command of the English language. Approximately thirty per cent can speak it with a fair to high degree of fluency. This can hardly be fortuitous.'

'It isn't,' Feuerfresser said approvingly.

'May one ask, Colonel, what the implications are from our own point of view?'

'For the moment, none, though I presume you can guess what lies ahead. Just as the combat techniques we have hitherto perfected and taught were tailored to the Russian and Polish theatres of partisan warfare, so it will probably become necessary to devise training programmes for the effective deployment of crack formations against British and American troops. We may even be required to set up special units of our own. This is still top secret, however. Not a hint of it must leak out.'

'In other words, Colonel, we carry on just as before – outwardly, at least?'

'You've hit it, gentlemen – I congratulate you both. Until I issue further orders, you officially know nothing.'

Once this conference was over, the first Russian class could proceed. It took place in the gymnasium and was attended by all the hundred and twenty trainees.

Major Kastor, with Natasha standing mutely beside him, watched his herd of pedigree cattle file into the gym carrying chairs clamped under their left arms in the regulation manner. Half-way through his eagle-eyed inspection he was distracted by the appearance of Captain Königsberger, who saluted him smartly and smiled at Natasha.

'Mind if I sit in on this lesson, Major?' The MO's tone was respectful. 'The Colonel always speaks so highly of your training methods, I feel they may do me some good. We medical men need to broaden our horizons.'

Kastor had a word with Pollandt, who was thumbing through some papers a few feet away. The MO's interest flattered them. Although they suspected him of trying to butter them up, this was not ungratifying because it signified that Königsberger had finally appreciated the desirability of cultivating proper interdepartmental contacts. Kastor returned wearing a cordial smile.

'Of course you'll be welcome, my dear Doctor. We both hope you'll learn something, and not only in your medical capacity. After all, you're an army officer as well as a doctor.'

Königsberger thanked him politely and beckoned to Singer, who had been hovering in the background. They went into the gym and made themselves comfortable on a rolled-up mat.

The first thing that struck them was the disciplined silence of the trainees, who stared straight ahead like so many lambs being led to the slaughter. Master-Sergeant Heinz, with his legs planted firmly apart and his thumbs hooked in his belt, surveyed them contentedly. Then he snapped to attention.

'On your feet! Come to attention! Eyes front!' He marched up to Kastor and Pollandt. 'All trainees present and correct for special instruction – sir!'

The majors acknowledged his report with a cursory salute. 'At ease, men. Sit down.' The order was executed like a drill movement. The trainees sat ramrod fashion, hands resting lightly on thighs. They were strictly forbidden to sit back or lean forward, let alone cross their legs.

Kastor and Pollandt scanned their heroic band at prodigious length, one by one, doubtless because they felt that thorough familiarity with their own countenances would engender respect in the men who gazed so obediently back at them.

Königsberger leant across to Singer. 'I don't see Lahrmann,' he whispered.

'Lahrmann's busy elsewhere,' Singer told him. 'He's going through the trainees' quarters with a fine-tooth comb, though I can't think what he hopes to find there.'

At a nudge from Pollandt, Kastor stepped forward. The attentive hush deepened to the point where a falling pin would have broken the spell. 'Men,' he said, 'as you have already been informed, more than once, this course is top secret. Not a word of it must be allowed to leak out. You may not, therefore, take notes. All you learn here must be stored in your hearts and minds.'

Another devout silence followed. Then Kastor introduced Natasha. 'This woman is employed by us. She acts on our instructions and will be treated with due respect. You are here to receive your first lesson in the language spoken by our principal enemy of the moment.' He meant the Russians. 'Your task will be to memorize certain basic phrases essential to the effective conduct of military operations. All of you must master these, so try your hardest. Anyone who doesn't has come to the wrong place.'

'And now,' said Major Pollandt, 'phrase number one: "Hands up!"'

Natasha, who had not been permitted to sit down,

reproduced the words in Russian, slowly and distinctly. The trainees chanted them after her in a full-throated chorus, syllable by syllable. They did so again and again, straining every nerve.

'I don't see the point of this,' Königsberger muttered. 'Does it have any practical value?'

Singer raised his eyebrows. 'You mean you doubt it?'

'I'm not qualified to judge, I suppose. I've never seen any action.'

Meantime, more verbal aids to combat were being given out, translated into Russian, and chanted in unison like war cries. 'Up against the wall!' roared the heroic glee club. 'You're surrounded! Move a muscle and you're dead!'

These renderings were noisy enough to enable Singer and the MO to converse in relative freedom. 'It must be very unpleasant for Natasha,' said Königsberger. 'Why does she lend herself to this sort of thing?'

Singer was surprised and showed it. 'Wouldn't you, in her position?'

'I can't help feeling sorry for the girl.'

'Sorry isn't good enough, Captain. She needs your help – in fact she'd welcome it.'

'She wouldn't accept a thing from me. We're worlds apart.'

'You could be making a big mistake. Meet her half way – speak to her. She may be able to explain some of the things you ought to know. Don't fight your better impulses.'

More apt commands in Russian were now being practised. 'Drop your guns!' bellowed a hundred and twenty eager voices. 'Hands on the back of your neck! Come forward one at a time!'

Singer turned to Königsberger with a wry smile. 'I can think of some far more topical phrases, like "Can you spare a cigarette, tovarich?" or "I was never a Nazi" or "My father was a communist before me" – that sort of thing. As aids to survival, they'd be a lot more use.'

The MO wearily shook his head. 'Stop playing the tempter, my friend. I'm no Faust and you're no Mephisto. Can't you think of anything better to do?'

'Can I! I'd sell my soul for a weekend pass to Munich, and the sooner the better.'

'Getting itchy feet?'

'You could call it that. I'd like to visit some friends. Will you fix it?'

'With pleasure,' said the unwitting MO, 'if only to see the back of you for a couple of days. You're starting to get on my nerves, Singer, like so many other people in this place.'

The choral concert finally came to an end. No sooner had Königsberger risen to his feet, looking dazed, than Major Kastor bore down on him. 'Well,' he crowed, 'how about that?'

Königsberger spoke the exact truth, neither more nor less, so he sounded utterly sincere. 'I'm quite overcome, Major.'

'You see?' said Kastor, who readily accepted this as a compliment. 'Our methods are unique!'

Which they were.

Before Singer could leave for Munich, Lieutenant Wagner summoned him to his office in the administration block.

It was as sparsely furnished as an interrogation room. The desk had a hard chair behind it and a stool in front. The end wall of this otherwise bare cubicle was adorned by a poster-sized four-colour reproduction of a stock portrait of the Führer and Supreme Commander. It depicted Adolf Hitler gazing with martial intensity into the far distance, rather like a male Mona Lisa executed in shades of gunmetal grey.

Beneath it sat Lieutenant Wagner, leafing self-importantly through some papers on his desk. He smiled at Singer and bade him be seated.

'In some strange way,' he began, 'our lives exhibit certain parallels. We both come from relatively humble homes – humble but highly respectable. In other words, we constitute the backbone of our nation. Social origins form a bond between those who share them.'

'You may be right, Lieutenant.'

'There's no maybe about it. As the Führer himself has said, "Tell me where you come from and I'll tell you where you belong." You, Corporal Singer, belong with us.'

'If you say so, Lieutenant.'

Wagner nodded. 'I gather from your personal record that you lost your father at an early age, in a road accident. There are several depositions to the effect that he was a staunch nationalist as well as a socialist – to put it another way, a National Socialist. I'm sure you've always felt that placed you under a patriotic obligation.'

'In a way, yes – very much so, Lieutenant.' Singer eyed his inquisitor warily.

'Life is an eternal challenge,' Wagner proclaimed. 'We must meet that challenge and surmount it – ruthlessly. *Necessitas non habet legem*, as the Romans used to say: necessity knows no law.' He had quoted the same tag in the mess the previous night – to great effect, so he fondly believed. 'Ah yes, my dear Singer, we're both in the same boat.'

'And where are we bound for, Lieutenant?'

'There's no mystery about that, compatriot.' Wagner's sudden resort to the Nazis' equivalent of the Communist's 'comrade' was a sign that he had come to the point at last. 'I trust you. Now that I'm satisfied of your total commitment to our common cause, we can work together.' Which, being interpreted, meant, 'You can work for me.'

Singer was not unduly surprised by Wagner's overture because he had been expecting something of the kind, though not quite so crudely put.

'Co-operation's a fine thing, Lieutenant, but what form would it take – in my case, I mean?'

'Any form that presents itself. Take your personal contacts, for instance.'

'The MO, you mean? You want me to keep tabs on him and report anything I see or hear?'

Wagner smiled approvingly. 'You're a smart fellow, I spotted that right away – just the kind of person our country needs. In a fight for national survival, we can't afford to leave a single stone unturned.'

'Is Captain Königsberger under suspicion, then?'

'Really, my dear Singer, you're jumping to conclusions! On the other hand, we must never drop our guard. As far as the MO is concerned, he's a brilliant doctor, a conscientious officer, and a not uncongenial companion. But is he also a devout National Socialist – is he unreservedly committed to our just and righteous cause?'

'You're thinking of the opinions he saw fit to express on the night of July twentieth, Lieutenant, is that it?'

Wagner firmly brushed this suggestion aside. 'Come, come, that's water under the bridge. Nobody mentions it any more.'

'So what would you like me to concentrate on?'

'I'll tell you, Singer. Our worthy MO suffers from a lack of ideological clarity which he mistakenly confuses with tolerance. He also appears to suffer from occasional bouts of un-German sentimentality. Being aware of these defects, we must do our comradely best to protect him from them. We owe it to ourselves as well as him.'

'You put it very convincingly, Lieutenant.' Singer paused. 'But what happens if I don't feel up to the job?'

'You will,' Wagner said with lofty self-assurance, 'because you know you can't afford not to – not if you want to survive here. I'm sure you're a man who prefers the sunny side of life. Well, aren't you?'

All Singer's doubts seemed to have evaporated. When

Wagner conspiratorially extended his hand, he shook it without hesitation.

CURRICULUM VITAE OF WERNER WAGNER
or, The Rewards of Perseverance

I was born on 21 August 1920, at Kalk, on the outskirts of Cologne. My parents were Willi Wagner, a clerical worker at the municipal gasworks, and his wife Veronika, who was also employed there. I was their first and only child.

Werner spent his childhood in a happy-go-lucky atmosphere. His parents, who shared a passion for choral singing, had met at an audition. They married and produced Werner soon after that. Active supporters of Cologne's annual carnival and rather less active church-goers, Willi and Veronika led an almost unclouded existence. Consistently cheerful and sometimes the worse for drink, they always contrived to have fun.

At carnival time, young Werner spent many nights alone in his parents' three-roomed apartment. This scared him stiff, but, like the true German youngster he was, he took care not to show it. Besides, he always received a hearty and affectionate good night from his party-going parents, Willi in a Prussian guard's uniform which he kept in trim himself, Veronika dressed as a female camp follower with garishly rouged cheeks and a well-filled canteen from which Werner was sometimes dosed with a hefty slug of brandy – a proven aid to sleep.

Politics was not a family topic. 'As a senior municipal employee,' his father said flatly, 'I steer clear of that sort of thing. I do my job and I do it well. Nothing else matters a row of beans.'

I started elementary school in 1926, and was fortunate

133

enough to be taught history, geography and German by Hans Peter Kern, our future Deputy Gauleiter. He ensured that I went on to high school, though I was forced to leave there after only two years, thanks to the political bias of a teacher with extreme left-wing views. Thereafter I attended business school.

Though rather one-sided in his interests, young Werner was a gifted pupil – at least in the opinion of Herr Kern, an ex-officer who had fought in the trenches and remained a staunch patriot. Werner read a great deal, not only between classes but under the bedclothes at night, by the light of a flashlamp. His favourite subject was history – knightly epics, tales of battle and biographies of the great. Kern, who spotted this interest in feats of manly endeavour, set him on the right road. 'You have hidden potentialities, my boy,' he told him. 'We must do our best to nurture them.'

'Cast-iron Kern', as his colleagues called this patriotic pedagogue, appointed his pet pupil head of the class. Werner was privileged to carry his books and briefcase, but Kern also devoted time to the boy out of hours. Purely on an intellectual plane, of course, even if he did give him an occasional hug of commendation or slap him playfully on the bottom. It was Kern who drew his attention to the edifying and uplifting qualities of Hitler's *Mein Kampf* – 'an absolute must', as he called it.

Thanks to some vigorous lobbying by his revered teacher, Werner got into a high school which continued to rejoice in the name of Germany's former emperor. To the great satisfaction of German traditionalists, Kaiser Wilhelm high schools still existed all over the country, but in this case the name proved deceptive – certainly where Werner was concerned. He ended up in the class of a so-called teacher who doubtless owed his post to an administrative blunder. This man – probably Jewish or at least half-Jewish – tested his knowledge of history with catastrophic results.

'Your brain has been systematically pumped full of hot air,' declared this individual. 'Either you can't think, or you aren't prepared to. You've studied Napoleon, but you don't have a clue about the French Revolution. You seem to be impressed by this man Hitler, but you've never even heard of Karl Marx.'

Werner felt miserably at sea. When he claimed, in all sincerity, that his previous studies had helped him to develop an unshakable belief in Germany's greatness, his asseverations were greeted with head-wagging and sarcastic laughter. 'Reactionary claptrap!' was the left-wing teacher's verdict. At this, Werner had the temerity to remark that events would prove which of them was the real reactionary. His fate at high school was thereby sealed.

Werner was expelled because of his 'incapacity for constructive thought', but also because of his allegedly inadequate marks in physics, mathematics and Latin – Latin, of all subjects, which he not only loved but often drew on, even in those days, for tags appropriate to any given situation. His only recourse was to enter a business school. Though deeply embittered by the turn events had taken, he was not discouraged. As he later declared, he had always known precisely what he wanted.

In summer 1932 I joined the Hitler Youth, where I received a comradely welcome. By winter of that year, I was helping to raise the tone of our evening meetings, mainly with readings from Faith in Germany *and apt quotations from the Führer's* magnum opus. *My promotion to the rank of section leader was only a matter of time.*

Werner devoted himself unstintingly to this patriotic task, even though it meant cutting lectures and neglecting divine worship. He knew, after all, where his priorities lay.

The elder Wagner obligingly declared himself sympathetic to Werner's new-found enthusiasm. 'I'm a broadminded man – always have been. You can take as much time off as you like, son, especially if you spend it in decent, upstanding company. Besides, it looks as if you weren't so wrong after all. These Nazis are going places. What's more, that Hitler of yours hasn't said a word against our carnival, nor against the Church.' – 'Nor against choral singing,' Werner's mother added knowledgeably.

So they tolerated his activities with some degree of generosity. His father financed the purchase of a uniform and his mother kept it spick and span. Werner cut a pleasing and promising figure. He trotted up hill and down dale with his Hitler youth detachment, underwent paramilitary training, and even took part in scuffles with members of rival socialist organizations.

On 30 January 1933, the day his beloved Führer came to power, a torchlight procession wound its way through Cologne, or at least through one or two outlying suburbs. Though not particularly large, it was not to be ignored. Werner marched in its ranks, of course, and so did his parents, who had decided to follow their boy's shining example and come down off the political fence. In March 1933, Werner's father applied to join the Nazi Party and his mother the National Socialist Women's Association. His active membership of the Hitler Youth guaranteed them ready acceptance, and his growing feats of organization and oratory, the latter founded on a rich store of Greater German ideas, soon attracted favourable attention. Beyond all doubt, Werner Wagner was destined for great things.

The Reich Youth Leader, Baldur von Schirach himself, summoned Werner to Berlin for a personal interview. 'Comrade,' he told him, 'your services have been outstanding. I have great plans for you – I even intend to take you on to my staff. Before I do, however, you must undergo a further test. Our armed forces seem badly in need of an ideological injection. I want you to become an officer – carry the banner of our beliefs into the military domain, as it were. Are you prepared to do so? You may rest assured that we shall smooth your path in every way.'

In 1937 I volunteered for military service. Being a veteran Hitler Youth leader armed with official Party testimonials to that effect, I was promptly accepted by the Army and, as expected, earmarked for a commission.

Werner's first year of training was no rest cure, but he endured it with the fortitude of one whose eyes are focused on a lofty goal. His exemplary conduct was noted and appreciated. No veteran Hitler Youth leader could have made less of an attempt to wangle preferential treatment, and nothing stood in the way of his rapid promotion to noncommissioned rank.

Werner did equally well as an NCO instructor in 1938. 'Keen as mustard but agreeably modest despite his exceptional achievements,' ran his confidential report. 'If he keeps it up . . .'

And keep it up he did. Werner was sent on an eight-week officer selection course, from which he emerged with outstanding success. After a triumphant spell at military academy, he seemed certain of a promising career as an officer. Then came 1939, and with it the threat of a patriotic war in defence of Greater Germany – allegedly forced on her peace-loving inhabitants by their hostile neighbours. Purely as a precaution, all personnel were medically examined to see if they were a hundred per cent fit for combat duty. Officer Cadet Wagner, too, had to submit to this examination.

The MO in charge, a Captain Berger, was unimpressed by Werner's physique. 'What?' he had the effrontery to say. 'If you're hoping to become an officer, forget it. You've a tendency to flat feet.'

Werner was outraged. Him, flat feet? He couldn't take a defamatory remark like that lying down, so he tapped his contacts with the Reich Youth Leader and Deputy Gauleiter Kern, as his former schoolmaster was now known. The result was predictable.

Captain Berger, the MO who had perpetrated this malicious act of sabotage, received a sharp rebuke from his immediate boss, a major. 'Stop nit-picking,' he was told. 'A tendency to flat feet can be corrected – you ought to know that. If Wagner's been earmarked for a commission, he'll get one.'

And get one he did. After graduating from military academy during the Polish campaign, he participated in the 'stroll' through France as a second lieutenant and infantry platoon commander. His unit suffered heavy casualties. He himself was awarded the Iron Cross Second Class. In the course of a convivial booze-up with his brother officers, which culminated in an impromptu *feu-de-joie*, he was hit by a ricochet which temporarily immobilized his left arm. This earned him the Wound Badge in Silver.

For a while he acted as a sort of liaison officer between the Party and the commander-in-chief of the Replacement Army, whose headquarters were in Bendlerstrasse, Berlin. From there he was transferred to AFSIC Kampfental. Having looked, long and closely, at his personal file, Colonel von Feuerfresser sent for him. 'I don't give a damn whether you're a National Socialist,' he said. 'You seem to be a reliable officer with an excellent record, that's all that counts with me.'

Corporal Singer had been granted some leave the following weekend – the last one in August 1944. This privilege, which was normally restricted to long-standing members of the permanent staff, he owed to a fortunate combination of circumstances.

Frau Klarfeld had asked the MO for some sleeping pills. Königsberger had promptly supplied them but added, in a tone of polite regret, that his stocks were running low. He had a friend and colleague in Munich who might be able to replenish them, but only if someone reliable were sent there – Singer, for instance – with a written requisition. Frau Klarfeld had made the appropriate recommendation to her admirer, Captain Tauschmüller, who acted on it. Singer himself ensured that Sergeant-Major Schulz put no difficulties in his way by allowing him to pocket a substantial win during one of their nocturnal card games. Schulz's response was almost human. 'Feeling like a quick screw in Munich, eh?' he said jocularly. 'Well, why not – but mind you bring me back some juicy phone numbers.'

And that was how Singer came to be given a pass covering the period 11 a.m. Saturday to midnight Sunday, destination Munich.

The slow train from Hölzbach, which was always jam-packed, took just under two hours to get there. Munich's central station was badly battered but still in commission. Allied bombs did not reduce it to rubble until some weeks later. Waiting for Singer at the end of the platform was a pretty young blonde with wide, lively eyes and a pert little tip-tilted nose. Totally unembarrassed, she darted forward and flung her arms round his neck.

'Lovely to see you, Barbara.'

'Glad you could make it, Sebastian.'

A fresh-faced young soldier kissing a pretty girl on a station platform – nothing could have seemed more commonplace in wartime, yet there was more to the scene than met the eye.

Barbara was dividing her time at Munich University between drama and law. She lived in Leopoldstrasse, which was still more or less intact, with an aunt who had long since become inured to the antics of her headstrong niece.

What was more to the point, Barbara happened to be the dearly beloved and only daughter of Field-Marshal Wedell. Although she always insisted that her parentage had no bearing on anything, least of all her private life, she had not entirely succeeded in dissociating herself from this ultra-powerful father figure – nor did she always wish to. Lingering inhibitions apart, however, she was a hot-blooded young woman who wanted to love and be loved.

Chance had brought Sebastian Singer into her life a few weeks earlier. One of her regular escorts, a handsome young lieutenant with a chestful of medals and a rather complex personality, had bought two tickets for a summer concert of Haydn, Mozart and Rossini serenades. He arranged to meet her but failed to turn up. Instead, his seat was occupied by a stranger – a corporal. And that was how it all began.

'Well,' he said, 'what shall we do with ourselves?' They were still inside the station.

'Whatever you feel like, Sebastian – as if I didn't know.'

Singer's spine tingled. It was a pleasant sensation.

It soon turned out that Barbara was quite prepared to take discreet advantage of her father's exalted position, especially as his chief-of-staff was only too happy to aid and abet her.

Colonel Schlumberger, whose promotion to major-general was in the offing, had a quasi paternal fondness – if not a masculine weakness – for his field-marshal's daughter, and loved doing her little favours. This time he had surpassed himself. Barbara and her boy-friend were showered with all the not inconsiderable luxuries that were still to be had in wartime Munich, ranging from an early supper at the Restaurant Walterspiel, to a pair of seats for *Figaro* in the royal box – now the Führer's box – at the State Opera, to a double room at the celebrated Hotel

Schottenhamel. Colonel Schlumberger had personally booked the latter by phone from Army Group Headquarters.

'A double room, please, in the name of Singer.'

'A gentleman on the Field-Marshal's staff?' the head receptionist enquired politely.

Schlumberger chuckled. 'No, a corporal.'

The head receptionist was one of the old school. He had seen generals, ambassadors and cabinet ministers come and go – he had even welcomed Hitler to the premises. At least this was a new departure.

'Certainly, Colonel. One double room in the name of Singer.' His own chuckle was inaudible as he added, 'A room fit for the Field-Marshal himself.'

It was a memorable night, filled with alternating passion and tenderness. Worn out, they slept through breakfast and did not wake till nearly midday.

Singer had no need to tell Barbara how happy he was – his face said it all. In her arms, he had managed to forget the war.

'Back in camp,' he said, 'we've got a lieutenant who quotes Latin tags all the time. If he were in my place, which God forbid, he'd probably say, "*Omnia vincit amor*" – love conquers all.'

Barbara laughed. 'Except that love isn't an uninterrupted process, not even with us. Everyone has to eat now and then.'

She consulted her watch on the bedside table. 'We ought to get dressed for lunch. Incidentally, I invited Konstantin to join us.' She glanced at him keenly. 'I hope you don't mind.'

'Why should I?' Singer said casually. 'We'd never have met if it hadn't been for him. Besides, I always enjoy his company. His kind don't grow on trees.'

She shook her head. 'I sometimes wonder what you

really are, Sebastian, broad-minded or calculating.'

'Just what I keep asking myself,' he said, 'but never where you're concerned. About you I'm selfish, ruthless and possessive. That's because I love you.'

Konstantin Kersten was already waiting for them in the dining-room of the Schottenhamel. Candles and flowers adorned their secluded corner table, which was regularly reserved for special guests and had been booked in the prestigious name of Wedell.

Lieutenant Kersten, with the German Cross in Gold on his chest and the Knight's Cross of the Iron Cross at his throat, was unimpressed by the privileges of rank. Smiling broadly, he kissed Barbara's hand and gave Sebastian a hearty hug.

'I took the liberty of ordering for us,' he said, 'just to pass the time. Bavarian broth to start with, then Wienerschnitzels with sauté potatoes and a green salad on the side. What comes next is up to you. Any complaints?'

He was obviously used to making decisions, as in combat so in hotel dining-rooms.

'You're looking moody, Konstantin,' said Barbara. 'Is it anything to do with us?'

Kersten grinned. 'You couldn't be more wrong, my girl. I know what friendship means.' He turned to Sebastian. 'Or have you been trying to persuade her that I don't?'

Singer parried this casual insinuation with a smile. 'Sure we're friends, and I'd like us all to stay that way if we can.'

'So would I, Konstantin.' Barbara squeezed his left hand and Sebastian's right, looking like a cream-fed cat. 'Now let's have some champagne,' she said, 'on Old Father Field-Marshal.'

'On the taxpayer, you mean,' Singer said drily.

Kersten rejected the idea out of hand. 'I wouldn't hear of it. This bottle's on me. Incorruptible, that's us. We don't take favours from anyone, not even an army group commander.' On his lips, it sounded like a profession of faith.

Sebastian regarded him intently. 'Barbara's right, you don't look too chirpy. What's up?'

'It's that chief MO at the field hospital – he's getting me down.' At long last, Kersten seemed to have broached the subject that was preying on his mind. It was like a dam bursting. 'You know the man I mean, Sebastian, you managed to give him the slip – him and his smarmy bedside manner.'

'He won't let you go, eh? No wonder, you're his star patient.'

Kersten wasn't amused. 'Know what I told that unctuous little quack? I said, unless you certify me fit for combat duty in double-quick time, I'll be forced to conclude that you're sabotaging the war effort.'

'Is that all you're worried about?' said Barbara. 'There must be several million men who'd swap places with you any day. Still – ' she raised her glass in a mock toast – 'if my father could hear you, I'm sure he'd give you another medal.'

They drank to each other. As soon as they had put their glasses down, Singer took up the thread again. 'So you bullied the chief medic. How did he take it?'

'He's a typical play-it-safer, that man. He rounded up a few more specimens of his breed and formed a makeshift medical board, just for my benefit. Their findings were unanimous, of course: quite unfit to be discharged.'

Singer shrugged. 'Maybe they're right. You were far more badly knocked about than I was.'

'It's not just that. The man actually dared to suggest that it might be necessary to give me a psychological check-up. I don't know what he meant, but I took the precaution of turning him down flat.'

As personal orderly to a medical officer, Singer could guess what the chief MO had been driving at, though he thought it inopportune to say so. Kersten wouldn't have been the first war hero whose mental state required investigation. 'I see,' he said, 'so they want to keep you in their hellhole for another few weeks.'

'Yes, but I'm not having it.' Kersten sounded pugnaciously sure of himself. 'I really rubbed that head quack's nose in it. I told him he'd deprived badly wounded men of hours of medical treatment by holding his witch doctors' convention for my sake. I also told him I'd have him court-martialled for wasting time, neglecting his patients and abusing his authority.'

'Congratulations!' Barbara smiled at both her companions in turn. 'As my father might say in one of his coarser moments, you chewed his balls off.'

'Good and proper,' said Singer. 'He must be itching to get rid of you now, but his hands are tied – he tied them himself by appointing that board. He'll have to put up with you for a bit longer – he doesn't have any choice.'

Kersten brushed this nonchalantly aside. 'Don't worry, I'll soon be on my way.'

'Where to?'

'The front, of course – where else? You know me as well as anyone, Sebastian. You not only claim you know what makes me tick, you really do.'

Their strange friendship had originated only a few weeks earlier at No. 9 Field Hospital, Munich District, where they had both been admitted in a critical condition. They occupied different wards and were treated by different doctors, but one day, when they had been reclassified as walking wounded, they met in the hospital grounds.

Beside one of the paths stood a stone table with an inlaid chessboard and some weatherproof men to match. Kersten was bending over it, brooding, though not about chess. He glanced up as Singer strolled past, then froze and stared at him with strange intensity.

'What's your name?' he asked. 'Excuse me, it's just that you remind me of someone.'

Singer introduced himself.

'Care for a game of chess?' The question sounded quite spontaneous and curiously intimate.

Singer accepted Kersten's invitation with the polite detachment which their difference in rank prescribed. He soon realized that the lieutenant was anything but a dogged, deliberate player. Bold and reckless, he seemed obsessed with capturing his opponent's men at all costs.

Singer gave him the first two games, but so skilfully that Kersten could congratulate himself on a pair of hard-won victories. The next game Singer decided in his own favour – quickly, convincingly, almost masterfully – because he was in urgent need of a visit to the men's room. Kersten's reaction came as a complete surprise: he was delighted.

'Very impressive, Corporal. You obviously have a first-class mathematical brain.' Almost inaudibly, he added, 'Just like Karl.'

Singer ignored the last remark, but from then on Kersten sought his company. They ate together, walked together, and swapped books. They also played chess regularly. The score after a week was four games all and four drawn. Singer won the next game hands down in record time. Far from being put out, Kersten beamed with pleasure and called him a genius. By now they were on first-name terms.

They often strolled through the hospital grounds to the fishpond. One day, when it was raining hard, they came across a number of disabled men in wheelchairs abandoned round the edge of the pool. There were no orderlies in sight. This offended Kersten's ever active sense of fair play.

'What's the meaning of this!' he bellowed in a commanding voice. 'These men have been left unattended. Orderlies, where the hell are you?'

The orderlies came scuttling up, followed by one of the hospital's three dozen medical officers. 'Please, Lieutenant!' he entreated. 'No need to shout. It isn't as easy as you think – there's a shortage of nursing staff.'

'But no shortage of wounded men!' barked Kersten. 'These comrades of ours risked their necks in action – they didn't knock off for a quiet smoke whenever they felt like it. The least you dozy medics can do is look after them now, do I make myself clear?'

The MO nodded mutely. The wheelchair cases seemed more surprised than grateful. Kersten's tirade was something outside their experience. Besides, there was every reason to fear that the targets of his abuse would make them suffer for their humiliation.

To Singer, however, the scene brought home the heroic obstinacy of the man whose friendship he had gained. Belatedly but not too late, he realized that Kersten was intent on doing battle with everything that struck him as suspect or unsavoury. The lieutenant had begun to intrigue him.

During one of their subsequent chess games, Singer said, 'I've been thinking of something you said the first time we met. "You remind me of someone," you said.'

'Did I?'

'Yes, and you said something else a bit later – something about someone named Karl. Is he your brother?'

Kersten's face darkened. 'I don't have a brother, not now. I used to have, and we were very close. He died young, but I'd rather not talk about it.'

Singer didn't pursue the subject. They continued to play chess, go for walks in the grounds and take their meals together. Although they exchanged personal and private confidences as their friendship matured, Kersten's dead brother was never mentioned again.

'Come on,' Singer said one day, 'let's have another game, but this time let's play for a prize.'

'Any suggestions?'

'Yes, you've got a date with Barbara Wedell tomorrow. Going to a concert, aren't you?'

'Not by choice. She insisted, but music doesn't mean a thing to me – it goes zooming in one ear and out the other. Concerts are wasted on me. Why, are you interested in the girl?'

'I only know her from the photos you've shown me, but I wouldn't mind meeting her some time.'

'All right.' Kersten grinned at him. 'We'll play, and the loser takes Barbara to hear Mozart and Co.'

Singer lost with pleasure, and the resulting encounter had strange and fateful consequences. He and Barbara fell for each other, but their mutual friend raised no objection.

True friendship ranked just below courage in Kersten's scale of masculine virtues. Friendship meant far, far more to him than love, which was secondary.

Situation Report No. 4

The Allied invaders pressed on irresistibly, in the south as well as the west. In the east, too, Soviet troops drew ever nearer the borders of Greater Germany, their primary objective being East Prussia. Although Hitler redoubled his injunctions to conquer or die in the attempt, desperate German counter-offensives soon petered out.

Rome was declared an open city, which preserved its unique art treasures from destruction. Static warfare raged around the monastery of Monte Cassino, where thousands of men shot, bombed and bayoneted each other in the grand old manner. Daring Allied airborne landings at Arnhem and Nijmegen proved immensely costly to both sides but contributed to the capture of Antwerp and, ultimately, to the complete liberation of Belgium and Holland.

German propaganda played such things down or placed its

own construction on them. Soldiers who still believed in final victory were bombarded with encouraging lies. 'Whatever happens in the east,' ran one line of argument, 'remember that your enemies are subhuman Asiatic hordes. Being as indisciplined as they are, they will end by killing each other off.' Or again: 'Current developments in the west are based solely on material and financial superiority, which cannot prevail in the long run. The Western Allies have no real fighting spirit. They are degenerates whose strength has been sapped by Negro jazz, capitalist Coca-Cola, and the Semitic effusions of Hollywood. They think money can accomplish anything, but this is a mistake that will cost them dear.' Finally: 'We alone are infused with creative energy and the spirit of invention.'

Precisely what that meant was soon apparent to all who could put two and two together. It signified the existence of a miraculous secret weapon – a long-range rocket which would, it was rumoured, clinch the war in Germany's favour.

Meanwhile, the Americans were working on an atomic bomb.

Singer's weekend leave drew to a close. Barbara and Kersten accompanied him to the station, where his train was already waiting. The three friends stood on the platform, heavy-hearted at the prospect of saying goodbye.

'Only seven minutes to go,' Kersten said tactfully. 'I'll nip off to the news stand and get you a *Völkischer Beobachter* to read on the journey.'

The lovers gazed after him, grateful for the chance of another few minutes alone together.

'I'll never forget this weekend,' Singer murmured. 'It was glorious. I hope you won't get into hot water.'

'With my father? No fear of that, he's too busy helping to run the war. He doesn't have time to worry about his daughter's private life as well. Anyway, he's delegated his paternal responsibilities to Colonel Schlumberger, and

Schlumberger's like a doting elder brother – he'd do anything for me.'

'Anything?'

'Almost anything. His word carries nearly as much weight as my father's. Why, what's on your mind?'

'It's Konstantin,' Singer said pensively. 'I'd like to keep him out of harm's way for as long as possible, wouldn't you?'

She nodded. 'Of course, but he's half-way to the front already, in spirit. You can't hold him back for ever.'

'No, not for ever, but how about arranging a little detour?'

'Via Kampfental, you mean?'

'You got me sent there, Barbara, so why not him too?'

'I'm sure I could fix it, but what if he found out? Wouldn't it be risky from your point of view? Konstantin may be your friend, but he's also a born hero – he'd be furious with you.' She shrugged. 'Still, if you insist, I'll do the necessary.'

Kersten rejoined them a minute before the train left for Hölzbach, carrying a bundle of newspapers and magazines. Singer shook his hand warmly, then gave Barbara a long and tender farewell kiss.

He climbed aboard and squeezed into an overcrowded compartment. Clambering over legs and assorted baggage, he reached the window just in time to wave goodbye.

5

A teleprinter message from Field-Marshal Wedell's army group headquarters reached No. 9 Field Hospital, Munich District, the same night. It was signed by his chief of staff, Colonel Schlumberger, and headed 'Urgent – For Immediate Action'. The text was as follows:

> As of now, Lieutenant Konstantin Kersten of Ward 2a is assigned to AFSIC Kampfental, Hölzbach District. He will report to the Commandant in person within twenty-four hours. Kindly issue a movement order to that effect.

The chief medical officer, who was specially woken with this news, could barely conceal his relief, but he took care to cover himself in the duty officer's presence. 'I can't be expected to certify that Lieutenant Kersten has made a full recovery,' he said. 'His extravagant behaviour may well be due to some form of mental disturbance, but there it is. Orders are orders, especially when they come from the top.'

Next day, AFSIC Kampfental seemed more than ever determined to justify its élite existence. The majors' first full-scale exercise – 'Detection and Extermination of Partisans' – was scheduled for that morning.

Lieutenant Lahrmann prefaced it by ordering his highly trained NCO instructors into the woods on the north side of the training area. There they were to deploy under Master-Sergeant Heinz's command, having previously exchanged their camouflage suits for a motley array of Red

Army uniforms drawn from AFSIC's special clothing store. They also carried captured Russian weapons, but no live ammunition.

Heinz surveyed his mock partisans with grim satisfaction. 'Right, men, let's make it feel like the real thing.'

'Not too real,' warned Lahrmann. 'Remember, Heinz, this is only an exercise.'

'But a tough one, Lieutenant. Correct?'

While the instructors were doubling off to their deployment area, cheerfully spurred on by Heinz, Lahrmann assembled his trainees on the outskirts of the wood and briefly explained what the morning held in store.

'You've already had several lectures on the nature of partisans and the tactics they employ when operating from positions of concealment. That was theory. Now to put what you've learned into practice. Concealed in the wood to our front, probably strung out across its north-east axis, are a number of partisans. Your task is to detect and dispose of them – silently. That's why no live ammunition has been issued. All-out, hand-to-hand combat is the only method open to you. Anyone pinned to the ground or otherwise immobilized will be counted as dead.'

He proceeded to divide Groups A and B into three squads each.

'And now, at intervals of thirty minutes, carry on!'

This sentenced the trainees to at least three hours' involvement in an exercise for which their previous combat experience, gained under totally different conditions, left them quite unfitted. One by one, in a disastrously unimaginative way, they plodded off into the trees. The shock treatment they received there was skilfully administered and thoroughly effective.

Once the unwitting novices had gone some distance, they were bushwhacked at lightning speed. Their partisan-instructors dropped out of trees or burst from the undergrowth and dragged them, with many a kick, punch and stranglehold, into camouflaged foxholes.

The trainees stood no chance against their rugged and experienced opponents, whose fiendish delight in the operation had been reinforced by the promise of three crates of beer and a carton of cigarettes.

The results of this ordeal were unsurprising. A couple of instructors displayed minor cuts and bruises; of the trainees, three sustained slight to medium injuries and two were hospital cases. Lieutenant Lahrmann registered extreme annoyance.

'Was this really necessary, Heinz?' he demanded.

'Couldn't be helped, sir,' said Heinz. He felt tempted to trot out his pet formula – 'This isn't a kindergarten' – but confined himself to adding, 'Besides, there's always Captain Königsberger. If he's as good as everyone says, he'll patch 'em up in no time.'

The same morning, Singer took a call from Munich on the MO's phone. The caller was Kersten, and Kersten was hopping mad.

'I don't know who's responsible for this piece of skulduggery, Sebastian, but if it was you or Barbara – and if I ever find out – I'll show you what it means to gang up on a friend.'

Singer didn't turn a hair. 'I don't follow you, Konstantin. What's all this about skulduggery? There's so much around these days, you'll have to be more precise.'

'I've been posted to Kampfental, that's what.'

'Terrific! This place is a regular playground for war heroes – you'll be right in your element.'

'Cut it out, Sebastian! All I wanted was a field command, and they send me to the back of beyond.'

'You never know, you may find it interesting. Unfamiliar ground always is.'

'Well, at least you'll be there too. I'm arriving by the midday train. Can you meet me?'

152

'I'll try, but I can't promise. We're fighting our own kind of war here, and it's got its own special rules.'

Singer put the phone down and went to see Mess Sergeant Gerner. 'They say there's a new officer on the way,' he told him. 'A Lieutenant Kersten.'

'A new officer?' Gerner frowned. 'That's news to me. What about him?'

'Well, Sergeant, every orderly's meant to look after two officers – all except Priewitt, who's the Colonel's personal property – so I'm one short. Maybe I could take on the new man as well as the MO.'

Still looking puzzled, Gerner called Sergeant-Major Schulz. 'There's a new addition to the mess,' he said, 'a lieutenant by the name of Kersten. Did you know?'

'Sure, why wouldn't I? There's a telex message about him on Tauschmüller's desk, not that he's seen it yet – too busy. Anyway, who told you?'

'I got it from Singer – the little skunk's here with me now.'

'And where did he get it from?'

'No idea.'

'Then bloody well ask him!'

Singer had a convincing explanation at his fingertips. He still kept in touch with a few of his fellow patients at No. 9 Field Hospital, and one of them had tipped him the wink that Lieutenant Kersten was being posted to Kampfental. Gerner transmitted the gist of this to Schulz, together with Singer's request.

'Sounds reasonable,' said Schulz. 'Maybe it's not such a bad idea at that. Tauschmüller likes to keep tabs on all his officers, and Singer could be just the man for the job – he's crafty enough, God knows. Ask him what he knows about this Lieutenant Kersten.'

Gerner did so without result. 'He says he doesn't have a clue, Sergeant-Major. What do you think?'

'I'm always open to intelligent suggestions, Gerner. If Singer's so keen to shine the man's shoes, let him.'

Lieutenant Lahrmann's bruised and battered trainees were in for yet another exercise that day, as he briskly informed them.

'You have just received your first practical lesson in anti-guerrilla tactics. We shall now move on to Training Area No. 2. Concealed there are a number of targets representing hostile elements. These are mechanically operated. They can appear without warning on either flank, bob up from the ground, or be lowered from above.'

Lahrmann benignly scanned his men's faces as this news sank in.

'You will be issued with a generous supply of live ammunition,' he went on, 'fifty rounds per rifle, three hundred per sub-machine-gun, and six hand grenades per man. This does not entitle you to blaze away wildly. You will crawl forward in groups, alert to any sign of enemy activity. And be careful of your fellow trainees. Anyone who gives his neighbour a spare arsehole will have to take the consequences.'

Lahrmann's admonition was tempered with a consoling incentive.

'At the conclusion of this exercise, there will be a get-together in the canteen with free beer all round – but only for those of you who survive.'

The trainees responded as Lahrmann undoubtedly meant them to. Their laughter at his virile jest was loud but mirthless. It was beginning to dawn on them that AFSIC Kampfental had not exhausted its store of surprises.

Situation Report No. 5

The war, German soldiers were led to believe, could still be won. All they needed was faith and courage; everything else

154

could safely be left to Adolf Hitler, Führer and Supreme Commander of the Armed Forces. And so they fought on, eager to defend their womenfolk and children from 'Asiatic hordes' and 'Jew-infected gangsters', and any generals who had survived Hitler's displeasure accompanied them on their march into the abyss.

London, where 'combat-shy' Allied staff officers were said to be 'skulking', was subjected to long-range bombardment from Peenemünde on Hitler's orders. The V1, or flying bomb, was quickly superseded by the more effective V2, a rocket immune to fighters and anti-aircraft fire. Both systems foreshadowed the conquest of space, years later, by America and the Soviet Union.

At the time, however, these newfangled weapons spread 'destruction, alarm and terror' – or so it was claimed, with undiminished bombast, by a Nazi propaganda machine which further alleged that whole tracts of London had been flattened, that its inhabitants were dying like flies, and that Allied morale had suffered a shattering blow. The truth was somewhat different. Although these unmanned jet- and rocket-propelled missiles inflicted numerous casualties, and although they destroyed individual buildings and city blocks, the phlegmatic British withstood their psychological impact.

Historians are not alone in drawing attention to the consequences of what was Hitler's greatest blunder and most fatal miscalculation. His blind, inveterate, and ultimately murderous anti-Semitism not only stripped Jewish patriots and war heroes of their citizenship but compelled some of Germany's most brilliant men of letters and science, from Stefan Zweig to Albert Einstein, to seek refuge abroad.

They were accompanied into exile by a substantial number of their non-Jewish friends and associates. The United States gave shelter to these homeless European intellectuals, granted them generous working facilities, and employed them to develop an atomic bomb which made the V2 look like a rather nasty little toy.

This raises the most difficult and delicate questions of all. What would have happened if Hitler had been less of a bigot – if he had not expelled, persecuted, and ultimately murdered the Jews of Germany? What would have happened if, on the contrary, he had allotted them an honoured place in his Greater German empire? Would Jewish officers and men have marched under his banner? Would the Jewish medical élite have tended his troops? Would Jewish writers have sung his praises?

Above all, would Jewish scientists have built him the atomic bomb that could hardly have failed to Germanize Europe and much of the rest of the world?

The fact is, they didn't.

After breakfast on that glorious early autumn morning, Colonel von Feuerfresser had summoned his adjutant and expressed a wish to savour the joys of the chase.

'Certainly, Colonel,' said Tauschmüller. 'Normal or full turn-out?'

'I don't know yet, my dear fellow.' Feuerfresser mused for a moment or two. 'Autumn is the finest time for hunting, but it remains to be seen whether I shall devote myself to it for a few hours or a couple of days.'

This, Tauschmüller realized at once, meant a full turn-out, and this in turn meant that he would have to muster an army of beaters, tent-pitchers, gun-bearers, security personnel, and kitchen staff. 'You wish to move off at midday, Colonel?' he enquired.

'No, fourteen hundred,' said Feuerfresser, who preferred to march on a substantial mess lunch. 'Please make the necessary arrangements.'

Tauschmüller did so with characteristic efficiency. He organized a party of twelve men and lectured them on their duties. Eugen Priewitt would as usual be in close attendance, carrying his master's private arsenal.

Also included in a hunting party of this type were half a

dozen sub-machine-gunners from Lieutenant Wagner's Security Platoon, who doubled as beaters and bodyguards. The Colonel's personal tent and camp bed, together with tents for his retinue, were loaded on to a handcart specially designed to be hauled across country by a team of four men, and the party's gastronomic welfare was assured by the presence of one of the three mess cooks.

Mess Sergeant Gerner, who was detailed to command the baggage train on this occasion, ventured to express certain misgivings to the organizer of the party.

'Pardon me for saying so, Captain, but the mess is my baby. You really think I ought to leave it unattended?'

Tauschmüller straightened him out at once. 'The mess is wherever the Colonel happens to be, Sergeant. You should know that by now.'

This presented Gerner with the problem of who was to deputize for him in his absence – an uneasy decision, given his extreme reluctance to delegate control over what he regarded as his personal property.

Priewitt, who would have made an ideal stand-in, merely said, 'If you don't want to carry the can for a balls-up at this end, you better pick someone good. I know who *I'd* choose.'

Gerner took the hint at once. He sent for Singer and handed over his bristling bunch of keys with Priewitt acting as witness to the transaction. 'Singer,' he said sternly, 'it's your job to see everything carries on as usual – and I mean exactly! One little goof and you'll wish you'd never been born, right?'

'Right, Sergeant.' Singer concealed his delight with an effort. 'In that case, have a good time.' He saluted Gerner, winked at Priewitt, and hurried off to meet Kersten's train at Hölzbach.

At 2 p.m. on the dot, the Colonel's favourite mount – a spirited dapple-grey named Baldur – was gracefully pawing the gravel outside the mess. Feuerfresser swung himself into the saddle and murmured a few soothing words in the restive beast's ear.

Gerner reported his party present and correct, three selected members of the chamber orchestra blew a melodious fanfare on hunting horns, and Captain Tauschmüller saluted.

'Permit me to wish you good hunting, Colonel.'

'Thank you, Captain. Escort, forward – march!'

Feuerfresser rode off at the head of his rank and file. Tauschmüller watched the party disappear into the woods with some relief. The shadow cast by his lord and master was a long one. He was free of it at last, if only for a while.

The midday train from Munich was only a few minutes late, war or no war. Kersten tossed his one piece of baggage, a sort of kitbag, on to the platform, and climbed out after it. Looking around for Singer, he saw him lolling against a pillar beside the station entrance. Singer, who was acquainted with Kersten's likes and dislikes in the field of protocol, made no move to help him carry his bag.

'There you are, you cunning little devil!' Kersten grinned pugnaciously. 'Good to see you again.'

They shook hands. Singer indicated a camouflaged sedan parked outside the station. 'Your carriage awaits.'

The lieutenant merely nodded. He scanned his surroundings as though gauging their tactical pros and cons.

'No sign of military activity,' he said at last. 'What the hell is this, a health resort?'

'No, the back of beyond – you said so yourself on the phone. Don't worry, you'll soon feel at home here.'

'You do, that's obvious. It's also suspicious. Maybe you'd better fill me in.'

'With pleasure.' Before leaving Hölzbach, Singer proposed a brief visit to the Brown Bear. 'The landlord's a hospitable type. We can have a quiet chat there.'

They were given a courteous welcome and ushered into a

side room. Kersten sniffed his beer tankard, took a swig, and slammed it down on the table.

'I don't believe it! Peacetime quality, when the rest of our boys are drinking dishwater!'

Singer grinned at him. 'That, my friend, is only a modest foretaste of the service we get here.' As though on cue, the landlord appeared with an outsize bowl of creamy, meaty goulash.

Kersten stared at it with mingled repugnance and rapture. He sampled some, then turned on the innkeeper, who was hovering over him in expectation of a bouquet. 'What goes on here, man? Our comrades at the front are starving – even in hospital they're fed on pigswill, but you live like kings. There's a war on, or hadn't you heard? It's been going five years.'

The landlord washed his hands with imaginary soap. 'One does the best one can, Lieutenant. Anything for our boys in uniform – anything at all . . .'

'Balls to that!' snapped Kersten. 'It's a disgrace!'

Although the disgrace of it didn't prevent him from wolfing all that was put before him, Singer could see that he did so with mixed emotions. He knew what Kersten's trouble was. Men in the heroic mould felt ill at ease so far from the front – out of place and bereft of chances to prove their mettle.

'Take it easy,' Singer told him. 'Don't be down-hearted, the war isn't over yet. Besides, you may see more action here than you think.'

The combat exercise in Training Area No. 2 ended late that afternoon – successfully, according to Lieutenant Lahrmann, despite the regrettable incidence of further casualties.

His two wounded men had come off lightly, one with a flesh wound in the rump, the other with a graze on the arm. Captain Königsberger was treating them at the medical centre, assisted by Melanie Mauerland. Their arrival had interrupted the first of his Russian lessons from Natasha, but she was still there when Lahrmann turned up with what at first appeared to be a bunch of flowers. It proved to be a bottle generously wrapped in tissue paper – not any old schnapps but some twelve-year-old French cognac which Singer, armed with Gerner's bunch of keys, had obligingly withdrawn from the mess cellar.

'And how are my wounded comrades?' asked Lahrmann, holding his bottle aloft. 'Here, they've earned a little pick-me-up.'

The MO frowned at him. 'I don't allow my patients hard liquor when they're in a state of shock.'

'Very well,' said Lahrmann, who refused to take umbrage, 'have a snort yourself – you and your harem.' He grinned amiably at Melanie and Natasha.

Königsberger was unmollified. 'Two men wounded in a single exercise under your command, Herr Lahrmann. How on earth can you justify such a casualty rate?'

'My dear Doctor,' Lahrmann said loftily, 'you don't understand these things. I regret the need for casualties, but higher issues are at stake.'

'Call them what you like, I don't see the point.'

'What's the matter with you these days?' A warning note crept into Lahrmann's voice. 'You've patched up plenty of my men in the past two years, and a damn good job you've always made of them, so why get squeamish now?'

'Everyone has to start some time.'

Königsberger's unwonted obstinacy puzzled Lahrmann until he thought he spotted the reason – a glance at the girls in the background seemed to explain everything: the MO was trying to impress them. The warning in Lahrmann's voice became a threat.

'If I were you, Captain Königsberger, I'd be more careful in my choice of words. Someone might get the wrong impression – someone in your immediate circle.'

'I have absolute faith in the judgement and discretion of all my staff,' Königsberger said gravely, 'male or female. In that respect, I draw no distinction between them.'

'Captain Königsberger's right,' Melanie chimed in, flushed with conviction. 'Frau Klarfeld takes just the same attitude, and I'm sure you wouldn't cast aspersions on *her*.'

'Of course not,' Lahrmann said hastily, 'but we're all entitled to our own opinions.'

'Quite so,' retorted the MO, 'and that includes me.'

Lahrmann retired, not forgetting to take the bottle of brandy with him. He reserved his parting gaze, which was rather aggrieved, for the two girls and Melanie in particular. The MO, that object of his righteous disdain, he deliberately ignored.

Later that afternoon, AFSIC Kampfental became the scene of three separate incidents which first mystified and then alarmed those involved. They were all provoked by the new arrival, Lieutenant Kersten.

Kersten's first port of call was the administration block, where Sergeant-Major Schulz was eagerly awaiting the latest addition to Feuerfresser's staff. Without an inkling of what he was in for, Schulz snapped to attention and saluted.

'Welcome to Kampfental, Lieutenant. Sergeant-Major Schulz at your service. If there's anything you want – anything at all – you only have to say the word.'

Kersten's eyebrows rose in surprise, then contracted with displeasure. 'I've no time for bootlickers, Schulz. I don't give a damn whether my presence is welcome or not, to you or anyone else. And what's all this guff about being at my service? In view of our respective ranks, that goes without saying. As for what I want, I want what any officer expects of his subordinates in wartime, no more and no less. Is that understood?'

Schulz swallowed hard. 'Yes, Lieutenant.'

Still escorted at a discreet distance by Singer, Kersten strode into another office in the administration block. Lieutenant Wagner, assistant adjutant, camp security chief and National Socialist Guidance Officer, rose to his feet with a flourish.

'Welcome, comrade!'

'I've no desire to be welcomed by anyone,' Kersten told him. 'I was posted here against my will. I wanted a field command. Instead, I find myself in this godforsaken dump.'

'This "dump" is an installation of the utmost military importance, Lieutenant, as I'm sure you'll very soon come to appreciate. First, however, I must ask you to read and sign our special security declaration.'

He handed Kersten a sheet of paper. Kersten read it through with growing surprise and disapproval. Finally, he spoke.

'No.'

Wagner was dumbfounded. 'What do you mean, no?'

'I mean I don't propose to sign this garbage – it's an insult to any self-respecting officer. I'm already bound by the usual oath of secrecy.'

'But I insist on your signing.'

'You insist? You can't give me orders, you know that as well as I do. Only my commanding officer can. If he does, I shall naturally comply – on the understanding that he takes full responsibility, which you can't. Have I made myself clear?'

'As daylight.' Wagner almost choked on the words.

The third stop on Kersten's itinerary was the medical centre, where he had to undergo a routine physical check-up. Singer came too.

Königsberger greeted them briskly. 'Right, Lieutenant, let's take a look at you. Strip off, please.'

'That won't be necessary,' Kersten snapped. 'I'm perfectly fit.'

'Glad you feel that way,' the MO said patiently. 'I'll be delighted to confirm your opinion, but not till I've examined you.'

'Doctor,' said Kersten, and his voice became a menacing growl, 'don't try pinning any medical labels on me. I know you quacks – always keen to find something wrong with a man, just to make yourselves look big. I'm a hundred per cent fit for combat duty. If that's what you want to check, you can do what you like to me. Otherwise, forget it.'

'Who said anything about combat duty? My job is to ascertain whether you're fit enough to be employed here.'

'Which is just what I don't want to be, not even temporarily.'

'In that case your eyesight must be defective. I'll have to make a note of that.'

'But there's nothing wrong with my eyesight!'

'There must be, if you're blind to the opportunities this place presents. I'm sure our friend Singer would agree.'

'Absolutely,' said Singer, who was lurking in the background.

Kersten pricked up his ears. '"Our friend", you called him. Was that just a figure of speech?'

'Not at all.' The MO smiled. 'I like to think our ties are more than merely professional. Yours are too, I suspect. Together, we might make a well-balanced team.'

Kersten laughed, but his expression remained wary. 'What the hell *is* this place, a military installation or a breeding ground for personal relationships? Either way, I'd feel wasted here, and that's the last thing I want.'

At that moment, as though by magic, a slender white-coated figure came tiptapping into the examination room. It was Melanie. One look at Konstantin Kersten – one long, searching look – and she froze in mid-stride with a faint blush mantling her lovely cheeks.

It was much the same with Kersten. He too seemed paralysed by the sight of her. Pervaded by a novel and unwonted thrill of delight, he stood there blushing like a schoolboy.

The French, who are experienced in such matters, would have called this phenomenon a *coup de foudre*. It was love at first sight, a bolt from the blue – an all-enveloping cloudburst of emotion.

Neither Melanie nor Kersten uttered a word; they simply continued to stand there, gazing fixedly into each other's eyes.

Königsberger beckoned to Singer, and they both beat a tactful retreat. Although they guessed what had happened, its consequences surpassed their wildest expectations.

Captain Tauschmüller, who had been hoping to spend some tranquil hours in his CO's absence, was slightly perturbed by Wagner's and Schulz's alarming accounts of the new officer's arrival – the more so because he himself had greeted the news of Kersten's posting with unease. Although he was privy to almost all the Colonel's plans, Feuerfresser had grown somewhat secretive of late. For tactical reasons, he decided to preface any action by calling on the majors and sounding them out.

Kastor and Pollandt received him with a courtesy which implied that, busy though they were, they were never too busy for him. Their official relations with Tauschmüller were largely undefined, and they were happy to leave them like that because, although they outranked him, he was the Colonel's adjutant and personal staff officer.

Tauschmüller came straight to the point. 'We've just been sent a Lieutenant Kersten. Any idea who asked for him and why?'

'None,' said Kastor.

'On the other hand,' Pollandt said thoughtfully, 'we're short of officer instructors – I mean, in view of these secret plans to extend the scope of our syllabus. I'm sure you're in the picture, Tauschmüller?'

'Of course,' said Tauschmüller, though the allusion meant nothing to him. He thought it wise to tread with extreme care. 'Very well, I'll give him the once-over. I suggest you both do the same – tonight in the mess, let's say.'

He promptly retired to his office and sent for Lieutenant Kersten. The newcomer's personal file, which had already arrived, lay open on his desk. A swift perusal of its contents intensified his vague forebodings. So did his first careful scrutiny of the man himself. Straight-eyed gaze, lithe movements, drawling enunciation with razor-sharp undertones – everything suggested that Kersten was a human dynamo.

'You arrived at Hölzbach by the midday train,' Tauschmüller said briskly, 'but you didn't reach camp for a good two hours after that. I'm merely stating a fact, Lieutenant, not rebuking you. We allow our officers as much freedom of movement as possible. The Colonel recommends such a policy, and I've always done my best to promote it.'

'How nice,' said Kersten. 'In that case, I shall take full advantage of the Colonel's recommendation.'

Tauschmüller deemed it inappropriate to pursue the subject. 'It has come to my notice,' he went on, still in the same coolly amiable tone, 'that you gave our sergeant-major a tongue-lashing – deservedly, no doubt, but somewhat unnecessarily. You also behaved outrageously towards Lieutenant Wagner. Of that I take a far more serious view. To underestimate Lieutenant Wagner's status here, as you so obviously did, can be dangerous. I trust you were labouring under a misapprehension.'

'Not at all, Captain. I always call a spade a spade – it's the way I'm made. I've spent too long in the front line, I suppose.'

'Well, now you're here with us.' The words carried a discreet warning. 'Kindly remember that in future.'

'I'll certainly remember it, Captain. Whether I can change my spots is another matter.'

Tauschmüller ignored this and leafed through Kersten's file with grudging respect. To judge by his list of decorations, the lieutenant was a born fighting soldier – an embodiment of the nation's unconquerable will to win.

'I'm sure the Colonel will appreciate your distinguished achievements in the field, my dear Kersten. He himself had an outstanding record in the first war.'

'I'm aware of that, Captain. I shall be honoured to make the Colonel's acquaintance.'

Still looking through his personal file, Tauschmüller came across something that struck him as downright monstrous. He had seen fit to accuse his former regimental commander, a Colonel Fillbringer, of cowardice in the face of the enemy and have him court-martialled.

'This Fillbringer business, Kersten – what on earth made you do it?'

'No choice. Read on and you'll see I did the same sort of thing more than once, when it couldn't be helped.'

Tauschmüller sat back, frowning. 'Well you'd better not try it here – not in the Colonel's orbit. You'd regret it, believe me.'

In the absence of Colonel von Feuerfresser, the dinner menu that evening in the mess had been chosen by Captain Tauschmüller. He had plumped for fried liver *à la mode de Berlin* preceded by cream of mushroom soup and followed by fruit jelly. This, as he alone knew, was Frau Klarfeld's favourite culinary combination.

Singer, the guardian of the cellar keys, had recommended that kir be served as an aperitif. This blend of dry white wine and blackberry liqueur proved universally popular because, though quite alcoholic, it irrigated the tonsils like a draught of refreshing lemonade.

It went without saying that, as Feuerfresser's adjutant,

Captain Tauschmüller should preside over the meal in his stead. With the Colonel's place vacant, he felt at liberty to regard himself and his table companion, Frau Klarfeld, as the undisputed focus of the entire gathering. Both were soon engrossed in intimate conversation.

The right-hand side of the refectory table was as usual occupied by Majors Kastor and Pollandt. Taking advantage of Feuerfresser's absence to do something that would have been utterly unthinkable in his presence, they came to table laden with schedules, personnel lists and performance charts. These they unashamedly studied between courses. Opposite them, like two wary tomcats, sat Wagner and Königsberger.

Lieutenant Lahrmann, who was attending his trainees' get-together in the canteen, had asked to be excused. Seated in his place at the bottom of the table, and watched with covert interest by all present, was the new addition to the mess. Lieutenant Kersten looked positively outlandish in such refined company. Improperly dressed, with his trouserlegs stuffed into boots and a ring of sweat round his shirt collar, he did not so much eat his food as capture it by frontal assault. Captain Tauschmüller shuddered at the thought of Colonel von Feuerfresser's probable reaction to this uncouth behaviour.

Pollandt was the first to address the stranger. 'Tell me,' he said casually, 'do you speak English?'

'Who, me?' Kersten replied through a mouthful of liver. 'I do anything I have to do, Major.'

Tauschmüller followed this up with a question of his own. 'Any idea why you were sent here?'

'None.' Kersten drained his glass and clicked his fingers for a refill. He seemed to be taking a ferocious delight in his meal. 'Friends in high places, maybe.'

'The Field-Marshal, you mean?' asked Tauschmüller.

'Never met him, but I do know his daughter. That could explain a lot of things.'

The others thought so too. There were smiles all round at this likely explanation of what had been troubling them. Tension eased, and the evening could now be enjoyed to the full.

Singer summoned up all his liquid resources. Champagne flowed like water, but to greater effect.

Meanwhile, fraternally seated side by side, the trainees and their instructors were holding their first major beer-and-togetherness session in the enlisted men's canteen.

'Comrades,' cried Lieutenant Lahrmann, 'off your butts and up with your glasses. I call upon you to drink to the Führer, the Fatherland, and the foregone conclusion for which all of us at AFSIC Kampfental are straining every nerve and sinew: final victory!'

They rose as one man, extended their brimming glasses in Lahrmann's direction, gazed at him through their golden contents, and drank deep.

'And now, comrades,' said Lahrmann, having proposed and drunk a further toast to Hitler, home and beauty, 'we come to the informal part of the proceedings.'

The camp orchestra, which had been strategically stationed at the rear of the canteen, broke into a medley that included almost every stirring item in the German choral repertoire – songs of home, songs of the happy wanderer, songs in praise of grape and hop, songs of the heart, of eventide and dawn's early light. All were bellowed with a vocal power proportionate to the amount of beer consumed.

As a reward for this wholehearted effort, Lahrmann circulated plates of grilled pork sausages – three brace per head – accompanied by dishes of sauerkraut, buckets of eye-watering mustard, and mountains of sliced bread.

'Tuck in, men!' called Lahrmann, and they did so, washing their fodder down with torrents of beer. The orchestra, which had switched to a selection from *Der*

Freischütz, was barely audible above the steady chomping and slurping of its intended audience.

Each man was treated to another two beers – but only two. Even this aspect of the course was subject to the strictest planning and supervision. Experience showed that one square meal and four large beers were sufficient to induce a restful night's sleep after an eventful day. Lahrmann glanced at his watch and banged the table for silence.

'Right, that's it for tonight. A most successful get-together – I'm sure you've all enjoyed yourselves as much as I have. If you keep up the good work, as I don't doubt you will, we may have a repeat performance some time.' He paused to let this sink in. 'That is, if you feel like one. Well, do you?'

The response was thunderous and unanimous.

'That's settled, then.' Lahrmann's voice became incisive. 'But now, comrades, off you go in double-quick time. I'll give you two minutes to be out of here and another fifteen to pee, wash, and clean your teeth. Lights out in half an hour. After that, nothing moves, understand?'

There was a stampede for the huts. Lahrmann found himself almost alone in the deserted canteen with Sergeant-Major Schulz.

'Will that be all, Lieutenant?'

'Yes, everything went like clockwork. First-class organization, Schulz – not that I'd expect anything else, from you.'

'Thank you, Lieutenant.'

'Get your men to clear away this mess. And tomorrow morning at reveille, pitch into 'em good and hard. You know my motto. A man can get drunk – blind drunk, for all I care – but you can only tell if he's a real man the morning after.'

'Quite right, Lieutenant. Beg permission to wish the Lieutenant good night.'

'My night isn't over yet. I'm off to the mess for a quick snort – they're sure to be waiting for me.'

His forecast wasn't entirely accurate. After polishing off their dinner and consuming more of the champagne with which Singer had generously plied everyone including the kitchen staff, Lahrmann's brother officers seemed too engrossed in their own affairs to pay him much attention.

The majors had bagged a window-seat and were talking shop. Captain Tauschmüller and Frau Klarfeld, with their heads close together, were conversing in a friendly undertone. The new officer, whose glass was never empty, roamed from one group to another, brazenly eavesdropping with one ear cocked like an inquisitive gundog.

Meanwhile, Captain (Med.) Königsberger was leafing through the *Völkischer Beobachter*, the Nazi Party's very own newspaper, with a studiously impassive expression. Lieutenant Wagner watched him, eyes peeled and ears pricked, until he thought he detected an exclamation that sounded like 'hm'. Then he pounced.

'May I enquire what you meant by that suspicious remark?'

Conversation ceased abruptly. Everyone stared – at Wagner with faint surprise, at Königsberger with faint concern. The MO slowly shook his head.

'What are you talking about, Herr Wagner? I'm not aware of having made a remark of any kind, suspicious or otherwise. I haven't opened my mouth for the last fifteen minutes, least of all to you.' Nothing could have sounded more provocative than Königsberger's polite restraint.

'Pardon *me,* Doctor, but my hearing is excellent. I distinctly heard you say "hm" in an unmistakably sarcastic way. What's more, you were reading the battlefront communiqué on page one.'

'Perhaps you're right,' Königsberger conceded, 'but only up to a point. If I said "hm" at all, my tone was far from sarcastic. Worried would be a better description.'

'What!' yelped Wagner. 'You read a communiqué from the Führer's headquarters and it *worries* you?'

'I can't help feeling slightly concerned, can you? I mean, we seem to be retreating all the time.'

'*Retreating?* What sort of language is that? We're merely straightening our front in accordance with the Führer's master plan. Look at it like this: Germany is an impregnable stronghold. Having sallied forth and inflicted enormous losses on our enemies in the past few years, we're now withdrawing to the shelter of our own ramparts and encouraging their pathetic remnants to bleed to death in a vain attempt to take what can never be taken.'

'I see,' the MO said drily. 'May I ask if your view coincides with the official one?'

Kastor and Pollandt had been holding a whispered conference. Presumably because they didn't want the evening spoiled, Kastor tried to lower the temperature.

'I know our worthy MO wears uniform, but he can't be expected to think along military lines.'

'Then he should try,' Wagner snarled, 'and try a whole lot harder than he has up to now. It's unpatriotic to indulge in negative conjecture. Positive thinking is the order of the day – positive thinking and devotion to the truth. The Colonel expects it of us.'

Königsberger was audacious enough to laugh out loud. He sounded genuinely amused. 'You really think you know what the Colonel expects, or what positive thinking means, or what the truth is? Absolute truth is one of the most elusive concepts known to the human intellect, but Herr Wagner claims to have pinned it down at last!' To rile his victim still further, he resorted to Latin. '*Ignoramus et ignorabimus*, gentlemen: we know not, nor shall we ever know.'

Wagner crimsoned with rage. He was still at a loss for words – a rare condition for him – when the new officer surprised everyone by putting his oar in.

'I'm sorry to have to say so in the presence of a lady, but you're both talking horseshit. Hot air won't get us anywhere. Facts are all that count. If a man doesn't back his country to the hilt, be damned to him! If a man concocts unfounded allegations, the hell with him too!'

Wagner swung round. 'The internal affairs of this camp are new to you, Kersten. Kindly don't meddle in things that escape your comprehension.'

'Take it easy, Wagner,' growled Kersten. 'I'm right behind you, in principle. No half measures! It's all or nothing with me. Why else do you think I've been risking my neck at the front?'

Wagner looked mollified. 'Glad to hear you say that, Kersten.'

'Nevertheless,' Captain Tauschmüller put in, 'there's a time and a place for everything.'

The majors chuckled in unison, though only briefly. They rose and announced their intention of limbering up for the grand Christmas chess tournament. Singer was instructed to dispatch a bottle of burgundy to the smoking-room and hold another in reserve.

Tauschmüller seemed to welcome this development. He glanced at Frau Klarfeld, who also rose, and offered to escort her to her quarters. Wagner, Königsberger and Kersten were left to themselves.

'Well,' said the MO, getting up, 'I don't suppose you're thirsting for my company. Anyway, I still have to look in on a couple of patients. Lahrmann's training methods have claimed another two victims.'

'I hope you realize what you did tonight,' Wagner snarled. 'This mess is a unique institution, and you poisoned the whole atmosphere.'

'One of us did, certainly, but I wouldn't care to say which.'

'Don't try and blame it on me, I warn you – and stop talking twaddle. What do you mean, "victims"? This isn't a nursery school – we're fighting a world war. If you've no stomach for it, why not say so straight out?'

'He's right,' said Kersten. 'You really ought to give us the benefit of your opinion, Doctor. After all, what are a few casualties? I've seen hundreds of fellow soldiers kick the bucket in a single engagement.'

'The price of victory,' said Wagner, nodding grimly. 'It's time you grasped that and accepted it, Doctor – unquestioningly.'

Königsberger feigned amusement. 'Spare me the empty phrases, gentlemen. Any more, and I'll begin to think you take me for a fool.' So saying, he left the room.

Wagner turned to Kersten and slapped him on the back. 'Spoken like a man, comrade. We're obviously on the same wavelength.' Undiscouraged by Kersten's lack of response, he bellowed for another bottle of champagne, which Singer brought at once.

CURRICULUM VITAE OF WOLFGANG KÖNIGSBERGER
or, The Imponderables of Chance

I was born in Bamberg on 4 December 1915. My father, Ernst Theodor Königsberger, was a veterinary surgeon specializing in domestic animals. My mother Agnes assisted him and kept house. My only sister, Konstanze, was born late in 1916.

The small half-timbered house, a sixteenth-century building, was situated near the cathedral square. Everything about it made an idyllic impression, inside as well as out, especially during the late afternoon and early evening. Herr Königsberger recited poems or read aloud from the works of E. T. A. Hoffman, who had also lived for a while in this romantic town. Frau Königsberger played the piano, and little Konstanze, who soon developed a love of the instrument, aspired to become a concert pianist.

Professionally speaking, Herr Königsberger laboured under a regrettable disability. Although extremely fond of animals and anxious to help them, he could not bear to see them suffer. Whenever one of his patients died on him, he lapsed into silence for days on end. The members of his household included a three-legged dachshund, four stray cats, a hamster, two budgerigars, and three rabbits.

Also in residence was a sleek black tomcat named Pluto, which had been bequeathed to Herr Königsberger by a brewery owner's widow. With it came two paintings by Spitzweg and a handsome annual allowance to cover the cat's upkeep. Pluto lived well, and so – thanks to Pluto – did his foster family.

Herr Königsberger had a mild passion for collecting pictures. Apart from the two Spitzwegs, he owned three paintings by Leibl, one by Paula Modersohn-Becker, and even a couple of Turners, *The Alps* and *Venice – the Grand Canal*. Although he spent a substantial proportion of his income in this way, his wife never complained, possibly because she guessed that the paintings were a hedge against the hard times her husband foresaw in years to come.

In July 1917, when the Kaiser could dispense with his services no longer, Ernst Theodor Königsberger joined the Army Veterinary Corps. He was sent to the Western Front and killed in the course of his very first engagement, while tending a disembowelled packhorse under fire. Even in his death throes, so an eyewitness reported, he flung one arm around the neck of the beast whose last moments he shared.

I started school in 1921. In 1928 my sister Konstanze succumbed to a blood disease which was then incurable. In 1930 my mother underwent several operations for the removal of intestinal tumours. As soon as I matriculated in 1932, I went to study medicine at Munich University.

Wolfgang's sister Konstanze had great musical talent. She gave her first recital at the age of eleven and was acclaimed by some as a child prodigy, but died after a short illness. Her mother, whose own health gave way soon afterwards, required several major operations. A Leibl and a Spitzweg had to be sold to pay for them.

This swift succession of blows left Wolfgang bemused and helpless. They might have cowed him completely but for Professor Jacob Lewin, a Jew who had held a chair of medicine at Berlin University before being ousted by political pressure. Lewin then retired to his home town, Bamberg, where he practised part-time in his small apartment near St Michael's Church.

Jacob Lewin and Ernst Theodor Königsberger had been close friends from their earliest childhood, and Lewin's affection for the dead veterinarian transferred itself to his wife and children. He was almost one of the family – always on hand when needed and always quick to offer help and advice. Wolfgang loved him dearly.

When Lewin asked him what he wanted to be, the boy's response was unhesitating.

'A doctor, of course.'

'Good,' said Lewin. 'I'll see what I can do.'

In the event, he did a great deal. It was Lewin's generous financial assistance that enabled Wolfgang to study for his profession.

I qualified in 1936. After that, I had to do military service for the regulation two years. I opted for the Army Medical Corps.

His duties consisted mainly in supervising the regular emptying of latrines, disinfecting male genitalia after sexual intercourse, and pumping injections into the buttocks of comrades suffering from clap. On one of his home leaves, he confessed that the whole thing made him sick.

Lewin and his mother regarded him with concern. His mother, who was still a very sick woman, summoned up an encouraging smile. Lewin produced a concrete suggestion.

'Disease is a universal phenomenon, my boy. The work you're doing may be tedious, but it isn't valueless. Still, perhaps you ought to extend your qualifications. Psychology seems a promising field at the moment. Why not give it a try?'

'They'll never release me.'

'Let me worry about that. I happen to know someone in a pretty influential position. We used to be friends, and he won't have forgotten the fact – he won't be able to, considering all I know about him.'

After a few minutes on the phone, Lewin returned with good news.

'About your new degree course – it's all arranged. If you ever run into trouble and don't know which way to turn, get in touch with Surgeon-General Peter Beauvais at Army Headquarters. Make a note of the name but don't write it down – and don't mention this to anyone but Beauvais himself. This may be the last thing I can do for you.'

It was. A few days later, Jacob Lewin was arrested and interrogated by the Gestapo. Then he was beaten up and carted off to a concentration camp. Surviving fellow inmates report that he never uttered another word. The exact time, place and manner of his death are unknown.

In 1939, though still a member of the armed forces, I started reading for another degree – psychology, with the emphasis on psychological warfare. My tutor and doctoral supervisor was Professor Gerhard Kramer of Berlin University. My mother died in 1940. In 1942 I graduated for the second time.

Professor Kramer was a little weasel of a man who spent his lectures scuttling back and forth between a handful of students and an array of blackboards thickly adorned with spidery writing. He did not seem at all put out by the size of his audience, which varied between twelve and eighteen.

'Ours,' he proclaimed, 'is an élite science with a great

future whose importance has yet to dawn on the general public. It is totally unconnected with the suspect theories of Sigmund Freud. Those are based on sexual functions, whereas I specialize in the field of intellectual response. My writings, to which we shall be devoting the most intensive study during the next three years, have succeeded in branding that Viennese head-shrinker as the Jewish charlatan he is.'

No one in Nazi Germany who proposed to lecture on psychology could afford to omit such a preamble. At least once a week, the students of the little man and great professor were also treated to a routine pep talk.

'I expect you to concentrate on the substance of my lectures to the exclusion of all else. I will not tolerate digressions or distractions of any kind. Fail to conform, and you're out on your ear.'

This was the fate that seemed to be in store for Wolfgang Königsberger. During one of Kramer's lectures he met an exchange student named Misha, a Japanese girl who was studying psychology under the auspices of the Berlin-Tokyo Axis. Wolfgang fell for her, and his feelings were reciprocated.

He helped Misha with her studies and perfected her knowledge of German. They spent many evenings in each other's company – many nights, too – and eventually set up house together.

It was not long before this case of 'immoral behaviour with an alien' came to the notice of the local block warden, who notified the secret police. Two Gestapo officers duly called on Professor Kramer and issued him with a stern warning. Kramer, in his turn, sent for Wolfgang.

'I don't propose to go into detail, Königsberger, but I'm bound to say I regard this incident as a disruptive factor – a serious threat to our joint efforts in the academic field. The Japanese girl is here for purposes of study, not exposure to moral danger. You will terminate your relationship at once. Otherwise, we shall have to part company.'

Wolfgang now turned, for the first and only time, to the man whose name Jacob Lewin had given him shortly before his arrest. He requested an interview with Surgeon-General Beauvais, who received him at once and heard him out. Then he gave his verdict.

'Your studies must come first, young man. That means we shall have to send the girl back to Japan. Any questions?'

Wolfgang could see that the die was cast. 'No, General, no questions.'

All at once, Beauvais struck a more human note. 'Young man, I always had the greatest respect for the – er, person who recommended you to me. He stood by me at one of the darkest moments in my life, and never asked for anything in return – only that I should help you if you ran into any problems.'

Before Wolfgang could thank him, the surgeon-general became businesslike again. 'That's it, then. Complete your course and chalk up another qualification. After that, I'll see you get a suitable appointment.'

After gaining his second degree, Königsberger was posted to Kampfental as Colonel von Feuerfresser's medical officer and expert on psychological warfare.

Corporal Hausleitner was sitting on a stool in Room 6 of the camp brothel. Sprawled on the rumpled bed was a dark-haired Polish beauty of nineteen or twenty.

'Help me!' she whimpered, trembling spasmodically. 'Help me – I can't go on!' They were a few of the two or three dozen German words she had picked up during her year in 'the Chapel'.

The elderly corporal put out a limp, wrinkled hand, and she clung to it like a drowning woman. 'Help me!' she implored.

Sonia had collapsed after her third customer of the night, spitting blood and calling frantically for

Hausleitner, who had been fearing the worst for weeks.

'Listen,' he said, 'calm down and get some sleep – I'll book you off duty for the rest of the night.' He was sure she understood every word. 'I feel the same myself, sometimes – right at the end of my rope. When I look at you or one of the other girls, I often think: Jesus, she could be my daughter. You bring out the father in me, Sonia. Well, fathers are there to do what they can for their kids, and that's what I try to do for you, God help me.'

'Mer—cy!' said Sonia, enunciating the word with difficulty.

It was not a word Hausleitner had ever heard uttered in these surroundings. He flinched at the sound of it, knowing that the sole purveyor of mercy on his premises was death.

'Help,' she moaned, 'please!'

Gravely, like a priest celebrating High Mass, he said, 'Here, take this glass of water.' He handed it to her. 'And here are some sleeping pills.' He gave her a cylindrical glass bottle. It was full. 'Mind you don't take more than two or three.'

'Thank you!' she said, and put her arms round his neck.

Very tenderly, Sonia embraced the man who had granted what she yearned for, and he humbly submitted to her embrace. He had done what he had to do. He could not have done otherwise.

That night in the mess, Lieutenants Lahrmann and Kersten met for the first time. Their Knight's Crosses seemed to flash a greeting as Wagner introduced them. They shook hands rather guardedly, much as a racehorse and a greyhound might sample each other's scent.

'Welcome to the outfit,' said Lahrmann. 'What's your job going to be?'

'No idea,' said Kersten, who was pretty plastered by now. 'S'pose I'll be told in due course.'

The fellow's drunk, thought Lahrmann – drunk as a

skunk in Colonel von Feuerfresser's mess! He did not have time to dwell on the thought because Kersten chose that moment to make a noisy exit.

'Going to hit the sack,' he said thickly. 'Had enough for one day.'

Lahrmann watched him totter out with an air of distaste. Wagner was more benevolent. 'Kersten may not know it yet,' he said, 'but he could be just what we need here. He's politically sound, anyway, and that's worth a lot. Care to split a bottle with me, comrade?'

'With you? Any time.'

Singer appeared like magic with a bottle of champagne and two glasses.

'Quick thinking, Corporal,' Wagner told him approvingly. 'And stick another bottle on ice – no, better make it two while you're at it.'

The lieutenants clinked glasses and drank. Then Wagner's face darkened.

'We're on the same wavelength, comrade. I wish I could say the same for everyone in this place.'

'Having trouble?' asked Lahrmann.

'Nothing I can't handle. Nobody crosses me and gets away with it.'

As though to ease some mental burden, he pulled out the Mauser 635 he always carried and slammed it down on the table. Being used to weapons of quite another calibre, Lahrmann was not unduly impressed by this dramatic flourish.

'What are problems for?' Wagner demanded, and supplied the answer himself. 'They're there to be eliminated!'

'I'm sure the Colonel would agree with you,' Lahrmann said sympathetically. 'Any particular problem in mind?'

'Alien, hostile elements are at work here,' said Wagner. 'We must root them out. We can't have our prospects of final victory blighted by soft, woolly-minded, idealistic civilians camouflaged as soldiers.'

The only member of the mess who fitted that description was Captain (Med.) Königsberger. Lahrmann, who shared Wagner's loathing of the MO, nodded in agreement.

'He actually thinks he's entitled to criticize our training methods. Instead of concentrating on the product they're designed to turn out, he kicks up a fuss about unavoidable casualties. Today he had the gall to do that with a couple of female camp followers in the room!'

Wagner's eyes narrowed. 'Tell me about it, comrade.'

This was more than a confidential request from one German patriot to another – it was an offer of friendship. Flattered, Lahrmann described the scene at the medical centre with mounting indignation.

'Well,' he concluded, 'how do you like that! Outrageous, wasn't it?'

Wagner sealed their new-found intimacy by using Lahrmann's first name. 'Just between the two of us, Heinrich, what I find even worse is the MO's totally un-German attitude.'

'You're right, Werner.'

'My dear Heinrich, you've always been a loyal, dependable comrade in arms. Now you're a friend as well.' Wagner indicated the Mauser on the table between them. 'You can have that if you like. It's almost brand-new.'

'Thanks, Werner.' On impulse, Lahrmann pulled out his own service automatic, a heavy nine millimetre handgun with great powers of penetration. 'Tested in action by yours truly! I blew away half a dozen Ivans with it, just before they gave me my Knight's Cross. Fair exchange is no robbery.'

'Thanks, Heinrich. How about a toast to victory and friendship?'

Ever alert, Singer bustled up with another bottle of champagne. It was not the last of the night.

*

Lieutenant Kersten was the first to appear for breakfast in the mess next morning, showing no signs of his recent devotion to board and bottle. He looked cheerful and well rested as he strode across to Singer, who was already performing his duties as deputy mess sergeant.

'Well, what's on offer this morning?'

'The Colonel likes his officers to eat a hearty breakfast.'

'Fine, dish up.' Kersten sat down, rubbing his hands, and Singer loaded a plate with ham and eggs. The lieutenant attacked it as though he hadn't eaten for a week.

Singer looked at him closely. 'Kampfental doesn't seem to have spoiled your appetite – yet.'

Kersten pointed at his opulent breakfast, chewing steadily. 'This reminds me of the extra rations they give us before a really rugged operation – except that we don't get ham and eggs, just canned meat and a mug of schnapps. This is a lot more classy, but what do we have to do to earn it?'

'You'll find out.'

'Any idea what job I'll be doing?'

'Only the Colonel can tell you that, but he's not here. I should fill in the time by taking a good look around.'

'Where do you advise me to start?'

'Try the "museum" – that's what they call the armoury here. Master-Sergeant Heinz looks after it. He's a man of action like you. Maybe you'll hit it off together.'

Kersten found Heinz on the road near the armoury, streaming with sweat as he ran through his daily work-out in splendid isolation. It was an impressive sight.

'From tomorrow, Sergeant,' said Kersten, 'I'll be joining you.'

'You're welcome, Lieutenant.' Heinz looked gratified. 'Anything I can do for you?'

'Yes, show me round your collection.'

Glowing with pride, the weapons expert took Kersten on

a guided tour of his domain. No. 1 Section's shelves were crammed with all the standard items in the German arsenal, plus innumerable boxes of ammunition. Kersten merely nodded and moved on to No. 2, an extensive and almost complete range of Red Army weapons. 'Seen 'em all before,' he said tersely.

But then came No. 3, the recently acquired collection of US military equipment which Heinz had sorted, labelled and arranged since its arrival at Kampfental. This time, Kersten was unmistakably impressed and enthralled. He gave an exclamation of delight and pounced on the weapons, turning them over and over like precious jewels.

'Very advanced models,' he said judicially. 'A bit hard to handle, mind you. Not designed for knuckleheads – more for experts.'

Master-Sergeant Heinz nodded approvingly. This new lieutenant appealed to him. He seemed to be a man after his own heart – a devotee of things lethal.

'Have you tried them out?'

'Not all of them, Lieutenant.'

'Then you'd better make up for lost time, Sergeant. I'll help you.'

Half an hour later, with the greatest relish, they loosed off a firework display on No. 2 Firing Range. It was only a foretaste of things to come.

Colonel von Feuerfresser returned from his jaunt the next afternoon. He rode into camp on his charger, Baldur, with his retinue trudging along behind under the command of Sergeant Gerner, who looked as if he felt he had earned promotion. The 'bag' was unloaded from the handcart and laid out on the drive in front of the mess. It consisted of two deer, one wild boar and three hares. They lay there with flaccid limbs and glazed eyes, like a microcosm of the slaughter occurring elsewhere in Hitler's historic new era. Königsberger, who was anxious not to miss the spectacle, had stationed himself at a window with Singer peering over his shoulder. From there they saw Captain Tauschmüller scamper down the steps and salute.

'Welcome back, Colonel! No problems to report at this end.'

'Thank you, my dear fellow,' Feuerfresser replied in measured tones. 'I knew I could trust you to hold the fort.'

'Glad to see you haven't come back empty-handed, Colonel.'

'I was lucky, that's all. In the long run, luck and skill amount to the same thing.'

Singer nudged Königsberger. 'I'm no hunter, but isn't there such a thing as a close season?'

'Yes, but not for him.' The MO might have been talking to himself. 'The Colonel makes his own rules. As far as his passion for hunting goes, it's a psychological enigma.'

One thing, at least, was certain: Feuerfresser's handiwork represented a handsome contribution to the mess cuisine – the makings of a dozen choice banquets. Singer was distracted from this thought by the sight of Eugen Priewitt, who was standing idly in the background, supervising the labours of others instead of toiling himself. His badges of rank explained why. Priewitt was a sergeant once more, having cancelled his recent demotion by ensuring that the Colonel did not lack for creature comforts under canvas.

Feuerfresser's sovereign calm was unshakable. It remained so even when Captain Tauschmüller dropped his bombshell.

'By the way, Colonel, two officers from Counter-espionage turned up this morning. They asked to see you.'

Feuerfresser dismounted with ostentatious nonchalance and gave Baldur a farewell slap on the rump, then turned to his adjutant.

'Of course I'll see them, if they think it's essential.'

'I took the liberty of directing them to Hölzbach and

ordering them a good lunch at the Brown Bear. They won't be in a hurry to cut our hospitality short.'

'Excellent,' said Feuerfresser, reflecting that Captain Tauschmüller was a pearl beyond price. 'First I propose to have a bath and a snack – fresh deer's liver fried in butter will do, so please inform the chef. After that, you can wheel the gentlemen in.'

Feuerfresser's visitors were Abwehr officers from the Munich section of Military Intelligence, Counterespionage Branch. The senior of the two was a Lieutenant-Colonel Wassermann, a sleek desk warrior with a professionally suspicious manner. His companion, a lieutenant whose name was never mentioned but didn't matter anyway, looked like an overworked but willing police dog.

The Colonel motioned them into a pair of chairs facing his desk and eyed them with a trace of condescension. Stationed behind him was Sergeant, formerly Corporal, Priewitt. The ever watchful Tauschmüller stood on his right, as befitted a right-hand man. On his left, but slightly to the rear, stood Lieutenant Wagner, who considered it a special mark of trust that he had been summoned to attend the interview.

'Well, gentlemen, what can I do for you?'

Lieutenant-Colonel Wassermann cleared his throat a trifle nervously. 'We're from Military Intelligence, Colonel. Our Counterespionage Branch used to be based in Berlin, as you know. It has since been transferred to Munich for – er, strategic reasons. As head of that branch, I hope I can rely on your full co-operation.'

Viktor von Feuerfresser looked supercilious. 'Co-operation – after all that's happened? Why, I'm surprised to hear your department still exists!' He glanced at Lieutenant Wagner, who reacted with predictable alacrity.

'A very shady outfit, sir. Speaking as a loyal National Socialist Guidance Officer, I'd point out that Military

Intelligence has been under investigation ever since the débâcle of July twentieth, if not before. The head of Military Intelligence himself, Admiral Canaris, is strongly suspected of complicity, and his chief associate, General Oster, has reportedly been arrested for high treason.' Wagner rounded on Wassermann with a look of scorn. 'How can you expect any patriotic German to trust your department?'

'We're trying to mend our fences,' said Wassermann. 'That's why we're here.'

Feuerfresser shrugged. 'Very well. Carry on, but you'd better make it convincing.'

Like any shrewd superior, Lieutenant-Colonel Wassermann, too, kept a mouthpiece handy. His anonymous sidekick stepped into the breach.

'Subsection Five – that's our radio monitoring and decoding service – has picked up a number of unauthorized transmissions in the past few weeks. They're definitely being sent in a Russian code – one we've already cracked. The messages are transmitted at regular intervals, using four or five frequencies at most. With the aid of direction-finding equipment, we've plotted the transmitter's position, though only to within five or six miles.'

Feuerfresser greeted this revelation with marked indifference, but his ghost of a smile was stiff. 'I hope I'm wrong,' he said, turning to Wassermann, 'but the lieutenant seems to be implying that someone in my own sphere of command – '

'No, no, my dear Colonel!' Wassermann broke in. 'I'd never countenance such a suggestion. At the same time, I must ask you to take note that, according to our readings, this clandestine transmitter is located in the Hölzbach area.'

Feuerfresser smiled again, even more superciliously than before, and left it to Tauschmüller to comment at length.

'We aren't the only military installation in the area,' Tauschmüller said sternly, 'as your department must be aware. There are also a garrison headquarters, a field hospital, a labour camp manned by prisoners of war, a naval research centre transferred from the north, and a hydrogenation plant producing gasoline from coal. Last but not least, there's an SS training establishment. That makes several thousand men in addition to our own.'

Wassermann gave the adjutant a nod of agreement before turning back to Feuerfresser. 'We're well aware of the existence of these units and their whereabouts. On the other hand – and I hope you'll pardon my saying so, Colonel – no other installation in this area possesses the same immense strategic importance.'

Though mildly flattered, Feuerfresser insisted, in a tone of chill reproof, that no slur on his personal fief would be tolerated. 'Not another word, do you hear, gentlemen? Not even a shadow of suspicion!'

Lieutenant-Colonel Wassermann could not fail to detect the menace in Feuerfresser's voice. What he did not know was that Feuerfresser had the memory of an elephant as well as the hide of a rhinoceros. He found out three months later, when his importunate little department was disbanded and its staff packed off to the front. But none of this was discernible now.

'Goodbye, gentlemen,' said Feuerfresser. 'I hope, if we meet again, that we shall do so under less distasteful circumstances.'

As soon as the Abwehr snoopers had gone, he looked at Tauschmüller and shook his head. 'These things are sent to try us.'

'Yes, sir,' said Tauschmüller. His thoughts, which had already turned to Lieutenant Kersten, sent a shiver down his spine.

6

Colonel von Feuerfresser's first encounter with Lieutenant
Kersten took place at dinner in the mess that evening.
Captain Tauschmüller had taken the precaution of briefing
him on the highly decorated newcomer and his nonexistent
table manners.

Kersten, who blithely persisted in his total disregard for
mess conventions, not only shovelled up his food like a
mechanical grab but commented on it in language better
suited to the front line. 'Terrific chow!' he exclaimed. 'You
don't get this kind of fodder from a field kitchen. Nothing
like a square meal for boosting morale!'

The others, their appetite temporarily spoiled, maintained a furtive watch on the Colonel from behind their
almost untouched plates. His reaction came as a surprise.
He merely wagged his head with discreet but indulgent
disapproval.

'What a waste,' he remarked to Tauschmüller, just
loudly enough to be overheard by his immediate neighbours. 'The boy's an officer and a gentleman, and how
does he conduct himself? Like a front-line private in a
foxhole!'

When dinner was over, Feuerfresser invited his latest
acquisition to a game of chess. It took him only a few
minutes to realize that Kersten had no use for long-range
planning or tactical finesse; his response to any situation
was that of an infuriated bull. The Colonel strove to amplify
this first impression with his other officers listening in.

'I've been glancing through your record, Kersten. It's

very impressive, but don't you feel there's room for improvement?'

'Of course, Colonel. I still have a few decorations left to aim for – not that I can ever hope to match your "*Pour le Mérite*".'

'You know about that?'

'I know every detail of your legendary charge at Douaumont, Colonel. It was magnificent – an object lesson to any fighting soldier. There was something really spectacular about the first war. This one doesn't have the same panoramic grandeur.'

Viktor von Feuerfresser found it hard to disguise the full extent of his pleasure at this unfavourable comparison. 'You may be right. However, there's more to the perfect soldier than gallantry in the field.'

'Really, Colonel?' Kersten said eagerly. 'May I ask what?'

'A great deal. On the one hand, dignity, self-control, and an appreciation of higher things. On the other, respect for the established order and an ability to conform. You follow my meaning?'

Kersten looked puzzled. 'No, Colonel,' he said truthfully.

'In that case, my boy, I shall try to enlighten you in due course. It's part of my job.'

'Thank you, Colonel.' Kersten's gratitude was as genuine as his reverence for a great hero of a great war. 'I'd appreciate that.'

To everyone's complete surprise, this seemed to presage the development of a father-and-son relationship. Viktor von Feuerfresser showed every sign of taking Konstantin Kersten under his wing.

Late that night, the Colonel held a confidential meeting in his office. Only Majors Kastor and Pollandt were invited.

'Gentlemen,' he said without preamble, 'I want you to form all your English-speaking trainees into a separate group. You will not, however, give them any hint of the purpose behind this move.'

The majors nodded as if they knew it themselves.

'Within the overall framework of our combat-training scheme, these men will be known as Group C. Kindly draft the relevant orders. I should add that Group C will be commanded by Lieutenant Kersten.'

'An extremely promising youngster,' said Kastor, and earned himself a fleeting frown from Pollandt, who considered the remark precipitate. It was never wise to volunteer an opinion in Feuerfresser's presence.

Feuerfresser merely gave a pensive smile. 'Very promising indeed,' he said, 'but rather a rough diamond.' Kersten's education had been criminally neglected, he went on, but he proposed to take him in hand and teach him the fundamentals of Prussian military philosophy. He further proposed to ask Captain Tauschmüller to instruct him in mess etiquette and Frau Klarfeld to give him a few tips on social conventions.

'I'm counting on you too, gentlemen. Lieutenant Kersten is a one-sided product of combat experience – an officer without an officer's cultural background. I doubt if he even has an adequate knowledge of military history. That's your speciality, so give him a crash course.'

Kastor and Pollandt, who also specialized in concealing what they really thought, nodded in a silent display of wholehearted concurrence.

Lieutenant Wagner, Kampfental's guardian of ideological purity, was never one to shirk the burdens of his office, one of them being to scrutinize the trainees' private correspondence. In this he was ably assisted by two NCOs from the Security Platoon, both of them Party members selected for their absolute reliability. One of them steamed the envelopes open while the other took notes at Wagner's dictation.

In performing this task, which also provided the raw material for morale reports submitted to the Colonel, Wagner proceeded systematically. Any comments and opinions that struck him as useful or illuminating were classified under the following headings:

1. Personal remarks. Phrases and passages conveying lack of enthusiasm or despondency on the writer's part were copied down and forwarded to Kastor and Pollandt in memo form.

2. Views on the current military situation, the state of the country and the fighting spirit of the trainees themselves. These, in turn, were subdivided into three categories. First, favourable and optimistic comments (the overwhelming majority). Second, comments of an equivocal or dubious nature (comparatively rare). Third and last, unfavourable and pessimistic comments attributable to ignorance or stupidity (very rare indeed).

3. Derogatory and defeatist remarks indicative of treasonable tendencies.

For once, Wagner had struck oil in the third category. One trainee's letter contained a passage that temporarily robbed him of speech.

'The man's just a jumped-up corporal,' he was appalled to read, 'taking it out on the world because the Army, which was commanded by morons and still is, never saw fit to make him an officer . . .'

There could be no doubt that the author of these lines was referring to the greatest military leader of all time, Adolf Hitler. Summoning the man who had been guilty of this monstrous aberration, Wagner glared at him with mounting contempt for a good two minutes. The culprit, whose uneasiness grew with every passing second, was a suspiciously intellectual-looking corporal named Korfeld.

'At long last, AFSIC's National Socialist Guidance Officer tapped the letter in front of him. 'Do you realize what this means?'

Corporal Korfeld hurriedly protested that he had been misunderstood. 'All I meant was, it took twenty years for the world to appreciate the Führer's true genius. If I didn't find the right words, Lieutenant, I can only apologize.'

'Corporal Korfeld,' Wagner said acidly, 'the personal qualities of our Führer and Supreme Commander are obvious to the meanest intelligence. Anyone who disputes them – anyone lacking in absolute loyalty to him and his cause – is either a madman or a traitor.'

So saying, Wagner marched his victim off to the adjutant's office and plunked the incriminating letter on Tauschmüller's desk like an ace of trumps.

'An open-and-shut case, Captain. We'll have to make an example of this man.'

Tauschmüller rose and beckoned Wagner into a corner. 'Can't you sort this out yourself – on the side, I mean?'

The lieutenant, who was prepared for this suggestion, rejected it out of hand. 'At this early stage in the course? No, Captain, I submit that his offence merits drastic and exemplary punishment – as a deterrent. I'm sure it's what the Colonel would want.'

Captain Tauschmüller forbore to reprimand Wagner for his presumption in claiming to know what a man like Feuerfresser might or might not think expedient. 'Very well,' he said, 'carry on.'

The words 'on your head be it' were taken as read.

Colonel von Feuerfresser was busily applying himself to Lieutenant Kersten's further education.

'I assume you know who Clausewitz was?'

'More or less, Colonel. He was a Prussian general who wrote a lot of books. Not exactly part of an officer's duties, but still, as long as it kept the old boy happy.'

Feuerfresser deliberately ignored the last remark because he himself had been engaged in writing a military treatise for years. Only his habitual attention to detail had prevented its completion.

'You must try to take a longer view.'

'In what way, Colonel?'

'Well, take me – take my family. Many of my ancestors were Prussian officers. I began my career in Imperial Germany. I now serve the Third Reich, Kersten, just as you do.'

'Meaning we both serve the Führer?'

'Meaning that we're soldiers obedient to a supreme commander, which isn't quite the same thing. We don't serve a political system or head of government; we serve an entity called the state. One of the functions of that entity is to guarantee our nation's survival and ensure that it prevails over outside forces.'

'So doing your bit at the front isn't enough?'

'Feats of heroism are the high-water marks in a soldier's life, my dear Kersten, but they aren't the whole of it. Readiness to do battle isn't enough in itself. Courage must go hand in hand with a sense of duty – and a knowledge of where one's duty lies.'

Kersten sighed. 'In that case, when I've finished Hitler's *Mein Kampf* I'll go on to Clausewitz.'

'And Kant, and Moltke, and Hegel. I shall lend you some selected reading matter and await your questions with interest.'

To Kersten, whose head was spinning, Captain Tauschmüller's appearance represented a welcome distraction. Feuerfresser swallowed his annoyance at being brought down to earth so abruptly.

'What is it, Captain Tauschmüller?' His expression softened. 'Unless it's a matter of supreme national importance, Lieutenant Kersten can stay. He may learn something of value.'

'It's Wagner,' said Tauschmüller. 'He requests permission to see you, Colonel. He's detected an enemy of the state and he wants to parade him for your inspection.'

. A quick sidelong glance reassured the Colonel that his dove-grey doeskin gloves were within reach. The significance of the look was not lost on Tauschmüller. After the unfortunate events of 20 July, Armed Forces High Command had issued an order replacing the conventional military salute with Hitler's favourite arm movement. Colonel von Feuerfresser, who could not get used to this novel practice, neatly evaded it with the aid of his gloves, which he flourished in a semblance of the prescribed gesture.

'Very well,' he said, 'if Wagner insists, send him in.'

Feuerfresser gave Corporal Korfeld a brief but searching stare, then leafed through Wagner's written report. Having swiftly absorbed its contents, he passed it to the adjutant. Tauschmüller, who knew what was expected of him, marshalled his findings.

'There are several possibilities, Colonel. We could simply ignore this ridiculous drivel – though that might be difficult, now it's a matter of record. Alternatively, the man could be charged and tried by court martial.'

. Although the Colonel's powers would have entitled him to set up a summary court martial and appoint himself president, he spurned dramatic gestures of this kind and preferred to deal with problems in a less obtrusive way. Knowing that his master was the last person to make waves unless he had to, Tauschmüller offered him another way out.

'On the other hand, in view of Corporal Korfeld's previous good character, we could give him a chance to retract his remarks and apologize. He would, of course, have to do this in writing.'

'I'd be glad to, Colonel,' Korfeld said eagerly. 'Put it any way you like and I'll sign it. After all, anyone could have made the same mistake.'

'*Anyone?*' snarled Wagner. 'I've never heard a more monstrous allegation! Are you seriously suggesting that *anyone – any* of his gallant and devoted soldiers – might have cast such vile aspersions on our beloved Führer? If that doesn't cry out for a court martial, I don't know what does!'

Feuerfresser turned to Kersten, who had been sitting in the background. 'Well, my boy, what would your decision be, a court martial or an immediate transfer to the front?'

Kersten didn't hesitate. 'A court martial, Colonel.'

'Why?'

'Because sending him to the front would be like giving him a medal, and no one as ideologically suspect as this man – ' he indicated Korfeld – 'deserves that kind of treatment.'

'Well said,' exclaimed Wagner. He could have hugged Kersten.

Silence fell as they all waited for the decision that mattered. Feuerfresser took his time before quietly and calmly announcing his verdict.

'If someone chooses to be one of us, we welcome him with open arms. If not, we must bid him farewell.'

Sentence had been passed on Corporal Korfeld. He was to be transferred out, sent to the front, pointed in an easterly direction.

Occasional transfers of this type were handled by Lieutenant Lahrmann, whose first move was to telephone Army Group Headquarters. Colonel Schlumberger's office – the official link between Field-Marshal Wedell and Colonel von Feuerfresser – had always proved accommodating, particularly of late.

Colonel Schlumberger, who knew that every available man was needed on the Eastern Front, ensured that all went smoothly. Troop trains left Munich at dawn every day, bound for destinations that were drawing ever nearer as the Russian advance progressed, and there was always room for an extra passenger.

Punitive transfers gladdened Lahrmann's heart for a very special reason. He was a frustrated racing driver, and only these trips to Munich enabled him to indulge his passion to the full.

Lahrmann regarded his exclusive entitlement to a jeep-style Mercedes 200 scout car as a privilege, which it was. Colonel von Feuerfresser, who could see through his underlings as a biologist scans bacteria under a microscope, had catered to Lahrmann's craze for speed and thereby earned his undying gratitude and devotion.

These moments when he crouched behind the wheel, savouring the pleasure of speed for its own sake, were among the finest in Lahrmann's existence. He felt this now, as he tore through the darkness from Kampfental to Munich. The masked headlights were poor aids to visibility, but he had eyes like a lynx and his reactions were worthy of a Le Mans veteran.

The driver beside him – a misnomer, because he seldom took the wheel himself – was ashen-faced, like the passengers on the rear seat. These were a sergeant on loan from Wagner's Security Platoon and the injudicious correspondent, Corporal Korfeld.

Lahrmann screeched to a halt outside Munich Central and handed Korfeld over to the officer in charge of the next eastbound troop train. His mission was accomplished.

After completing his duties in the mess, Corporal Singer took a nightcap to Kersten's quarters. He found his friend ensconced behind a pile of books.

'Well, my old mental gymnast, how goes it?'

'Need you ask?' groaned Kersten. 'I feel like a fish out of water in this place.'

196

Singer sat down uninvited. 'Look, Konstantin, the Colonel's taking a personal interest in your further education, you're living off the fat of the land and drinking more than you can carry, and tomorrow morning you'll be putting Group C through the mill. What more do you want?'

Kersten shut his book with a snap. 'Something smells here, but I don't know what.'

'It's Melanie Mauerland, isn't it?' said Singer. 'You aren't getting anywhere with her, that's your trouble.'

'She's been avoiding me, God knows why. Won't she, or can't she?'

'She'd like to, but rules are rules in this outfit.'

'Damn the rules!'

Singer welcomed this outburst but didn't show it. 'Melanie's like all the other girl auxiliaries here – she's kept in purdah by the Klarfeld woman. Still, even Klarfeld drops her guard occasionally. It's just a question of knowing when.'

'And you do?' Kersten demanded eagerly.

'Yes, I happen to know she's taking a trip in the next few days. Then you'll be able to get your paws on Melanie – maybe.'

'Don't be so crude, Sebastian. I worship that girl.'

'Call it what you like. I'll see you get a crack at her, anyway. The rest'll be up to you.'

Lieutenant Lahrmann's early morning treat wasn't over yet, nor were the torments it inflicted on his remaining passengers, the sergeant from the Security Platoon and his non-driving driver. Their return trip to Kampfental became a race against the clock – against Lahrmann himself.

His existing record for the eighty-mile drive along dusty, tortuous country roads and winding village streets stood at eighty-five minutes. It had been achieved without regard for casualties such as maimed dogs or mangled geese and chickens.

This morning's whirlwind dash through the dawn improved on Lahrmann's personal best by a full four minutes. Far too proud of his latest feat to waste a glance on the waxen-cheeked pair in whom it had inspired such mortal terror, he felt that his efficiency had been duly rewarded.

This did not, of course, prevent him from promptly reassuming his role as senior instructor in anti-guerrilla warfare – in fact it only spurred him on. Having roared into camp at seven, he was back in front of his trainees by eight, an erect and virile figure.

'And now, men,' he cried, 'dig the sleep out of your eyes. The show must go on!' Those who knew him realized that he was being mildly humorous.

Immediately after lunch on the next of these lovely autumn days in 1944, a small party left Kampfental Camp on a special mission scheduled to last several hours. Although it was an official trip, the cloudless sky and sun-drenched South Bavarian landscape, which was still untouched by war, lent it something of the atmosphere of a carefree peacetime excursion.

The leader of the party, Captain Königsberger, had originally been bold enough to request the use of Lieutenant Lahrmann's precious Mercedes. Predictably, Lahrmann rejected this idea point-blank.

'You've got a nerve, Doctor!' were his actual words.

'Pardon me,' the MO said blandly, 'but the Mercedes isn't your private property. Besides, Frau Klarfeld will be going too.'

'Number one, the Mercedes is an official vehicle reserved for my exclusive use and personally assigned me by the Colonel. Number two, if Frau Klarfeld cares to inform me when and where she wishes to go, I'll be happy to drive her there myself. Number three, you're the last person I'd trust with my car.'

'Perhaps we should request a decision from the Colonel.'

They tried, but did not get past Captain Tauschmüller, that inescapable channel of communication. Tauschmüller headed them off politely but firmly, displaying considerable diplomatic skill.

'Frau Klarfeld in an open car? Most inadvisable – these autumn nights can be really chilly. You'd better take my staff car.'

Lahrmann beamed. 'Thank you, Captain – I'm indebted to you.' He was indeed, and he soon got a chance to pay him back.

The party, which consisted of Königsberger, Frau Klarfeld, Natasha, and the adjutant's personal driver, a Private Baumgartner, showed their passes at the main gate and drove off. The MO sat back with a sigh of relief.

'Head for Garmisch, driver.'

Frau Klarfeld, who was sitting beside him, raised her eyebrows. 'I understood we were going to the hydrogenation plant at Isaraubach.'

'So we are, but we can't get down to work there until the night shift comes on at six this evening. We're going to fill in the time by making a little detour – an authorized detour, in case you're worried.'

'Worried?' Frau Klarfeld dimpled at him. 'Of course not, Doctor, I trust you implicitly.'

This was no exaggeration. Frau Klarfeld entertained the highest regard for Captain Königsberger. He had given her several thorough check-ups, discreetly advised her on a matter of some delicacy, and kept her lavishly supplied with pharmaceutical products of a quality almost unobtainable after five years of war.

'Our port of call at Garmisch will be a medical research centre transferred there to escape the bombing. The director used to be a professor of mine, but he's more of a personal friend these days. Our medical supplies are running low. I'm hoping he can top them up.'

'Whatever you say, my dear Doctor.'

'In that case, let's make the most of our day out.' The MO indicated Natasha, who was sitting beside the driver. 'At least we can show off the beauties of Bavaria to our visitor from abroad.'

'Thank you,' Natasha said softly, and even Frau Klarfeld was gracious enough to smile.

CURRICULUM VITAE OF ERIKA KLARFELD
or, The Waywardness of Woman

I was born in Leipzig on 19 August 1912, and was the second of three daughters. My parents were Erich Marunke, who owned a printing and publishing house, and his wife Elfriede. As a young woman, my mother had published a small volume of poetry, Tame the Wild Wind, *under her maiden name, Elfriede Odenwald. She died in 1915, giving birth to her third child.*

Soon after 1918, Erich Maria Marunke – the 'Maria' which completed his nom de plume was an afterthought of his own – developed from a self-styled 'ardent aesthete' into a 'libertarian idealist'. His one-time enthusiasm for war having swiftly evaporated, he now entered upon a phase of 'humane enlightenment' and 'philanthropic self-criticism'. Ever quick to spot a budding trend and sense the climate of the times, Marunke kept a weather eye open for any commercial opportunity.

During the early 'twenties his publishing house specialized in 'documents of our time' and 'personal confessions'. In other words, there was almost nothing he wouldn't publish as long as it promised to pay off. A 'victim of the law' recounted his experiences in gaol, a Red-baiting streetfighter hymned his heroic deeds, and a

Weimar politician issued dire warnings to the world at large. Through the medium of his own literary review, *Dawn*, Marunke distinguished himself as an equivocator of visionary brilliance, a master of the not only but also, the nevertheless and notwithstanding, the possibly but possibly not.

Marunke became a widely esteemed and respected figure, partly because his ownership of a lucrative printing empire enabled him to entertain on a lavish scale in the house which was run, after his wife's death, by his loving sister Irene. It turned into a haunt popular with all who claimed membership of the cultural élite in the Leipzig-Dresden area.

Marunke's eldest daughter, Gertrude Marion, a young woman of practical bent, worked on the production and distribution side of his business. The youngest girl, Anneliese Melinda, who seemed to have inherited her mother's literary gifts, planned to augment her father's list with a slender volume of her own.

But Erika Margot, who was addressed like both her sisters by the second of her given names, attended to her beloved father's home comforts. She made his bed, ensured that his toothpaste and cologne never ran out, and looked after his suits, shoes and underwear. Such was her devotion to his welfare that she sometimes joined him between the sheets when overtiredness robbed him of the ability to sleep.

These ministrations were frowned on by his sister and indefatigable housekeeper, whose displeasure soon culminated in a time-worn threat. 'Either she goes or I do!' Irene told him. 'Don't worry,' said Marunke, 'we'll think of something.' And they did.

In 1930, while still in my teens, I became engaged to Jörg Thomas Reiner, a poet whose work was then highly regarded. Our betrothal was announced just after the

appearance of Into the Eye of the Sun*, a volume of
poetry which bore my father's imprint and was hailed by
reviewers as 'the publishing coup of the century'.*

Jörg Thomas Reiner was probably Marunke's most
important discovery, and Marunke was determined to
hang on to him. It was therefore in the interests of his
publishing house, as well as his sister, that he encouraged a
match between Erika Margot and this promising young
poet.

But their engagement soon turned out to be a monu-
mental error. Once betrothed to his publisher's daughter,
Reiner stopped work and flung himself into a life of
debauchery – much to the distress of Erika, who was
nauseated by his verbal diarrhoea, heavy drinking and
unsavoury personal habits.

So she put up the first, though not the last, of the barriers
between herself and the opposite sex. Another and more
important one was erected years later at Kampfental, but
that lay far in the future.

Erika broke off her engagement and fled from Leipzig to
Dresden, where her mother's only sister, who was married
to a conductor, welcomed her with open arms. The ensuing
months were one long cultural feast – concerts, operas,
theatres, museums – but none of these aesthetic delights
could permanently dispel young Erika's new-found
restlessness.

Next on her road through life came Berlin. Here she
shared an apartment with one of her schoolfriends, who
was studying drama. The two girls became inseparable, at
least in the eyes of the world. No art exhibition or film
première, no riotous studio party or profound coffee-house
debate on the meaning of existence was complete without
them, but Erika soon found these occasions stale and
superficial too.

Then, at a press reception, she met a man who attracted

her as magically as she attracted him. He was Count Von Klarfeld, a celebrated wartime pilot who had been one of the youngest members of Baron von Richthofen's 'Flying Circus', the most select and successful of all Imperial Germany's fighter formations.

Count von Klarfeld had until recently earned his living as a stunt flyer. Malicious rivals called him an aerial acrobat – a mere clown – but to Erika he seemed like something out of a child's book of Nordic fairy-tales: blond and blue-eyed, with broad shoulders, slender hips, and the springy stride of a conquering hero.

He was the only man for her, and she the only woman for him.

On 21 July 1937, I married Eberhard, Count von Klarfeld, who was by then a major in the Luftwaffe. Our witnesses were two of his oldest comrades: Hermann Göring, the future Reich Marshal, and Ernst Udet, who already held the post of Inspector-General, Air Force Ordnance. In 1939, at the start of the Polish campaign, my husband was shot down over Warsaw on his very first mission. He died when his fighter burst into flames.

But nothing could detract from the splendour of the preceding two years – the receptions at the Chancellery, the annual fighter pilots' banquet at Göring's palatial country seat, the seaside holidays on Sylt, the soirées with friends, the gala evenings at the State Opera and State Theatre. How gloriously fraught with promise everything had been!

One of the high-spots was the first anniversary of their wedding. Eberhard von Klarfeld, who had since been promoted lieutenant-colonel and entrusted with the testing and development of Germany's latest fighter aircraft, received a special tribute to mark the occasion. He and his young wife were allocated a lakeside house on the fashionable outskirts of Berlin – a miniature country mansion standing in its own grounds. Made available by Göring and presented to them by Udet, it was elegant rather than ostentatious. A cook, housemaid and gardener went with it. 'Make yourselves at home,' Göring told them. 'The previous owner decided to go abroad in a hurry. For good.'

What distinguished company they entertained! Udet plus friends and girl-friends; Count Helldorf, Berlin's police chief, usually accompanied by the pretty blonde starlet who was his life's companion of the moment; and Göring himself, together with wife Emmy. 'You're a remarkably German young woman,' he told Erika with elephantine gallantry. 'In other words, my dear, one of us.'

And then came the death – the heroic death – of her husband. Udet turned up in full-dress uniform to express his sympathy. 'My friend Eberhard was one of our very best men – irreplaceable, unforgettable!' Göring sent her a personal letter, as did the Führer himself, and their words of condolence were published in the *Volkischer Beobachter*. Every obituary contained the same recurrent phrases: 'Ever ready to sacrifice himself in the cause of victory . . . carve his name with pride . . . a shining example to us all . . .'

All that remained was to accept this truly German stroke of fate and endure it with becoming dignity – a challenge to which Erika proved more than equal.

Early in 1940, after my beloved husband's death, I volunteered my services to the Greater German Armed Forces, confident that I was doing as he would have wished. I was determined that he should not have died in vain.

Erika gave up her house beside the Wannsee and placed it at the state's disposal.

From now on, she seemed to shun the Luftwaffe. Her

wish to work for the Army was fulfilled by a staff officer who had once been a visitor to her house – a sympathetic and helpful man with exquisite manners. This acquaintance, whose name was Schlumberger, found her employment in the area controlled by the army group whose chief of staff he was.

Throughout her service in a variety of military establishments – garrison headquarters, supply depots and training centres – Erika Klarfeld demonstrated that she was a woman of many parts. She performed her duties so efficiently that Schlumberger got her appointed head of all the women auxiliaries assigned to the top priority project known as AFSIC Kampfental. Transferred there in summer 1942, she soon attracted the attention of Colonel von Feuerfresser. She was not immune to his aura of lofty grandeur. As for Feuerfresser, he courted her as ardently as he could, but his efforts at a crucial stage in their relationship proved sadly abortive.

He endured this with serene resignation, just as she had to. 'Dear lady,' he told her, 'we mustn't try to force the pace. When a fact is inescapable, it should be accepted with equanimity.'

Neither of them ever mentioned the incident again. The Colonel, tended by his ever faithful and wholly uncomplicated minion, Eugen Priewitt, redevoted himself to tasks of national importance. Erika sought consolation in her work and, temporarily, in the company of Melanie Mauerland.

She continued to do so until she thought she perceived certain possibilities in the Colonel's adjutant, Hermann Tauschmüller. Though anything but a Wagnerian personality, he was undeniably intelligent and sensitive – rather like a half-way house between her artistic but intemperate fiancé and her heroic husband.

And so she became involved with him.

*

Mess Sergeant Gerner was prowling the cellar of the officers' mess like a caged tiger.

Despite its rigours, his two-day outing with the Colonel had gone so smoothly that he felt confident of promotion. After celebrating his prospective advancement with Sergeant-Major Schulz for most of the night, he had finally run a check on his mess supplies – of drink in particular. The result was a nasty shock.

He yelled for Singer, who appeared with suspicious alacrity, looking thoroughly ingenuous.

'What's up, Sergeant?'

'We're two dozen bottles of champagne short, that's what!' Gerner's parade-ground bellow was a work of art. 'Two dozen of the best! Who snitched them? Was it you, you creep?'

'I didn't snitch them, Sergeant, I issued them.' Singer shrugged. 'The officers asked for champagne and I served it, that's all.'

'Are you crazy? Don't pretend you don't know the form. Only the Colonel gets champagne, and now you've gone and used up most of his personal reserve. When the others ask for champagne, you give them German fizz.'

'Live and learn, Sergeant.'

Gerner glowered at him. 'I'm beginning to get your measure, you little turd. Suck up to the officers while my back's turned, would you? Well, I don't take that from anyone, least of all a creep like you!'

Eugen Priewitt, himself a sergeant again, elbowed his way through the mess waiters who were avidly eavesdropping on Singer's latest altercation with Gerner.

'Pipe down, you fellows, the Colonel's having his afternoon nap.'

'Don't blame me,' said Singer. 'I'm being as quiet as a mouse.'

'Sure,' Gerner said contemptuously, 'quiet as a silent fart!'

Priewitt flapped his hands in entreaty. 'Cool it, I've got something to tell you.'

'Why butt in, Priewitt?' Gerner demanded. 'Are you ganging up on me?'

Priewitt dismissed this suggestion with a sweeping gesture. It wasn't a question of personalities, he said. All that counted was the Colonel, right? Right.

'And the Colonel told me to pass the word. He's giving a slap-up dinner in honour of a lady visitor.'

'You don't say!' Gerner looked incredulous. 'A lady, here? I mean, apart from Frau Klarfeld.'

'Yes,' said Priewitt, 'and if I were you, I'd put on a really good show – give 'em everything you've got.'

'Will do,' Gerner reassured him. 'Mind you, we could be in trouble on the champagne front.'

'I hope not, friend,' said Priewitt. 'Nothing but the best – that's what the Colonel told me.'

'Look, if there isn't enough champagne to go round, blame your pal Singer here – you wished him on me. He had the gall to raid the Colonel's personal reserve, and we won't be getting another delivery till next week.'

Priewitt grinned serenely. 'Singer's *our* pal, not mine, and I didn't wish him on you – you picked him yourself. Besides, why should I beat my brains out over your problems? I've got plenty of my own.'

'Shit!' said Gerner, stung by the smirk on Singer's face. 'What the hell am I going to do?'

'Do like we did on New Year's Eve when the bubbly started running out. We saved the real stuff for the Colonel and gave the rest of them fizz decanted into empty champagne bottles. They never noticed – or if they did, they didn't show it.'

Gerner's brow cleared. 'It's an idea.'

'Who's the lady?' asked Singer, intrigued.

'Shut your trap!' barked Gerner. 'I ask the questions round here. All right, Priewitt, who is she?'

'Frau Tauschmüller,' said Priewitt. 'Yes, that's right – the ever-loving wife of our respected adjutant.'

'What brings her here?'

'She's on her way to take over a field hospital in Garmisch – she's a bigwig in the Army Nursing Service. She politely asked if she could stop off here, and the Colonel said he'd be honoured. That's why he's ordered this special dinner.'

'For a captain's wife?'

'Don't be so dumb, Gerner. She's out of the top drawer – a tycoon's daughter, or something. Besides, she's married to the Colonel's right-hand man.'

'What about Frau Klarfeld?'

'Never you mind about her, just concentrate on your own problems. Anyway, Frau Klarfeld's away for the day. She won't be back before midnight, and by then it'll all be over. Right?'

'Right,' said Gerner. He turned to Singer. 'Well, what are you standing around for? Take your thumb out of your bum and get cracking!'

That afternoon, work began on what later became known as 'Kersten's Coconut Shy'. It was jointly supervised by Lieutenant Kersten and Master Sergeant Heinz, who made an excellent team.

On the open ground between the sports field and the firing ranges, they got the trainees of Group C to erect a circular edifice of sandbags some ten feet in diameter. By the time it had grown to the height of a man, it resembled an outsize, topless beehive.

'What's that supposed to be?' demanded Sergeant-Major Schulz, who was making one of his periodic tours of inspection.

'You'll see,' Heinz told him cryptically. 'Everyone's in for a big surprise, believe me.'

As one who prided himself on never missing a trick,

Schulz was exasperated by this response. He had asked for a straight answer and been fobbed off with a dark hint. Nobody talked to *him* that way! Fuming, he withdrew to a more distant vantage point.

Kersten and Heinz, who were too busy to bother about the sergeant-major's sensibilities, proceeded with the second phase of their construction project. Under their guidance, the Group C trainees enclosed the sandbag beehive with three concentric rings of foxholes, the earth from which was heaped into protective mounds.

'Will there be enough grenades to go round?' Kersten asked anxiously. 'We'll use at least a hundred an exercise, so you can multiply that by four or five.'

'I've got more than enough in stock, Lieutenant.' Heinz spoke with a touch of pride. 'Don't worry, everything's going to go with a bang. I can hardly wait.'

'That makes two of us,' said Kersten.

Captain Königsberger's little party took about two hours to reach the Army Medical Corps research centre that had been evacuated from Berlin to the outskirts of Garmisch in southern Bavaria. The inevitable checkpoint was manned by two sentries armed with sub-machine-guns.

'No admittance without special authorization from the Führer's headquarters,' called the guard commander.

'Unless,' said Königsberger, 'a permit has been issued by the officer commanding this establishment, Surgeon-General Meller.'

'Correct. Do you have one?'

'No, but kindly tell the General I'm here. My name is Königsberger.'

A brief telephone call did the trick. The car and its occupants were waved on at once. General Meller, who was waiting for the party outside the main building, bade them a hearty welcome. He hugged Königsberger, who had once been his favourite student, and hailed his female companions with professorial delight.

'Whom have we here? What glamorous beings deign to shed such lustre on my unworthy domain? Juno and Venus in person! It's enough to gladden an old man's eyes and fan his waning passions into a blaze! Welcome, welcome!'

He directed the driver to the canteen. The others he showed into a pleasantly furnished sitting-room next door to his office.

'Please make yourselves comfortable. I can offer you some Abyssinian coffee, thanks to an Italian colleague of mine. We have a business arrangement: half a pound of coffee for a litre of pure alcohol.'

Meller's eyes twinkled as he spoke. His plump, rosy cheeks might have belonged to the bon-vivant president of a thriving business corporation. Having seated Natasha and Frau Klarfeld at either end of a capacious sofa, he subsided into the space between them with a contented grunt.

'Don't begrudge me my little treats, ladies – I get so few nowadays.' He heaved a histrionic sigh. 'However, my dear Königsberger, I'm sure you didn't come just to feast me on the sight of these lovely creatures. How can I repay you?'

'In the usual way, General. You can probably let me have a few of the medical supplies I've been unable to obtain elsewhere.' Königsberger produced a list and handed it to Meller, who skimmed through it with greater attention than his casual manner suggested. Then he nodded, said 'Excuse me, ladies,' and phoned for one of his aides.

Once the aide had gone, Meller devoted himself wholeheartedly to his visitors, and the ladies in particular. The next two hours sped past in a flurry of entertaining conversation about the world and his wife, the pleasures of earthly existence, and the dear dead days before the war.

'What a charming man,' Frau Klarfeld said admiringly,

as she climbed back into the car. 'A very exceptional person,' Natasha agreed, as she followed suit.

Their host drew Königsberger aside, looking uncharacteristically grave. Not a word had passed between them on the subject of Hitler and the war. Now, Meller made up for lost time.

'You know what we're in for, don't you? Total destruction. We never wanted it, but we're all partly to blame.'

'My sentiments entirely, General. I suppose we'll just have to grin and bear it.'

'Not necessarily, my dear boy. Certain loopholes do exist, even in a predicament like ours. If you're ever at your wit's end, make a dash for this place and bring the ladies with you.'

'You've enough on your plate as it is.'

'Don't underestimate me. I'm not unprepared. As soon as the front collapses, as it undoubtedly will, this centre will convert itself into a large-scale isolation hospital teeming with highly infectious diseases. No enemy will dare to darken its portals, least of all the Americans. They have an absolute horror of bugs, so they'll give this place a wide berth. Anyone on the inside – you and the ladies, for instance – will be quite safe.'

'You mean you've actually planned all this in advance?'

'For months now, I've been shifting the focus of our research to epidemic diseases. I've also collected some suitable patients – nearly three dozen of them housed in two special wards in the grounds. By the time we're liberated, as the Allies call it, I shall be able to produce over a hundred cases requiring intensive care and strict isolation.'

'I see. One way of surviving the war is to be gravely ill and undergoing treatment from a doctor like you.'

'War's an illogical business, my boy – but I don't have to tell you that.'

Profoundly impressed, the MO gave Meller's hand a farewell shake. 'I always knew you were a good teacher, Professor, but I didn't know just how good till now.'

Situation Report No. 6

Acts of deception, self-deception included, are common to the final phase of all heroic ages. Any historical 'precedents' and bugbears that may come in handy are exhumed and put to work. Hitler and his cronies were unstinting in their efforts to keep Germany's warriors up to the mark and boost the morale of soldiers, civilians and Party members. World history was reinterpreted accordingly by Alfred Rosenberg, Hitler's ideologist-in-chief, and sundry others.

Hitler, for example, likened himself to Frederick II of Prussia, surnamed 'the Great' – something he had often done before but never with such a grim sense of purpose. Because Frederick's predicament had resembled his own, he declared, what mattered was to emulate the king's unique brand of perseverance during the Seven Years' War.

Heavy losses, military setbacks and seemingly irreversible defeats – Frederick the Great had survived them all and gone on to inscribe a glorious final victory in the annals of warfare. He had done so in the knowledge which Hitler now made his sacred motto: the true soldier lays down his arms only when twelve has struck, not at the eleventh hour.

Fortitude and faith in God being essential to victory, Hitler often invoked 'the Almighty' without ever defining what he meant by the term. Just as fortune favoured the bold, so miracles were a prerogative of genius, and Hitler believed himself as much a genius as Frederick the Great.

Just when that most Prussian of all kings seemed done for, from the purely military aspect, death claimed one of the two warlike women who had been fighting him so doggedly. Not Maria Theresa of Austria, but Elizabeth, Empress of Russia. Her successor was a military nonentity who played with soldiers as a girl plays with dolls. An admirer of Frederick the Great, he made peace with him and placed his forces at the Prussian monarch's disposal.

That, Hitler believed, was the way history worked. One had to wait – and be able to wait – until the right moment came. As he saw it, several very encouraging factors were already in operation:

1. Stalin was an old, inflexible, much-hated man who savagely decreed the murder of all potential enemies inside the régime. Serious friction existed between him and his generals, the Politburo, and those who were jostling to step into his shoes.

2. Roosevelt, thrice re-elected President of the United States, could be expected to suffer another stroke at any time. Opposition to him was steadily increasing. One of his keenest critics was General Douglas MacArthur of Far East fame, an inordinately ambitious man with his own designs on the Presidency.

3. Churchill had degenerated into a hopeless old toper and spent more time asleep than at work.

4. General de Gaulle, the pig-headed Frenchman, was nothing more than a strutting puppet whom the Allies indulgently tolerated.

5. Tito and his confederates were merely upstarts intent on feathering their own nests and covetous of the prestige enjoyed by those more powerful than themselves.

By taking this view of the international scene and broadcasting it loud and clear, Hitler and his paladins sought to keep up their people's spirits. Victory, they proclaimed, would go to those with greater faith, fortitude, and staying-power.

Late on the afternoon of the same day, Lieutenant Kersten turned up at the camp medical centre. Singer had hinted to him that the time was ripe, and he didn't want to miss his chance.

Peering into the absent MO's office, Kersten was

delighted to see Melanie Mauerland at work on some papers. He hurried over to her.

'I've been dying to see you again, and here you are – all by yourself.'

Melanie smiled demurely. 'Good afternoon, Lieutenant, what can I do for you?'

'Plenty,' he said, squeezing her hand rather than shaking it. 'For a start, you can call me Konstantin.'

She blushed. 'We hardly know each other.'

'Then we'd better make up for lost time,' he said briskly. 'War's no picnic – anything could have happened by tomorrow.' He turned to close the door.

'Please don't, Herr Kersten, that door has to stay open. It's regulations.'

He stared at her with a mixture of surprise and pique. 'What's the matter, don't you feel like a tête-à-tête?'

'My feelings don't come into it.'

'So what's stopping you?'

Her big brown eyes craved sympathetic understanding. 'I told you – regulations. We all have to obey them, and that includes you.'

'Regulations be damned! The question is, where can we have a quiet chat? What about a stroll, or shall we go to your quarters?'

'It's no use, Herr Kersten.' The regret in her voice was quite unmistakable. 'Informal contact between male and female personnel is forbidden except at public functions such as concerts, film shows or football matches.'

'Are you being serious?' Kersten said incredulously. 'Anyone'd think this was a nunnery. Who dreamed up all these rules?'

'Commandant's orders.'

Lesser men might have admitted defeat, but not Kersten. 'Does he really think he can regulate everything in this place, even people's emotions?' He paused. 'We do feel something special for each other, don't we?'

'Maybe,' she conceded. Then, screwing up her courage, she added, 'I'd like to get to know you properly too, but I don't see how we're ever going to manage it. Perhaps we could start by writing to each other.'

'Become pen pals, you mean?' Kersten's face was a study in utter bewilderment. 'But that'd be a complete waste of time.'

For once, she didn't contradict him.

Frau Tauschmüller's official chauffeur-driven car purred into camp shortly after 5 p.m.

Her husband – captain of infantry and HQ Company commander, but first and foremost the Colonel's personal staff officer – had been waiting at the main gate for almost half an hour. He advanced on the car, opened the passenger door, and helped his spouse to alight.

'Here you are at last, my love! Welcome to Kampfental!'

They embraced, not passionately but with due affection – this was, after all, a public proceeding. Frau Tauschmüller stepped back a pace, still holding her husband by the upper arms, and searched his face.

'Am I really welcome?' she asked. 'I'd hate to think I was intruding on your official duties.'

'A husband must always make time for his wife, dearest. Thanks to the Colonel's generosity, I've been able to do so.'

They had met only once in the past year, and then under rather inauspicious circumstances. Frau Tauschmüller had been nursing at a military hospital in East Prussia, and he – once again with the Colonel's gracious permission – had fitted a three-day detour into an official trip to Berlin. Feuerfresser was always concerned for his senior subordinates' physical and mental well-being.

They dismissed the car and set out for the officers' mess on foot.

'You're looking the picture of health,' said Frau Tauschmüller.

'That's because you're here.' Glancing fondly at his wife, Tauschmüller was transfixed by the sudden realization that she bore an uncanny and hitherto unnoticed resemblance to Frau Klarfeld. Though slightly stouter and more austere-looking, she had the same majestic poise.

'I'm very grateful to your commanding officer for making this reunion possible,' she said. 'He must be a kind-hearted man.'

'Uniquely so,' Tauschmüller assured her. 'He wants to welcome you in person – he's even giving a dinner in your honour.'

As they approached the main terrace, they were sighted by Priewitt, who obviously had orders to look out for them. He scuttled back into the mess. A moment later, the double doors swung open. Priewitt and Gerner posted themselves on either side, flunkey fashion, and Colonel von Feuerfresser emerged like Frederick the Great appearing on the steps of his palace at Potsdam.

He waited for the Tauschmüllers to draw nearer, then took two or three paces in their direction.

'My dear Frau Tauschmüller!' he exclaimed. Something in his voice conveyed that her resemblance to Frau Klarfeld had struck him too. 'Permit me to welcome you to our humble abode.'

He seized her right hand, drew it towards him, bent over it, and kissed it with old-world ceremony. Frau Tauschmüller was enchanted.

'My dear Colonel, I do hope my presence hasn't caused you any inconvenience.'

'On the contrary, madam, it's a pleasure to see you here. You are, after all, the wife of my most trusted subordinate.'

'Thank you, Colonel.' Frau Tauschmüller glowed with pride.

'I should also like to express my appreciation of the Colonel's kindness,' said her husband, deeply moved.

'Come, come, what could be more natural?' Feuerfresser graciously offered Frau Tauschmüller his arm and escorted her into the mess. 'Please make yourself at home, dear lady. I have had your husband's quarters equipped with everything necessary for your personal comfort. I shall look forward to the honour of your presence at dinner in the mess this evening. Music will be provided by our resident orchestra.'

The official purpose of Captain Königsberger's excursion was to procure replacements for those inmates of the camp brothel who had recently departed this life. One convenient source of supply was the hydrogenation plant at Isaraubach, a strategically vital establishment whose foreign labour force was supervised by Hauptsturmführer Breitenbach, an SS captain. The Hauptsturmführer had always proved extremely accommodating, the more so because he and his football team were invited to Kampfental every other month to play a 'friendly' against the latest batch of trainees, and every such sporting event was followed by a memorable binge in the mess. Breitenbach appreciated the scale on which AFSIC Kampfental entertained its visitors, so his response to Königsberger's request was bluff and unhesitating.

'Of course I'll let you have some more of my foreign floozies,' he said. Breitenbach was a staunch believer in the master-race theory. 'They're useless, these subhuman Slav scum. Sturdy peasant stock, that's what they're supposed to be. In fact, they're a threat to my workers' morale – plain idle and downright promiscuous. As far as I'm concerned you can take the whole bunch, just as long as your people supply me with a few reasonably able-bodied prisoners of war in return, the way they've done before.'

Königsberger was familiar with the SS captain's

attitude. Although he found it repugnant, he refrained from saying so. Frau Klarfeld preserved a fixed smile and Natasha just stood there, stiff and impassive. They all had a job to do.

Breitenbach was a man of considerable importance, at least in his own estimation. He presided over two dozen large huts occupied by nearly two thousand human ants whom he easily kept in order with his two hundred SS guards. The latter included thirty hand-picked, well-trained footballers, and their victorious guest appearances throughout the local military district were a permanent feather in Breitenbach's cap.

The SS captain himself lived on the outskirts of the hydrogenation plant, in a luxurious country house that had once belonged to its original owner, since deceased in a concentration camp. This villa, which stood on a hill and commanded a magnificent view of the surrounding country side, was littered with Persian carpets and plastered with valuable paintings – all of them quite unappreciated by the new occupant.

Breitenbach ushered his visitors inside with an expansive gesture. 'Be my guests. 'Fraid I can't compete with that splendid cellar of yours at Kampfental, but you won't go thirsty. What'll it be?'

'Whatever you suggest,' the MO said politely. 'But first, Hauptsturmführer, perhaps you'd allow our colleague here – ' he indicated Natasha – 'to visit the huts occupied by your female personnel and make a preliminary assessment?'

'Of course, of course!'

Königsberger turned discreetly to Natasha. 'In that case,' he said, 'would you carry on?'

Natasha, who knew that her task was to pick out four or five suitable candidates, nodded and left the room. The other two were offered some Crimean champagne.

'Spoils of war,' Breitenbach explained. 'We're sent it by

the truckload. Not bad stuff – slips down like lemonade. Now if your Colonel'd like some for the mess . . .'

Königsberger gave a thin smile. 'A charming thought, but I'm sure you and your men need all the liquid refreshment you can get.'

'You never said a truer word, Doctor.' Breitenbach sounded grateful for the implied refusal. 'It's a tough job, keeping these idle foreign swine on their toes. Still, anything for the sake of higher output and final victory.'

'Quite so. Am I wrong, or did we pass three corpses on a gallows as we drove into your compound?'

'You bet you did! I keep 'em dangling near the main gate. That's so my workers see them twice a day, going on shift and coming off. We make a practice of it -- you'd be surprised what a deterrent effect it has.'

'Deterrent?'

'Yes, and productive. Our output rises in proportion to the length of time they hang there. It's the stench, you see.'

'And you find such measures unavoidable?'

'Not only unavoidable, Doctor – absolutely essential. We may be in the middle of Germany, but we're manning an outpost of civilization here. There's more than shirkers in my work force. Some of these foreign labour conscripts are spies and saboteurs, and they've got to be warned off. It's as simple as that.'

'You mean you hang a few at random now and then?'

'Correct. The Reichsführer's issued a directive to that effect.' Breitenbach uttered Himmler's title with a hint of reverence. 'They're easily led astray, these people, and it's one way of keeping them up to the mark. Besides, what's a trio of stinking corpses to two thousand employees? As a percentage, it's insignificant.'

Königsberger made no further comment. Frau Klarfeld's silence seemed to imply that she hadn't heard a word. Her interest in the proceedings did not revive until

Natasha returned with the news that she had found four likely recruits.

The girls were promptly inspected in Breitenbach's office. They were young and, despite the filthy, shapeless smocks they wore, not unattractive.

Frau Klarfeld's job was to assess their potential feminine appeal and racial attributes, weeding out any alien and undesirable elements in the process. For his part, the MO conducted a preliminary medical examination. In the case of Natasha's candidates, no grounds for rejection seemed justified.

'All clear, Hauptsturmführer,' Königsberger said at last. 'Kindly have these women transferred to Kampfental as soon as possible, preferably tomorrow.'

'Will do.' Breitenbach beamed at him. 'Always glad to be of service to you and your CO, Doctor. Please give him my best and tell him I look forward to our next away match.'

Königsberger and his party boarded their car and drove off. The SS captain waved them goodbye, but they didn't look back. They didn't speak, either, until their car was clear of his well-run hellhole and back on the open road. Then Frau Klarfeld broke the silence.

'What now?' she said brightly. 'To be honest, I feel like a little rest and relaxation.'

'So do I,' said Natasha, almost inaudibly.

Königsberger smiled. 'In that case, I suggest a visit to the Brown Bear at Hölzbach. AFSIC personnel are always welcome there, thanks to certain arrangements between camp headquarters and the landlord. Shall we take advantage of them?'

Frau Tauschmüller sat on the Colonel's right at dinner, a change in protocol which presented no problems because Frau Klarfeld, who would otherwise have claimed that privilege, had fortunately failed to return in time. As

220

Feuerfresser's right-hand man, Tauschmüller occupied his time-honoured place on the Colonel's left.

The atmosphere was jovial and relaxed, not least because the MO had also failed to show up. Lieutenant Wagner, who positively blossomed in his absence, was quick to fire off one of his gems of wisdom. '*Pax est tranquillitas ordinis*,' he proclaimed. 'That's a Roman proverb, meaning roughly: "Peace reigns where calm and good order prevail." How appropriate to the present occasion!'

Wagner's effusions still drew nods of assent, even from Majors Kastor and Pollandt, though theirs had lately betrayed a hint of impatience. The majors were not to be impressed by any pronouncements save those of the Colonel, but he was wrapped in oysterlike silence.

Feuerfresser's gaze rested on Lieutenant Kersten, whose junior status condemned him to the place at the bottom of the table. In spite of his brooding, preoccupied expression, Kersten was eating with habitual gusto.

As an apt accompaniment to the meal, which consisted largely of delicacies provided by the Colonel's recent expedition, the chamber orchestra played the fourth movement of Haydn's Symphony No. 37, 'The Chase', an allegretto embodying fanfares played on French horns and oboes. Nobody noticed that this work was performed twice because something nutcrackerish by Tchaikovsky was sandwiched between the twin renditions.

'Wonderful,' breathed Frau Tauschmüller, 'simply wonderful!' Her husband smiled at her across the Colonel. Her evident sense of pride and gratitude was in part a tribute to himself.

'My dear madam, my dear Captain Tauschmüller,' said Feuerfresser, 'for tonight, you must treat this place as your home. That being my most earnest wish, you may withdraw.'

Almost simultaneously, a no less convivial dinner was in

progress at the Brown Bear in Hölzbach. The venue was not fortuitous. The inn and the neighbouring camp carried on a brisk two-way trade. The landlord's own brewery supplied Kampfental with 'Hölzbacher Special', which even now maintained its pre-war quality and strength. In return, the landlord received brandy, meat, game and produce from AFSIC's kitchen garden and poultry farm. The growth of this business relationship was yet another achievement on the part of that assiduous fixer, Captain Tauschmüller.

It was only natural, therefore, that Königsberger and his little party should be heartily welcome at the Brown Bear. The landlord bustled up, greeted Königsberger and Frau Klarfeld effusively, and even extended his massive paw to Natasha and the driver.

'What can I offer you, ladies and gentlemen? Beds for the night? A private room? The menu?'

'A private room, if possible – somewhere nice and quiet,' said Königsberger. 'And then, perhaps, something to drink and a modest meal.'

'Say no more.' The landlord drew himself up proudly. 'First, a well-chilled beer – one of my special extra-strong brews – and then some tasty smoked ribs of pork with sauerkraut. For pudding, apple pie, with or without custard.'

Königsberger turned to Frau Klarfeld. 'Would that suit you?'

'Admirably, thank you.'

'One more thing: would it bother you if our driver and interpreter joined us for dinner?'

'Why should it bother me, Doctor? Quite apart from the fact that this is a private function, the Führer himself is a Socialist – a National Socialist, but still.'

'Fine,' said the MO. 'Then that's settled. Would anyone like a wash and brush up?'

They were allotted the so-called 'Mayor's Parlour', a

room that boasted a certain rustic magnificence. Numerous hunting trophies adorned its wainscoted walls -- roebucks' antlers, mountain goats' horns, stuffed birds, and a brace of massive boars' heads.

Königsberger was the first to take his place at table, closely followed by Frau Klarfeld. She leant towards him with a confidential smile.

'Your budding interest in Natasha has not escaped me, Doctor.'

'If I were interested in her – and I repeat, *if* – would you have any objection?'

'A whole host of objections,' she replied, presumably in her role as mistress of AFSIC's women staff auxiliaries. 'However, please rest assured that my attitude isn't unsympathetic.'

'Really? May I ask what makes you say that?'

Frau Klarfeld succumbed to a rare attack of feminine frailty. 'I myself know all too well how strong the pull of emotion can be, whatever the obstacles in its path. Love is like a prison sentence passed by fate -- one can't evade it.'

The MO had no chance to follow up this interesting but not wholly unexpected revelation because Natasha and the driver appeared.

The meal was ample and delicious, and universal applause greeted the old zither-player whom the landlord sent in to enliven the occasion with a medley of Bavarian folk tunes. When the party left for camp just before midnight, Frau Klarfeld surprised Königsberger with a magnanimous gesture which confirmed his suspicion that she was more than a little tipsy.

'For a change,' she announced, 'I shall sit in front beside the driver.'

This meant that Königsberger and Natasha had the back seat to themselves. 'If you must, you must,' she told them archly. 'But remember, one thing can lead to another!'

*

223

As though intent on relaxation, Corporal Singer went for a brief stroll through camp after the gala dinner in Frau Tauschmüller's honour. His route took him to the northernmost – and darkest – corner of the fence enclosing the women auxiliaries' compound. Waiting for him on the far side was the austerely uniformed figure of Melanie Mauerland.

'You wanted to speak to me, Herr Singer, or so you said on the phone. Why here and at this hour?'

'So we can have a chat – so I can explain a couple of things. We can't go to your room or borrow Frau Klarfeld's quarters, worse luck, not with this damn great fence between us, but I wouldn't take the liberty even if we could. Lieutenant Kersten might get the wrong idea.'

'Did he send you?'

'To play Cupid, you mean? No, if you're expecting chocolates or flowers, forget it. I'm here because I'm by way of being a friend of his.'

'Somehow, Herr Singer, I feel I can trust you.'

'Don't be too sure. Look at it this way: we've all got our own axe to grind, but there's just a chance we're working on the same one. I'm thinking of Erika Klarfeld. She obviously means a lot to you.'

'I treasure her friendship,' Melanie said fervently, 'but don't misunderstand me. Erika's a wonderful person – she treats me like a younger sister. I'm scared she might disapprove if she found out that some kind of – ' she struggled for the right word – 'affair was developing between me and Lieutenant Kersten.'

Singer chuckled in the darkness. 'You must be joking. Don't you really have any idea what your worthy boss gets up to in the small hours, over at the officers' mess?'

'She goes there on duty – she works late.'

'Sure, that's one way of putting it. The plain truth is, you poor sweet innocent lamb, she's having an affair with Captain Tauschmüller.'

'Never! That's quite impossible – not with him, he isn't worthy of her. Besides, he's a married man.'

It was all Singer could do not to burst out laughing. 'Good God, girl! Worthy or unworthy, married or single, stop kidding yourself.'

Melanie digested this for a moment or two. 'Was that why he sent Erika off for the day, so she wouldn't be here when his wife came?'

'Ah!' said Singer. 'Your brain's beginning to tick over at last, even though you're wrong about your lady-friend's excursion. That was fixed up long before Frau Tauschmüller decided to pay her surprise visit.'

Dimly, he saw her shake her head in bewilderment. 'It's all so terribly confusing,' she said.

'Unscramble the situation and you'll have a free hand.'

'But how?'

'It's now or never, Melanie. The captain's lawful wedded wife will be gone by tomorrow morning.' Singer explained his plan in detail, then paused. 'Well, is it a deal?'

Melanie nodded.

It was midnight, almost on the dot, when the car drove into camp and Frau Klarfeld turned to Private Baumgartner.

'Stop here, please.' She leered at Königsberger over her shoulder. 'I take it, Doctor, that you'd like to escort our interpreter to her quarters – as far as the gate, that is.'

The MO was taken aback. 'I can always do that later, Frau Klarfeld. What about you?'

'Never mind me, you look after Natasha. The driver will see me home.'

Königsberger and Natasha got out and said good night. Frau Klarfeld shook hands with them both, Natasha first. 'Well, Doctor,' she said with alcoholic bonhomie, 'thank you for an extremely enjoyable day. If you can't be good, be careful.'

They stared after the departing car. Königsberger

scratched his head. 'Well, well! Our *grande dame*'s becoming positively human these days.'

'Happy people are always generous,' said Natasha, 'and Frau Klarfeld seems unusually happy at the moment, I don't know why.'

'I do. Like me to tell you, or are you too tired?'

'More overexcited than tired.'

'So am I, for some reason. Shall we smoke a last cigarette?'

She smiled at him ruefully. 'Where? Nobody's allowed to stand around in the middle of camp after midnight. You can't come to my quarters and I can't come to yours. As for the brothel, I wouldn't go there even with you, Doctor.'

The atmosphere between them had become charged with a kind of devil-may-care gaiety which showed no signs of flagging.

'There is another possibility, Natasha: my office at the medical centre – I have to go there anyway, to check up. Anything could have happened while we've been out, and I may need your services as an interpreter. Would you mind coming along?'

She accompanied him readily – gladly. She also let him slip his arm through hers, though not as yet around her waist.

Frau Klarfeld reached her quarters looking slightly cock-eyed but far from jaded, let alone exhausted.

'Erika! There you are at last!'

She was relieved to note that Melanie Mauerland, who had been waiting for her, sounded curious rather than reproachful. 'You waited up for me? You really shouldn't have.' She sat down at her dressing-table, with its serried rows of pots and jars, and studied her reflection in the triptych mirror. 'Why did you bother, my dear?'

'Because I've got a message for you, Erika. I think you can guess who from.'

She could indeed – it had to be Hermann Tauschmüller. 'I see. Well, go on.'

'He wants to see you.'

'At this time of night?'

'It doesn't matter how late. He'll expect you when he sees you – it's urgent.'

'Did he say that?' Frau Klarfeld's eyes had begun to dance.

'He sent a message to that effect. Corporal Singer passed it on by phone.' Melanie reflected that she would be able to qualify this next day: she'd thought it was Singer's voice, but she couldn't swear to it. 'Anyway, Erika, he's expecting you. Any time.'

'How nice.' Frau Klarfeld drew a deep breath, got undressed and disappeared into the bathroom. She re-emerged a few minutes later, naked but unashamed. 'Be a darling and comb my hair for me – comb it back really hard and pin it up tight. A severe hairstyle tends to look forbidding, but it can also hint at something altogether different. You ought to bear that little tip in mind, my dear.'

Frau Klarfeld massaged some fragrant face cream into her cheeks while Melanie combed away, then dabbed the inside of her ear-lobes with a drop or two of French perfume. She rose and swathed herself in a pink bathrobe. Finally, to keep the chill night air at bay, she donned a heavy Bavarian cloak in hunting green.

'My God,' she confided, 'how happy I am!'

'I'm glad for you,' Melanie assured her, 'but I only hope you aren't making a mistake.'

It was nearly 1 a.m. by the time Erika Klarfeld made her way to the officers' mess, recognized and saluted by all the sentries she passed.

Once there, she padded down the long corridor that led to the officers' private quarters. The route was so familiar that darkness presented no problems. Quietly opening the door of Captain Tauschmüller's room, which was also in darkness, she tiptoed inside and closed it behind her. Then she threw off her cloak, slipped out of her bathrobe, and dived into bed with a glad cry.

'Here I am at last, beloved!'

Abruptly wrested from the land of sweet dreams, Captain Tauschmüller gave a yelp of consternation and sat up. On his other flank, a second stark-naked female did likewise and switched on the bedside lamp.

'Who are you? What are you doing here?' Frau Tauschmüller glared irately at Erika Klarfeld's inviting tracts of unclothed flesh. 'You – you unutterable bitch!'

'A mistake!' her husband wailed. 'There's been some mistake, my love!'

Frau Klarfeld, too, was beside herself with rage. She pointed at the plump, bare-breasted female in bed with her Hermann like an archangel banishing a sinner from paradise. 'What's *she* doing here?' she demanded.

At this juncture, instinctively taking refuge in social conventions, the captain sprang a surprise performance of his own. 'Ladies, permit me to introduce you. Countess von Klarfeld, my wife. My dear, meet Countess von Klarfeld.'

'So that's who you are,' said Frau Tauschmüller, mindful of her dignity even under present circumstances. 'And now that *you* know who *I* am, madam, I trust you'll acknowledge my right to be here. Perhaps you'll also be good enough to explain what prompted you to enter my husband's quarters in a state of undress.'

Erika Klarfeld shot a look of inquiry at her lover, who reacted swiftly. 'As I already said, my dear, there's been a mistake, nothing more. I'm sure the countess will confirm that – won't you, Countess?'

Erika just stared at him, first in disbelief, then with

boundless contempt. 'Very well,' she said, 'that's what it was: a mistake, nothing more.'

Without wasting another glance on the two naked Tauschmüllers, she swept up her clothes from the floor and strode majestically out, not forgetting to slam the door behind her.

'You see?' Tauschmüller told his wife, when the echoes of her vigorous exit had died away. 'There's nothing to it. Pure coincidence, that's all. You really must have a little faith in me, my dear.'

'Faith, Hermann, after *that* scene?' Frau Tauschmüller looked sourly sceptical. 'Absolute candour would be more to the point, and that's what I'm waiting for now.'

'Of course, dearest. Allow me to explain – '

'Absolute candour, I said, and I insist on it. Unless you make a clean breast of things, I shall be forced to ask the Colonel to investigate this affair in the morning.'

'But in the meantime – '

'In the meantime I think it better that you leave this bed at once. You may take your underclothes and a blanket and spend the rest of the night in the bath. Until the air has been cleared to my complete satisfaction, I refuse to exchange another word with you.'

7

For once, Colonel von Feuerfresser had expressed a desire to breakfast with the members of his staff. The gala dinner of the night before had precluded their usual discussion of current business. To remedy this omission, they were instructed to parade at seven-thirty sharp.

Majors Kastor and Pollandt appeared first, carrying paper-laden clipboards. Then came Lieutenants Wagner and Lahrmann, who seemed highly amused by something unbeknown to the mess at large. Frau Klarfeld, whose attendance had not been requested, was missing. The MO, whose presence was equally superfluous, turned up anyway. Kersten, too, was there on time.

Captain Tauschmüller put in a wholly unexpected appearance on the stroke of seven-thirty. This caused something of a stir because he had been given leave to enjoy a conjugal breakfast in his quarters. With a curt but comradely nod and an earnestly official expression, the adjutant strode to his accustomed place.

Colonel von Feuerfresser saved him from having to answer any embarrassing questions by appearing precisely sixty seconds after the appointed hour – his usual practice. Priewitt opened the door for him and his officers came to attention behind their chairs.

The gloves in Feuerfresser's hand flapped as he raised his right arm in a travesty of the Hitler salute. Then he sat down. While the others were following suit, he turned to Captain Tauschmüller.

'You here, my dear fellow?' he said amiably.

Tauschmüller bowed his head in solemn resignation. 'I thought it advisable, Colonel.'

Feuerfresser sensed at once that he was in for some unwelcome news. His steely gaze belied the smile that continued to hover on his lips. 'I thought I had given express instructions that you and your wife were to be served breakfast in your quarters.'

'Yes indeed, Colonel, and I couldn't be more grateful. However, something has occurred in the interim – something of a rather delicate nature.'

The Colonel reacted like lightning. He turned to Priewitt. 'All enlisted men are to leave the room at once.'

As soon as the room had been cleared, he readdressed himself to Tauschmüller. 'You are not, I take it, requesting a private interview? That would scarcely be appropriate. In the first place, I have no secrets from my officers. Secondly, I know from experience that embarrassing incidents soon become common knowledge in any case. Let us try to resolve the matter as quickly as possible.'

Tauschmüller gulped and took the plunge.

'Last night, Colonel, when I and my wife were asleep in bed, Frau Klarfeld entered my quarters in a state of – er, undress. It was an unforeseen, embarrassing and regrettable occurrence. Although I disclaim all responsibility for it, my wife insists on a thorough investigation.'

'I see.' Feuerfresser surveyed the rest of the table. 'We are obviously dealing with a personal entanglement of some kind. Although it has no direct bearing on official matters, it could detract from the good name of my staff. I therefore want it promptly, thoroughly and resolutely investigated. In the interests of our unblemished reputation, gentlemen, I expect you to produce some concrete and conclusive results. I shall give you plenty of time to do this – an hour, let's say. We'll discuss the matter again at zero nine hundred.'

*

Lieutenant Kersten had been dismissed half-way through the above conference. After hurriedly consulting his fellow major and obtaining the Colonel's consent, Kastor had sent him off to supervise the trainees.

'Keep 'em busy,' Kersten was told. 'Physical jerks are the thing – the more exercise you give 'em the better.'

'Certainly, Major,' said Kersten. Before quitting the table, however, he calmly buttered two pieces of bread, covered them with a thick layer of sliced sausage, folded them into sandwiches, and wrapped them up in a napkin. The others watched him askance with a mixture of revulsion and fascination, but he ignored them.

The NCO instructors – three sergeants and seven corporals – were drawn up on the sports field with their charges. Kersten addressed them briskly.

'Right, I want Groups A and B kept busy – major's orders. Chivvy them round the assault course till they don't know whether it's Christmas or Easter. Group C will report to Master-Sergeant Heinz at the coconut shy.'

He briefly watched the antics of the first two groups before joining the third. Heinz was awaiting him with an air of conspiratorial glee. Kersten, who set no store by 'present-and-correct-sir's' or heel-clicking formality, slapped him on the back and turned to face the thirty members of Group C.

'Morning, all!' he called.

'Morning, Lieutenant!' they replied in unison.

Kersten pointed to the mysterious ring of sandbags. 'Familiarize yourselves with that thing and the area round it. You've got fifteen minutes.'

While his men were dutifully exploring the terrain, Kersten motioned to Heinz to sit down on a stack of hurdles and perched beside him. He opened his napkin-covered bundle.

'Here, help yourself.'

Heinz took a sandwich, beaming gratefully, and sank his teeth in it.

'All set?'

The master-sergeant, with both cheeks bulging, merely nodded.

'Fine. Let's see how long it takes before one of them shits himself.'

Precisely fifteen minutes later, Kersten gathered his flock around him again. 'Well, any idea what we're going to do now?' Everyone looked mystified. 'No? Then I'll show you.'

Kersten clicked his fingers and Heinz passed him a practice grenade. After tossing it playfully from hand to hand, he suddenly pulled the pin, waited a full two seconds, and lobbed it into the ring of sandbags from a distance of ten yards. It landed plumb centre and went off with a sound like a toy popgun.

'That was kids' stuff,' said Kersten. He winked at Heinz, who grinned back. The trainees were looking more mystified than ever. 'Now we'll do the whole thing again, but properly this time.'

The master-sergeant handed him a live grenade. The sequence of events was identical: Kersten pulled the pin, waited a couple of seconds, and lobbed his missile into the topless beehive, where it exploded with a muffled but incisive report. Splinters ripped into the surrounding sandbags.

Some of the trainees had ducked or looked around for cover – two, in fact, had flung themselves into foxholes – but the majority felt duty-bound to emulate Kersten. Like Heinz, he had remained erect and unflinching.

'Get the idea?' said Kersten. 'Usually, grenade-throwing is practised from trenches or foxholes, but that's plain stupid. Our way's the right way. We're going to stand round the target in a circle and aim at the button – and no edging away, is that clear?'

233

'Yes, Lieutenant!' came the still unwitting chorus.

'We'll start at six or seven yards and increase the range progressively. Of course, some grenades may fail to land inside the protective screen – they may hit the lip, or fall short, or go right over the top. What then?'

Yes, thought Group C, what then?

'Then,' Kersten told them with relish, ' – then it'll be a matter of split seconds. You'll have to move like greased lightning – but only then, mind you. I've fixed you up with plenty of cover. Right, let's get started. Practice makes perfect.'

Sergeant-Major Schulz, whose natural curiosity was compounded with mistrust of the new lieutenant who treated him like dirt, soon turned up to watch the proceedings. He did so with growing apprehension. 'Jesus,' he muttered, 'this isn't grenade-throwing practice – the man's training himself a suicide squad. Just wait till the Colonel hears!'

CURRICULUM VITAE OF PAUL SCHULZ
or, The Will to Succeed

I was born on Christmas Eve, 1914, at Hohenstein in East Prussia. My father was a fisherman. My mother and my four elder brothers all worked with him.

Drudgery and deprivation were the salient features of Paul's boyhood. Being the youngest and smallest member of the family circle, he invariably acted as a sort of valet to his father and the four elder brothers whose cast-off clothing he wore. He had to clean their boots, make beds, wash dishes and swill out chamber-pots. Betweentimes, he went to school, where he soon proved good at figures and made a favourable impression in Bible class.

On reaching the age of ten, however, Paul had to play a far more active part in the family team than before. He

234

learned to mend nets, gather wood for the smokehouse and get boats ready for sea. Sometimes he was allowed to accompany his mother to market when she went there to sell the family's output of golden-yellow, kippered fish. Paul not only enjoyed these jaunts but became a skilful salesman. His mother had a soft spot for her 'little one', as she continued to call him for the rest of her life, and slipped him an occasional malt or honey candy.

Paul realized, even as a schoolboy, that the family trade didn't pay. They all toiled day and night, yet they barely earned enough to make ends meet, even if his mother did own a Sunday dress, his father a dark serge suit, and his brothers a pair of shirts apiece. Paul himself had six, but they were all hand-me-downs. He broached the subject of their poverty at supper one night.

'We work like blacks,' he said, 'but we never get anywhere. It doesn't make sense.'

'Use your mouth for eating,' snapped his father. 'The rest of the time, keep it shut!'

In 1925, when Paul was through with elementary school, the headmaster called on his parents. 'That's a really bright lad of yours,' he told them. 'You've kept him away from school far more often than police regulations allow. Even so, he's got an excellent grasp of German, written as well as spoken, and he's outstandingly good at mathematics. You ought to put him in for a commercial apprenticeship.'

'Headmaster,' Herr Schulz replied with dignity, 'my father was a fisherman like his father before him. My sons are fishermen too, and that's the way it's going to stay.'

But Paul had no intention of remaining an impoverished fisherman all his life. He started to jib at the prospect and argue his case.

'Look,' he said, 'here we are, slaving away for twelve or more hours a day, when any normal person knocks off after eight hours of far lighter work and stretches his legs, or lifts his elbow, or goes to bed – never mind who with.'

'Shut your trap,' roared his irate father, 'or I'll shut it for you!' But Paul was too big to whop by now, so Herr Schulz decided to turn a deaf ear in future. The ears that *did* begin to absorb Paul's propaganda, albeit slowly and laboriously, were those of his elder brothers.

'He'll spoil our other lads,' his father told his mother in bed one night, 'he'll turn their heads.'

'Paul wants to make his way in life,' she pleaded. 'Why not let him go?'

'As far as I'm concerned,' he retorted, 'he can go to the devil!'

At the end of 1932 I applied to join the Reichswehr – the Republican Army, as it then was. On 1 April 1933, after passing several physicals and intelligence tests, I signed on for twelve years. I did my primary training at Königsberg, with the 1st Infantry Regiment.

Paul Schulz quickly made his mark as a willing, efficient and adaptable soldier. The word 'reliable' cropped up in his very first assessment. Whatever he was ordered to do, he did. In short, his superiors found him a very congenial subordinate to work with.

This paid off. In 1934 Paul was promoted corporal and appointed a junior NCO instructor. Having so far been bullied, he now became a licensed bully himself. Now it was he who ordered recruits to crawl through mud, empty latrine buckets, bellow marching songs and clean his boots. 'You can always depend on Schulz,' was his superiors' unanimous verdict. By 1935 he was a sergeant.

It was only now that Paul Schulz began to enjoy his weekend passes, which usually ran from midday Saturday to midnight Sunday. He frequented several hostelries in Königsberg with a gang of cronies, sank vast quantities of beer, devoured huge helpings of jellied meat and fried potatoes, and disported himself in suburban dance halls patronized by army personnel. As soon as a fracas developed, for instance between the infantry and the artillery, he ingeniously fanned the flames until the two sides came to blows. Then he made a rapid and unobtrusive exit.

His love-life was not especially active. To the extent that it was, he adopted what he saw as a robust and manly approach: quick off the mark and as quick to subside. Gretel he 'banged' up against a war memorial; Paula he 'screwed' in the back yard of a dance hall; Hilde he 'poked' in a darkened doorway – after all, he had more important things than sex on his mind. In 1936 he was promoted staff sergeant, in 1937 master-sergeant. He was steadily approaching his goal.

Soon after this latest promotion, a sergeant-major's post fell vacant in his battalion. Paul Schulz swotted hard for the written examination and passed it with high marks.

In 1938 I was promoted sergeant-major. That made me probably the youngest man in the Army to wear the two silver cuff bands. Being a good shot, I was also entitled to a plaited silver marksman's lanyard draped across my chest. The company I took over was No. 3 Company, 1st Infantry Regiment – in other words, the outfit I was already serving with.

Paul Schulz had now gone as far as he had always hoped to go. He tended and supervised his men like two dozen sheepdogs rolled into one. He turned up in unexpected places, was a stickler for detail, and took drastic steps to deal with shirkers, whose tricks he knew inside out.

Most important of all, perhaps, he came to recognize the incompetence of certain officers. In his own company, for example, two lieutenants were supposedly responsible for combat training. In practice, they limited themselves to a supervisory role and left their senior NCOs to do the real work. If the latter were uncertain about anything, they consulted Schulz; if they had a report to make, they made it via him.

Sergeant-Major Paul Schulz was also quick to discover that his first company commander, like most of his subsequent ones, had little knowledge of service regulations or disciplinary procedure and no gift at all for official correspondence. This company commander was a captain named Federlein – a human clothes-horse with the friendly condescension of an oriental potentate. Federlein far preferred sipping hock in the officers' mess to watching the evolutions of his men on the parade ground. He was also blessed with excellent connections from which his sergeant-major was one day destined to benefit.

'No matter what crops up, my dear Schulz,' he used to say, 'you always seem to cope with it. I know I can depend on you all the way.' And he could. Schulz coped with absolutely everything. He drew up duty rosters at his own discretion, recommended punishments and leave passes, engineered promotions and transfers. No. 3 Company was *his* company.

Before long, Captain Federlein was promoted major and appointed to command a battalion on the grounds that he had run his company in an exemplary manner and made it by far the most efficient in the regiment. Federlein did not forget Schulz while celebrating his promotion in the mess. Via an orderly, he sent him a bottle of choice Moselle whose label bore the inscription: 'In grateful appreciation of all your efforts.'

Spring 1939 saw the approach of the next world war, for which timely preparations had been made by conscientious German staff officers working on their Führer's instructions. Within months, the Army trebled, then quadrupled its strength. Companies blossomed into battalions and battalions into regiments, greatly increasing the demand for sergeant-majors. Schulz realized that men of influence like himself were threatened with a disastrous bout of inflation.

He decided to look up 'his' Major Federlein – 'his' in the sense that Schulz had made him what he was – and voice his concern. Federlein not only greeted him with un-diminished warmth but gave him a very sympathetic hearing.

'My dear Schulz, a talented organizer like you could get a commission on his head – I'd root for you hard, believe me. You don't fancy becoming an officer? Very well, you must have your reasons. The essential thing, in that case, is to get you transferred to a job that matches up to your special qualifications. Leave it to me.'

In August 1939 I was posted to the Military Academy at Wiesbaden, as sergeant-major of the HQ Company there. The commandant was Colonel, later General, von Brandeisen, who left his bones in Russia. I stayed with the Academy for nearly three years, during which my rank and appointment remained unchanged.

After his first six months at Wiesbaden, Schulz was sent for by Colonel von Brandeisen, a rugged old war-horse with a stentorian voice and a wry sense of humour.

'You were recommended to me by Major Federlein, Sergeant-Major. Know who he is? He's my son-in-law. He may be a tailor's dummy, but at least he's got good taste – must have, or he wouldn't have married that filly of mine. He also seems to be a fair judge of character. You're the living proof of that. You're a good man, Schulz – a damned good man. Keep it up.'

Schulz didn't always find it easy, not in a military hothouse where ambition ran riot and hordes of officer cadets were all intent on gaining commissions. Hundreds of them were put through the wringer every year – three four-monthly intakes divided into twelve batches of approximately company strength and supervised by officer instructors, all of whom, in turn, were rivals for official commendation.

The trainees' general and physical welfare was catered for by HQ Company under Sergeant-Major Schulz, whose qualities of leadership became steadily more apparent. Thanks to his administrative efficiency, the officer cadets were adequately nourished, well clothed, and housed in relative comfort. One commandant succeeded another – Colonel von Brandeisen handed over to a Colonel Bauer, who was relieved by a Colonel Andersen – but Schulz stayed put, seemingly determined to outlast all comers. Once, after he had juggled the duty rosters with more than usual success, it was again suggested to him that he could become an officer any time he chose. Politely and with every outward sign of humility, Paul Schulz declined once more.

'No need for that, Colonel. I feel quite at home where I am.'

Early in 1942, however, a staff lieutenant-colonel named Schlumberger paid the Academy an extended visit. Although his manner could not have been more urbane, Schulz identified him as a tenacious and persevering sleuth-hound. For the first time in years, he felt a pang of alarm.

Then, one evening, Schlumberger asked Schulz to join him for a stroll round the parade ground.

'Your name was recently brought to my attention by a brother officer of mine, Sergeant-Major – your former company commander, Colonel Federlein. Remember him?'

Schulz pricked up his ears. 'Of course, sir.'

'In his opinion, you're an extremely able and versatile man. I now endorse that opinion. I could find you a job in a special unit we're forming, with the same rank and function but considerably greater influence. As of now.'

Which was how Paul Schulz came to join AFSIC

Kampfental and take on yet another professional challenge.

As soon as Feuerfresser had left the mess, his officers debated the problem confronting them.

'One thing seems certain,' began Major Kastor, the intellectual. 'The Colonel expects us to produce an explanation of what happened last night, and it'll have to be convincing enough to dispose of the matter permanently.'

'But first,' said Major Pollandt, the man of action, 'we should make something absolutely clear: Captain Tauschmüller, to whom we all owe so much, can count on our full and unqualified support. Whatever we can do for him will be done.'

'Hear, hear!' said Lieutenant Lahrmann, who was quickly seconded by Lieutenant Wagner. The others echoed this sentiment, and even Captain Königsberger was heard to murmur sympathetically.

Captain Tauschmüller looked round the table, moist-eyed. 'Thank you, gentlemen,' he said, 'thank you all.'

'However,' said Major Kastor, reverting to the point at issue, 'what form would such an explanation take? Any ideas on the subject, Captain Tauschmüller?'

'I'm hardly in a position to answer that, Major. It all happened so suddenly – so unexpectedly. As to the underlying reasons, I couldn't even hazard a guess. Perhaps you should ask my wife or Frau Klarfeld.'

'In view of the Colonel's obvious desire to set her mind at rest,' Pollandt said quickly, 'I think it would be wiser to leave your wife out of this. On the other hand, a really effective reconnaissance of the terrain – as we tacticians say – might render it appropriate for someone to have a discreet word with Frau Klarfeld.'

Kastor cleared his throat. 'I will, if necessary.' Armed with the consent of all present, he rose and departed for the women auxiliaries' compound.

Conversation waned in his absence because nobody wanted to commit himself too soon. The officers silently sipped their tea or coffee until, some fifteen minutes later, Major Kastor returned.

'I asked the lady if she'd care to comment,' he reported, 'but she declines to do so. She considers it beneath her dignity, she says.'

'That's bad,' was the almost unanimous verdict, but Kastor firmly contested this. 'I take the opposite view, gentlemen. If Frau Klarfeld remains silent, for whatever reason, it may be her way of leaving us free to settle the matter as we see fit.'

'A wonderful woman,' Lahrmann said fervently. The others looked equally admiring, even Königsberger, who now made his first major contribution to the debate.

'As I see it,' he said, 'this whole ridiculous business must be due to a straightforward error of some kind – an understandable mix-up for which some simple explanation exists. To put it baldly, Frau Klarfeld mistook one door for another.'

Captain Tauschmüller heaved a sigh of relief. 'Much the same idea had already occurred to me. If you're right, our troubles are over.'

'Not quite,' said Kastor. 'Not unless we can point to the lady's intended destination.'

'I'd be prepared to shoulder that burden of suspicion,' Königsberger said obligingly. 'I'd volunteer my services without a second thought.'

'Thank you!' Tauschmüller's voice was husky with emotion. 'Thank you, Doctor.'

'Then that's the way it was,' Lahrmann exclaimed. 'We owe it to the adjutant and Frau Klarfeld to clear them of this imputation. Solidarity is our national watchword – "each for the other and all for Germany," as our beloved Führer so aptly puts it.'

'Bravo!' Königsberger applauded vigorously. 'As I said

just now, I'd be only too happy to volunteer my services for friendship's sake. In this particular case, though, I'm afraid I can't.' He paused to savour the stunned silence that greeted this volte-face. 'Unfortunately, my quarters are some distance from the adjutant's, so the mix-up theory wouldn't hold water. In my view, only the room next door would fill the bill.'

It was obvious whose room he meant. All eyes swivelled in Lahrmann's direction.

'However,' the MO went on, 'I'm not sure it would be fair to foist such a thing on the logical candidate, in spite of his proven capacity for self-sacrifice.'

'What do you mean, "foist" it on him?' Wagner protested. 'It would be an act of chivalry and comradeship, performed for the sake of communal harmony. Personally, I'd consider it an honour.' This gave him the cue for one of his tags. '*Cui honorem, honorem.*'

'Which is a Roman proverb,' Königsberger said sarcastically, 'meaning "Honour be to him who deserves it."'

Robbed of his punchline, Wagner glared angrily at the MO. The majors said nothing, which was a tribute to their age and experience, but Tauschmüller couldn't contain himself.

'My dear Lahrmann,' he said, 'it would be unseemly of me to recommend such a course, but I'd be eternally grateful . . .' His voice trailed away.

Lieutenant Lahrmann's dignified bearing was almost worthy of Feuerfresser himself. 'Once I have assumed a responsibility, Captain, I never shirk it. That's the way I'm made.'

It was indeed. Lahrmann's brother officers gathered round and pumped his hand appreciatively. Not for the first time, all at AFSIC seemed to be back on an even keel.

While the officers were still in conference, Kersten's

coconut shy claimed its first casualty – a fatal one.

'Hell and damnation!' Kersten bellowed. 'What are you, a bunch of deadbeats, or what?'

In the middle of grenade-throwing practice, one of Kersten's budding heroes – a sergeant named Grimm, though his identity was immaterial – had allowed his mind to wander. A fellow trainee missed the sandbags by a mile and lobbed his grenade into a foxhole, whereupon Grimm was stupid or inattentive enough to dive in after it.

Kersten was unperturbed. 'The man wasn't up to scratch. Haul him out of the way and sling a tarpaulin over him, then carry on.'

When their allotted time was up, Colonel von Feuerfresser rejoined his officers in the mess dining-room.

'Well, gentlemen, what are your findings? I'm listening.'

Major Pollandt, who evidently felt called on to act as spokesman for the rest, clicked his heels. 'Though delicate, Colonel, this affair has turned out to be less of a problem than we feared. It all stems from an elementary mistake – a comedy of errors, one might say.'

Feuerfresser brightened. 'Really?'

'Yes, Colonel. The person responsible has been identified. To be more exact, he has owned up like a true man, voluntarily and with laudable frankness. The said person admits to having had an assignation with Frau Klarfeld, who then mistook his door – understandably, in view of the prevailing darkness and the fact that he occupies the room immediately adjacent to that of Captain Tauschmüller – '

'Yes, yes,' Feuerfresser broke in. 'Who was it?'

'Colonel,' said Lieutenant Lahrmann, 'I admit to being the person concerned.'

'You mean it?'

'Absolutely, Colonel.'

'Good,' said Feuerfresser, 'that sounds convincing enough. I don't, of course, approve of such goings-on, but anyone under my command may take it for granted that I sympathize with those whose emotions get the better of them. In return, I expect them to be ready at all times to accept the consequences of their behaviour.'

He inserted a well-gauged pause for effect and scanned the room. Lahrmann was sitting there pouter-chested with pride, rejoicing in the sensation that he had become the hero of the hour. Tauschmüller was registering boundless relief and Wagner nodding approval. Kastor, Pollandt and Königsberger were looking thoughtful.

Feuerfresser smiled, confident that they had all taken his point. After expressing his appreciation of their efforts, he turned to Tauschmüller, who was obviously finding it hard to collect his wits now that the danger had passed.

'Kindly bring your lady wife to see me in my office at midday, Captain. Once her doubts have been dispelled by an explanatory chat, I trust she'll join us for lunch before she leaves.'

Melanie eyed Frau Klarfeld fearfully. 'You aren't angry with me, are you?'

Frau Klarfeld shrugged. 'No, not angry. I suppose I should be grateful to you for opening my eyes. I needed it, but the way it happened was too shocking for words. That's why I'm so sad that you – you, of all people – should have conspired against me.'

'Please, Erika – '

'I'm not reproaching you, Melanie. Thanks to you, I've been brought face to face with the truth. I'd never have known it otherwise.'

'The truth about what, Erika?'

'Two people in my life. I loved that man and he claimed to return my love, but he didn't have the courage to confess it when it came to the pinch. As for you, Melanie, I was mistaken enough to believe in your utter devotion. Why did you get mixed up in this unsavoury little plot?'

'Perhaps because I'm in love myself.'

'Fiddlesticks, girl! You don't know the meaning of the word.'

'Yes, I do – I'm in love with Konstantin Kersten, but we never get a chance to be alone together. That's why we need your help.'

Frau Klarfeld froze at this surprise announcement, then swiftly recovered herself. 'Send the MO to me,' she said resolutely. 'I mean to get to the bottom of this business – and you can put Lieutenant Kersten out of your pretty little head. He isn't worthy of you.'

Colonel von Feuerfresser motioned the Tauschmüllers into some heavy leather armchairs near his office window and sat down himself.

'Dear lady,' he said, addressing himself exclusively to Frau Tauschmüller, 'so glad you could come. I thought you might be interested to see my quarters – the paintings are said to possess some merit. I also welcome this chance of an informal chat.'

'Good of you to invite me, Colonel.' Frau Tauschmüller sounded faintly ill at ease.

Feuerfresser studied his nails for a moment, then looked up. 'My dear Frau Tauschmüller, would I be safe in assuming that you trust me?'

'But of course, Colonel, that goes without saying.'

'Delighted to hear it.'

He smiled at her and she smiled back. They might have been alone in the room. Tauschmüller humbly accepted his non-speaking role in the knowledge that everything his Colonel said and did was the product of careful fore-thought.

'It has come to my ears,' Feuerfresser went on, 'that an extremely embarrassing incident occurred here last night. Since absolutely nothing in my sphere of command escapes me, I was duly informed of it. Being naturally disinclined to let matters rest, I appointed a board of inquiry. Would its findings be of interest to you?'

'They certainly would, Colonel.'

'Then I can tell you, madam, that these nocturnal happenings were the result of a misapprehension. Frau Klarfeld had no thought of visiting your husband, she merely mistook one door for another. It has been established beyond doubt that her intention was to visit Lieutenant Lahrmann, whose quarters are situated next door.'

'You say you have proof of this?'

Viktor von Feuerfresser drew himself up. 'When I offer someone a personal assurance, madam, I do not expect it to be doubted.'

'No,' she said, flinching, 'of course not.'

'In that case, dear lady, it gladdens my heart to have succeeded in persuading you of your husband's innocence. May I now request the honour of your company at luncheon?'

In high delight, Frau Tauschmüller seized her husband's hand with a conciliatory flourish. Tauschmüller himself gazed gratefully at his commanding officer, who nodded benignly at the reunited couple.

Situation Report No. 7

Unswerving devotion to Führer and Fatherland – that was the watchword in times like these. Even though the German frontiers were under threat, even though German forces had been driven out of the Balkans and Finland had signed an armistice with the Soviet Union, even though Italy was a write-off and the French Resistance a growing thorn in the Germans' side, the really decisive turning-point in the war – it was claimed – had yet to come. No German could be allowed to have died in vain.

Even at this stage, artists felt impelled to continue working, presumably in the hope and belief that their world was indestructible. While millions were dying around them, they wrote, composed, and painted. Most of their works disappeared into limbo.

Meanwhile, spurred on by their national governments, scientists were also toiling day and night. The British succeeded in building jet engines capable of powering aircraft with an operational range of five hundred miles. The Germans sent their V2 rockets soaring to a height of over a hundred miles and brought them down on London with greater accuracy than ever before.

In one of America's deserts, scientists of various nations – many German expatriates among them – began to grasp the potential of the bomb they were assembling: a weapon that could obliterate whole cities and kill a hundred thousand people at a stroke. Some of these 'fathers of the atom bomb' were initially reluctant to bring such a weapon into operation, but they bowed before those who argued that the need to end the horrors of the present war left them no choice.

What even these people could not guess at, and what remained almost incomprehensible decades later, was a gruesome process which, though not dependent on large-scale military operations, killed human beings by the million. The decision to embark on this terrible venture was taken by a handful of men and prompted by 'conviction'.

Never in recorded history has there been a deed so monstrous and atrocious as the settlement of the Jewish question by means of what was termed the Final Solution.

It was a scheme devised and put into effect by Germans.

Conscientious officer that he was, Lieutenant Kersten took advantage of the Tauschmüllers' audience with Feuerfresser to pay a quick visit to his trainees. He was waylaid by Sergeant-Major Schulz, who had obviously been waiting to intercept him.

'Someone's just bought it, Lieutenant – one of yours.'

'Impossible! Nobody gets killed round here.'

'They do with Lieutenant Kersten in charge.'

As soon as Schulz had briefed him on the bare bones of the incident, Lahrmann hurried off to inform Majors Kastor and Pollandt. Predictably shocked and outraged, they sent for Kersten, who came at once. His Hitler salute was agreeably off-hand, but that was the only agreeable feature of the interview.

'It is really true, Kersten,' Kastor demanded, 'that while practising with live grenades – '

'Sure,' Kersten said tersely. 'You can't make an omelette without breaking eggs.'

'But you don't have to kill people in the process.'

'There's a war on, Major. War's a lethal business.'

'You'll have to answer for this, Kersten.'

Kersten shrugged. 'Naturally.'

'To the Colonel, I mean.'

'Why not? He's a fighting man – he'll understand.'

'And if he doesn't?'

'Then he doesn't know anything about the latest combat-training techniques – but that I can't believe.'

Every member of Feuerfresser's staff was present at the lunch he had ordered. Kersten, who seemed wholly indifferent to the interest that centred on his person, could hardly wait for the first course to arrive.

'An army marches on its stomach,' he said loudly. 'Mine needs a re-tread right now.'

The MO apologized for Frau Klarfeld's absence. 'A temporary indisposition,' he explained, 'a touch of flu, actually. She asked me to make her excuses.'

'Send the lady some flowers,' Feuerfresser magnanimously decreed, 'on my behalf. But first, the soup.'

Priewitt bore in a tureen of mushroom soup, heavily blended with cream, and Singer ladled it out. Everyone wielded their spoons in reverent silence. Mess Sergeant

Gerner rewarded his senior chef with the sort of congratulatory nod that sometimes exempted its recipient from the next field training session. During the main course, an equally delectable offering of braised wild duck with red cabbage and dumplings, Colonel von Feuerfresser fixed Lahrmann with a stern but sympathetic gaze and addressed him in fatherly tones.

'Congratulations, Lieutenant. I was delighted to learn of your courageous decision to make a clean breast of things. It was the act of an officer and a gentleman.'

'Thank you, Colonel.' Lahrmann's radiant expression betrayed his total unawareness of what lay in store.

'I'd have expected no less of you, just as I know you're never a man to do things by halves. Am I right?'

'Absolutely, Colonel.'

'Your attitude confirms my existing impression, which is that your relations with Frau Klarfeld are of the closest and most intimate nature. Is that correct?'

'If you say so, Colonel, they must be.'

'I therefore conclude,' Feuerfresser went on, 'that you and Frau Klarfeld are as good as engaged. If so, I expect you to take the appropriate action.'

Even Lahrmann knew what that implied: formal betrothal, if not impending matrimony. He was deeply affected by the prospect but far from downcast, having long been an admirer of the lady in question. To him, she seemed the epitome of ultra-German womanhood.

'Of course, Colonel,' he said, 'but I can't help wondering how Frau Klarfeld will view the matter.'

Feuerfresser made a dismissive gesture. 'That's up to you. In view of your past achievements in other fields of endeavour, I'm sure you'll clear any remaining hurdles with ease. Your brother officers will give you all the help and advice you need – isn't that right, Captain Tauschmüller?'

'We certainly will, Colonel.' Tauschmüller looked

round the table, quite unabashed. 'Won't we, gentlemen?'

They nodded, almost to a man. Lieutenant Kersten gave vent to some muttered remarks, but they were inaudible to all save the MO, who was sitting beside him. 'Good God,' Königsberger heard him growl through a mouthful of duck, 'what a dump! Dip your wick a couple of times and you're sentenced to life.'

Feuerfresser looked up sharply. 'You said something, Kersten?'

Kersten was still chewing hard, as luck would have it, so Königsberger answered for him. 'The Lieutenant isn't fully acquainted with the facts of the case.'

'That's one way of putting it,' said Kersten.

Everyone frowned at him – everyone except the Colonel, whose eyes twinkled indulgently. 'My boy,' he said, 'you still have a lot to learn, but never mind – I'll gladly take you in hand. There's an old trainer's motto: "Never hurry a young horse." You follow my meaning?'

'I'm trying to, Colonel.'

'How are you feeling?' asked the MO. 'Any better?'

'Neither better nor worse.' Erika Klarfeld's tone was ominously aloof. She was sitting in an armchair near the window of her private sitting-room and seemed to have been dipping into a book. Picking it up, Königsberger saw that it was the second volume of Bismarck's political memoirs.

'What an unusual choice of reading matter,' he said. 'Don't tell me you're making a comparative study of the Iron Chancellor and his present successor in office?'

She made no comment, just stared at him coldly. 'What do you want?'

'Melanie told me you might appreciate a visit, so here I am. Speaking in a professional capacity, I'm bound to say you're looking slightly under par. I've brought you something from the dispensary. Quite apart from that, it's always a pleasure to talk to you.'

'What topic do you propose to discuss this time, Doctor?'

He pulled up a chair and sat down close beside her, then felt her pulse. 'Fast and irregular,' he commented.

'Can you wonder? You may think you know how I feel, Doctor, but you don't – nobody does! The last thing I want is another emotional trauma.'

'And you think I've got one up my sleeve? Any idea what it could be?'

'Whatever it is, you'll inflict it on me. I presume that's why you're here.'

Königsberger came straight to the point. 'Did you know that Lieutenant Lahrmann has been requested to make you a proposal of marriage?'

To his surprise, Frau Klarfeld failed to inquire the source of the request. 'Not that too!' she said scornfully. 'So he'd even stoop to that, great and noble soul that he is! He never forgets a grudge, not when something touches him personally – not when it affects what he calls his sense of honour. Anyone who offends him, deliberately or inadvertently, has made an enemy for life.'

'You're referring to the Colonel, I suppose.'

She left this conjecture unanswered. 'What about Captain Tauschmüller? How did he react to the idea?'

'With his wife and the CO breathing down his neck – how do you think? All he could do was run for cover.'

'No matter,' said Frau Klarfeld. 'As far as I'm concerned, he's dead. By spurning me and my love for him, he forfeited all my respect. You can tell that to him and his commanding officer. You can also convey how touched and honoured I am that an officer of Herr Lahrmann's calibre should have asked for my hand. I see no reason whatever to reject his proposal.'

Almost imploringly, Königsberger argued against

252

taking such a precipitate step when the situation might be transformed overnight – when even Tauschmüller might have a change of heart – but in vain.

'Doctor,' Frau Klarfeld said firmly, 'you may regard your mission as successfully accomplished. I'm extremely grateful for your interest and consideration. If I can ever do you a favour in return, let me know.'

'Ah,' said Königsberger, 'now you come to mention it, I'd like to employ Fräulein Mauerland as an official full-time receptionist and assistant. She's already helped me out on a number of occasions, to my entire satisfaction. I find her capable and ideally suited to the job. Would you be willing to endorse the appointment?'

'I don't see why not, but only if you promise to discourage her relationship with Lieutenant Kersten.'

'Oh, him,' the MO said evasively. 'I'm not too crazy about him myself – human volcanoes don't appeal to me – but what if Melanie's in love with him?'

'There's no question of that. She's a little mixed up at present – a little emotionally confused, which is why you'll have to watch her. Do you promise?'

Königsberger was incautious enough to do just that.

The same afternoon, Majors Kastor and Pollandt presented Feuerfresser with a detailed report on the 'Kersten case'. The Colonel received it impassively. 'Thank you, gentlemen,' he said, when they had finished. 'Send Kersten to me at once. I shall read him the riot act – he seems to need it badly.'

The majors departed and Kersten marched in. He came to attention before his commanding officer, looking more than ever like a heroic statue.

Feuerfresser treated him to a long, searching stare. 'What on earth were you thinking of, my boy?'

'When, Colonel?'

'One of the men in your charge died today. Was it absolutely unavoidable?'

'Absolutely, Colonel.'

'But why? I'm waiting for an explanation.'

'That's easy, Colonel. Anyone with my amount of combat experience would sooner have two or three of his men killed in training than two or three dozen in action. I've seen too many ill-trained rabbits gutted in my time.'

'No form of training, however tough and intensive, should result in fatal casualties.'

'As I told Major Kastor, Colonel, you can't make an omelette without cracking a few eggs. That's my belief, anyway.'

'What if I disagree?'

'In that case, Colonel, one of us must be mistaken.'

Feuerfresser sat back and brooded in silence for a considerable time. Then he said, 'I can only advise you to give the matter more thought. I've been striving to understand your point of view, but mine is what counts here. That, Kersten, is the way of the world.'

Early that evening, Singer strolled into the MO's office. Königsberger's attempts to seem busy with some paper-work did not conceal his greater interest in Natasha and Melanie, now installed as his full-time assistant.

'I hope I'm intruding,' Singer said brightly. 'I always do my best to.'

'You're out of luck,' Königsberger told him. 'We're bringing our case histories up to date.'

The corporal sat down uninvited. 'Maybe I can help.'

'How?'

'By leaving you alone with Natasha, Captain. I could take Fräulein Mauerland next door and give her a few useful tips.'

'On what?'

'Oh, the world in general and Lieutenant Kersten in particular. Would you like that, Melanie?'

She nodded. 'If it's all right with the Captain.'

Königsberger tried to look stern. 'Actually, Singer, you've no real business to be here.'

'Why not, Captain? I'm your personal orderly.'

'Yes, but don't get too personal.' He turned to Melanie. 'And don't let him sweet-talk you into anything.'

'Never again, Captain.'

Singer took Melanie by the arm and led her into the dispensary next door. He switched on the lights and checked the blackout screens before perching on a crate and patting the one beside it. Melanie accepted the invitation.

'Do you know Herr Kersten well?' she asked with ill-concealed curiosity.

'Pretty well,' he said. 'I don't know why, but we react to certain things the same way. We're on first name terms too, not that that means much in itself.'

'What sort of person is he?'

'Well to start with, he's a hero. You'll have to accept that, Melanie, but don't let it worry you. It doesn't mean he's immune to deeper feelings, even if he's incapable of showing them. He wanted to know a lot about you – everything, in fact.'

She looked apprehensive. 'What did you tell him?'

'All I know, or think I know.' Singer smiled at her. 'I said you're a very special kind of girl, very shy and reserved, very self-absorbed - till now, I mean. I also told him there was nothing in the rumours about you and a certain lady.'

'They've been going the rounds, I know.'

'In this cosy little snakepit, everyone gets bitten. With so much venom being squirted around, rumours are bound to circulate. Ignore them, that's the best policy.'

'Even when they're to do with Herr Kersten?'

'I suppose a little bird told you he's having an affair with Field-Marshal Wedell's daughter.'

'Yes, and I wouldn't put it past him.'

'Except that it isn't true, Melanie. Barbara Wedell's as good as hitched – to me.'

She breathed a sigh of relief. 'You mean I can go on seeing him with an easy mind?'

'Yes. It's all up to you, though. Konstantin's just as much of a sentimentalist as you, in many ways, but that could be a lucky break for both of you.'

A phone call from Singer brought Kersten, too, hurrying to the medical centre. The first people he saw there were Königsberger and Natasha.

'Sorry,' he said with unwonted courtesy, 'I hope I'm not butting in.'

'Not at all,' said the MO. 'My professional services are always at your disposal.' He glanced at Natasha, who rose and disappeared into the room next door. 'Very well, what's the trouble?'

Kersten looked almost bashful. 'It's more of a private matter, really. I was hoping for a chat with Fräulein Mauerland.'

'On official premises? Out of the question, Lieutenant.'

'I can't but Singer can, is that it?'

The MO could see that Kersten had been fully briefed. 'Corporal Singer is entitled to be here because he's my personal orderly.'

'Perfect!' exclaimed Kersten, slapping his thigh. 'He's mine too, which gives me an official reason for coming. If I happen to bump into Fräulein Mauerland as well, so much the better.'

'It isn't as simple as that, Herr Kersten. Fräulein Mauerland works here.'

'Twenty-four hours a day?'

'She's just going off duty.'

'Fine, I'll see her back to her quarters.'

'No need, she's being collected. Frau Klarfeld's orders.'

Kersten swore under his breath. 'They're plain abnormal, all these rules and regulations.'

'Except,' the MO said reprovingly, 'that they're the fruit of careful deliberation on the Colonel's part. You ought to have grasped that at lunch today, if it hadn't dawned on you before. Under his moral code, which is universally binding, the only way you'll get near Melanie is by announcing your engagement to her – with his approval, of course.'

'He must be off his rocker!' Kersten's oversimplified verdict on the Colonel's mental state was brutally outspoken. 'What's he trying to do, make a war widow out of every woman on this base? If he expects *me* to help him, he's picked the wrong man!'

One of the ensuing autumn days was crisp and sunny. 'Just the weather for my boys,' said Breitenbach, the SS captain from the hydrogenation plant, as he arrived at Kampfental with his football team. He was driving a Mercedes scout car like Lahrmann's. Grinding dependably along behind him came a Henschel truck.

Captain Tauschmüller, who was waiting to greet him at the main gate, had an attractive suggestion to make. 'The sooner we get started, Hauptsturmführer, the sooner we can retire to the mess for some refreshment. Let's kick off right away – or do your men need a breather first?'

'No, no,' was the brisk response, 'we're all set to go. My boys are itching to get their own back for the last defeat.'

'And the two before that,' Tauschmüller said blandly, 'but we won't mind your winning for a change.'

Breitenbach ordered his team out of the truck – eleven players plus four reserves, all in jet-black SS track suits – and doubled them to the scene of their previous humiliations. Here he put them through their warm-up routine.

The spectators who had been detailed to attend the match began to fill the wooden benches. Camp personnel, headed by Sergeant-Major Schulz, sat on the right. Trainees, shepherded by their NCO instructors, sat jam-packed on the left. The best places near the half-way line were reserved for the women auxiliaries, who marched to them under the majestic leadership of Frau Klarfeld.

The atmosphere was cheerful and expectant. Spirits rose still higher when Lieutenant Lahrmann, uniformed like Breitenbach but with the Knight's Cross bobbing at his throat, doubled into the arena at the head of his white-clad gladiators. The benevolent applause that greeted them subsided as soon as Colonel von Feuerfresser appeared. On his left, Captain Tauschmüller; immediately behind him, Priewitt, followed by the two majors, the MO, and Lieutenant Kersten, whose own Knight's Cross vied in splendour with his German Cross in Gold. Lieutenant Wagner, accompanied by a section drawn from his heavily armed Security Platoon, brought up the rear like members of the Führer's bodyguard.

For the Colonel, a folding canvas armchair had been erected in front of the foremost row of benches. The one on his left was reserved for Captain Tauschmüller. The one on his right he offered to Frau Klarfeld, who was still sitting with her flock.

'May I invite you to sit with me, dear lady?' he called. 'Here on my right, where you belong.' She joined him without demur.

The two team coaches, Hauptsturmführer Breitenbach and Lieutenant Lahrmann, marched up to the Colonel's chair, saluted him smartly, and reported their men ready to kick off. Feuerfresser shook hands with them in turn, first the visitor, then Lahrmann.

'May the better side win!' he proclaimed.

Play could now commence. A referee on loan from

Garrison HQ, Hölzbach District – an officer, naturally – blew his whistle. Both teams attacked vigorously from the outset, concentrating on their opponents rather than the ball. Only ten minutes into the first half, Breitenbach was compelled to replace his fleet-footed outside left, who had been badly mauled. After another dangerous foul, his outstanding centre half had to be borne off on a stretcher with the MO in close attendance.

'You'll never get anywhere like this,' said an amiable voice in Breitenbach's ear.

The SS team coach tore his gaze away from the field long enough to see who had spoken. It proved to be an insignificant corporal. He sounded interested and sympathetic rather than ingratiating. 'Mind if I give you a tip, Hauptsturmführer?'

'Don't bother,' growled Breitenbach, 'we've got it made this time.' He still felt confident because his latest team had been reinforced by several first-class players and trained to within an inch of their lives. They were in peak condition.

'You'll lose for a certainty,' said the unknown corporal. 'You obviously haven't grasped the way our side operates. Their tactics are quite straightforward: any potential threat gets eliminated. The same principle applies to everything else in this place.'

'What's that supposed to mean?' snapped Breitenbach. 'Are you trying to stir it?'

'I merely took the liberty of offering you some advice.'

The SS officer glowered. 'Damned backhanded advice, from the sound of it.'

He clung to his brusque rejection of Singer's hints for the remaining thirty minutes of the first half, during which the SS team seemed destined for another even more catastrophic defeat. They conceded two goals and lost their viciously effective right back, who retired hurt and hobbled off the field. Then, just before half-time, their goal-keeper had to make a third journey to the back of the net.

More than content with such a clear-cut margin, Feuerfresser rewarded Lahrmann with a gracious wave during the interval. Then he turned to Frau Klarfeld. 'Splendid fellow, Lahrmann – one of the finest young officers I've ever come across. Magnificent, the way he keeps our team up to scratch. I congratulate you, dear lady.'

Meanwhile, Lahrmann had gathered his team around him. 'That's the spirit,' he told them. 'Keep it up, and the game's as good as won.'

Breitenbach was simultaneously trying to reinject some pep into his own men. 'Pull your bloody socks up! You're going to win because you've damn well got to. If you don't, God help you!'

His players, who had no idea how to pull the match out of the fire, looked utterly at a loss. Breitenbach felt equally at a loss until he caught sight of the corporal who had accosted him earlier, now hovering on the outskirts of the crowd.

'All right,' he said, striving hard to sound conciliatory, 'where have we been going wrong, and what's it to you?'

Singer ignored the second question. 'It simply struck me that your team was being steam-rollered after losing its best players through injury. Why not take a leaf out of the other side's book?'

'Meaning what?'

'For a start, there's that hulking great centre forward of theirs – the ex-international. Then there's the right half, who's the real brains of the side and an expert at disguised fouls. Finally, there's that rugged left back. His job is to cripple your strikers, not mark them.'

Singer's implicit advice produced sensational results. The visitors devoted most of the second half to a deliberate and successful elimination campaign. In the seventieth minute they levelled the score at three all, and one minute before full-time they clinched the match in their favour. Three Kampfental players had sustained injuries requiring overnight treatment in the medical centre's sick bay.

The Colonel waxed philosophical during the subsequent celebrations in the mess. Instead of saying, 'The better side won,' he confined himself to a brief monologue on the vicissitudes of fortune. It was only a game, after all.

The players were generously regaled in the NCO's canteen, for which Sergeant-Major Schulz was responsible. Several dozen roast chickens were dismembered, devoured, and washed down with three barrels of Hölzbacher Special.

Fare in the officers' mess was equally plain and unpretentious because Hauptsturmführer Breitenbach was known to be no great lover of gastronomic refinement. Here, a species of cold buffet had been set out, including wedges of rare roast beef, man-sized ribs of smoked salt pork, thick slices of blood and liver sausage, pigs' trotters, and calves'-heads in aspic. A wide range of drink was freely available.

The hosts accepted their surprising, almost staggering defeat by the visiting team with studious equanimity. They made no further mention of it and dedicated themselves to their food as if acting on the Colonel's instructions. Seizing what he thought was a favourable opportunity, Lieutenant Wagner paraded his Latin again. *'Civis Romanus sum,'* he announced. 'I am a Roman citizen.'

'Really?' Kersten looked mystified. 'How does that apply to a game of soccer?'

'Cicero was emphasizing that all Roman citizens shared a common national identity,' Wagner explained. 'In our case, that means it doesn't really matter who wins as long as he's one of us. If he is, we all have a share in his victory.'

'You've hit the nail on the head,' Breitenbach chimed in. 'We're all in the same boat, now more than ever – I mean, now we've reached such a crucial turning-point in our country's historical development.'

'Indeed?' said Feuerfresser, who had pricked up his ears. 'What sort of turning-point?'

'It's absolutely definite, Colonel.' The SS captain was clearly delighted to flaunt his inside information and pass it on for comradeship's sake. 'At long last, the Führer has tackled the Final Solution. It's no holds barred from now on.'

Few of those present seemed to know, or want to know, what Breitenbach was driving at. The majors registered tactical indifference and Captain Tauschmüller awaited further developments. The MO looked as apathetic as he often did these days. Lahrmann gulped down a big hunk of meat, almost as if he were choking on his own defeat and that of his men. As for Kersten, he looked drowsy and pleasantly replete. The one word that escaped his lips sounded vaguely like 'Bullshit!'

The Colonel narrowed his eyes and focused them on Wagner, who couldn't fail to construe this as a request for still more inside information.

'The process known as the Final Solution,' he said, 'may be defined as the most systematic and essential measure ever taken in our country's history. It was intimated at a top-secret, high-level Party conference which I was privileged to attend that the Final Solution will be the ultimate stage in the purification of the Greater German Reich.'

'He's right,' said Breitenbach. 'It entails the elimination of all pathological, diseased and subversive elements. In other words, Jews – Jews first and foremost, plus anyone else in the same category.'

'At last!' cried Wagner, flushed with enthusiasm. 'And high time too! We can't be expected to harbour those vermin in our midst any longer.'

'This Final Solution,' said Feuerfresser, 'is it still in the planning stage, or have things gone further than that?'

'Himmler has already transmitted the relevant directive from the Führer,' Breitenbach told him. 'We've been ordered to exterminate the rats without mercy, once and for all. I'm speaking in the strictest confidence, of course, because the order's top secret.' He smiled, exposing a fat gold tooth. 'Not that I need to stress that in this select company.'

Wagner was enraptured. 'There's no one to touch our Führer for absolute and unflinching determination. We ought to drink a toast to his incomparable greatness of spirit.'

The Colonel raised his glass. 'To the Fatherland,' he said, 'and all who have its best interests at heart.'

With minds enlightened and bellies well lined, the revellers briefly dispersed to answer calls of nature or assist the digestive process by strolling on the terrace. In honour of their SS guest, it was planned to serve a midnight snack of caviar and Crimean champagne – several cases of which he had brought as a gift – with orchestral accompaniment.

Feuerfresser and his adjutant withdrew to the smoking-room, where Priewitt served them brandy. The Colonel was looking thoughtful.

'A final solution on that scale?' he mused. 'Millions of people? A direct order from the Führer? The mind boggles!'

'Fundamentally,' said Tauschmüller, 'it's nothing at all to do with us. We aren't involved in any way. Our own functions are clearly defined and altogether different.'

Feuerfresser nodded. 'Very true. Our world remains intact – inviolate. Every king needs an executioner, as our forefathers used to say, but we're soldiers. Plain soldiers and nothing else.'

They brooded in silence for a while. Then, in a pensive

and confidential tone, Feuerfresser changed the subject. 'My real headache at the moment is Kersten.'

'I can understand that, Colonel,' said Tauschmüller. 'He's a disruptive element – an exceptionally pig-headed young man.'

'If that were all, my dear fellow, he could be dealt with one way or another. He's a living contradiction, that's what worries me – brave as a lion but blind to higher things. He may well come to grief unless I manage to instruct him in his duties as an officer and a gentleman.'

'But wasn't Lahrmann like that to begin with, Colonel? Look what a sound type he's become, thanks to your tuition.'

Feuerfresser slowly shook his head. 'Lahrmann's another kettle of fish. His fighting spirit stems from conviction, whereas Kersten's is instinctive. He's like a bull intent on destroying everything in its path.'

'Then he'll have to be slaughtered – to borrow your imagery, Colonel.'

'Not without a final effort on my part. Honour demands it.'

Meanwhile, Majors Kastor and Pollandt had embarked on a rather half-hearted game of chess. Wagner and Breitenbach were swapping personal reminiscences and holding a highly constructive conversation on what the Final Solution entailed in practice. They agreed that it was a question of all or nothing, them or us. The MO disappeared in the direction of the medical centre, but not for the injured footballers' sake alone. Kersten looked round for Singer, who seemed to have been lying in wait for him.

'Now's your chance,' he said.

'Where is she?'

'As the medical centre, but don't go bumping into the MO again – make sure the coast's clear first. And if you do manage to get the girl alone, remember who you're dealing with. Compared to our mutual friend Barbara, Melanie's a shrinking violet.'

'Women are women and men are men,' scoffed Kersten, who was nicely tanked up by now. 'You're talking crap.'

'Sure, and you sound capable of believing any stupid cliché that pops into your head.'

Kersten found Melanie alone in the dispensary, ostensibly unpacking a new consignment of medical supplies. She looked at him as if she'd been waiting for him all her life.

'It's nice to see you,' she confessed.

He advanced on her with easy familiarity, clearly intending to kiss her, but she shrank away.

'No,' she said sternly, 'not just like that. I warn you, Konstantin, you can't treat me as your personal property. If you're looking for easy meat, go somewhere else. I won't be rushed off my feet by anyone, and that includes you.'

Kersten managed to corner her between two crates. 'Come off it, girl. Anyone'd think you didn't fancy me.'

Melanie gave him a sudden, violent shove that sent him reeling backwards. 'It isn't as simple as you think, Lieutenant,' she hissed. 'What sort of a girl do you take me for?'

With surprising vigour, she hustled him outside. He stood there in the inhospitable darkness, feeling cheated and angry.

'How dare she do that to me,' he said thickly. '*Me!*'

Natasha and the MO were sitting side by side in the MO's office, gazing long and deep into each other's eyes. Their hands had met, as though by accident, in the middle of the desk.

'I don't know quite how to put this,' Königsberger said, 'but we hit it off pretty well, don't we?'

'You mean a lot to me,' she said. 'I admit that, but isn't it all rather pointless – not to mention dangerous?'

'Pointless and dangerous?' he repeated. 'Tell me what isn't, in wartime. We love each other, that's the main thing.'

She gently released her hands. 'Don't forget I'm Russian. And Jewish, to make matters worse.'

'I don't mind – but I expect you've noticed that. All that worries me is your personal file. Is there any chance you're registered as Jewish?'

'No idea – it's quite possible. Why?'

'I have my reasons, but don't ask me to go into them. If there is such an entry in your papers, we must try and get it deleted at once. There mustn't be any record of what you told me just now.'

'But why?' she insisted.

Königsberger decided to tell her the truth. 'Because Hitler has personally decreed the final solution of the Jewish question, as he calls it. Have you any idea what that means?'

She shook her head.

'It means wholesale brutality and barbarism – the mass extermination of the Jewish race.'

'Does that include me?'

'Not if I can help it. I want you safe – safe by my side for ever.'

And then, as passion overcame them on what was probably the most wonderful night in two short lifetimes, the world and its horrors faded into oblivion.

Intense activity reigned in the brothel because Sergeant-Major Schulz had, on orders from above, granted every member of the SS team a free visit. Having gorged and swilled themselves to a standstill, the victorious footballers stormed the former chapel in quest of further entertainment.

Corporal Hausleitner, who was highly resentful of this disorderly invasion, succeeded in bringing it under control. Not even a horde of tipsy SS men could be allowed to disrupt the smooth running of his 'recreation centre'.

Meanwhile, Singer was mingling with their defeated rivals, who were moping in the smoke-laden fug of the NCOs' canteen. Although they had been allotted as much beer as they could drink, they seemed to have lost their taste for it.

'Nothing the matter with your game, boys,' Singer told them. 'You lost all right, but you didn't deserve to.'

Everyone nodded. 'Bastards!' the captain said indignantly. 'They spent more time fouling than playing in the second half.'

'Yes,' said Singer, 'and now it's paying off. They're even getting a free ride in the brothel – *our* brothel, mark you! They don't have any right to be there, if you ask me.'

Tempers were getting short by now. 'Bloody cheek!' – 'Why should we stand for it?' – 'It's a downright disgrace!'

'Then you'd better do something about it,' shouted Singer. 'Otherwise those SS thugs'll think you're fairies as well as losers. Which you aren't – or are you?'

That did it. They rose as one man and headed resolutely for the brothel, where Hausleitner tried to stem the flood.

'Easy, boys! Everything follows a system here.'

'Yes,' he was told, 'our system!'

They thrust him aside so roughly that he hit his head on the doorpost and slid to the floor, half stunned. Then they strode over his prostrate form, thundered up the stairs, and stormed the cubicles in their thirst for vengeance.

Shrill screams rang out, fists flew, bed frames collapsed. The girls, most of them naked, fled into corners while the battle raged with undiminished ferocity. By the time it was over, the brothel had been reduced to a shambles and several men were injured.

'Oh, my God,' wailed Hausleitner, 'it's like the end of the world!' He hauled himself painfully to his feet. 'I could see this coming a mile off. Another few months, and the whole country will look like this . . .'

Still smarting at Melanie's brusque rejection of his advances, Kersten went for a lengthy stroll through camp and returned to the mess in time for the 'feast of friendship' that had been set for midnight.

For those who preferred more rib-sticking fare than caviar and Crimean champagne, there was some thick, nutritious pea soup fortified with fat bacon and slices of farmhouse sausage. There was also beer of every hue from molasses brown to urine yellow. Nobody took any notice of the string serenade in progress next door.

Everyone was there except the MO, whose absence was ascribed to the brisk demand for his services, and Frau Klarfeld. This time, the chair on the Colonel's right was occupied by his SS guest.

Perhaps because he was working off his resentment at Melanie's behaviour, Kersten seemed unusually aggressive, even for him. He weighed into Lahrmann on the grounds that he bore the blame for Kampfental's defeat. To Lahrmann's fury, he described his team's performance as a 'ninety per cent flop'.

'What do *you* know about football?' Lahrmann retorted.

Colonel von Feuerfresser, who had been following the incipient row with interest, gave Kersten a glance of benign expectation. Intercepting it, Kersten went for Lahrmann bald-headed.

'Our team had the game wrapped up, but they weren't given the proper guidance and backing. Inadequate staff work, that was their problem.' He turned on the SS captain. 'Or would you claim your men are better players?'

'I never said that,' Breitenbach protested, thoroughly taken aback. Being a man with a simple and straightforward cast of mind, he had no inkling of what he was up against. 'Still,' he added, 'we did win.'

'It's utterly absurd to draw conclusions like that,' said Lahrmann, still striving to defend himself against Kersten's verbal onslaught. 'My men did their best. They had bad luck, that's all.'

'Bad management, you mean.' Kersten gave a scornful laugh. 'You had three really tough and effective players in your original side, Lahrmann, but you didn't back them up – you left them unsupported. Militarily speaking, that breaks every rule in the book.'

'Nonsense!' snapped Lahrmann. 'What are you talking about?'

'I'm talking about the most important lesson a field commander's ever likely to learn: pick out your best men and give them all the covering fire you've got. It's the only way to win.'

Colonel von Feuerfresser nodded as though he now knew something that had so far eluded him. 'Gentlemen,' he said, rising to his feet, 'I have some business to attend to. Kindly excuse me.'

Tauschmüller and Priewitt followed him out. 'Just as I thought,' they heard him mutter. Quite suddenly, he looked like a tired old man.

8

The nuptials of Lieutenant Heinrich Lahrmann, born Wiesbaden 1914, holder of the Knight's Cross and sundry other coveted orders and decorations, and Erika, Countess von Klarfeld, *née* Marunke, born Leipzig 1912, war widow and woman auxiliary of major's rank, likewise several times decorated, *inter alia* with the Distinguished Service Cross, Classes I and II, were to be 'a unique and unforgettable occasion'. This had been expressly requested by Colonel von Feuerfresser, and the Colonel's requests were tantamount to orders.

He was shrewd enough not to give Captain Tauschmüller official charge of the preparations. Tauschmüller's brief ran as follows: 'Naturally, my dear fellow, you'll supervise everything to ensure there are no slip-ups, but only from behind the scenes. Keep an eye on my staff, especially the MO and Kersten. For the rest of the time, concentrate on your lady wife. I shall invite her to be my partner at table.'

'Thank you, Colonel,' said Tauschmüller, vastly relieved that his responsibilities were to be confined to his spouse, his brother officers, and the camp orchestra – not to mention the kitchen and cellar, which would naturally be expected to give of their best. In this respect, he was fortunate enough to command the services of his three master chefs and Mess Sergeant Gerner's reliable team, with Priewitt and Singer in the van. A quick inspection of mess stores disclosed that they would be fully equal to the demands made on them.

It was semi-officially decreed that the wedding should be, first and foremost, 'a patriotic occasion imbued with spiritual and cultural significance'. Lieutenant Wagner was responsible – or rather, willingly assumed responsibility – for this aspect of the proceedings. His grand design took the form outlined below:

1. Camp personnel. To mark the occasion, members of the permanent staff will be excused duties for the day. Afternoon: film show. Evening: party in the gym, with free beer, instrumental accompaniment and choral singing – German folksongs only – under the direction of Sergeant-Major Schulz.

2. Trainees. Groups A, B and C will undertake supervised "walks" in the immediate vicinity of camp. Late afternoon: route march. Destination: the Brown Bear at Hölzbach. Purpose: social get-together. Organization: Master-Sergeant Heinz. Overall supervision: Majors Kastor and Pollandt. Security: Lieutenant Wagner plus Security Platoon.

3. Instructors. Training personnel under Lieutenant Lahrmann's direct command – 1 master-sergeant, 3 staff sergeants, 9 sergeants, 27 other ranks – will be permitted to participate in the ceremony itself, first as a guard of honour, then as a choir. They will also be privileged to extend personal congratulations to their immediate superior, to wit, the bridegroom. Evening facility: one visit to the camp recreation centre, free of charge.

Tauschmüller's reaction to this logistical exercise was extremely favourable. 'Excellent, Wagner – really first-class,' he said. 'Just what the Colonel wants, I'm sure. Go on.'

Wagner's face darkened slightly. 'The Colonel has fixed the wedding for eleven hundred hours. The first phase will be a religious ceremony. Protestant,' he added.

'What's wrong with that?'

'Nothing, Captain, not if the Colonel wants it that way.'

'He doesn't *want* it that way, he merely thinks it appropriate to accede to Frau Klarfeld's personal wishes.'

'Which have to be respected, I suppose,' Wagner said grudgingly. 'Still, even though a church wedding isn't exactly in the spirit of the new Germany, at least the officiating priest will be Senior Chaplain Niedermayer of our own army group. I presume he's a loyal German as well as a Christian.'

'Not only that but a lover of good cheer, by all accounts, so make sure he's well looked after. The same goes for the registrar from Hölzbach, of course. Everything's got to go with a swing. That's your job, Wagner. We have the utmost confidence in you, the Colonel and I.'

'I'll do my best, Captain.'

'Fine, so you don't have any problems. Or do you?'

'Only one,' said Wagner. 'Lieutenant Kersten has been detailed to act as best man, but he's trying to back out. He describes the whole affair as a load of bullshit – among other things.'

'Tell him I want him,' Tauschmüller said firmly.

Kersten appeared, wearing a faintly belligerent grin. When asked the reason for his uncooperative behaviour, he replied, 'Because it's all a load of bullshit.'

'I'm already acquainted with your views, I regret to say, and they're clearly based on insufficient thought.'

'What gives you that impression, Captain?'

'There are three points to bear in mind, Lieutenant Kersten. Number one, the Colonel wishes this occasion to pass off in a dignified and harmonious manner, and I'm sure you wouldn't want to poison the atmosphere. Number two, Lieutenant Lahrmann will soon be vacating his post in the Training Wing. Just between ourselves, it's yours for the asking.'

'That's no incentive,' said Kersten, though he hesitated for a split second. 'What else?'

Now it was Tauschmüller's turn to grin. 'Just a minor

point, but one that may possibly hold some interest for you. Your own allotted role in the wedding ceremony has a female counterpart. The bridesmaid will be Fräulein Mauerland.'

'Fair enough,' said Kersten. 'Count me in.'

Having been given the good news by Tauschmüller, Wagner felt free to proceed. He asked the MO to entertain the chaplain and the registrar, which he agreed to do and later did with the aid of two bottles of champagne.

Lieutenant Wagner's schedule was a document containing points of detail worthy of the German General Staff. In his eyes, it was cogent testimony to his strategic talents.

Part 1: Preparations. 0800 onwards: fir branches to be cut and dismembered into sprigs of a size suitable for scattering by fatigue parties assigned by Sergeant-Major Schulz. 0945: scattering of foliage to commence along path from women staff auxiliaries' compound to mess entrance. 1015: above operation to be completed. 1020: guard of honour, wearing battle dress and steel helmets, receives preliminary briefing from Lieutenant Wagner.

Chamber orchestra to be divided into component sections. Outside: hunting-horn quartet. Officers' mess: string quartet plus piano, with augmented camp choir in background. Latter to sing rehearsed selections from *Der Freischütz*, including 'We deck thee in the bridal wreath'.

Part 2: Prelude to ceremony proper. 1030: the bridegroom's best man, Lieutenant Kersten, joins Lieutenant Lahrmann. Both officers proceed in full-dress uniform, complete with orders, decorations and medals, to the main entrance of the mess, where they report to the Commandant at 1045. Together with him, but one pace to the rear, they then proceed to the bride's quarters. 1050: collection of bride, accompanied by her bridesmaid, Fräulein Mauerland. Solemn silence to be preserved.

1055: bride proceeds to officers' mess on Commandant's arm, followed by bridegroom, best man and bridesmaid. Guard of honour presents arms, hunting-horn quartet blows fanfare based on theme from Mozart's Concerto No. 4 for French horn and orchestra, camp choir strikes up. Eighty-eight milli-metre anti-aircraft gun on roof of administration block, manned by members of the Security Platoon, fires seven-gun salute at five-second intervals.

1100: arrival in banqueting hall . . .

There, an altarlike edifice had been erected – a row of trestle tables draped in white damask, decked with burning candles, and backed by a semi-circle of potted bay trees. In front of this stood the leather armchairs reserved for the principal actors: Colonel von Feuerfresser in the centre, the bride on his right, the bridegroom on his left. Flanking them were Majors Kastor and Pollandt, Captain Tauschmüller and his wife, Lieutenant Kersten, and Fräulein Mauerland. Everyone else was disposed in the background.

The musicians were playing some Bach. Although Wagner had taken the precaution of warning them to exercise self-restraint where the length of their offering was concerned, they showed sings of turning the ceremony into a protracted concert. Colonel von Feuerfresser, who had graced the occasion by donning his 'Pour le Mérite' and sundry other decorations earned in two world wars, nipped this danger in the bud. During the very first lull between movements, he crisply and commandingly set the ball rolling.

Noticeably flushed by the MO's hospitality, Senior Chaplain Niedermayer lurched into action. He faced the congregation and delivered himself of a resounding preamble.

'Comradeship is the essence of a soldier's life, my friends. We are a community united by a common destiny, for Germany must live even if we have to die in the fight for her survival.

'As a soldier, you must accept that you are no longer your own master. Your whole heart, your entire existence, belong to someone else. For God has given us his word of honour and binding pledge: "Fear not, I am with thee."

'Germany knows she has been summoned by God to reshape the history of Europe. All of us have heeded the Führer's call. Such is the spirit in which I now see you, my beloved children, united here before me.'

Remarkable though they were, these pseudo-Christian bromides were not the work of the chaplain himself. He had taken them, word for word, from 'higher authority' – in this case, from an official Protestant chaplains' pamphlet entitled *Virtues of the Christian Soldier*.

As soon as this ordeal was over, and before the chamber orchestra could butt in again, Feuerfresser said, 'Proceed with the civil ceremony.'

The registrar needed no second bidding. Because it had been conveyed to him that brevity would be appreciated, he came straight to the nub of the matter.

'Heinrich Lahrmann, do you take this woman, Erika, Countess von Klarfeld, to be your lawful wedded wife?' He repeated the question, *mutatis mutandis*, to the bride. Both parties replied in the affirmative.

Erika Klarfeld did not forget to give Tauschmüller a quick, reproachful glance which her erstwhile lover affected not to notice. He put his arm round his wife, who ostentatiously nestled closer.

Melanie Mauerland's cheeks were aflame, but not with a bridemaid's natural emotion. Kersten, who was sitting beside her, had been unmannerly enough to put his hand on her thigh and give it a squeeze.

'In that case,' the registrar briskly concluded, 'I pronounce you man and wife in the name of the Führer and the Greater German Reich. Herr Lahrmann, Frau Lahrmann, my heartiest congratulations.'

The Colonel smiled his most gracious smile. 'And now,' he said, 'let the festivities commence.'

CURRICULUM VITAE OF HEINRICH LAHRMANN
or, A Decent Man's Devotion to Duty

Name: Heinrich Lahrmann. Date and place of birth: April 20, 1914, Wiesbaden-Biebrich. Father: Heinrich Lahrmann, detective-inspector. Mother: Helene, née Henrici, housewife and part-time thermal bath attendant. One younger brother named Heinz.

Heinrich felt content with his surroundings from the first. His father was a worthy man, his mother the soul of kindness, his brother fraternally affectionate. They lived in a neat, clean, comfortable three-room apartment overlooking the Rhine, ate simply but well, and spent cosy family evenings together. His father used to leaf through the newspaper and read bits aloud – mostly crime reports, on which he would comment in a way that revealed his expert knowledge and capacity for human understanding. Heinrich did crossword puzzles while brother Heinz, who planned to become an architect, drew structural elevations. Frau Lahrmann darned socks and smiled at her menfolk.

In 1924, however, Heinrich's father was gunned down on duty while trying to arrest a fugitive wanted for political murder. He merely fired a warning shot when the man ran off, but his quarry emptied a magazine straight at him with fatal results.

Inspector Lahrmann's fellow policemen not only bought him an imposing wreath but collected a substantial sum for their colleague's widow. A representative from the Ministry of the Interior conveyed his 'deep personal sorrow' and 'sincerest condolences' to the three surviving members of the victim's family. 'He died in the execution of his duty, like a soldier in battle. You can be truly proud of his memory.' The widow was further informed, in a confidential whisper, that an adequate pension would be forthcoming.

In 1926, brother Heinz was killed on a school outing. By scrimping and saving, his mother had enabled him to go on a guided tour of some historic castles and mansions. While homeward bound, the school coach was rammed by a freight train on an unprotected level crossing. As a result of this appalling accident, five children were killed and twenty-one injured, nine of them seriously.

Heinrich burst into tears over his beloved brother's grave. His mother hugged him to her. 'Don't cry, my son. "Men never cry" – that's what your poor dear father would have said, I'm sure.' And that, God knew, was what Heinrich wanted to be: a man his whole life through.

In 1928 his mother was drowned at the thermal baths in Leibnitzstrasse, where she worked as an attendant. Alerted by the cries of a big fat woman who was wildly thrashing around in the water, Frau Lahrmann dived in at once. The woman clung to her in mindless panic, drowning them both. At her funeral, Heinrich's eyes remained dry.

His mother's sister, a war widow, moved into the Lahrmann home to look after him. 'From now on,' she told him, '*I'm* your family.'

I attended Biebrich Elementary School from 1924 onwards and went on to high school in Wiesbaden in 1930. There I remained until I got my junior diploma.

277

Although it was suggested that I stay on and try for a place at university, financial considerations made this impossible.

As a schoolboy, Heinrich showed a remarkable aptitude for almost every subject. His school reports confirmed this. He was, they declared, an extremely self-effacing, serious-minded youngster, easy to teach and eager to please.

His eagerness to please could be excessive. On three occasions in the years that followed, calculations and translations of his turned up in other pupils' exam papers. 'Did you crib off them,' his teacher sternly demanded, 'or did they crib off you? The latter, presumably, but I'd like to hear the truth from your own lips.'

Heinrich declined to answer. Rather than sneak, he preferred to shoulder the burden of suspicion himself. His clear-cut attitude of mind made it impossible for him to save himself at the expense of others. Whatever the circumstances, Heinrich was a stickler for solidarity.

At home, his aunt not only looked after him but took complete possession of him. She would climb into his bed at night, fold him in a speciously protective embrace, and clasp him to her. 'I only want the best for you,' she told him, 'you know that.' Being dependent on her, he submitted. Craving warmth and security, he yearned to rediscover the close-knit family atmosphere of his early boyhood.

He searched in vain at first, because all the women and girls he met aroused a latent fear that they would turn out to be aunt-like creatures whose one desire was to possess him utterly.

In 1937 I joined the Army as a volunteer and signed on for two years, a term which was extended when the war broke out. I became an officer cadet in spring 1939 and was commissioned in autumn of that year. I took part in the Polish, French and Russian campaigns.

278

Bereft of everyone and everything he loved, Heinrich Lahrmann came to look on the Army as his home and family. He was correspondingly prepared to regard his superiors as surrogate fathers: strict, but always kind and just. In his determination to see them as such, he saw them as such – a fact which they naturally appreciated.

Heinrich soon became known as a decent, dependable type who could be trusted all the way – and not only with men and equipment. He was, for instance, privileged to escort his company commander's wife and her woman friend to the theatre and see them home, but staunchly resisted the brazen invitations made him on these and other, similar occasions.

'Lahrmann,' stated one glowing personal assessment, 'is a born soldier with an unremitting urge to prove himself. He should be given every opportunity to do so.'

During the Polish campaign, he and his platoon spearheaded the assault on a strategically important Warsaw suburb. His company commander, who had overslept the operation in the arms of a Polish camp follower but turned up just in time for its successful conclusion, was awarded the Iron Cross First Class. He was gracious enough to make the real hero a promise. 'I – ' he stressed the 'I' – 'am personally recommending you for a Second Class.' Heinrich duly got one, which filled him with confusion and gratitude.

During the French campaign, he played a humble but none the less important part in driving the British back across the Channel. His battalion commander received the Knight's Cross, but this time Heinrich was assured of an Iron Cross First Class. The divisional commander pinned it on his chest, shook his hand, and told him, 'Officers like you are the Army's pride and joy. Keep up the good work.'

In winter 1941-42, when the German High Command still believed it could overrun the Soviet armies, Heinrich Lahrmann, by then a first-lieutenant and company commander, hurled himself and his surviving men into an assault on the city of Tula. He penetrated its defences at what was mistakenly believed to be a key point. Although the Russian line was only dented, not broken, the operation was prematurely described – by the Führer among others – as decisive.

In recognition of his brilliant tactical achievement, Lahrmann's regimental commander was recommended for the Knight's Cross – an occasion which naturally had to be celebrated. Looted Crimean champagne flowed like water in a makeshift mess just behind the front line.

The night was far advanced when Lahrmann's CO, already nicknamed 'the hero of Tula', decided to have some fun of a manly, military kind. Completely plastered, he pulled out a hand grenade and flourished it with jocular menace at his officers, who dived for cover. Unfortunately, he omitted to part with it in time. The grenade exploded in his hand and blew him to bits.

Heinrich Lahrmann received the Knight's Cross in his place. It was draped around his neck by a general – Russia was crawling with them by then – in a field hospital. Heinrich had been hit several times during the siege of Tula: a bullet through the shoulder, grenade splinters in his left leg, and a wound in the testicles. Being the possessor of a Knight's Cross, he was nursed with special care and patched up with some degree of success.

Then came a long spell of convalescent leave. He spent it at the Black Horse, a luxury hotel in Wiesbaden, and not at his old family home, where his aunt was still living. He avoided her like the plague and spent many hours beside the graves of his beloved father, mother, and brother.

Finally, he received another posting. His movement order read: 'AFSIC Kampfental, Hölzbach District.' The very name sounded like an accolade because it referred, he knew, to a special military establishment of the highest security rating. The movement order further instructed him to report to a Captain Tauschmüller and was signed 'Schlumberger'.

Little though he guessed it, his life's fulfilment was at hand.

The 'festivities' began with a general exodus on to the terrace of the former country mansion. As though to order, a wintry sun pierced the clouds.

The hunting horns blew another fanfare. Then, while the choir gave tongue once more, the first noncommissioned guests were permitted to offer their congratulations. On behalf of the permanent staff, Sergeant-Major Schulz stepped forward with a basketful of wine bottles. 'Lots of luck,' he said crisply. 'Long life and happiness to you both.' Master-Sergeant Heinz, representing the NCO instructors, proffered an engraving of the Brown Bear at Hölzbach, an embroidered swastika flag, and a leather-bound copy of Hitler's *Mein Kampf* inscribed 'To Our Lieutenant, In Abiding Respect and Loyalty.' On behalf of the women staff auxiliaries, Melanie Mauerland handed the bride an enormous bouquet.

Kersten was convulsed with mirth. 'Aren't they a scream?' he demanded of the MO, who was standing next him. 'A charade like this in wartime? It's downright insane!'

Königsberger shushed him. 'Who's to say what's sane or insane, Lieutenant – you? Don't overestimate yourself. And take care – your behaviour isn't going down too well with Fräulein Mauerland.'

The climax of the first phase came when Mess Sergeant Gerner marched up with a shiny silver key on a dark blue velvet cushion. 'Compliments of the Colonel,' he announced. 'The happy couple have been assigned a first-floor suite, freshly redecorated and fully equipped with all mod cons.' Lahrmann took the key and handed it to his bride, whose cheeks turned pink. Applause rang out.

Meanwhile, a fatigue party was hard at work in the mess. Under Priewitt and Singer's joint direction, the altar-like centrepiece had been dismantled and transformed into a banqueting table of horseshoe design.

To describe the ensuing meal as sumptuous would have been a gross understatement. Via Captain Tauschmüller, the head chef had mobilized all his contacts in the culinary world. A Luftwaffe supply unit based in Munich had flown in fresh lobsters from Holland and salmon from Norway. Even at this late stage in the war, a fellow chef and old friend employed by SS Headquarters, Munich, had managed to conjure up Russian caviar by the pound.

The remaining items on the menu came from the camp's own kitchen garden and the Colonel's game larder. Out of them, the chefs had fashioned a seven-course banquet lasting three hours. Now banished to the room next door, the chamber orchestra was able to toot and fiddle to its heart's content.

'Well, Captain,' said Singer as he refilled the MO's champagne glass, 'how are you feeling?'

'Like someone on another planet.'

An understandable sensation, except that this other planet was in the midst of Germany, whose starving, bombed-out inhabitants subsisted on ration cards that entitled them to a third of an ounce of fat, one-and-a-half ounces of meat or sausage, and seven ounces of bread a day, plus any vegetables that were going. Tobacco was scarce, coffee a thing of the past, and hard liquor almost unobtainable. Even servicemen were beginning to feel the pinch.

Armed with his bottle of champagne, Singer bent over Kersten and asked him the same question.

'Like a sleepwalker,' Kersten said musingly. 'What happens when we all wake up?'

'You tell me.'

'I can't, Sebastian. All I know is, these people wouldn't

know shit from shaving cream. They make me want to vomit.'

'Peeved, eh?' Singer bent still lower and whispered in his ear. 'Peeved because you can't get near that girl of yours.'

Kersten gave a snort of indignation. 'Maybe I don't even want to any more. She doesn't seem to have heard about the birds and the bees.'

Over dessert, Colonel von Freuerfresser turned and smiled gallantly at each of his table companions in turn: Frau Lahrmann-Klarfeld on his right, Frau Tauschmüller on his left.

'A great and memorable day,' he observed. 'As the wives of two fine officers, both you ladies possess the sense of duty that belongs to a relationship – a union – such as yours: you, Frau Tauschmüller, as a senior member of our Army Nursing Service, and you, Frau Lahrmann, as commander of our women staff auxiliaries. You both know the meaning of self-sacrifice.'

'Quite so,' his adjutant said crisply. Tauschmüller knew what Feuerfresser was leading up to. Lieutenant Wagner did not, but his unerring yes-man's instinct prompted him to echo the Colonel's sentiments. 'Ah yes,' he said, 'in a great age like ours, what could be more natural and laudable than self-sacrifice?' He was mortified that the wedding preparations had left him no time to memorize a new Latin tag.

The Colonel sailed blithely on. 'Life for a serving officer's wife is not, I fear, a bed of roses. You, my dear Frau Tauschmüller, will soon have to bid your husband farewell and resume your official duties – not that you mayn't have another opportunity to visit us in the near future. There is, however, an unwritten but invariable rule that married couples may not be employed within the same military establishment.'

By now, even Lahrmann had caught the Colonel's drift.

He laid a hand on his bride's arm and said, 'May I inquire, sir, what inference I'm to draw from that remark?'

Konstantin Kersten hadn't been listening. All his attention was centred on the girl beside him. 'You must be dying for a pee,' he said bluntly. 'I'll come with you, if you like.'

Melanie looked aghast. 'How dare you make such an obscene suggestion – now, of all times?'

'Because it's the ideal moment,' he retorted. 'Nobody'll notice if we run out on the party. They're all too busy listening to the Old Man talking hot air.'

'Hot air?' She stared at him in utter consternation and disgust. 'He's talking about Erika – my dearest friend – and her future. Don't you have *any* finer feelings?'

'Not interested, old girl. It's our future that interests me.'

Melanie must have failed to appreciate his undoubted sincerity. She edged her chair as far away from his as possible. Kersten felt his lips shaping an uncomplimentary word. Fortunately, he didn't say it.

'Inference? What inference, my dear Lahrmann? Come, come, we haven't reached that stage yet, not by a long chalk.' The Colonel's tone was more paternal than ever. 'Let's all sleep on the subject – each in his own way.'

His jest drew subdued male laughter, though not from everyone present.

'In the first place,' he pursued, 'the festivities in your honour are still far from over. Secondly, your honeymoon begins tomorrow morning – seven whole days of it, and all at public expense. Climb into your pet Mercedes and whisk Frau Lahrmann off to the mountains and lakes. After that – well, we'll see.'

'But I can't, Colonel. I mean, I'm extremely grateful for the kind suggestion, but I can't run out on my trainees.'

'Yes you can, with an easy mind. Lieutenant Kersten will deputize for you – won't you, Kersten?'

'Delighted, Colonel,' said Kersten, sounding anything but.

'Good.' Feuerfresser glanced at his watch. 'I suggest we call a halt till twenty hundred hours. Then comes the second part of the festivities – dinner and dancing by candlelight. Until then, ladies and gentlemen, feel free to amuse yourselves as you wish.'

There were various possibilities. Wagner enumerated them: mounted excursions on horses provided for the occasion, walks beside the lake, boat rides, the film show in the gym . . .

'I myself,' said Feuerfresser, 'have some urgent paperwork to attend to. I should also like a word with Lieutenant Kersten in due course.'

Before long, the officers' mess was wrapped in postprandial lethargy. The newly-weds, it was generally assumed, were stealing a march on their wedding night. Tauschmüller manfully devoted himself to his wife, but not before he had instructed Kersten to remain in the mess until the Colonel sent Priewitt to fetch him.

Königsberger retired to the medical centre, where Natasha was waiting for him. Melanie hurried off in his wake without bestowing another glance on Kersten, who watched her go with masculine contempt. While he was standing there, Singer sidled up.

'Feel like a drop of something to cool you down after that jamboree?'

'No, thanks, got to keep a clear head for my interview with the Colonel.'

'Very wise,' said Singer. 'Watch your step, Konstantin. He can be an awkward customer.'

Kersten merely shrugged. 'So can I.'

Meanwhile, Majors Kastor and Pollandt were in their planning centre, labouring over the draft of a definitive work provisionally entitled *Manual of Anti-Partisan Warfare: A Practical Guide Based on Annotated Case Histories.*

'I have a feeling, Konstantin, that you don't feel entirely at home here.' Feuerfresser eyed Kersten with sympathetic concern. 'Or am I mistaken?'

'No,' Kersten said tersely, 'you aren't.'

'Would you care to tell me why?'

'Lots of reasons, Colonel.'

For a moment, Viktor von Feuerfresser debated whether there was any point in pursuing the conversation. 'Very well, let's get down to cases. What don't you like about this place?'

'For a start, the general atmosphere. I don't care whether it's here in the mess or out on training, there's too much emphasis on social refinements and too little tough talk, as if the war didn't exist.'

'War isn't everything, my boy.' Feuerfresser's smile conveyed fatherly understanding. 'Your generation has grown up to the sound of gunfire. Quite clearly, none of your previous commanding officers ever took the time to instruct you in what it really means to be a soldier – to be part of a military tradition. I still hope my efforts in that direction may have borne some fruit.' He paused to give Kersten time for thought. 'What else do you object to?'

'Our training methods, Colonel. Some of them are obsolete and inadequate, to put it mildly. They've been dreamed up by armchair warriors – they aren't rugged enough to be of any practical use.'

Feuerfresser nodded. 'I mightn't be averse to the introduction of certain changes.'

'Changes of my own?' Kersten demanded swiftly. 'Any changes I see fit?'

With considerable difficulty, the Colonel restrained himself from pouncing on this piece of bare-faced presumption and rejecting it out of hand. Not that Kersten seemed to mind, his voice became a trifle sharper.

'Any changes *you* see fit, Lieutenant? Not exactly. Any changes *I* see fit. Nobody lays down the law here but me.' Feuerfresser hurrumphed briefly. 'Nevertheless, I'd be interested to hear what you have in mind.'

'The systematic adjustment of our training methods to conform with conditions prevailing at the front. That grenade-throwing exercise of mine is only one example. I've got lots more ideas up my sleeve. May I try them out?'

'You go too fast and too far, Kersten. Any attempt to reinforce discipline, increase physical efficiency and widen the scope of our syllabus can be certain of my approval, but not a risky and fundamentally pointless gamble with human lives. You must accept that.'

'But I can't, Colonel. What I know from experience, and what I keep telling everyone, is that it's better to sacrifice a couple of men on a tough, realistic exercise than ten times as many in combat. I've seen scores of decent soldiers die as a result of namby-pamby training.'

The Colonel had risen to his feet. He stood there like a graven image, eyes veiled. 'No,' he said softly, more to himself than Kersten, 'we aren't on the same wavelength.' Then he looked Kersten full in the face. 'Thinking as I do, Lieutenant Kersten, I'm bound to reject your proposals. I must therefore ask what action you intend to take.'

'Thinking as *I* do, Colonel, I don't have any choice.'

'You mean you'd be prepared to oppose my wishes, if you thought it imperative?'

'Yes.'

Colonel von Feuerfresser's disappointment was so intense that he longed to turn on his heel, but he braced himself for one last all-important question.

'Can you reconcile such an attitude with your conscience?'

'I know I can, Colonel.'

'In that case, you must do so.' Feuerfresser drew himself up, looking every inch an officer in the classic Prussian mould. 'Conscience is a yardstick to be dismissed by no one, least of all a man of my principles.'

That was Viktor von Feuerfresser's final farewell to a dream – a great dream – that had defied fulfilment. He left Kersten standing where he was and summoned Priewitt.

'Tell Wonnegut to saddle Baldur for me.'

Mounted on his favourite stallion, he rode northwards into the solitude of the forest.

Eugen Priewitt was deeply dismayed and highly irate. He dashed off to find Singer.

'That friend of yours! What the hell's he been doing to my Colonel? The Old Man had tears in his eyes.'

'Come again?' said Singer. 'Tears? You're pulling my leg.'

'You don't know him – nobody here does, with the possible exception of me.'

Singer was still lost in wonder. 'Well, fancy that. I'd never have believed it of him.'

'I can tell you one thing, Sebastian: I'm going to pay your buddy back for upsetting the Colonel like this. I'll set the dogs on him – all of them, from Tauschmüller and Wagner down to Schulz – and if that doesn't work I'll take him apart myself. I've never seen the Old Man in such a state.'

Singer was genuinely worried now. 'Look, Eugen, before you go off half-cocked, let me have a word with Kersten. Maybe I can fix things.'

Just before 4 p.m., Lieutenant-Colonel Wassermann of Military Intelligence presented himself at the main gate escorted by his anonymous lieutenant and a uniformed squad of six armed men.

Wagner, who was holding the fort and had been

promptly notified, hurried out to meet them and exchanged a snappy Hitler salute with Wassermann. He could sense that something big was in the wind.

The Abwehr colonel left it to his sidekick to explain, which he did as though reading the weather forecast.

'I regret to inform you that the suspicions we voiced not long ago have turned out to be correct. Further radio messages have since been picked up and decoded. They confirm our belief that a clandestine transmitter is situated inside your camp.'

'Damnation!' exclaimed Wagner. 'That's all we need. Are you sure?'

'Absolutely. In the past few days, our monitoring trucks have been converging on Kampfental in an attempt to pinpoint its exact location. After intercepting further messages last night and this morning, they finally succeeded. Our bearings indicate that it must be in the central section, somewhere to the left of the main road.'

'I see!' Wagner's voice rang with menace. 'So the swine must be operating from the women auxiliaries' compound, the brothel, or the medical centre.'

'Wherever they are, we've come to pick them up.'

'Good luck to you, but I'm afraid I don't have the authority to permit outside personnel to operate on camp premises.'

'Then get it, Lieutenant. Every second counts.'

Wagner got on the phone at once. The Colonel was out riding, Priewitt informed him. Captain Tauschmüller was also unavailable, having taken his wife for a walk round the lake. Majors Kastor and Pollandt disclaimed the requisite authority. That left Wagner holding the baby. He metaphorically clutched it to him in the belief that his greatest hour had struck.

'Very well, gentlemen,' he said briskly, 'let's smoke out this wasps' nest ourselves.'

Wassermann rubbed his hands. 'You know your own

people, Lieutenant. Any idea who the guilty party may be? If you want my guess, it's a person of some intelligence with a knowledge of Russian and considerable freedom of movement inside camp.'

Wagner snapped his fingers triumphantly. 'Of course! It must be Natasha, our interpreter.' He scowled. 'I've never trusted that girl.'

'Right,' said Wassermann, 'let's pay her a social call.'

Wagner conducted the Abwehr officers and their bloodhounds to Natasha's quarters. Her door was locked, so they kicked it open.

Then they embarked on a methodical search of her room. Her wardrobe and bed they reduced to matchwood without success. It was only when they started ripping out the pinewood walls and tearing up the floorboards that something came to light. It was an easily assembled, battery-powered radio transmitter tuned to a frequency known to be employed by Soviet agents.

'Fine,' said Wassermann. 'Now all we need is the lady herself. Where do we find her, Lieutenant?'

Wagner hazarded an informed guess. 'At the medical centre, the double-dealing Russian bitch. She's been spending a lot of time there lately, and I know who with.'

Guided by Wagner, the two intelligence officers and their party headed for the medical centre. They burst into the MO's office without knocking.

Wagner levelled his finger at Natasha, who had been working on some papers with Königsberger. 'That's her!'

The MO looked indignant. 'How dare you barge in here unannounced! Perhaps you'd have the courtesy to tell me what I can do for you?'

'For the moment, nothing.' The Abwehr lieutenant was again acting as spokesman while his boss held a watching brief. 'It's this lady here. We're taking her in for questioning.'

Königsberger interposed himself between the lieutenant and Natasha. 'By what right?'

'Don't make trouble,' snarled Wagner. 'You can't afford to, not any longer. That girl-friend of yours is under arrest.'

'On what grounds?'

The Abwehr lieutenant laughed contemptuously. 'We just found a clandestine transmitter in her room.'

The MO blinked. Then he said, 'So what? You may have found one there, but it doesn't mean she owns or operates it. You'll have to prove that first.'

'Why so keen to get her off the hook, Doctor? You're only casting suspicion on yourself, don't you see?'

Now it was Natasha's turn to rise and stand in front of Königsberger.

'No need to waste any more of your time, gentlemen,' she said. Her voice was proud and unflinching. 'I'm the one you want, nobody else. I admit it.'

'Now I've heard everything,' said the Abwehr lieutenant. He gave another mocking laugh. 'So she admits it, the dirty little Soviet spy. Take her away, Sergeant.'

A hand seized her by the arm, but Natasha shook it off and strode out of the room with her head held high. She didn't look at anyone, not even the MO, which hurt him.

Wassermann turned to him. 'I've a good mind to arrest you too, Doctor – there's enough circumstantial evidence to warrant it. Or would you be prepared to assist us with our inquiries? A voluntary statement might count in your favour.'

'By all means,' said Königsberger, outwardly acquiescent. 'As soon as I get the green light from Colonel von Feuerfresser.'

'There's no need for that.'

'Oh yes there is.' Königsberger looked at Wagner. 'Isn't there, Lieutenant?'

Wagner fidgeted slightly. He avoided the MO's eye

and addressed himself to Wassermann. 'Well, yes – he is a member of the Colonel's staff.' Much as he would have liked to see his pet aversion summarily arrested, the point was a valid one. 'We'll have to consult him first, I'm afraid.'

'Very well, let's do that.' Being already acquainted with Colonel von Feuerfresser, the intelligence chief thought it wiser not to bypass him.

The interview took place in Feuerfresser's office as soon as he returned from his ride. Fully briefed, he sat ensconced behind his desk with an air of majestic calm which conveyed that nothing special was afoot. He seemed unconscious of the MO's presence.

'What's this I hear?' he began, in a quiet and menacing tone. 'Did you really carry out an operation in my sphere of command? Without consulting me first – without even informing me?'

'It was an emergency,' Wassermann replied. 'There was a grave danger that other military secrets would be betrayed, so we couldn't wait. Besides, Colonel, we felt satisfied that we were acting in your own best interests.'

'*My* interests?' said Feuerfresser, cold as a fish. 'Not knowing what they are, you can't possibly claim to have acted in accordance with them. Despite that, I'm prepared to give you a hearing.'

The Abwehr chief launched into a detailed account of how the clandestine transmitter had been pinpointed. 'The agent has already made a full confession,' he wound up. 'It's an open-and-shut case.'

'I see.' Feuerfresser looked unimpressed. 'And where does Captain Könisberger fit into the picture?'

'The radio messages we monitored and decoded contained details of a highly classified operation known as the Final Solution. This poses an obvious question. How did the agent come to hear of it? Who furnished her with the relevant information? From all we know so far, Captain Königsberger must be regarded as the prime suspect.'

'Pure conjecture,' said Königsberger, trying to keep the tremor out of his voice. 'I categorically deny it – the whole idea's absurd.'

'In my view, Colonel, there's no room for doubt.' Wagner uttered this grave accusation without a blush. 'May I remind you that details of the Final Solution were discussed in the mess – in the presence of a handful of officers whose loyalty the speaker took for granted? The MO was one of them.'

'And you were another,' Königsberger retorted.

Wagner gave him a withering glance. 'But only you were in close contact with the girl. You were on intimate terms with her – you may even have slept with her, for all I know. I don't say I blame you, humanly speaking, but that could account for a lot of things.'

'Is this true, Captain Königsberger?' the Colonel demanded sternly.

'Well, yes,' said Königsberger. 'A certain relationship did exist between us, but it was purely physical.' He longed to cry his love aloud, but stopped himself in time.

'In that case,' said Feuerfresser, 'I regret that I can no longer extend you the personal protection to which every member of my staff is normally entitled.'

'But Colonel, I never supplied the enemy with classified information – never, on my word of honour!'

'That may or may not be true. Either way, you must fend for yourself. Until this matter is settled, I cannot regard you as one of my officers.'

On that note, Königsberger was led away.

Singer, who had gone in search of Kersten, ran him to earth in the armoury. The lieutenant and his right-hand man were sitting on some ammunition boxes with an almost untouched bottle of schnapps between them.

Any friend of Kersten's being a friend of his, Master-Sergeant Heinz was accustomed to Singer's privileged status. 'Have one?' he asked, indicating the bottle.

'Next time, thanks, Sergeant.' Singer looked at Kersten. 'Somebody's got to keep a clear head around here. You're in trouble.'

Heinz tactfully stood up. 'Permission to fall out, Lieutenant?'

'Sure, and take the bottle with you.' Kersten gave him a comradely slap on the arm. 'And don't worry about that grenade-throwing business. We'll make out, one way or another.'

As soon as Heinz had gone, Singer took over his ammunition box. 'For God's sake, Konstantin, what have you been doing to the Colonel? Priewitt's mad as hell – he says the Old Man's out of his mind.'

'Bullshit! I told him what I thought about a couple of things, that's all.'

'Nobody can afford to do that, not with Feuerfresser.'

Kersten merely grunted.

'Did you hear about the MO?'

'Yes, I heard. If he's innocent, he'll be cleared. If not . . .' Kersten drew a finger across his throat. 'In case you didn't know, there's a war on.'

'You don't sound very sympathetic.'

'I'm not a bleeding heart.'

'What if I were involved too?'

Kersten hesitated, but only for an instant. 'Are you?'

'"If," I said.'

'Then you'd have to take what was coming to you. What else d'you expect me to say?'

'I see,' said Singer. 'That's clear enough. Anyone who's in the way has to go – anyone in your line of fire gets clobbered. Natasha's just vermin, is that it?'

'I wouldn't put it quite like that. She must have guts, and people with guts impress me.'

'Can it, Konstantin.' Singer stared at his friend intently. 'I've got no time for people who find the sight of certain death impressive. I know your views on the subject, but they're your own affair. Don't try and impose them on people who think otherwise.'

'What do you mean, otherwise? The whole thing's as plain as the nose on your face. We're at war, we've got enemies, and it's either them or us. There's nothing in between.'

'Is that what you told the Colonel?'

'More or less. You only need to take a look around you.' With a sweeping gesture, Kersten indicated the shelves full of arms and ammunition. 'First-class stuff, but it's gathering dust. As for our training methods . . .'

'You don't approve of them?'

'They make me puke. We're meant to be turning out combat troops, not nancy boys. Now I'm here I'm going to pump a bit of fresh air into this place.'

'How?'

'By drafting a report and submitting it through channels. I know the form, Sebastian. Last time I put in a report, somebody's head rolled. There was enough dynamite in it for a dozen courts martial.'

'Don't be too sure. This time your bomb could backfire. You obviously don't know what sort of a place this is.'

'Who says I don't? It's a rotten, stinking club for professional survivors. That's why I'm going to put a squib under them.'

'You're taking on more than you can handle, Konstantin. The Colonel carries a lot of guns. He's a personal friend of the Field-Marshal's – even Hitler thinks highly of him. Then there are Kastor and Pollandt – two really shrewd tacticians – and Tauschmüller, who's as slippery as an eel when it comes to backstage diplomacy. Finally, there's that bloodhound Wagner. How do you plan to tackle *that* bunch?'

'With my powers of persuasion and a few hard facts,' said Kersten. 'Plus your help, Sebastian. I'm counting on that.'

'I thought you might be,' Singer said drily. 'Look, don't underrate these people. They've dumped Frau Klarfeld, crapped on Lahrmann – who was one of their own – and dropped Königsberger like a hot potato. If that doesn't tell you something, it ought to. They'll wipe the floor with you, Konstantin. And me as well.'

'We'll see. Personally, I rate our chances pretty high. I'm raring to go.'

'How heroic of you,' said Singer, ' – and how goddamned premature. If you're smart, you won't make a move till you've taken out as much insurance as you can. There is one possibility.'

'Meaning?'

'Meaning we're both under an obligation – one we can't duck. You know we didn't land here by accident, even if you pretend you don't. We got posted to this weird and wonderful outfit because somebody engineered it. My transfer was voluntary, but yours was made at my suggestion. Barbara fixed them both.'

'So? I'm fond of Barbara, but she shouldn't have done it.'

'She did, though, and she did it through her daddy's friend, Colonel Schlumberger. It wouldn't be smart to spring this on him. From all I've heard about the man, you'd be asking for trouble if you bypassed him.'

'So what do you suggest?'

'Have a word with Schlumberger first – be as outspoken as you like, but talk to him.'

'What's this, delaying tactics?'

'Not at all. I simply think you'd be wise to consult him first, and as soon as possible.'

'If I see him at all, it had better be tomorrow.'

'I'll get in touch with Barbara. She'll arrange it, you bet.'

'All right,' said Kersten, 'but then the fur's going to fly.'

Despite everything, the evening banquet in the mess had gone ahead. Although a certain uneasiness was apparent among the partakers of this candlelit feast, Colonel von Feuerfresser did his best to dismiss the day's events as a mere bagatelle. Like Hitler, whom he never referred to as 'our Führer', the Colonel had a penchant for lengthy monologues at table.

'No one can evade his duty,' he began, 'least of all in this establishment. None of my officers would embark on such a course, nor would I recommend them to try. We belong, after all, to a German community – a Greater German community. Let us drink to the obligations that imposes.'

Having done so, everyone was left in peace until the turtle soup had come and gone. Then:

'We are members of a uniquely powerful nation, ladies and gentlemen. Tempered like steel by two thousand years of glorious Germanic history, we can give as good as we get. Living, as we do, in an imperfect world where unforeseen and undesirable developments can never be ruled out, we are forced to prove our mettle again and again. But this should come as no surprise to a race whose motto is, "That which fails to kill us only strengthens us."'

The sucking-pig brought him to the boil yet again:

'We have a lifelong duty to preserve and enrich our historic heritage. Membership of our nation confers responsibilities as well as privileges. A handful of individuals fail to grasp this because they lack the strength of character to do so. We must cast them out – amputate them like gangrenous limbs.'

This, as all present realized, was an allusion to Captain (Med.) Königsberger, who had proved unworthy of their comradeship. The majors nodded like a pair of mechanical toys in a window display. Tauschmüller stared meditatively at his wife, who was worshipping at the Colonel's shrine. The newly-weds sat there rather forlornly, forgotten or ignored by everyone.

Wagner surveyed the scene with an air of grim resolve. His gaze travelled to the far end of the table and lingered there. Lieutenant Kersten was wolfing everything within reach, perhaps to fortify himself for the coming fray. His appetite seemed unaffected by the absence of Melanie Mauerland.

'In a life-or-death struggle like ours,' Feuerfresser continued over the apple tart and whipped cream, 'we must cling to the traditional Prussian virtues exemplified by Frederick the Great: discipline, good order, and sovereign calm, coupled with a German faith in God and final victory. Armed with them, we can overcome the direst of disasters – or what appear to be such.'

'*Per aspera ad astra!*' cried Wagner, carried away. 'A Roman proverb, meaning roughly, "Stony is our path to the stars."'

'Captain Königsberger,' said Kersten, 'recently quoted another old Roman proverb: *Sapere aude*, meaning "Dare to be wise."'

No one deigned to acknowledge this clumsy gaffe – the uttering of an unutterable name. Not even a pitying smile came Kersten's way, especially as the Colonel had begun his peroration.

'Ladies and gentlemen, we have just spent a memorable day – memorable for its comradeship and conviviality. Now the time has come to say goodbye. We bid farewell, first, to Frau Tauschmüller, whose patients await her ministrations. Next, we bid adieu to the newly married couple, who embark on their brief honeymoon accompanied by our warmest good wishes for their future happiness. And now, ladies and brother officers, let us adjourn to the terrace to watch the fireworks.'

This display, which could hardly have been more in tune

with the times, was staged above the lake by Lahrmann's NCO instructors. It opened with an eruption of tracer from half-a-dozen machine-guns. Then, from a pontoon moored offshore, coloured signal rockets soared into the air. Next, heralded by a salvo of gunfire, an illuminated barrage balloon began to rise. While ascending, it was suddenly captured by the beam of a searchlight. Precisely fifteen seconds later, light anti-aircraft guns opened fire, likewise with tracer, and blazed away until they had shot it to shreds. Darkness and silence returned.

A concerted sigh of satisfaction went up. 'Magnificent!' said someone. 'Superb!' said someone else.

'A tribute to our standard of training,' commented Feuerfresser, ' – though I say it myself.'

Kersten's verdict – 'Fireworks are fine but fire-power's better' – was naturally ignored.

Everyone trooped back into the warmth and comfort of the mess. 'One for the road,' said Feuerfresser. 'Two or three, if you wish, but forgive me if I don't join you.' He saluted the assembled company with a casual flourish of the gloves in his right hand, and strode out. Priewitt hurried after him, looking worried. He alone knew how close to collapse his Colonel really was.

Utter silence reigned in the brothel that night, though light could be seen escaping from chinks in the blackout curtains, which had not been drawn as regulations prescribed. In the view of a patrolling sentry, this was not only an offence but a waste of national resources.

He entered the building to investigate. The foyer was deserted. So was the bar, though all the lights were on. 'That made me suspicious,' he stated in evidence. 'I thought it my duty to look upstairs, so I did. I had a nasty feeling.' Not only nasty but justified, it soon turned out.

Sub-machine-gun at the ready, he kicked open the door of the first 'recreation room'. A girl was lying slumped on the bed, half naked. She had evidently vomited. 'The place stank like a field latrine in July,' was the sentry's graphic description.

Fighting back his nausea, he took a few steps towards the bed and prodded the girl with the muzzle of his gun. 'Had a drop too much, darling?' he asked, but she didn't move. She was dead.

The discovery of another three corpses decided him against pursuing the matter on his own responsibility. He reported it to his immediate superior, a sergeant in the Security Platoon, who promptly telephoned Wagner.

'Seal the place off,' he was told. 'Not a word to anyone. Keep your mouth shut and your eyes open. I'll be right over.'

Wagner was there within ten minutes, wearing a greatcoat and boots over his pyjamas. 'Sergeant, take two men and follow me. Safety-catches off, but don't get itchy-fingered. Nobody fires unless I give the word.'

Wagner and his party marched into the brothel with a clumping of boots and a creaking of leather. One of the men behind him coughed, another farted resoundingly.

He found a total of twelve dead bodies, or the entire female complement of the recreation centre. 'Where's Hausleitner?' he asked, and his men took up the cry. 'Hausleitner, where are you? You're wanted right away!' It relieved them immensely to join in the chorus.

'Find him,' snapped Wagner. 'Fetch him here at the double.'

Though soon located, Hausleitner was past doubling anywhere. The elderly corporal lay wedged between the wall and the extremity of the plinth that had once supported the chapel altar but now functioned as a bar counter. His corpse brought the total to thirteen. Wagner eyed it with distaste.

'Two men guard the entrance, four patrol the outside of the building and another four cordon off the medical centre. Nobody goes in or out without my say-so, Sergeant.'

As soon as the sergeant had barked the regulation 'Yessir!' and bustled off, Wagner, now alone in the brothel, went over to the altar-cum-bar. Here, after briefly scanning the bottles, he treated himself to a tumblerful of brandy. He drained it and shook himself violently, like a wet dog.

Then he picked up the field telephone on the bar counter and cranked the handle hard. The switchboard operator answered at once. 'Wagner here. Put me through to Captain Tauschmüller right away. It's urgent.'

Tauschmüller was on the line some five seconds later, presumably speaking from his matrimonial couch. The adjutant sounded sleepy but unresentful. He made a point of being present and correct at all times. 'Anything wrong, my dear fellow?'

'That's putting it mildly, Captain. We've got thirteen stiffs on our hands.' To Wagner's satisfaction, Tauschmüller was momentarily at a loss for words. Wagner went on to give details. 'From the look of it,' he wound up, 'there's been a mass abuse of dangerous drugs.' In other words, one more nail in the MO's coffin.

The last remark seemed to dispel Tauschmüller's stupefaction. He responded in an entirely normal voice. 'Think you can handle this on your own, Wagner?'

'Certainly, captain.'

'Good man, then do your stuff for the second time in twenty-four hours. And don't leave any loose ends – I want the whole case wrapped up tight. Better call in a quack. Lieutenant Kramer from Hölzbach might do. He owes us a lot of favours, especially now. The Colonel's earmarked him for Königsberger's job.'

'Thanks for the tip, Captain. Don't worry, I'll sort this out.'

Though roused untimely from his slumbers in Hölzbach, Lieutenant (Med.) Kramer was quick to promise every assistance. He reached Kampfental, where Wagner welcomed him 'on the Colonel's behalf', within thirty minutes.

'How can I help you, Lieutenant?'

'Give this place a thorough going-over, and take your time. I want a detailed and authoritative medical report. Something along these lines: "Suicide occasioned by the misappropriation or unlawful administration of dangerous drugs." Right, get on with it.'

Wagner's requirements were met in full. After examining the bodies, Lieutenant Kramer submitted his preliminary findings.

'There's no doubt about it,' he announced. 'The cause of death in every case was an overdose of barbiturates – the sort of drug that can only be prescribed by a qualified physician.'

'In other words,' snarled Wagner, 'Königsberger. *Him* again!'

'I have also ascertained that the women died at about the same time, which definitely points to some kind of suicide pact or collective decision on their part. In the case of the man, death did not supervene until roughly an hour later. None of the thirteen bodies displays any marks of physical violence.'

'They must have been lunatics,' Wagner said suggestively. 'Either that or spies and traitors trying to escape their just deserts.'

'I can certainly confirm that they took their own lives.'

Wagner gave the doctor an appreciative pat on the back. 'Good work, Lieutenant. I'm sure the Colonel will wish to express his thanks in person.'

'Delighted to be of service, Lieutenant.'

'Meantime, Captain Tauschmüller has asked me to offer

you a bed in the mess – that and a stiff nightcap. We'll see what develops in the morning.'

Next morning, Captain Tauschmüller, Lieutenant Wagner and Lieutenant (Med.) Kramer called on Colonel von Feuerfresser to present their combined report. He received them in his spacious office, looking pale but majestic.

'Well,' he said, 'I'm listening.'

Wagner, who acted as spokesman for the trio, outlined what had happened. 'It has since been ascertained,' he went on, 'that the said Corporal Hausleitner reported to Sergeant-Major Schulz late last night, as usual, to submit his weekly accounts. They each drank two bottles of beer. According to Schulz, Hausleitner seemed very agitated about something. He even made the following remark – and I quote his actual words: "We're for it, every last one of us." This statement has been taken down in evidence.'

'And how do you interpret it?'

'As an indication that the arrest of the interpreter and the MO caused panic among their confederates. That Russian creature had obviously succeeded in building up a sizeable spy ring, employing the girls in the brothel to glean information from their clients.'

The Colonel nodded thoughtfully. 'Go on.'

'The girls were under the supervision of Hausleitner, who was clearly a fellow conspirator, and also of Captain Königsberger, whom the Russian agent lured into her bed and pumped for military secrets. Once they were arrested, the other members of the ring knew their time was running out. They decided to cheat the executioner by committing suicide.'

'That explains everything,' said Tauschmüller.

'None of my findings conflicts with anything the Lieutenant has said,' Kramer chimed in.

'In other words, Colonel,' Wagner concluded, 'justice has been done. These thirteen cowardly creatures have proved that by taking the easy way out.' Contemptuously he added, 'They knew they had to die one way or another – they had no choice.'

The Colonel nodded again, even more thoughtfully. 'The finest and noblest things in life – ' he clearly meant himself and his command – 'are constantly under attack by the forces of evil and destruction. This presents us with a challenge which must and will be met. I thank you, gentlemen. That will be all.'

Situation Report No. 8

During the last year of World War II, almost every theatre in Europe remained dark and deserted. No exhibitions took place and few books were published. Opera companies and symphony orchestras ceased to perform. Apathy reigned throughout the arts. Some artists were conscripted into the armed forces and others into munitions factories, while others helped to evacuate the contents of museums and libraries. Unique works of art were destroyed, churches and palaces demolished, irreplaceable private collections looted and broken up.

The Nobel Prize for physics went to Isidor Rabi of the United States, for his work in the field of atomic research. Otto Hahn of Germany was awarded the chemistry prize for effecting a form of nuclear fission by means of neutron bombardment. An American astrophysicist named Jordan claimed that our universe had come into being about ten million years ago and expanded since then at the speed of light, constantly producing new stars known as supernovae.

Allied troops politely stood aside while General de Gaulle entered Paris in triumph and formed a provisional French government. Liberia, Romania, Hungary – even San Marino – announced that they were in a state of war with Germany. In return for American petroleum, Franco Spain stopped supplying Germany with strategic materials.

On the Western Front, 209 German bombers faced an overwhelming force of 2,682 British and American machines. The Allies had 4,573 fighters, the Germans less than a quarter of that number. Gone were the days when Reich Marshal Göring had grandiloquently invited everyone to call him Maier if a single enemy warplane penetrated German air space. It was a joke that had long since ceased to amuse the inhabitants of the steadily, inexorably shrinking Fatherland.

But it was only now that the war divulged its most fearsome secret. The horrors that came to light far surpassed the wildest imaginings of normal human beings, even those who believed Nazi Germany capable of almost anything – almost anything, but not that.

Although the whole world knew that Hitler abominated the Jews, people had assumed that he was trying to segregate them and set up Jewish reservations where they could pursue their 'verminous' existence without obstructing the fulfilment of his grand design.

Historians have since established that no less than 524,277 concentration camp inmates had already been liquidated by August 1, 1944. Most of them were Jews, but others were undesirable foreigners, refractory prisoners of war, political opponents, gypsies, and homosexuals.

As in the case of all crimes, the unrecorded figures must have been equally staggering. One has only to think of the thousands upon thousands of people who were done to death in the street or in their homes, during interrogation or while being shipped off for extermination.

But even this was only a modest prelude to what happened subsequently. The death factories were soon working flat out. By the time they ceased 'production', an estimated total of six million people had been murdered – shot, gassed, lethally injected, beaten to death – and buried or burned like briquettes.

Nothing comparable had occurred in the previous course of human history.

*

Late that afternoon, Kersten requested the use of an official car and was granted it with surprising alacrity. Notified in advance by Singer, Captain Tauschmüller loaned Kersten his gleaming Opel sedan and wished him a successful trip.

Kersten didn't pause to wonder what he meant. He roared off in the direction of Munich with Singer lolling comfortably on the back seat.

Their destination was Barbara Wedell's favourite hotel, the Schottenhamel, near the central station. Kersten unceremoniously parked Tauschmüller's car just outside the main entrance, with two wheels on the sidewalk.

Barbara was waiting for them in the lobby. Impulsively, she ran to meet Singer and flung her arms round his neck. The corporal got a long, loving embrace, the lieutenant a friendly hug.

'It's all arranged,' she told them. 'We're going to have a slap-up meal, and he'll be joining us.'

She led the way to the restaurant, where a table for four had been reserved in the far corner – reserved, so to speak, by Army Group Headquarters. Even at this late stage in the war, the Schottenhamel preserved its traditional standard of service. This was obvious from the snow-white tablecloth, crisp linen napkins, elegant china and dazzling silverware, not to mention the single red rose in a slender cut-glass vase. 'For the lady of the party,' the maître d'hôtel said in a discreet murmur, as he personally poured apéritifs from a pre-dinner bottle of Franconian wine – a Kitzinger-Mainleite 1939.

They were joined in time for the meal by Colonel Schlumberger, a tall, distinguished-looking man in a dark civilian suit of elegant cut. Barbara extended both her hands and he clasped them, gazing fondly down at her. Not until she introduced the others did he turn and give them each a dignified inclination of the head, a brief but interested glance of appraisal.

'Please address me as Herr Schlumberger,' he said, sitting down. His voice was surprisingly soft. 'I'd prefer you not to use my rank. Pretend I'm simply here in a private capacity, at Barbara's invitation. In case you're ever asked, that's the only reason for my presence.'

Kersten and Singer exchanged a surreptitious wink. Even senior staff officers played the Greater German self-insurance game, so it seemed, but the arrival of food left them no time to dwell on the thought. Kersten, who found his helping of grilled calves' liver on the small side, calmly demanded more and got it. Once this problem had been solved, Schlumberger showed signs of coming to the matter in hand.

'I gather from Barbara that you have some information which you think may interest me.' He fired an inquiring glance at Kersten and Singer in turn. 'What's it about?'

'A military shambles,' said Kersten, munching with gusto, 'otherwise known as AFSIC Kampfental.'

'Easy, Lieutenant,' said Schlumberger, and went on to make it clear that he had done his homework. It never did any harm to impress one's juniors with the extent of one's omniscience. 'Raising hell is one of your hobbies, I gather. At least two of your previous commanding officers caught a nasty cold, thanks to you.'

Kersten shrugged. 'They had it coming.'

Schlumberger turned to Singer. 'You, on the other hand, are something of an unknown quantity.'

'I only came along for the ride, Colonel – sorry, Herr Schlumberger. My friend here has something to tell you and I can confirm it if necessary, but I'm just a humble corporal. I wouldn't claim to know the full picture.'

Schlumberger nodded at them both. One, he realized, was an incorrigible hothead and the other a cool customer. 'Well,' he said, 'let's have it.'

'Herr Schlumberger,' said Kersten, 'directly under your command, or rather, under the command of Army Group

Headquarters, there's a so-called military installation like something out of the last century. Its training methods are years out of date and totally unproductive. As for its staff, they're parasites or worse. The place is a hellhole – everything goes on there from plain skulduggery to mass suicide.'

'Now, now, Lieutenant,' Schlumberger said reprovingly. 'You're one of our most highly decorated young officers, which entitles you to a certain latitude, but you can hardly hope to impose your front-line mentality on every military backwater.'

'I not only can, I intend to do precisely that.'

Schlumberger raised his eyebrows and glanced at Barbara as if to ask what he had done to deserve such a problem child. Barbara parried his unspoken question with a smile.

'Most men have a screw loose somewhere,' she said. 'They dream of playing God, but not these two – I can vouch for that. It might pay you to give them a hearing. You personally, I mean.'

'You're wasting your breath, Barbara,' Singer said acidly. 'It's the same old story. Anything that shouldn't exist, doesn't. Anything you'd rather not hear is inaudible.'

'All right,' said Schlumberger, 'fire away, but don't let's have any emotional outbursts or unfounded accusations. Hard facts are all I want. Can you produce some?'

Kersten nodded. 'Plenty. I've already drafted a detailed report. It runs to half a dozen sheets of typescript.'

'May I see it?'

'Of course.' Kersten pulled a sheaf of paper from his pocket. 'This is a copy – one of several.'

Schlumberger skimmed through the document while coffee and brandy were being served. His sang-froid had been acquired in the course of many an interdepartmental skirmish, but it cost him something of an effort to display it now. His face remained quite immobile, his hands slightly less so.

'I don't have to tell you that your allegations will be thoroughly checked out. If any one of them fails to stand up, you may well be court-martialled for preferring false, frivolous and malicious charges against highly respected officers of previously unblemished character.'

Singer grimaced. 'I think Lieutenant Kersten's prepared to run that risk.'

'You bet I am,' said Kersten.

'Very well, but you must give me time to institute inquiries.'

Kersten hesitated for a moment. 'As long as you don't try and shelve the whole affair.'

'Certainly not,' Schlumberger assured him. 'I intend to go through your report tonight, point by point. Once I receive the information I need from Military Intelligence and other departments, I may think it necessary to notify the Field-Marshal. I shall be paying Kampfental an official visit tomorrow, so hold yourselves in readiness. You may be required to give evidence. Are we all agreed?'

Singer looked at Kersten, who nodded.

'How about a glass of champagne?' said Barbara. 'Surely we've time for that?'

'Of course,' said Singer, smiling tenderly at her. 'After all, every glass could be our last.'

9

Colonel Schlumberger reached Kampfental at lunch-time next day. Captain Tauschmüller, who had been warned of his impending arrival by Army Group Headquarters, met him at the main gate and conducted him to Colonel von Feuerfresser.

Feuerfresser was waiting outside on the terrace. 'Welcome, Schlumberger! Delighted to see you again – it's been far too long. How are you, my dear fellow?'

'Blooming, all things considered.'

They exchanged a firm handshake.

'To what do I owe the honour of this visit?'

'Just a routine tour of inspection. Army Group likes to keep its finger on the pulse.'

'I assume you're here with the knowledge and approval of my old friend the Field-Marshal?'

'Naturally. He sends his warmest regards, by the way.'

'Thank you.' Feuerfresser looked gratified. His self-esteem precluded the asking of any more questions. 'We took the liberty of waiting lunch for you, Schlumberger. I do hope you'll join us. It will give me an opportunity to introduce any members of my staff who haven't yet had the pleasure of meeting you.'

No duel could have opened more urbanely.

Immediately after lunch, which was frugal by AFSIC standards, Colonel Schlumberger expressed a wish to inspect the training centre.

'My officers are entirely at your disposal,' Feuerfresser assured him.

'Please don't put yourself out. I'm simply here on a fact-finding mission.'

'May one ask for what purpose, Colonel?' Captain Tauschmüller had reacted as his CO was entitled to expect. Considering it beneath his dignity to ask such questions himself, Feuerfresser had schooled his adjutant to do so for him.

'My task,' Schlumberger said deliberately, 'is to gain a general picture of your work and assess the full extent of your resources and potential.'

Tauschmüller refused to give up. 'With a view to what, Colonel?'

'Everything's still in the melting pot – still in the primary planning stage. However, it's not beyond the bounds of possibility that changes may be made in the basic structure of this establishment. It may even be expanded and entrusted with tasks of a still more vital nature.'

Schlumberger's audience greeted this announcement with considerable relief. Kersten alone was lost in silent admiration of the smokescreen he had managed to lay with such skill.

'In that case,' said Feuerfresser, 'I won't hold you up any longer. Go where you like, take a look at anything that interests you. Captain Tauschmüller is second only to me in his local knowledge and familiarity with our administrative set-up. He'll be glad to give you a guided tour.'

Schlumberger thanked him politely. Feuerfresser acknowledged his thanks with a comradely nod and retired. The other officers also brought their lunch-hour to a close – Wagner with a crisp 'Duty calls!'

'Where would you like to start, Colonel?' asked Tauschmüller.

'In your office. I presume that's where you keep your organization charts and so on?'

After studying them closely, Schlumberger delighted the adjutant by saying, 'Excellent – very informative indeed.' He then stuffed them into his briefcase without asking.

'And now,' Schlumberger went on, 'let's take a stroll through camp.'

Their first stop was the stable block behind the officers' mess, which by now housed a dozen horses. Sergeant Wonnegut had been reinforced by a stableboy of private's rank. The post of Fodder Procurement NCO had also been created and filled by a corporal.

'Very impressive,' was Schlumberger's comment.

'Yes,' said Tauschmüller, 'and a tribute to the Colonel's breadth of vision. These animals are valuable breeding stock. But for him, they might be broken-winded hacks by now – hauling ammunition, or something of the sort.'

Second stop: the Agricultural Section, with its kitchen garden and greenhouses, its twelve superb dairy cows and palatial, well-stocked piggery, its goats, henhouses, and staff of twenty men.

Tauschmüller felt called on to elaborate. 'We try to be as self-supporting as possible, Colonel, so as to relieve the strain on our hard-pressed national economy. The bulk of the cows' milk goes to local hospitals.'

Third stop: the canteen, where the chamber orchestra was just rehearsing a Strauss waltz with stamina and dedication. The musicians were quite uninhibited by the presence of Tauschmüller and his visitor, who was steadily losing the power of speech.

'Look at it this way, Colonel,' said Tauschmüller. 'We feel we owe an obligation to our cultural heritage. That's why we recruit these first-class musicians – to prevent them from being unsuitably employed elsewhere.'

Fourth stop: the deserted brothel, a building of no

312

intrinsic importance but one that merited a visit for completeness' sake. Schlumberger remained as imperturbable as any senior staff officer should. He listened closely to his guide, but his questions became more and more infrequent.

'An inescapable necessity,' Tauschmüller explained. 'We were compelled to install a recreation centre of this type because no such facilities exist in the neighbourhood. I regret to say that it failed to function to our complete satisfaction, which is why we closed it down.'

Schlumberger pointed to the trim-looking huts in the south section of camp. 'What are those?'

'Trainees' quarters, Colonel. They've got running hot and cold water, central heating, well-equipped shower rooms, ample sanitary facilities. Would you care to inspect them?'

'I'll take your word for it.'

Tauschmüller warmed to his theme. 'Our courses of instruction have proved an outstanding success. We're currently processing our thirteenth intake, and we're constantly perfecting our techniques. The men are given close-combat training and brought to a peak of physical fitness, but we're also active in the field of psychological warfare. The majors are experts on that subject.'

'I'm sure they are.'

'Would you like to sit in on a training session, Colonel?' In default of any immediate response, Tauschmüller went on, 'Alternatively, you might prefer to glance through our syllabus. It's not unimpressive.'

'I'm quite impressed enough as it is, Captain.' Schlumberger meant it. Tauschmüller's attempts to blind him with science displayed a certain perverted skill. The slippery captain had made enormous strides in the two years since their last meeting.

'I'd be happy to show you round some of our other facilities, Colonel – the sports centre, for instance. It has a multipurpose hall suitable for ceremonial functions, National Socialist Guidance lectures and film shows. Or is there something else you'd like, Colonel?'

'Yes, two minutes on the phone. In private.'

Having assured Schlumberger that he could telephone in complete privacy from his office in the administration block, Tauschmüller escorted him there and left him to himself. Then, like the dutiful adjutant he was, he darted off to the central switchboard, which was only two doors down, and avidly eavesdropped on the Colonel's conversation.

Schlumberger asked for a priority call to Field-Marshal Wedell at Army Group Headquarters. Wedell answered within seconds.

'Well, Schlumberger, how does it look?'

'Pretty much as I expected, Field-Marshal.'

'I see.' Wedell paused for a moment. 'You mean you think I ought to show up in person?'

'It might be desirable, under the circumstances. The radical changes we discussed should be put into effect right away. There's no time like the present.'

'Very well,' said Wedell, 'I'll come. I'm backing your judgement, Schlumberger – but then, I always do. Warn Colonel von Feuerfresser to expect me this evening.'

CURRICULUM VITAE OF KONSTANTIN KERSTEN
or, Born Heroes Never Waver

Born? Of course I was, or I wouldn't be here now. Where? Nuremberg. When? Nineteen twenty-three. The exact date doesn't matter. All right, if you think it's that important: May 1 – Labour Day. Very appropriate for a birthday. Father? Sure I had a father, who hasn't? Who cares what he was? It's the end product that counts.

Konstantin's father ran a state-owned mental home, ably assisted by his wife Käthe. They both regarded the care of the mentally sick as their mission in life and were profoundly devoted to their work.

Their elder son soon developed a very low opinion of this philanthropic fad which cost the state so much and paid such meagre dividends.

Because his parents' official residence was situated inside the walls of the 'bughouse', as he insisted on calling it, Konstantin acquired a thorough knowledge of what went on there. 'I don't see the point,' he told them one day. 'Why waste time and money on creatures who play snowballs with their own turds, throw up all over themselves or plaster their hair with food? They don't have any right to exist.'

His father attempted to explain. 'We're doing a humanitarian job, my boy – one we believe in. We try to help the mentally ill to bear their sad affliction. It's what we live for, your mother and I. It also earns us a living – all of us, including you – and not a bad one at that.'

In 1932 a riot broke out on the premises. Allegedly because of poor food, a group of inmates went berserk in the dining hall. They smashed up the furniture and vandalized the washrooms and lavatories. Brandishing chair- and table-legs, they charged their attendants with bloodcurdling yells and put them to flight. Before the police and fire brigade could get there, the frenzied mob headed for the director's residence. Konstantin's father, who completely lost his head, prepared to evacuate the premises.

At this point, Konstantin stepped in. Not yet ten, he prevented the demoralized staff from taking refuge in the director's house and ordered them to run out the fire hoses. Attaching one to a hydrant, he turned the water full on and aimed a powerful jet at the oncoming horde. When the attendants followed his example, the rebels retreated and were finally subdued.

Konstantin's father was congratulated by a senior official from the Ministry of Public Health. 'Only your determined and courageous stand saved the day,' he was told. 'Please accept my deep appreciation.'

That night, the director put an arm round his son's shoulders and gave him a grateful hug. 'I'm proud of you, my boy. Carry on this way, and I always will be.'

Did I take an early interest in the Party and its affiliated organizations? What a damnfool question – of course I did. We were a normal, decent German family.

Except that nothing was 'normal' in those dynamic days when the sheep and goats were beginning to go their separate ways. Konstantin himself was alive to this process. There were liberal teachers at his school whom he despised for being cowardly prevaricators, but there were also teachers to whom he felt drawn – World War I veterans with a staunchly nationalistic belief in the dawning of a new German era. As for the handful of socialists and pacifists among the staff, he favoured their eradication.

Konstantin soon joined the Hitler Youth, in which he gave evidence of his very special aptitudes. He proved indefatigable on the parade ground, tireless on the running track, and able on the athletics field. Before long, he was put in charge of premilitary training.

It never embarrassed him in the least to attend school in full Hitler Youth uniform, nor did he ever miss a chance to probe his teachers' political attitudes. Some were evasive and pronounced themselves neutral. Others claimed to have supported the Party from the outset. Only a certain Herr Birnbaum had the nerve to dismiss Konstantin's questions as nonsense and the Hitler Youth as a bunch of silly, inexperienced little boys. 'You don't have a clue what's going on,' he said. 'Use your brains for a change!'

Konstantin declared war on Birnbaum from then on. He instructed his schoolmates to punish the man by ostracizing him, which they did to frightful effect.

Unheeded by his silent, unresponsive pupils, condemned by his headmaster as a total failure and shunned by his colleagues, Herr Birnbaum committed suicide. He hanged himself from a beam in the gymnasium.

Konstantin's verdict: 'Who cares? The man was a deadbeat.'

Military service from 1937, as duty demanded. Officer cadet 1939, then second-lieutenant. When I was doing my stint at a military academy near Berlin – successfully, needless to say – my supervising officer was a Captain Pollandt and my tactical instructor another captain named Kastor. Strange . . . When I ran into them again at Kampfental, years later, neither of them seemed to remember me. I'd never forgotten them.

Konstantin quickly proved himself an able soldier and a devotee of justice.

In 1939, during the Polish campaign, he found two NCOs trying to rape a girl captive. He gave them a good hiding and handed them over to a court martial, which sentenced them to a term in a penal battalion.

In 1940, just after the French campaign, he accused his company commander of tolerating looters and engaging in black market activities. The company commander, who was also court-martialled, found himself reduced to the ranks.

In Russia in 1941, Konstantin charged his battalion commander with cowardice in the face of the enemy. He, too, was tried and sentenced.

Konstantin could afford to do these and other things because he himself was an enterprising and successful field commander who had proved his worth in the most dangerous situations. Perceptive superiors sent him into action as often as possible because they knew that he relished tough assignments. He also had the luck of the devil – or the efficient – on his side.

It was not, however, until he started to specialize in anti-tank tactics that he really hit form. After studying the wrecks of Red Army tanks and self-propelled guns for weak points, he constructed mobile mines and explosive charges that could be hauled into their path on cable-drawn sledges. He also devised a species of mortar for firing Molotov cocktails.

His first tank earned him the Iron Cross Second Class, his third the Iron Cross First Class. After knocking out another three of the monsters in a single morning, he was invested with the German Cross in Gold – probably the most coveted decoration awarded for outstanding gallantry while in close personal contact with the enemy.

His Knight's Cross fell due when he had destroyed over a dozen tanks. Although it gratified him to wear it, especially in the presence of envious superiors, his cup of joy was not yet full.

Why? Because the Knight's Cross itself existed in three higher classes – with Oakleaves, with Oakleaves and Swords, and with Oakleaves, Swords and Diamonds – and Konstantin aspired to the lot.

His progress was interrupted by several involuntary respites from combat duty occasioned by wounds – four of varying severity sustained within two years. For these he was additionally awarded the Wound Badges in Gold and Silver.

Being a 'national hero', Konstantin always received the best of medical attention and nursing – as in summer 1944, when he was admitted to No. 9 Field Hospital, Munich District.

While convalescing there, he made the acquaintance of Barbara Wedell. He also met Sebastian Singer, a fellow patient who became the only friend he ever made in his life. Thanks to them, his consuming desire to return to the front was temporarily frustrated. They shunted him off to AFSIC Kampfental. No act of friendship could have been more unforgivable.

Herbert Wedell, field-marshal and army group commander, reached Kampfental on the evening of the same day. His black Mercedes limousine was escorted by four heavily-armed MP outriders mounted on BMW motorcycles. The cortège swept through the main gates, which had been flung wide, and drove straight up to the officers' mess.

Colonel von Feuerfresser greeted his old friend and comrade with a formal salute, then pumped his hand warmly.

'Good to see you again, Herbert.'

'And you, Viktor.'

'Come inside, Herbert. Make yourself at home – have a bite to eat. There's a snack waiting.'

'Thank you, Viktor, but business first, if you don't mind. There'll be plenty of time for pleasure later.'

Laughing as if Wedell had just delivered himself of a *bon mot*, they disappeared into the mess.

The conference in the Commandant's office was an exclusive affair. Apart from the two principals, only Colonel Schlumberger and Captain Tauschmüller were seated round the table near the window.

'Whatever brings you here, Herbert, I'm glad you came.'

'Good of you to say so, Viktor.'

Feuerfresser took the bull by the horns. 'Field-Marshal,' he said, and his sudden use of Wedell's rank was not a thing to be ignored, 'if you feel I've let you down in some way, I request an immediate transfer to the front.'

'No, no, Colonel,' Schlumberger cut in, looking pained, 'we aren't here to criticize the running of this camp, let alone condemn it. On the contrary, we feel that your experiments in the field of combat training merit wider application.'

Tauschmüller pricked up his ears. 'In what way, Colonel?'

'Let's get one thing straight,' said Wedell in a commanding tone. 'I should like to stress that my old friend and esteemed brother officer, Colonel von Feuerfresser, assumed command of this establishment at my personal request. He was appointed because I had the fullest confidence in him. I still do.'

Feuerfresser bowed his head. 'Thank you, Herbert.'

'Not at all, Viktor.'

That settled it, Tauschmüller told himself. Things couldn't be half as bad as he had feared after eavesdropping on the afternoon's telephone conversation.

'What lies ahead of us,' said Schlumberger, in response to a nod from Wedell, 'may be described as the final phase of the war. If we're to win it, all our available resources must be mobilized. "Total war demands total commitment," as the Führer has so rightly said.'

'Of course,' said Feuerfresser.

'Which means in effect,' Schlumberger went on, 'that all our reserves of manpower must be rounded up as quickly as possible and sent to the front.'

'Is that the reason you're here?' Feuerfresser asked Wedell.

'The only reason.'

Feuerfresser glanced at his adjutant, who was smiling happily because no brickbats had been flung, as he had feared they might be, at AFSIC's administrative system. Being an exponent of grand strategy, Wedell obviously accepted that trivialities had to be overlooked in the

interests of higher things. The man had style, Tauschmüller reflected.

'And you wish me to act accordingly?' Feuerfresser was
saying.

'Administratively speaking,' Wedell replied, 'this is an
extremely tough assignment. I wouldn't entrust it to
anyone but you, Viktor.'

'Have any guidelines been laid down for its implement-
ation?'

At another nod from the Field-Marshal, Schlumberger
started to elaborate. 'Army Group's area of operations
contains a large number of heavily manned garrisons,
training centres, supply depots, administrative offices,
field hospitals, et cetera. Some of them are totally
unproductive, I regret to say. Too many military personnel
are happy to twiddle their thumbs in soft jobs, inspired by
an unsoldierly urge to survive the war at their comrades'
expense. In all, these establishments must harbour several
thousand men who might otherwise be available for
combat duty. We intend to pry them loose.'

'And that,' said Wedell, 'is a task that should be ideally
suited to your forward-looking mentality, Viktor. Knowing you as I do, I'm sure you won't be able to resist such a
challenge.'

'Mind you,' said Feuerfresser, who was beginning to see
light at the end of the tunnel, 'it would require very, very
far-reaching powers.'

Wedell smiled. 'I've already discussed that in detail with
the Führer. If would-be defenders of the Fatherland and
deliberate shirkers are to be released for combat duty in the
largest possible numbers, this can only be achieved by
someone prepared to take vigorous action with backing
from higher authority. That someone, the Führer told me
in confidence, would have to be a general directly
responsible to his headquarters. He would also enjoy the
full support of my own command.'

'A general, did you say?'

'I did, Viktor. If we – that is to say, the Führer and I – can count on your wholehearted co-operation, you will be promoted forthwith.'

'Why should I hesitate? I've always been prepared to do my duty, though I admit it hasn't always been easy. Some of today's officers aren't the men we used to be.'

'How true,' said Wedell, 'but need that stand in our way?'

'If any problems crop up,' Schlumberger promised, 'we'll dispose of them together.'

'Some of them could be quite close to home,' Tauschmüller said meaningfully.

Schlumberger didn't even blink. 'If that's a reference to Lieutenant Kersten and Corporal Singer, they can scarcely be said to represent a problem – not to the likes of us.'

'Ah yes,' said Wedell, who was clearly in a mellow mood, 'I'd like to meet those two young men.'

Kersten, who was sent for first, marched in and snapped to attention. When invited to adopt a less formal stance, he spread his legs and flexed them slightly as though about to leap into an imaginary saddle.

Wedell regarded the much bemedalled lieutenant with gracious interest. Colonel von Feuerfresser eyed him sadly, and not only because he had just been informed of his peculiar role in the current proceedings. As for Schlumberger, he demonstrated his talent for reducing knotty problems to manageable proportions.

'My dear Kersten,' he said blandly, 'I'm sure you'll be interested to learn that AFSIC Kampfental, in its present form, is to be disbanded a few days from now. That means its training activities will cease as of now.'

'I'm glad to hear that, Colonel.'

'Even though your job as Lieutenant Lahrmann's replacement will go by the board?'

'That's secondary, sir.'

'From what I've been told, Kersten, your heart is set on another field command.'

'Very much so, Colonel.'

'The Field-Marshal has decided to grant your request. You're not only being sent to the front – you're getting a fully trained combat unit to take with you. How does that appeal?'

Kersten positively glowed. 'It's all I've ever wanted, Colonel. May I ask what form my assignment will take?'

'You'll move out at once, taking most of the current batch of trainees with you, as well as the pick of the permanent staff here. With this well-equipped force under your command, you'll report to General Werner on the Eastern Front. General Werner has been instructed to form a mobile reserve division whose role will be to counter-attack enemy spearheads threatening key sectors of the front. Just your cup of tea, I fancy.'

'Many thanks, Colonel.' Radiant with pride and satisfaction, Kersten marched out. Nothing but a few Russian bullets now stood between him and the next rung on the Knight's Cross ladder.

'There goes a genuine hero,' said Wedell, rewarding Schlumberger with an appreciative nod. 'And now for our next little problem.'

Sebastian Singer entered promptly. Feuerfresser and Tauschmüller gave the corporal an icy glare, Schlumberger a covert wink.

To everyone's surprise, Wedell spoke first. 'Come closer, Corporal – no, closer. I want to take a good look at you.'

He studied Singer closely, with growing surprise and amusement. 'Strange,' he said at last, 'I'd pictured you quite differently, even though I've seen photos of you and been forced to listen to a lot of anecdotes about you. I suppose you know who from?'

Singer preserved a tactful silence, which seemed to please Wedell. Smiling, the Field-Marshal sat back in his chair and turned to Schlumberger. 'Very well. Solution number two, as arranged.'

His chief of staff came straight to the point. 'Being a shrewd young man, Corporal, you must be aware that few people here would mourn your departure.'

'Too bad, Colonel. I don't think they realize just how co-operative I can be.'

'Really? That's nice to know.' Schlumberger was privately amused to see Feuerfresser wince at this piece of impertinence on the part of a mere corporal. Tauschmüller, who was girding himself for a curt retort on Feuerfresser's behalf, he quelled with a warning glance. To his great satisfaction, he noted that the Field-Marshal seemed to be enjoying himself immensely.

'So you're willing to co-operate,' he went on quickly. 'We welcome your attitude, Singer, which is why we propose to offer you a choice between two alternatives. You can either join your friend Lieutenant Kersten, who is taking command of a combat unit in accordance with his motto, which seems to be, the more gunfire, the more glory.'

'And the other alternative, Colonel?'

'You can come with me – quite why, I leave you to work out for yourself. I shall find some use for you in my immediate entourage. Is it a deal?'

Singer realized that he was being offered a slightly greater chance of survival. He was no hero, but he was no fool either.

'It's a deal, Colonel.'

With the main business of the day disposed of, relaxation set in. Priewitt went the rounds with a bottle of champagne.

'So we're agreed in principle, Viktor,' Wedell said happily.

'Will the Führer endorse your recommendation, Herbert?'

'He was presented with a short-list of possible candidates. At my request, your name headed that list. I was authorized to offer you the appointment. I did so, and you accepted.'

Feuerfresser gratefully inclined his head.

'Then we'll phone him at once.'

They were through to the Wolf's Lair, Hitler's East Prussian headquarters, within minutes.

'My Führer,' Wedell told his supreme commander, 'as foreseen, we can count on Colonel von Feuerfresser's wholehearted support in respect of Operation Barrel-scrape.'

'Good, very good. Put him on the line.' Adolf Hitler's voice became even harsher and more imperious as he addressed himself to Feuerfresser. 'You, Feuerfresser, are being entrusted with a great and historic task of crucial importance to the outcome of the war. I'm confident that you will prove fully equal to all the demands made on you. As of now, you're under my personal command, though Field-Marshal Wedell's army group will retain administrative responsibility. Is that understood?'

'Absolutely, my Führer.'

'Good. I shall expect to receive a progress report in the very near future. First, however, I promote you major-general. My congratulations.'

With a click, the line went dead. Although the ex-colonel and freshly hatched general bent a look of gratitude on his old friend and comrade, he could not help feeling slightly apprehensive.

'Congratulations, Viktor,' said Wedell, who had listened in on the extension earpiece. 'Nobody deserves promotion more. I'm sure you'll prove worthy of it.'

'I'll do my best, Herbert.'

'Then start on your planning right away. Report to me in Munich when you've roughed something out, but remember: time is of the essence.'

As soon as Field-Marshal Wedell had left Kampfental accompanied by his chief of staff and Corporal Singer, who had packed his belongings at top speed, Colonel von Feuerfresser gathered his officers around him.

The only absentee was Kersten, who was already drafting movement orders with Sergeant-Major Schulz. In addition to the trainees, two-thirds of AFSIC's permanent staff had also been instructed to join his task force, and Kersten insisted on taking all the NCOs and men of long experience. He curtly dismissed every one of the sergeant-major's protests. 'Stop blathering, Schulz!' was his standard retort. 'I'm acting on the Field-Marshal's orders.'

In the mess, Feuerfresser made his announcement with becoming modesty. 'Gentlemen, I'm pleased to be able to inform you that, earlier this evening, the Führer personally promoted me major-general.'

Once the universal buzz of surprise and pleasure had abated, Major Kastor offered his own and his brother officers' warmest felicitations, concluding with the words, 'If anyone deserves it, General, you do.'

Feuerfresser thanked him in measured tones. Champagne from his personal reserve was already on ice. He waited until his officers' glasses had been charged and raised in his honour before continuing.

'One promotion brings others in its train, gentlemen. First the commanding officer, then his subordinates. We're living in a unique era – one that presents exceptional challenges. The ability to meet them successfully is what counts – and what pays.'

Lieutenant Wagner was hugely impressed that Adolf

326

Hitler should have spoken to his boss in person. 'Führer command, we obey!' he proclaimed, confident that this hackneyed slogan would go down well under present circumstances.

'In consultation with my old friend and comrade, Field-Marshal Wedell,' Feuerfresser went on, 'the Führer has decreed that AFSIC Kampfental shall cease, as of now, to fulfil its current role.'

He paused to savour his officers' surprise and consternation. Most of them registered deep anxiety. Tauschmüller alone was calm personified, but he, of course, already knew the score.

By visual prearrangement with Major Kastor, Major Pollandt was the first to speak. 'Unless I'm mistaken, the General spoke of disbanding AFSIC in its present form.'

'Quite right, Major.' Feuerfresser nodded approvingly. 'But just to clear up one important point, let me say this: even though our unit is changing its role, I intend to retain the services of my closest and most experienced associates. By that I mean all of you, without exception.'

This news evoked a concerted sigh of relief, quickly followed by a thirst for action.

'What will our new role be, General?'

Feuerfresser's team was back into its stride. With evident satisfaction, he left it to his adjutant to fill in the details.

'Our General's instructions from the Führer,' said Tauschmüller, 'are to comb the home front for all redundant, superfluous or underemployed personnel and release them for combat duty.'

'What about the administrative structure?' Kastor inquired.

'The General has already roughed it out,' Tauschmüller told him. 'You'll be responsible for the fine brushwork.' He went on to expound the plan in broad outline.

'1. Majors Kastor and Pollandt, assisted by a skeleton staff of orderly-room personnel and women auxiliaries, will begin by drawing up a list of military establishments suitable for pruning, complete with accurate estimates of their present strength.

'2. A quota of fifty per cent will be applied during the weeding-out phase, which means that the units affected will be cut by half. Selection will be carried out in a rigorous and purposeful manner, regardless of any objections on the part of unit commanders, garrison headquarters and other authorities. In the event of major difficulties, the General will be informed.

'3. Our base of operations will be Kampfental, where a communications and information-gathering centre will be set up, with a switchboard manned twenty-four hours a day. Officer in charge: myself. Lieutenant Wagner will be responsible for forming a security and transportation section.'

Natasha did not survive her fifth night in custody. Though brutally tortured by interrogators from the Secret Field Police, a branch of Military Intelligence, she divulged no names or information. To the very last, she merely eyed her inquisitors with contempt and said nothing.

Her death certificate read: 'Deceased due to heart failure.'

Captain Königsberger was visited in his cell by a doctor acquaintance who had been officially instructed to give the prisoner a medical examination. His findings, as conveyed to the officer in charge, sounded ominous:

'I don't like the look of him. A high temperature doesn't mean much in itself, but there are definite signs that he's contracted a highly infectious disease. All direct contact with the prisoner should be avoided. I'll call an ambulance and have him transferred to the isolation hospital at Garmisch.'

Kersten, who had completed his own part in the preparations, loaded Schulz and his orderly-room clerks with a stack of paperwork which the sergeant-major, for all his muttered protests, was forced to accept.

'It's just before midnight, Schulz. I want all these equipment lists and movement orders neatly typed and ready for signature by reveille, so pull your finger out.'

So saying, Kersten joined Master-Sergeant Heinz for a midnight stroll along the camp road.

'You see, Heinz? We did it after all. Action at last.'

Heinz gave a contented grunt. 'And not before time, Lieutenant.'

Kersten had brought along a bottle of malt whisky, guaranteed ten years old – a parting gift from Sebastian Singer, who had left it under the table in his quarters with a scribbled note. The two warriors swigged at it from time to time.

'I'm stripping this place of all I can – men, weapons, equipment. The only remaining question is, are you coming too?'

'Just what I was going to ask you myself, Lieutenant.'

At Army Group Headquarters, a somewhat dilapidated baroque palace north of Munich, Singer was personally assigned his new quarters by Colonel Schlumberger. They consisted of one small room above the colonel's suite of offices – an attic room that looked like a dump for unwanted files and stationery. The only home comforts were a mattress and a couple of blankets on the floor.

'Very cosy,' Singer said drily.

'Be thankful for small mercies,' Schlumberger told him. 'You could still be languishing at Kampfental or heading for the front. The main reason I'm taking you under my wing is to see you don't perpetrate any more youthful indiscretions. All else apart, there's Fräulein Wedell to consider. From now on, you're not to see her without my say-so.'

'Aren't you underestimating her, Colonel? She's never been known to model her behaviour on anyone's say-so, not even yours – she goes her own sweet way.'

'Who knows, Singer? With the job I'm giving you, you may be less open to distraction by that headstrong young lady.'

'Job, Colonel? What job?'

'I'm setting up a liaison office to keep in touch with Kampfental. For that I'll need a staff officer and half-a-dozen men. In view of your unrivalled local knowledge, you'll be one of them. What do you say?'

Singer said nothing. He was too suspicious to speak.

Situation Report No. 9

What the conspirators of July 20, 1944, had foreseen and tried to prevent – the devastation of Europe and Germany's downfall – had finally come about.

Large tracts of territory had been laid waste and many cities reduced to rubble. The sufferings, hardships and privations of the people who roamed them were boundless, yet still they failed to grasp the full extent of what had been done to them. They lusted after scraps of bread and bowls of watery soup, fought each other for handfuls of rotten potatoes.

Marshal Zhukov captured Berlin. The British and Americans stopped short at the Elbe. Himmler vainly tried to negotiate an armistice with them before committing suicide. Hitler turned on Göring and ordered his arrest for high treason.

Cornered in the Berlin Chancellery, Hitler at last married Eva Braun. Next day, their lifeless bodies were drenched with gasoline and burned on his orders to prevent them from falling

*into Russian hands. Goebbels followed the Führer's example,
together with his wife and six children.*

*At a conservative estimate, some 24.4 million men were
killed on the battlefields of World War II. Between the
fighting fronts, roughly the same number of civilians died too.
But this gruesome tally is incomplete because, as always
in time of war, death defied its book-keepers' efforts to keep
pace.*

*In all, the war may have cost as many as a hundred million
lives.*

*It was later claimed, seriously and with scant sense of
shame, that few Germans had foreseen the catastrophe to
come.*

*Yet the road to doom and disaster had been clearly
signposted, years before, by those agents of death known as
soldiers.*

Feuerfresser was attired as a general when he joined his subordinates in the mess next morning. Priewitt had arranged
this with the aid of an experienced tailor who had worked
all night to sew on the scarlet shoulder straps, collar
patches and trouser stripes. Priewitt himself had been
awarded another silver pip and was now a staff sergeant.

Once his officers had demolished a hearty breakfast *à
l'anglaise*, Feuerfresser sat back and said, as he had been
wont to do when a colonel, 'Right, gentlemen, I'm
listening.'

Kastor led off. 'We've worked out an effective division of
labour as instructed, General. In our view, the most
practical course will be for Major Pollandt to concentrate
on local garrisons and field hospitals while I specialize in
training centres and supply depots. All these facilities
display certain common features in the personnel sector.
They ought to yield a rich harvest.'

'Fifty per cent or even more,' said Tauschmüller, who
had given the matter thought overnight. 'In my experi-

ence, they maintain manning levels dating from the palmy days of the Polish and French campaigns.'

'Quite so,' said Wagner, also striving to be practical. 'In fact, they may even have artificially inflated their strength in the interim, just for the sake of extra ration allocations. Their only aim is to sit out the war in comfort.'

'Which is why,' Major Pollandt put in, 'we propose to adopt the following procedure:

'1 When visiting each of the establishments listed in our master plan, our first step will be to request an up-to-date personnel list.

'2. We shall then inform the local commander what he's required to do, namely, halve his existing strength, and invite him to submit appropriate recommendations.

'3. Since he will almost certainly try to fob us off with misfits and rejects, we shall demand to inspect his entire unit and take a very close look at the men he proposes to retain.'

'Good thinking, gentlemen,' said Feuerfresser.

Wagner had a further suggestion to make. 'So as to make it abundantly clear that we're not to be trifled with, General, I recommend that the mobile selection boards be made up as follows: Majors Kastor and Pollandt each to travel in a staff car with one aide, one driver, and one of my security men equipped with two-way radio. Each vehicle to be escorted by two outriders armed with sub-machine-guns.'

'Go on.'

'That way, radio communication with base can be permanently maintained. To deal with any really intractable cases, I would hold a fully motorized, heavily armed assault detachment in readiness — a sort of flying squad which could escort the General to the scene if it became imperative for him to intervene in person.'

Feuerfresser approved this recommendation with a nod

and glanced at Tauschmüller, who presented a progress report of his own.

'Our administrative and communications centre will soon be fully operational, General. All the requisite equipment – weapons, vehicles, radio sets, and so forth – has been or is being procured. Special passes and permits are already in preparation.'

'What is more,' said Feuerfresser, looking smug, 'we ourselves are starting things off with a bang. By the day after tomorrow, nearly two hundred highly trained men will have left for the front under Lieutenant Kersten's command.'

'Is he getting all the men he asks for?' someone discreetly inquired.

'All I choose to give him, but none from Group C. They will receive separate marching orders whose details I shall announce in due course.'

'Has this got something to do with their knowledge of English, General?' asked one of the majors.

'Don't worry about that now, gentlemen, not even if I request you to continue selecting men with special aptitudes of the kind you refer to. They will be attached to Group C for possible use in a top-secret operation.'

Feuerfresser knew what he was talking about. The purpose of these measures became clear when the so-called Ardennes Offensive was launched on 26 December, 1944 – a breakthrough effected by German units wearing American uniforms, armed with captured weapons, and answering to words of command delivered in English. Surprise was complete, but the offensive failed to maintain its early momentum and petered out by 16 January, 1945.

'At all events, gentlemen, I shall regard our own initial contribution as a yardstick. In other words, I'm counting on a daily success rate of one hundred men.'

The majors nodded simultaneously, but Kastor spoke for them both. 'That ought to be possible, General.'

Feuerfresser rose. Staff Sergeant Piewitt, who had been standing behind him like a statue, pulled his chair back. 'We shall meet again this evening, gentlemen. I look forward to receiving further constructive suggestions then.'

Supper in the mess – pea soup with smoked ham and pigs' trotters – was positively spartan compared to what had been on offer there before. The only authorized beverage was half a bottle of Franconian wine a head.

'Very well,' the General said again, 'I'm listening.'

'Our co-ordinating centre,' Captain Tauschmüller reported, 'has now been installed in the gymnasium and is in fair working order. It incorporates the operational planning section, intelligence evaluation section, radio station, and telephone exchange – all of them under my personal supervision. The centre is staffed partly by Sergeant-Major Schulz's orderly-room clerks but mainly by women staff auxiliaries.'

His sudden frown was not lost on Feuerfresser. 'Problems, Captain Tauschmüller?'

'Only one, General. I've put Fräulein Mauerland in charge of the female personnel – I had no choice, since she's Frau Lahrmann-Klarfeld's second in command. From what I've seen so far, however, she lacks self-confidence. She may develop some in time, but she won't be up to the job till she does.'

Wagner gave a knowing, mocking laugh. 'She also lacks the attributes of a truly German female – doesn't know the meaning of total commitment, so I've heard.'

Everyone ignored this rather indelicate remark, especially as the majors had a more welcome contribution to make.

'According to the schedules we've drawn up,' said Pollandt, 'each of us should be able to carry out at least one operation a day. A considerable amount of time will be wasted in transit, of course, but it may be feasible, if the establishments to be inspected aren't too far apart, to fit in two operations.'

'Two if you possibly can,' said Feuerfresser.

'The only thing is, General,' Wagner interposed, 'a higher turnover would pose logistical problems. We can't ship the whole of our haul straight off to the front. One way out might be to set up a transit camp of our own, here on the premises. I'm pretty sure we could form some effective combat units out of the men we rake in.'

'And who'd take charge of them?'

'I'd be glad to, General, at least from the ideological angle. Their morale could be boosted by skilful handling. After a course of National Socialist Guidance lectures from me, many former shirkers might beg to be sent to the front right away.'

'It's an idea,' Feuerfresser conceded.

Wagner now had the bit between his teeth. 'And another thing, General. It's quite conceivable that our selection boards will flush out units which cannot only be cut by fifty per cent but are redundant enough to be disbanded altogether.'

'What facilities do you have in mind, Wagner?'

'Well, isolated supply depots, out-of-the-way ammunition dumps, and so on. We could simply amalgamate them – mobilize their personnel and take over their stores.'

'Excellent, Wagner!' Any such praise from the lips of Feuerfresser was rare enough to give promise of imminent promotion.

'First-class,' Tauschmüller chimed in, but went on to voice a few discreet misgivings. 'Except that I doubt if our existing organization could cope with the additional burden. We might dissipate our resources – unless, of course, we expanded our operational staff.'

'No need to, my dear fellow,' said Feuerfresser. 'After all, we're holding something in reserve – something we can now fall back on, given the change in our role. I'm referring to our experienced and versatile brother officer, Lieutenant Lahrmann – not to mention his charming wife, who has always commanded her women auxiliaries with such efficiency.'

Everyone nodded as though in receipt of an edict straight from Mount Sinai. Although another equally authoritative verdict had been passed, only a few days before, on the subject of employing married couples in the same military establishment, exceptional circumstances warranted exceptional measures.

'But General,' said Tauschmüller, 'the Lahrmanns aren't due back from their honeymoon for another three days. You really want me to recall them?'

'Of course. Their country needs them here and now.'

Almost on the dot of midnight, the first two hundred men released for combat duty paraded below the main terrace of the officers' mess. Parked beside the road was a convoy consisting of ten Henschel trucks and the elderly Mercedes scout car assigned to Lieutenant Kersten. Air-raid precautions forbade the use of lights, so the scene was eerily illuminated by the moon alone.

With solemn, measured tread, General von Feuerfresser came out on to the terrace flanked by his majors. Tauschmüller, Wagner and Priewitt brought up the rear.

Kersten's voice rang out. 'Task force, atten – shun! Eyes – right!' He mounted the steps, marched up to Feuerfresser, and saluted. 'Task force present, correct, and ready to move out, General.'

'Thank you, Lieutenant Kersten.' Raising his voice, Feuerfresser projected it at the serried ranks below. 'Men,' he cried, 'all of you have successfully undergone a tough and intensive course of combat training here. It will enable you to weather the storms that lie ahead. The only ones with anything to fear are the ill-trained, the inexperienced, the bunglers and ditherers – and you are none of those.

'Times are hard, men. This war was forced on us, but we shall win it none the less. We owe it to our mothers, wives and children to defend Greater Germany, our beloved homeland, on behalf of Western civilization.

'We shall do our duty, you and I. We shall willingly accept any hardship demanded of us. We shall press on regardless, even if the road we tread is one that calls for supreme self-denial and self-sacrifice. And now, men, I shall detain you no longer. Goodbye and Godspeed!'

'Task force!' bellowed Kersten. 'On the command "Move!", fall out and double to your trucks. Move!' He saluted the General again and headed for his scout car.

'One moment, Kersten,' said Feuerfresser.

Kersten retraced his steps. Stationing himself in front of the General, he looked him full in the face.

'Well, my boy, are you satisfied now?'

'A hundred per cent, General.' There was no doubting Kersten's sincerity.

'I wish I could have done more for you – far more. One day, perhaps, you may realize what our brief encounter meant to me.'

'Whatever it was, General, everything's fine. I'll do my best to justify your faith in me.'

Feuerfresser extended his hand and Kersten clasped it firmly. Like father and son, like hero saluting hero, they held each other's gaze for five long seconds.

Then Kersten hurried off to join his men and Feuerfresser retired to his office. He sat down at the desk, propped his head on his hands, and stared ruminatively at the leather blotter.

Priewitt brought him some champagne. He raised the first glass in a silent toast and drained it at a single draught.

'You know,' he said to his trusty acolyte and long-time

confidant, 'that sort of occasion calls for every ounce of self-control a man can muster.'

'Yes, General,' said Priewitt, refilling his glass.

Champagne in hand, Feuerfresser sat back and studied Priewitt through the ascending bubbles. 'Eugen,' he said after a while, 'you must have noticed that I've never been known to criticize our Supreme Commander.'

'Yes, General.' Even Priewitt had been struck by the fact that his farewell address had contained no reference to the Führer.

'Lately, though, I get the ominous feeling that he's lost all appreciation of the Army's true value. He seems prepared to misuse and squander his finest officers – infect them with a sort of suicidal mania, even. Like that splendid young man Kersten, who could have been my own son. It fills me with foreboding.'

Priewitt made a point of ignoring such remarks. His unique position of trust was based on deliberate deafness.

Captain Lahrmann and his bride returned to Kampfental next day. They were warmly greeted by Feuerfresser at dinner in the mess.

'Welcome to you both,' he said. 'I'm delighted to see you back – we all are. You're badly needed here, so thank you for your prompt response to my call. Kampfental has been given a new and vital role during your absence. We shall meet its requirements in our time-honoured fashion, by which I mean: as a team. That's why I can't do without you.'

The meal was a subdued affair. Although the diners ate with gusto, they somehow missed the background music. The members of the chamber orchestra were already on their way to the front.

Over pudding, the General addressed Frau Lahrmann-Klarfeld in a discreet undertone. 'I hope I can count on your continued support, dear lady. You alone can give our women auxiliaries the effective leadership they need. Just between ourselves, the job is proving too much for your deputy, Fräulein Mauerland. She can't hold a candle to you.'

'If I may venture a suggestion, General, she ought to be transferred to another unit without delay.'

'Agreed.' Their voices had sunk to a whisper by now. 'I shall be happy to accommodate you in every way, just as long as I can be assured of your fullest co-operation from now on. Is there anything else?'

'Only a minor matter, General. I was badly let down by a certain member of your staff. I should like to be spared the embarrassment of working in close conjunction with him.'

'Of course.' The General took this unmistakable reference to Captain Tauschmüller as read. 'You will, of course, be directly under my command. It won't be possible to avoid all purely official contacts with the person in question, but I shall ensure that they're kept to a minimum.'

'Thank you, General,' she said, surreptitiously glancing in Tauschmüller's direction.

Once this hurdle had been cleared, Feuerfresser turned with relief to Lieutenant Lahrmann. 'I've always been able to depend on you, Lahrmann, but the task that lies ahead will keep you at full stretch. You'll be away for days on end, operating independently under conditions requiring the ultimate in guts and initiative. I think you're up to the job. Do you?'

Lahrmann looked ingenuously heroic. 'Certainly, General.'

And that, Feuerfresser told himself happily, was just about that.

At Field-Marshal Wedell's headquarters, Corporal Singer was kept busy with the stream of progress reports that flowed from Kampfental to his own department, the

Special Operations Section. Their tone was bombastic enough to fill him with apprehension.

The latest message informed Army Group that Operation Barrelscrape had dispatched another sixty men to the front, corralled forty in Wagner's transit camp, and disbanded two administrative facilities. Singer deposited it on Schlumberger's desk.

'What do you think of that, Colonel?'

Schlumberger digested the contents of the report with grudging admiration. 'Pretty good going.'

'But isn't it all a gigantic mistake?'

Wedell's chief-of-staff grinned indulgently. 'Perhaps, but it's absolutely logical. These things always happen at the tail-end of a war. Establishments like Kampfental get out of hand, assert their independence, run wild. In the end, their destructive urge turns in on itself.'

'And there's nothing to be done?'

'Every war ends in an orgy of destruction, Singer. Potential winners start to feel like licensed executioners, potential losers run amok. One's only hope of survival is to play Pontius Pilate.'

'The way you're doing with Kampfental, you mean? It's obvious what's going on there. You've set a thief to catch a thief, haven't you? Those people are totally unscrupulous – they're greedy, corrupt and power-crazy. They've made the most horrendous, lethal blunders and they're still hard at it – by your kind permission.'

'I repeat, Singer, it's all part of the standard finale. Sad as it may seem, philanthropy and idealism are out of place in a situation like this. Besides, you aren't the world's greatest moralist yourself. You know that damn well, or you wouldn't have jumped at my offer of a safe billet here.'

'Maybe, Colonel, but it doesn't stop me from feeling an utter swine when I think of all the other poor devils who haven't a clue what's being done to them.'

'I offered you a chance of survival. You accepted it as a

matter of course, so act accordingly. Stop flaunting your conscience at me. We're up to our necks in manure, both of us, and we've no choice but to wade through it as best we can. That is, unless you can suggest another way of extricating ourselves without committing suicide?'

Sebastian Singer was forced to admit defeat.

Being the fruit of painstaking preparation and sedulous staff work, the operations mounted by Kampfental's élite produced results which far surpassed those of their competitors.

While General von Feuerfresser was at work in the south and west of what remained of Greater Germany, the same objective was being pursued in its dwindling northern and eastern territories by a certain General von Gabelsdorf, known to the rear echelon troops on whom he preyed as 'Grabber Gabelsdorf'. It was an apt nickname which Feuerfresser was soon privileged to share.

But whereas Gabelsdorf usually operated in person, escorted by a small retinue, Feuerfresser brought the whole of his brilliantly co-ordinated team into play. On the few occasions when he himself was forced to intervene – as, for instance, when officers of senior rank proved obdurate – he did so with striking and invariable success, like a martial *deus ex machina*.

The members of his staff fully justified his confidence in them. The majors, for example, developed a form of multiphase attack which they put to effective use with Lahrmann's co-operation. Its underlying principle was that old strategic precept beloved of the Prussian Army: 'March separately, strike together.'

This was how, by skilfully deploying their forces, they contrived to 'inspect' no less than three army posts in a single day. Before long, Feuerfresser's organization was releasing a weekly average of five hundred men for combat duty in newly formed divisions.

Just over half of all those rounded up were packed into troop trains at once. The rest spent some days in Kampfental's own transit camp, and thus in the hands of Lieutenant Wagner, who was at the top of his form. Wagner moulded them into combat units of company strength and armed them to the teeth, not only with the finest available weapons but also with Roman proverbs and quotations from *Mein Kampf*.

Kampfental's material resources – primarily food but also arms and ammunition – were continuously augmented by the disbandment of entire rear echelon units and the seizure of their stores. Its vehicle fleet, too, had vastly increased, necessitating the establishment of a substantial fuel depot on the former football field. Every vehicle used by camp personnel for purposes of reconnaissance, security, inspection, communications and transportation was brand spanking new.

And all these things were made possible by the Führer's blanket order to the effect that Kampfental's requisitions were made in his name, carried top priority, and should be acted on without delay. Thanks to this ukase, General von Feuerfresser was able to chalk up some phenomenal successes. Field-Marshal Wedell expressed his appreciation in the warmest terms, though rather wearily, and promised to inform the Führer at once.

He did so, with the result that Feuerfresser received a phone call from on high. 'Keep it up, General,' Hitler told him. 'The Fatherland is in your debt. You and your men may rest assured of my sincere gratitude.'

This was more than a passing word of encouragement. The two majors were promoted lieutenant-colonel. Captain Tauschmüller could henceforth call himself major. Lieutenant Wagner got his captaincy, as did Lieutenant Lahrmann. Sergeant-Major Schulz was awarded the Distinguished Service Cross, First Class, with Swords. Sergeant Gerner picked up one without Swords but could congratulate himself on his promotion to staff sergeant. Colonel Schlumberger became Major-General Schlumberger. He felt momentarily tempted to make Corporal Singer a sergeant but resisted the inclination.

At Kampfental, a big mess party was held to celebrate these marks of honour, but few of the assembled company looked particularly satisfied, let alone pleased with life.

Only Captain Wagner was in really high spirits. '*Moritur et ridet*,' he declared, ' – as the Romans used to say. Roughly translated, that means, "If you must die, die laughing."'

Final Report

Only a few weeks later, fighting officially ceased. As though seen in a distorting mirror, the images of the war and of those who had waged it acquired a strangely ambiguous quality as time went by.

Field-Marshal Wedell, faced with the imminent collapse of the Greater German Reich, the end of his professional career and the destruction of the armies under his command, chose suicide and shot himself with his service automatic. Hitler decreed that the name of 'that man' was never again to be mentioned in his presence.

Lieutenant Kersten was killed in action during his very first engagement on the swiftly crumbling Eastern Front. Though hit in the stomach, he bellowed encouragement to his men as they plodded past him through a hail of bullets. Curtly rejecting all offers of assistance, he died in agony several hours later.

Master-Sergeant Heinz ended his ultra-military existence within a few feet of his lieutenant, mangled past recognition by a mortar bomb.

Of their two hundred AFSIC-trained men, little more than fifty survived this first assault. Disheartened, they tried to withdraw. Only a couple of dozen got back to the German lines, but some of them claimed – long after the event – to feel a justifiable sense of pride and achievement.

Captain (Med.) Königsberger recovered overnight. Out of gratitude to his friend and teacher, the surgeon-general, he took over the isolation wards and tended their inmates until he really did contract a dangerous infection. He died on 9 May, 1945, the very day when the official surrender of the German armed forces came into effect.

Only a few days before the Americans arrived, Major Tauschmüller handed over Kampfental Camp to Captain Lahrmann with orders to defend it to the last. He himself, he announced, was leaving for the front on a special mission for the General, who had already departed. In reality, he headed for the Garmisch hospital where his wife was senior nursing officer. There he exchanged his uniform for a medical orderly's smock.

Captain Lahrmann stoutly insisted that his wife Erika, née Marunke, formerly Countess von Klarfeld, should withdraw to a place of safety. She obeyed his injunction and went to see Frau Tauschmüller, who overcame her initial reluctance and took her in. The Tauschmüllers and Frau Lahrmann survived the war à trois in an atmosphere that might almost have been described as harmonious.

Three years later, in 1948, Frau Tauschmüller died a 'natural' death from causes never wholly explained. After a suitable period of mourning, her bereaved husband and heir, the ex-major, got married again – to Erika Lahrmann-Klarfeld. He did so as the proprietor of an undamaged machine tool plant whose products were soon in great demand.

Their union presented no problems on Erika's side because she had long been a widow. Ever obedient to orders, Heinrich Lahrmann had faithfully attempted to defend Kampfental against a squadron of American tanks. He faced them at the main gate with a Luger in his hand and half a dozen machine-gunners at his back. 'Over my dead body!' were his last heroic words. He was killed instantly.

Corporal Singer fled to safety in the nick of time, taking Barbara Wedell with him. They billeted themselves on one of her father's sisters, who owned a substantial house near Schongau.

Here Singer began by working as his hostess's janitor, gardener and handyman. Her house was later requisitioned by a colonel in the US forces of occupation. He took a benevolent interest in Singer, the son of a man whom the Nazis had killed, and his fiancée, who could hardly be blamed for any crimes or misdemeanours committed by a father whose services to Hitler had been expiated by suicide. So benevolent was the American colonel's interest that he insisted on acting as a witness at their wedding.

Melanie Mauerland, who disappeared almost without trace, is reported to have died of cancer in 1950.

With his usual strategic finesse, General von Feuerfresser had also decamped at the opportune moment. Accompanied by Priewitt, he descended on his beloved mother's sister, who owned an estate in the south-west corner of what remained of Germany. She welcomed him with open arms, not least because ten thoroughbred stallions and brood mares had been sent to her – as a form of advance guard – when AFSIC Kampfental was obliged to change its role.

Feuerfresser proceeded to build up a new racing stable which quickly proved a commercial success and a valuable foreign exchange earner – not that he was overinterested in the financial aspect. 'Horses are the best kind of people,' he used to say. 'They're natural officer material.'

Some years later, when a change had occurred in the post-war climate which erstwhile defenders of the Fatherland found so depressing, the great ex-general's services were called on once more. Veterans' and displaced persons' associations invited him to address their rallies, and at least three publishers urged him to write his memoirs. Suggested title: A Simple Soldier – *in other words, an anti-Nazi from first to last.*

But Feuerfresser sternly rejected all such requests. 'I did my utmost for Germany,' he declared, 'only to discover that all my efforts were wasted. Any man could be forgiven for gagging on that sort of experience.'

Ex-Lieutenant-Colonels Kastor and Pollandt did not spend long as American prisoners of war. They underwent a brief spell of confinement in the former mountain infantry barracks at Garmisch, where US Army interrogators were agreeably impressed by their co-operative attitude. Their early 'Notes on East-West Relations' found widespread favour and were forwarded to the central US authorities in Frankfurt, who classified them as highly informative. This may have been attributable to growing American mistrust of the Russians, on whom Kastor and Pollandt could claim to be experts.

They worked for the US authorities as 'free-lance advisers', a capacity in which they drew salaries that were princely by contemporary West German standards. Kastor later embarked on an academic career and taught classical German philosophy at Tübingen University. Kant, Herder and Hegel he held in high esteem; Nietzsche, Heidegger and Jaspers he deprecated. Pollandt, always the more practical of the two, became managing director of an Essen-based truck-building firm which later started turning out tanks.

Of the others implicated in the foregoing events, little remains to be told. Ex-Mess Sergeant Gerner, promoted staff sergeant shortly before the end of the war, went to Munich and tried his hand as a nightclub manager, pimp, washroom vending-machine salesman, liquor manufacturer's representative – even as a chef – but not with any great success. Having gone bust a couple of times and had a minor brush with the law, he ended up managing a snack bar with a fried chicken take-away counter. When last heard of, he was feeling quite happy in his work.

Ex-Sergeant-Major Schulz started up a used car business with a few assorted vehicles purloined from the Army. He then took over a dealership in the Rosenheim area, where he opened a service and gas station. Within a few years, he had become the proprietor of a large garage and two service stations on the Munich-Salzburg Autobahn. He now employs a staff of over fifty people, all of whom – on his own submission, which seems entirely credible – he keeps 'on the hop'.

Erwin Schlumberger, last rank major-general, made no attempt to evade capture. He spent two years in a senior officers' camp south of London, where he learnt the English language with characteristic perfectionism and studied law in his own time.

When released, he went back to Germany to see his sister, whose husband owned a flourishing paper mill near Wuppertal. It was her financial assistance that enabled him to go to university. He completed his law studies there and graduated summa cum laude *at the age of forty.*

He then practised, with no great success, as an attorney specializing in reparation claims by victims of Nazi persecution. For whatever reason, he was quick to obey the call of duty when it came. Federal Germany's newly formed armed forces had urgent need of him, he was told, so he joined the Ministry of Defence. There he remained for years, serving on the staff of successive ministers. Universally esteemed for his professionalism and spirit of compromise, he was earmarked as a future Inspector-General of the Federal Armed Forces.

Werner Wagner, erstwhile captain of infantry and purveyor of National Socialist ideals, was adroit enough to procure some false papers and bury himself in a remote Bavarian township. He became town clerk, borough surveyor and highway superintendent in turn, consorted with the mayor and parson, and endeared himself to the local brewery owner.

Wagner then began to do some part-time journalism for a Munich daily licensed by the US authorities. He wrote several articles for the feature section in which he ridiculed the late Dr Goebbels's efforts with stylistic brilliance and deep sensitivity to the climate of the times. Next, he levelled his razor-sharp pen at some less exalted but still surviving beneficiaries of the Nazi régime, not forgetting Leni Riefenstahl.

He did not, however, really make his mark in the infant Federal Republic until rearmament became an object of impassioned debate. When that time came, he hurled himself at the authors of books and articles designed to warn the inhabitants of a country scarred by two world wars against taking on any new military commitments.

Arguing that self-defence is the inalienable right of any nation, Wagner flayed his opponents relentlessly. His scathing and virulent articles indicted them on three counts: first, they themselves had taken part in Hitler's war of aggression; second, they themselves were compromised by membership of some National Socialist organization or other, be it only the Hitler Youth; and third, they were merely belated war profiteers.

Wagner's unequivocal stand attracted the attention of a major political party which enabled him to enter parliament by offering him a safe provincial seat. He soon acquired great influence in the Bundestag. He sat on important committees, rated as a 'constructive' – or hawkish – expert on defence matters, and became joint deputy leader of his parliamentary group.

His line of argument, which he never tires of repeating, even now, runs: 'In the best of good faith, we Germans were badly led astray. Our nation suffered terrible reverses, but they are a thing of the past. We now know the meaning of true democracy. What's more, we're ready to defend it.'

The Hotel Schottenhamel remained in existence for years. Though bombed, it was rebuilt by the proprietor and his sons, only to be sentenced to demolition under a real estate development scheme. Before it was finally pulled down, General Schlumberger and the Singers met there for a farewell dinner.

'Well,' said Singer, once the hugs and handshakes were

over, 'we've certainly come a long way since the old days.'

It was a remark that applied to himself as well as the West German general. Thanks to his wife's connections, not to mention his own head for business, the ex-corporal had acquired a small Munich construction company and steadily expanded it during the postwar boom. Not that he set any store by titles, Sebastian Singer was now the president of a large corporation. He was also on the board of a leading bank and an engineering company, the first of which had financed him and the second employed him to build its plant.

'Still,' he went on, 'my personal motto is no publicity.'

Schlumberger said he subscribed to it too. He had turned down the Inspector-General's job, even though the Federal Chancellor had privately urged him to take it.

'It's crazy to court the limelight. All you do is lay yourself open to a host of know-it-alls and opinion-makers – party politicos, gossip columnists, TV commentators, reporters, lobbyists, pressure groups, et cetera. I'd sooner be one of the silent minority – the influential minority. That's what counts.'

'How modest and self-effacing of you, General.' Barbara's smile was almost sorrowful. 'I'm bound to say I've often been puzzled by your attitude – no, depressed would be a better word. After all, you and Sebastian saw the whole sordid business at first hand. You not only saw it – you saw through it, but you've always remained silent on the subject, at least in public. Shouldn't you have given your experiences an airing for the benefit of others?'

'Honestly, Barbara!' The president of the Singer Construction Company gave a rather mirthless laugh. 'If we did that, our friend here would find himself described as an ex-Nazi militarist. As for me, anyone can prove I'm married to the daughter of one of Hitler's favourite cannon-fodder merchants – very happily married, too, but there's no need to spread it around.'

'You've always been good at excuses, both of you.'

'Speaking for myself,' Schlumberger said in a subdued voice, 'I've often felt tempted to broadcast my own version of the truth. I'm afraid Sebastian's right, though. Those days have left their mark on us both – they've reduced us to humiliating silence. We're two of a dwindling number who saw what happened and survived, but who cares? It's all so long ago now.'

'Yes,' Singer said gloomily, 'our kind are dying out. It's ancient history, what we went through – it's already being analysed and interpreted by people who weren't even born till years after the event.'

'Does that make them wrong?'

'Not necessarily. Only when they speak of Hitler and Napoleon in the same breath. Only when they hail them both as misjudged men of genius who were thwarted by the scheming mediocrities around them, betrayed by short-sighted generals – left in the lurch by their cowardly compatriots.'

'Wholesale oblivion, that's what lies ahead.' Schlumberger reached for Barbara's hand as though to steady himself. 'Which is why our successors are in danger of falling into precisely the same trap. No one seems to have learned much from our mistakes.'

Barbara shrugged. 'But need we accept that as final?'